About the Authors

Sharon Kendrick once won a national writing competition by describing her ideal date: being flown to an exotic island by a gorgeous and powerful man. Little did she realise that she'd just wandered into her dream job! Today she writes for Mills & Boon, featuring often stubborn but always *to die for* heroes and the women who bring them to their knees. She believes that the best books are those you never want to end. Just like life…

Sandra Marton wrote her first novel while she was still in primary school. Her doting parents told her she'd be a writer some day, and Sandra believed them. She wrote a novel, her very first, and sold it to Mills & Boon Modern Romance. Since then she's written more than sixty books, all of them featuring sexy, gorgeous, larger-than-life heroes. A four-time RITA® award finalist, she's also received five *Romantic Times* magazine awards, and has been honoured with RT's Career Achievement Award for Series Romance. Sandra lives with her very own sexy, gorgeous, larger-than-life hero in a sun-filled house on a quiet country lane in the north-eastern United States.

Maisey Yates is a *New York Times* bestselling author of more than fifty romance novels, including the Copper Ridge and brand new Gold Valley series. She has a coffee habit she has no interest in kicking and a slight Pinterest add̶ r̶ research, she swea̶ h̶ her three children d̶ jaw and arresting f̶ . When Maisey isn'̶ ̶g̶ in the grocery store, online shopping for shoes and probably not doing dishes.

A Bride for the
Playboy Prince

SHARON KENDRICK

SANDRA MARTON

MAISEY YATES

MILLS & BOON

First Published in Great Britain 2018 by Mills & Boon, an imprint of
HarperCollins*Publishers*1 London Bridge Street, London, SE1 9GF

A BRIDE FOR THE PLAYBOY PRINCE © 2018 Harlequin
Books S. A.

Crowned for the Prince's Heir © 2016 Sharon Kendrick
The Ice Prince © 2011 Sandra Marton
At His Majesty's Request © 2012 Maisey Yates

ISBN: 978-0-263-26874-4

05-0518

MIX
Paper from
responsible sources
FSC™ C007454

This book is produced from independently certified FSC™ paper
to ensure responsible forest management.

For more information visit: www.harpercollins.co.uk/green

Printed and bound by
CPI Group (UK) Ltd, Croydon, CR0 4YY

CROWNED FOR THE PRINCE'S HEIR

SHARON KENDRICK

With special thanks to a dear friend - the wildly talented and inspirational Stewart Parvin – who designs amazing clothes and wedding dresses for discerning royals and women everywhere!

CHAPTER ONE

THE NAME LOOMED up in front of him and on the back seat of the limousine, Luc's powerful body tensed. He knew what he ought to do. Ignore it. Drive on without a backward glance. Forget the past and accept the future which was waiting for him. But the dark voice of his conscience was forgotten as he leaned forward to speak to his driver, because sometimes curiosity was just too damned strong to resist.

'Stop the car,' he ordered harshly.

The car slid to a halt in the quiet street of London's Belgravia, a street full of unusual restaurants and tasteful shops. But only one of these caught his eye—which was surprising, since Luciano wasn't the kind of man who had ever featured shopping as a hobby. He didn't need to. Even the expensive baubles discreetly bought as compensatory keepsakes for departing lovers were purchased on his behalf by one of his many staff.

But there had been no purchase of baubles for quite a while now and no heartbroken lovers to pacify. He had recently undertaken two long years of celibacy—not exactly happily, but because he'd recognised it was something he needed to do. And he had risen to the challenge. His mouth hardened at the unintended pun. He had channelled his considerable energies into his work. He had worn out his hard body with exercise. His mind had been clear, strong and focussed—yet he wondered where that focus was now as he read the two words scrolled in fancy letters above the shop across the street.

Lisa Bailey.

He could feel the sudden throbbing of his groin as her name whispered into his memory just as her soft voice had once whispered urgent little entreaties into his ear as he drove deep inside her. Lisa Bailey. The hottest lover he'd ever known. The talented designer with the unblinking gaze. The tumble-haired tempt-ress with the delicious curves.

And the only woman to kick him out of her bed.

Luc shifted in his seat, locked in an uncharacter-istic moment of indecision because ex-lovers had the potential to be complicated—and complications he didn't need right now. He should tap on the glass and tell his chauffeur to drive on. Continue the journey to his embassy and deal with any last-minute queries be-fore he returned to his island home after the wedding. He thought about what awaited him in Mardovia, and a sudden stillness settled over him. He had a duty to fulfil, or a burden to carry. It all depended which way you looked at it, and if he preferred to look for the posi-tive rather than the negative—who could blame him?

His gaze returned to the shop front, and it was then that he saw her walking across the showroom and the pounding in his heart increased as he glimpsed the tumble of her curls. She turned slightly—showcasing the swell of her magnificent breasts. Lust arrowed sharply down into his groin, and stayed there.

Lisa Bailey.

His eyes narrowed. It was strange to see her here in this expensive part of town—far away from the edgier area of London where their paths had first crossed, in the tiny studio where she had designed her dresses.

He told himself it didn't matter why she was here because he didn't care. *Yet he was the one who had directed his driver to take this route, wasn't he?* And all because he'd heard some woman mention her name and had discovered that Lisa Bailey had come up in the world. His tongue snaked out over suddenly dry lips. What harm could it do to drop in and say hello, for old times' sake? Wasn't that what ex-lovers did? And wouldn't it convince him—as if he needed any convincing—that he was over her?

'Wait down the road a little,' he told the driver, opening the door himself and stepping onto the pavement. A few discreet yards away, a second car containing his bodyguards had also stopped, but Luc gave an almost imperceptible signal to tell them to keep their distance.

The August sun was hot on his head and there wasn't a whisper of wind in the leaves of the trees in the nearby square, despite the fact that it was getting on for five o'clock. The city had been caught up in a heatwave so fierce that news bulletins had been featuring clips of people frying eggs on the pavement and lying sprawled in the city's parks in various states of undress. Luc was looking forward to getting back to the air-conditioned cool of his palace in Mardovia. There white doves cooed in the famous gardens and the scent of the roses was far sweeter than the clogging traffic fumes which surrounded him here in the city. If it hadn't been for Conall Devlin's wedding party this weekend then he might have taken an earlier flight. Back to begin the process of embracing his new future—which he intended to do with whole-hearted dedication.

He pushed open the shop door and there she was, crouched down beside a rail of dresses with a needle in her hand and a tape measure around her neck—worn in the same way as a doctor might wear a stethoscope.

'Hello, Lisa,' he said, his tongue curling around the words as once it had curled around the soft swell of her breasts.

Lisa glanced up and narrowed her eyes against the light and at first she didn't recognise him. Maybe because he was the last person she was expecting to see, or maybe because she was tired and it was the end of a long day. A hot day at the end of August, with most people away on holiday and the city overrun by tourists who weren't really interested in buying the kind of clothes she was selling.

She felt the clench of rising hope as the doorbell gave its silvery little tinkle and a tall figure momentarily blotted out the blaze of the summer sun as the man stepped inside. She was due to close soon—but what did that matter? If this was a customer then he could stay until midnight for all she cared! She would switch on her best smile and persuade him to buy an armful of silk dresses for his wife. As he moved towards her she got an overwhelming impression of power and sensuality, and she tried to keep the cynicism from her smile as it crossed her mind that a man like this was more likely to be buying for his mistress than his wife.

But then he said her name and she stiffened because nobody else had an accent quite like his. She could feel the painful squeeze of her heart and the sudden rush of heat to her breasts. The needle she was holding fell to the carpet and vaguely she found herself thinking that she *never* dropped a needle. But then the thought was gone and the only one left dominating her mind was the fact that Luc was standing in her shop. His full name was Prince Luciano Gabriel Leonidas—head of the ancient royal House of Sorrenzo and ruler of the island principality of Mardovia.

But Lisa hadn't cared that he'd been a prince. She had known him simply as Luc. The man who had—unbelievably—become her lover. Who had introduced her to physical bliss and shown her that it had no limits. He'd made her feel things she'd never believed herself capable of feeling. Things she hadn't *wanted* to feel if the truth was known—because with desire came fear. Fear of being hurt. Fear of being let down and betrayed as women so often were—and that had scared the life out of her. He'd told her he wasn't looking for love or commitment and that had suited her just fine until she'd started to care for him.

She'd done her best to hide her growing feelings and had succeeded, until the day she'd realised she was fighting a losing battle with her heart. And that was when common sense had intervened and she had shrunk away from him—like someone picking up a pan to discover that the handle was burning hot. Telling him it was over hadn't been easy—and neither had the sleepless nights which followed. But it was easier than getting her heart broken and she hadn't once regretted her decision. Because men like Luc were dangerous—it was written into their DNA.

Her gaze flickered over him and immediately she became aware of the powerful sex appeal which surrounded him like an aura. His black hair was shorter than she remembered, but his eyes were just as blue. That brilliant sapphire blue—as inviting as a swimming pool on a hot day. Eyes you just wanted to dive straight into.

As always he looked immaculate. His handmade Italian suit was creaseless and his silk shirt was unbuttoned at the neck, revealing a tantalising triangle of silken skin. Lisa wished she didn't feel so warm and uncomfortable. That she'd had a chance to brush her wayward curls or slick a little lipstick over lips which suddenly felt like parchment.

'Luc,' she said, and the name sounded so right—even though it was two years since she'd spoken it. Two long years since she'd gasped it out in delight as he'd filled her and her body had splintered into yet another helpless orgasm around his powerful thrust. 'You're…' She swallowed. 'You're the last person I expected to see.'

He closed the shop door behind him and Lisa glanced over his shoulder, wondering where his bodyguards were. Lurking out of sight, probably. Trying to blend in to the upmarket location by peering into windows, or melting into the dark shadows of a shop doorway as they controlled access to their royal boss. And then she saw two low black cars with tinted windows parked further down the road and she was reminded of all the protocol which surrounded this charismatic man.

'Am I?' he questioned softly.

His voice was velvet and steel and Lisa felt a rush of desire which made her feel momentarily breathless. Against her lace brassiere her nipples hardened and her skin grew tight. She could feel the instant rush of heat to her sex. And it wasn't fair. How did he manage to provoke that kind of reaction with just one look?

So stay calm. Act like he's a customer. Maybe he *was* a customer—eager to commission one of her trademark silk dresses for one of his countless girlfriends. After all, wasn't that how she'd met him, when he'd walked into her workroom near Borough Market and she hadn't had a clue who he was? Her designs had just been taking off—mainly through word of mouth and thanks to a model who had worn one of her dresses to a film premiere. All sorts of people had started coming to see her, so it hadn't been that surprising to see the imposing, raven-haired man with a beautiful blonde model on his arm.

She remembered the blonde trying to draw his attention to one of the embroidered cream gowns Lisa had been making at the time and which women sometimes wore as wedding dresses. And Lisa remembered looking up and witnessing the faint grimace on Luc's face. Somehow she had understood that he was no stranger to the matrimonial intentions of women, and their eyes had met in a shared moment of unwilling complicity until she had looked away, feeling awkward and slightly flustered.

But something had happened in that split second of silent communication. Something she could never entirely understand. He had dumped the blonde soon afterwards and laid siege to Lisa—in a whirlwind of extravagant gestures and sheer determination to get her into his bed. He had turned all that blazing power on her and at first she'd thought she had been dreaming—especially when she'd discovered that he was a prince. But she hadn't been dreaming. The amazing flowers which had started arriving daily at her workshop had borne testament to his wealth and his intentions. Lisa had tried to resist him—knowing she had no place at the side of someone like him. But it had turned out he hadn't really wanted her by his *side*— he'd just wanted her writhing underneath him, or on top of him, or pushed up against a wall by him, and in the end she'd given in. Of course she had. She would have defied any woman to have held out against the potent attraction of the Mediterranean Prince.

They had dated—if you could call it that—for six weeks. Weeks which had whizzed by in a blur of sensuality. He'd never taken her to any of the glitzy functions featured on the stiff cards which had been stacked on the marble fireplace of his fancy house, which she had visited only once, under the cloak of darkness. He had been reluctant to be anywhere which didn't have a nearby bed, but Lisa hadn't cared. Because during those weeks he had taught her everything he knew about sex, which was considerable. She had never experienced anything like it—not before, and certainly not since.

The memory cleared as she realised that he was standing in her shop, still exuding that beguiling masculinity which made her want to go right over there and kiss him. And she couldn't afford to think that way.

'So you were just passing?' she questioned politely as she bent and picked up her fallen needle.

'Well, not exactly,' he said. 'I heard in a roundabout way that you'd moved premises and was interested to see how far up in the world you've come. And it seems like you've come a long way.' His eyes glittered as he looked around. 'This is quite some change of circumstance, Lisa.'

She smiled. 'I know.'

'So what prompted the transformation from edgy designer to becoming part of the establishment?'

Lisa kept her expression neutral as she met his curious gaze and even though she owed him no explanation, she found herself giving him one anyway. He probably wouldn't leave until she told him and she wanted him to leave, because he was making her feel uncomfortable standing there, dominating her little shop. 'I was selling stuff online and from my workshop—but it was too far out of the city centre to appeal to the kind of women who were buying my clothes.'

'And?'

She shrugged. 'And then when the opportunity came up to lease a shop in this area, I leapt at the chance.' It had been a bad decision of course, although it had taken her a while to see that. She hadn't realised that you should never take out an expensive lease unless you were confident you could meet the charges, and she'd chosen a backer who didn't know a lot about the fashion industry. But she had been buoyed up and swept away on a wave of acclaim for her dresses—and had needed a new project to fill the void left in her heart after Luc had gone. And then when her sister had announced she was going to have a baby, Lisa's desire to increase her income had become less of an ego-boosting career move and more of a necessity...

He was looking around the shop. 'You've done well,' he observed.

'Yes. Very well.' The lie slipped with practised ease from her tongue, but she justified it by telling herself that all she was doing was protecting herself, though she wasn't quite sure from what. And everyone knew that if you talked yourself up, then people might start to believe in you. 'So what can I do for you?' She fixed him with her most dazzling smile. 'You want to buy a dress?'

'No, I don't want to buy a dress.'

'Oh?' She felt the unsteady beat of her heart. 'So?'

He glittered her a smile. 'Why am I here?'

'Well, yes.'

Why indeed? Luc studied her. To prove she meant nothing? That she was just some tousle-haired tempt-

ress who had made him unbelievably hot and horny—
before she'd shown him the door.

But wasn't that what rankled, even now? That she
had walked away without a second glance—despite his
expectation that she'd come crawling back to tell him
she'd made the biggest mistake of her life. His pride
had been wounded in a way it had never been wounded
before, because no woman had ever rejected him—and
his disbelief had quickly given way to frustration. With
Lisa, he felt like a man who'd had his ice cream taken
away from him with still half the cone left to lick.

As his gaze roved over her, the sheer individuality
of her appearance hit him on a purely visceral level. He
had dated some of the world's most desirable women—
beautiful women whose endlessly long legs gave him
the height he preferred in his sexual partners. But Lisa
was not tall. She was small, with deliciously full breasts
which drew a man's eyes to them no matter what she
was wearing, or however much she tried to disguise
them. She was none of the things he usually liked and
yet there was something about her which he'd found
irresistible, and he still couldn't work out what that
something was.

Today she was wearing a simple silk dress of her
own design. The leafy colour emphasised the unusual
green-gold of her eyes and fell to just above her bare
knees. Her long, curly hair was caught in tortoiseshell
clips at the sides, presumably in an attempt to tame the
corkscrew curls. Yet no amount of taming could disguise the colour of her crowning glory—a rich, shiny
caramel which always reminded him of hazelnut shells.

A glossy tendril of it had escaped and was lying against her smooth skin.

But then he noticed something else. The dark shadows which were smudged beneath her eyes and the faint pinching of her lips. She looked like a woman who was short on sleep and long on worry.

Why?

He met question in her eyes. 'I'm often in this part of town and it seemed crazy not to come in and say hello.'

'So now you have.'

'Now I have,' he agreed as his mind took him off on a more dangerous tangent. He found himself remembering the silken texture of her thighs and the way he had trailed slow kisses over them. The rosy flush which used to flower above her breasts as she shuddered out her orgasm. And he wondered why he was torturing himself with memories which had kick-started his libido so that he could barely think straight.

His mouth hardened. Soon his life would follow a predictable pattern which was inevitable if you were born with royal blood. Yet some trace of the man he would never be called out to him now with a siren voice—and that siren's name was Lisa Bailey. For this was the woman who had fulfilled him on almost every level. Who had never imposed her will on him or made demands on him as so many women tried to. Was that why the sex had been so incredible—because she had made him feel so *free*?

And suddenly the self-imposed hunger of his two celibate years gnawed at his senses. An appetite so long denied now threatened to overwhelm him and he didn't feel inclined to stop it. What harm could there be in one final sweet encounter before he embraced his new life and all the responsibilities which came with it? Wouldn't that rid him of this woman's lingering memory once and for all?

'I've just flown in from the States and I'm here for a party this weekend,' he said. 'And on Monday I leave for Mardovia.'

'This is all very fascinating, Luc,' she observed drily. 'But I fail to see what any of this has to do with me.'

Luc gave a short laugh, for nobody had ever spoken to him as candidly as Lisa—nor regarded him quite so unflinchingly. And wasn't that one of the things which had always intrigued him about her—that she was so damned *enigmatic*? No dramatic stream of emotion ever crossed *her* pale face. Her features were as cool as if they had been carved from marble. The only time that serene look had ever slipped was when he'd been making love to her and it was then that her defences had melted. He'd liked making her scream and call out his name. He'd liked the way she gasped as he drove deep inside her.

He smiled now, enjoying the familiar lick of sexual *frisson* between them. 'And I thought I might ask you a favour,' he said.

'*Me?*'

'Well, we're old friends, aren't we?' He saw her pupils dilate in surprise and wondered how she would respond if he came right out and told her what was playing in his head.

I want to have sex with you one last time so that I can forget you. I want to bend my lips to those magnificent nipples and lick them until you are squirming. I want to guide myself into your tight heat and ride you until all my passion is spent.

His pulse pounded loudly in his ears. 'And isn't that what old friends do—ask each other favours?' he murmured.

'I guess so,' she said, her voice uncertain, as if she was having trouble associating their relationship with the word *friendship*.

'I need a date,' he explained. 'Someone to take to a fancy wedding with me. Not the ceremony itself—for those I avoid whenever possible—but the evening reception afterwards.'

Now he had a reaction.

'Oh, come on, Luc,' she said quietly. '*You* need a date? You of all people? I can't believe you're revisiting an old lover when there must be so many new ones out there. There must be women lining up around the block to go out with you—unless something is radically different and you've had a complete personality change.'

He gave an answering smile and wondered what she would say if she knew the truth. 'I cannot deny that there are any number of women who would happily accompany me,' he said. 'But none of them entice me sufficiently enough to take them.'

'So why not go on your own?'

'Unfortunately, it is not quite that simple.' He glanced out of the window, where he could see the shadowy shapes of his bodyguards standing beside one of the waiting limousines. 'If I turn up without a woman, that will leave me in a somewhat vulnerable position.'

'You? *Vulnerable?*' She gave a little snort of a laugh. 'You're about as vulnerable as a Siberian tiger!'

'An interesting metaphor,' he mused. 'Since, in my experience, weddings are a prime hunting ground for women.'

'*Hunting ground?*' she repeated, as if she'd misheard him.

'I'm afraid so.' He gave an unapologetic shrug. 'Some women see the bride and want to be her and so they look around to find the most suitable candidate for themselves.'

Her eyebrows arched. 'You being the most suitable candidate, I suppose?'

Luc looked at the tendril of hair still lying against her pale cheek and wanted to curl it around his finger. He wanted to use it like a rope and pull her towards him until their lips were mere inches apart. And then he wanted to kiss her. He shifted his weight a little. 'I'm afraid that being a prince does rather put me in that category—certainly amongst some women.'

'But you think you'd be safe with me?'

'Of course I would.' He paused. 'Our relationship was over a long time ago, and even when it was in full swing neither of us was under any illusion that there was any kind of future in it. You were probably the only woman who truly understood that. You can protect me from the inevitable predators.' He smiled. 'And it might be fun to spend the evening together. Because we know each other well enough to be comfortable around each other, don't we, Lisa?'

Lisa looked at him. *Comfortable?* Was he insane? Didn't he realise that her pulse had been hammering like a piston ever since he'd stepped inside the shop? That her breasts were so swollen that it felt as if she'd suddenly gone up a bra size? Slowly, she drew in a deep breath. 'I think it's a bad idea,' she said flatly. 'A very bad idea. And now if you don't mind—I'm about to shut up shop.'

She walked over to the door and turned the sign to *Closed* and it was only afterwards that she wondered if it was that gesture of finality which suddenly prompted him to try a different approach, because Luc was nothing if not persistent. Because suddenly, he began to prowl around the shop like a caged tiger. Walking over to one of the rails, he slowly ran his fingertips along the line of silk dresses, a thoughtful expression on his face as he turned around to look at her.

'Your shop seems remarkably quiet for what should be a busy weekday afternoon,' he observed.

She tried not to look defensive. To replicate the same cool expression he was directing at her. 'And your point is?'

'My point is that a society wedding would provide an excellent opportunity for you to showcase your talent.' His blue eyes glittered. 'There will be plenty of influential people there. You could wear one of your own designs and dazzle the other guests—isn't that how it works? Play your cards right and I'm sure you could pick up a whole lot of new customers.'

And now Lisa really *was* tempted, because business hadn't been great. Actually, that was a bit of an understatement. Business had taken a serious dive, and she wasn't sure if it was down to the dodgy state of the economy or the more frightening possibility that her clothes had simply gone out of fashion. She'd found herself looking gloomily at magazines which featured dresses which looked a lot like hers—only for a quarter of the price. True, most of the cheaper outfits were made from viscose rather than silk, but lately she'd started wondering if women really cared about that sort of thing any more.

She kept telling herself that the dip in her profits was seasonal—a summer slump which would soon pick up with the new autumn collection, and she prayed it would. Because she had responsibilities now—big ones—which were eating into her bank account like a swarm of locusts rampaging through a field of maize. She thought about Brittany, her beloved little sister. Brittany, who'd flunked college and become a mother to the adorable Tamsin. Brittany, who was under the dominating rule of Jason, Tamsin's father. Lisa helped out where she could, but she didn't have a bottomless purse and the indisputable fact was that Jason wasn't over-keen on earning money if it involved setting the alarm clock every day. Just as he seemed to have a roving eye whenever any female strayed into his line of vision. But Brittany trusted him, or so she kept saying.

A bitter taste came into Lisa's mouth. Trust. Was there a man alive who could be trusted—and why on earth would any woman ever want to take the risk?

'So pleased you're giving my proposal some serious consideration,' Luc said, his sardonic observation breaking into her thoughts. 'Though I must say that women don't usually take *quite* so long to respond to an invitation to go out with me.'

'I'm sure they don't.'

'Though maybe they would if they realised how much a man enjoys being kept guessing,' he added softly. 'If they knew just how irresistible the unpredictable can be.'

Lisa looked at him. Instinct was telling her to refuse but the voice of common sense was suddenly stronger. It was urging her to stop acting as if millions of offers like this came her way. She thought about the kind of wedding someone like Luc would be attending and all the upmarket guests who would be there. Women with the kind of money who could afford her dresses. Women who wouldn't *dream* of wearing viscose. Surely she'd be crazy to pass up such an opportunity—even if it meant spending the evening with a man who symbolised nothing but danger. She swallowed. And excitement, of course. She mustn't forget that. *But she could resist him. She had resisted him once and she could do it again.*

'Who's getting married?' she questioned carelessly.

He failed to hide his triumphant smile. 'A man named Conall Devlin.'

'The Irish property tycoon?'

'You've heard of him?'

'Hasn't everyone? I read the papers like everyone else.'

'He's marrying a woman named Amber Carter.'

Lisa nodded. Yes. She'd seen pictures of Amber Carter, too—a stunning brunette and the daughter of some industrial magnate. Someone like that would be unbelievably well connected, with friends who might be interested in buying a Lisa Bailey dress. And mightn't this wedding serve another purpose at the same time? Mightn't it get Luc out of her system once and for all if she spent some time with him? Banish some of her dreamy recollections and reinforce some of the other reasons why she'd finished with him. It would do her good to remember his fundamental arrogance and in-built need to control. And while she had shared his bed for a while, she realised she didn't really *know* him.

Because Luc hadn't wanted anything deeper—she'd understood that right from the start. He'd made it clear that the personal was taboo and the reason for that was simple. He was a royal prince who could never get close to a foreigner. So there had been no secrets shared. No access to his innermost thoughts just because they'd been sleeping together. He'd said it would be a waste of their time and make their parting all the more difficult if they became more intimate than they needed to be. She had understood and she had agreed, because her own agenda had been the same—if for different reasons—and she had also been determined not to get too close. Not to him. Not to anyone. And so they had just lived in the present—a glorious present which had been all about pleasure and little else.

She returned his questioning look. 'Where is this wedding happening?'

'At Conall's country house at Crewhurst, this Saturday. It's only just over an hour out of London.'

She looked directly into his eyes. 'So it would be possible to get there and back in an evening?'

He held her gaze and she wondered if she'd imagined another flicker of triumph in his smile. 'Of course it would,' he said.

CHAPTER TWO

WHY THE HELL was she *here*? Lisa's fingers tightened around her clutch bag. Alone in a car with the handsome Prince as they approached a stately mansion which was lit up like a Christmas tree.

Had she been crazy to accompany Luc to the A-list wedding of two complete strangers? Especially when she wasn't even sure about his motives for asking her. And meanwhile her own motives were becoming increasingly muddled. She was *supposed* to be concentrating on drumming up new business, yet during a journey which had been short on words but high on tension, all she'd been able to think about was how gorgeous Luc looked in a dark suit which hugged his powerful body and emphasised the deep olive glow of his skin.

The summer sky was not yet dark but already the flaming torches lining the driveway had been lit— sending golden flames sparking into the air and giving the wedding party a carnival feel. On an adjacent field Lisa could see a carousel and nearby a striped hut was dispensing sticks of candyfloss and boxes of popcorn. A smooth lawn lay before them—a darkening sweep of emerald, edged with flowers whose pale colours could still be seen in the fading light.

It looked like a fairy tale, Lisa thought. Like every woman's vision of how the perfect wedding should be. *And you're not going to buy into that.* Because she knew the reality of marriage. She'd witnessed her stepfather crushing her mother's spirit, like a snail being crushed beneath a heavy boot. And even though they weren't even married, she'd seen Brittany being influenced by Jason's smooth banter, which had changed into a steely control once Britt had given birth to Tamsin. Lisa's lips compressed into a determined line. *And that was never going to happen to her. She was never going to be some man's tame pet.*

A valet opened the car door and out she got. One of her high-heeled sandals wobbled as she stepped onto the gravel path, and as Luc put out his hand to steady her Lisa felt an instant rush of desire. Why was it *still* like this? she wondered despairingly as her nipples began to harden beneath her silky dress. Why could no other man ever make her feel a fraction of what she felt for the Prince? She looked into his eyes and caught what looked like a gleam of comprehension and she wondered if he could guess at the thoughts which were racing through her head. Did he realise she was achingly aware of her body through the delicate fabric as she wondered whether he was still turned on by a woman with curves…?

'Look. Here comes the bride,' he said softly.

Lisa turned to see a woman running towards them,

the skirt of her white dress brushing against the grass, a garland of fresh flowers on top of her long, dark hair.

'Your Royal Highness!' she exclaimed, dropping a graceful curtsey. 'I'm so happy you were able to make it.'

'I wouldn't have missed it for the world,' answered Luc. 'Amber, do you know Lisa Bailey—the designer? Lisa, this is the brand-new Mrs Devlin.'

'No.' The bride shook her head and smiled. 'I don't believe we've met. I've heard of you, of course—and your dress is gorgeous.'

Lisa smiled back. 'So is yours.'

She was introduced to Amber's new husband Conall—a tall and striking Irishman, who could barely tear his eyes away from his wife.

'We're not having a formal dinner,' Amber was saying, her fingers lacing with those of her groom as they shot each other a look which suggested they couldn't wait to be alone. 'We thought it much better if people could just please themselves. Have fun and mingle. Ride on the carousel, or dance and eat hot dogs. You must let me get you and Lisa a drink, Your Highness.'

But Luc gave a careless wave of his hand. 'No, please. No formality. Not tonight,' he said. 'Tonight I am simply Luc. I shall fetch the drinks myself, which we will enjoy in this beautiful garden of yours, and then I think we might dance.' His eyes glittered as he turned his head. 'Does that idea appeal to you, *chérie*?'

Lisa's heart smashed against her ribcage as his sapphire gaze burnt over her skin and the unexpected French endearment reminded her of things she would prefer to forget. Like the way he used to slide her panties down until she would almost be pleading with him to rip them off—and his arrogant smile just before he did exactly that. But those kinds of thoughts were dangerous. Much. Too. Dangerous.

'I like the sound of looking round the garden,' she said. 'Not having any outside space is one of the drawbacks of living in London, and this is exquisite.'

'Thanks,' said Amber happily. 'And, Luc, you must look out for my brother Rafe, who's over from Australia and prowling around somewhere. I thought you might like to talk diamonds and gold with him.'

'Of course,' said Luc, removing two glasses of champagne from the tray of a passing waitress and handing one to Lisa. But he barely noticed the newlyweds walk away because all he could focus on was the woman beside him. She looked... He took a mouthful of the fizzy wine, which did nothing to ease the dryness in his throat. She looked *sensational*, in a silvery dress that made her resemble a gleaming fish—the kind which always slipped away, just when you thought you might have captured it. Her shoulders were tense and she was sipping her champagne, determinedly looking everywhere except in his direction.

With a hot rush of hunger he found himself wanting to reacquaint himself with that magnificent body. To press himself up against her. To jerk his hips—hard—and to lose himself inside her as he had done so many times before. He swallowed. Would it be so wrong to sow the last of his wild oats in one glorious finale, before taking up the mantle of duty and marriage which awaited him?

They moved before he had time to answer his own question, making their way across a lawn washed deep crimson by the setting sun where many of the other guests stood talking in small groups. Some of these Luc recognised instantly, for Conall moved in similarly powerful circles. There were the Irish Ambassador and several politicians, including an Englishman rumoured to be the next-but-one Prime Minister. There was a Russian oil baron and a Greek hotel magnate, and Conall's assistant, Serena, came over with Rafe Carter, the bride's brother—and somehow, in the midst of all the introductions, Lisa slipped away from him.

Yet even though she wasn't next to him, Luc knew exactly where she was as he went through the mechanics of being a dutiful guest. He accepted a bite-sized canapé from a passing waitress and popped it into his mouth, the salty caviar exploding against his tongue. It was an unusual situation—for *him* to be doing the watching, rather than for a woman's eyes to be fixed jealously on him. But she seemed completely oblivious to his presence as she chatted to a clutch of trust-fund babes.

He watched her long curls shimmering down over her tiny frame as she laughed at something one of the women said. He saw a man wander up to the group and say something to her, and Luc's body grew rigid with an unexpected sense of possessiveness.

And suddenly he wanted to be alone with her. He

didn't want small talk—or, even worse, to get stuck with someone who was hell-bent on having a serious conversation about his island principality. He didn't want to discuss Mardovia's recent elevation to join the ranks of the world's ten most wealthy islands, or to answer any questions about his new trade agreement with the United States. And he certainly didn't want one of Hollywood's hottest actresses asking quite blatantly whether he wanted her telephone number. Actually, she didn't really put him in a position to refuse—she just fished an embellished little card from her handbag and handed it over, with a husky entreaty that he call her...*soon*. Not wanting to appear rude and intending to dispose of it at the earliest opportunity, Luc slipped the card into his jacket pocket before excusing himself and walking over to where Lisa stood.

There was a ripple of interest as he approached, but he pre-empted the inevitable introductions by injecting an imperious note into his voice. 'Let's go and explore,' he said, taking her half-drunk champagne from her and depositing their glasses on a nearby table. 'I can hear music playing and I want to dance with you.'

Lisa felt a flicker of frustration as he took her drink away, wondering why his suggestions always sounded like *commands*. Because he was a prince, that was why, and he had spent his entire life telling people what to do. Not only was he interrupting her subtle sales pitch, he also wanted to dance with her—an idea which filled her with both excitement and dread. She knew she should refuse, but what could she say? *Sorry, Luc. I'm terrified you're going to hit on me and I'm not sure I'll be able to resist.*

The trouble was that everyone was looking at her and the other women weren't even bothering to hide their envy. Or maybe it was disbelief that such an eligible man wanted to dance with a too-small brunette with an overdeveloped pair of breasts. She wanted to make a break for it, to run towards that copse of trees at the end of the lawn and to lose herself in their darkness. But she hid her insecurity behind the serene mask she'd perfected when her mother had married her stepfather and overnight their world had changed. When she'd learnt never to let people know what you were thinking. It was the first lesson in survival. Act weak and people treated you like a weakling. Act strong and they didn't.

'Okay,' she said carelessly. 'Why not?'

'Not the most enthusiastic response I've ever received,' he murmured as they moved out of earshot. 'Do you get some kind of kick from making me wait?'

Her eyes widened. 'Why? Is it mandatory to answer immediately when spoken to by the Prince?' she mocked.

He smiled. 'Something like that.'

'So why don't you just enjoy the novelty of such an experience?'

'I'm trying.'

'Try harder, Luc.'

He laughed as they walked across the grass to the terrace and up a flight of marble steps leading into the ballroom, from where the sultry sound of jazz filtered out into the warm night air. Lisa's chest was tight as Luc led her onto a quiet section of the dance floor, and as he drew her into his arms she was conscious of the power in his muscular body and the subtle scent of bergamot which clung to his warm skin.

It was hard not to be overwhelmed by his proximity and impossible to prevent the inevitable assault on her senses. This close he was all too real and her body began to stir in response to him. That pins-and-needles feeling spiking over her nipples. That melting tug of heat between her thighs. What chance did she have when he was holding her like this? I haven't danced with a man in a long time, she realised—and the irony was that she'd never actually danced with Luc before. He'd never taken her to a party and held her in his arms like this because their affair had been conducted beneath the radar. And suddenly she could understand why. The hard thrust of his pelvis was achingly evocative as it brushed against her. Dancing was dangerous, she thought. It allowed their bodies to be indecently close in a public place and she guessed that Conall's tight security was the only reason Luc was okay with that. Anywhere else and people would have been fishing out their cell phones to capture the moment on camera.

Yet somehow, despite her misgivings, she couldn't help but enjoy the dance—at least up to the point where her throat suddenly constricted and her breathing began to grow shallow and unsteady. Had he pulled her closer? Was that why the tips of her breasts were suddenly pushing so insistently against his chest?

And if *she* could feel her nipples hardening, maybe so could *he*.

'You seem tense,' he observed.

She moved her shoulders awkwardly. 'Are you surprised?'

'You don't like dancing? Or is being this close to me again unsettling you?'

Lisa drew her head back to meet the indefinable expression in his eyes. 'A little,' she admitted.

'Me, too.'

She pursed her lips together, wishing she could control the thundering of her heart. 'But you must get to dance with hundreds of women.'

'Not at all. I'm not known for my love of dancing.' His finger stroked distractingly at her waist. 'And no woman I've ever danced with makes me feel the way you do.'

'That's a good line, Luc.' She laughed. 'Smooth, yet convincing—and with just the right note of disbelief. I bet you hit the jackpot with it every time.'

'It's not a line.' His brow furrowed. 'And why so cynical?'

'I'd prefer to describe it as having taken a healthy dose of realism and I've always been that way. You never used to object before.'

Reflectively, his finger stroked her bare arm. 'Maybe I was too busy taking off your clothes.'

'Luc—'

'I'm only stating the truth. And please don't give me that breathless little gasp and look at me like that, unless you want me to drag you off to the nearest dark corner.'

'Carry on in that vein and I'll walk off all by myself.'

'Okay.' He sucked in a deep breath before moving his hands to her waist—the slender indentation of her flesh through the delicate silk feeling almost as intimate as if he were touching her bare skin itself. 'Let's keep things formal. Tell me what's been happening in your life.'

'You mean the shop?'

A faint frown arrowed his dark eyebrows together, as if he hadn't meant the shop at all. 'Sure,' he said. 'Tell me about the shop.'

Lisa fixed her gaze on the tiny buttons of his dress shirt. Did she tell him about how empty she'd felt when they'd split, which had made her throw herself headlong into her work—not realising that her ambition was outpacing her and that by aiming so high, she'd made the potential crash back to earth all the harder? 'People kept telling me I ought to expand and so I found myself a backer,' she said. 'Someone who believed in me and was willing to finance a move to a more prestigious part of the city.'

'Who?'

His voice had suddenly roughened and she looked up into his face. 'Is that really relevant?'

'That depends.' There was a pause before he spoke again. 'Is he your lover?'

She screwed up her nose. 'You're implying that I started a relationship with my new backer?'

'Or maybe it was the other way round? Your change

in fortune seems a little…dramatic,' he observed. 'It would make sense.'

Her feet slowed on the polished floor and Lisa felt a powerful spear of indignation. Was Luc really coming over as *jealous*—when he'd told her from the get-go that there was never going to be any future in their relationship? Was that what powerful princes did—played at being dog in the manger, not wanting you themselves, but then getting all jealous if they imagined someone else *did*? But she wasn't going to invent a closeness with her backer which did not extend outside the boardroom door. She and Martin were business buddies and nothing more.

She gave a laugh. 'Everyone knows you should never mix business and pleasure, and I'm afraid there hasn't been time for much in the way of recreation.'

'Why not?'

Again, she moved her shoulders restlessly. 'The stakes are much higher now that I've got the shop and then there's Brittany…'

Her words trailed off but he picked up on her hesitation.

'Your sister?'

Amazed he'd remembered the little sister he'd never even met, Lisa nodded. 'Yes,' she said. 'She had a baby.'

He frowned. 'But she's very young herself, right?'

'Yes, she is and…' Her voice faded because Luc wouldn't be interested in hearing about Brittany's choice of partner. And even though part of her despised Jason and the way he lived, wasn't there still some kind of stubborn loyalty towards him because he was Tamsin's father? 'I've been pretty tied up with that,' she finished.

'So you're an aunt now?' he questioned.

She looked up at him and Luc watched her face dissolve with soppy affection—her green-gold eyes softening and her mouth curving into a wistful smile. He felt a beat of something unfamiliar because he'd never seen her look that way before and a whisper of something he didn't understand crept over his skin.

'Yes, I'm an aunt. I have a little niece called Tamsin and she's beautiful. Just beautiful. So that's my news.' She raised her eyebrows. 'What about you?'

Luc's throat thickened with frustration, because ironically he felt so at ease in her company that Lisa would be the perfect person to confide in. To reveal that soon he would be marrying another woman—the Princess from a neighbouring island who had been earmarked as his bride since birth. A long-anticipated union between two wealthy islands, which he couldn't continue to delay.

And Lisa was a realist, wasn't she? She'd told him that herself. She might even agree that arranged marriages were far more sensible than those founded on the rocky ground of romance, with their notoriously high failure rate. If he hadn't wanted her quite so much he *might* have confided in her, but the truth was that he *did* want her. He wanted her so badly that he could barely move without being acutely aware of his aching groin, and he was glad she was standing in front of him, concealing his erection from any prying eyes.

But something stopped him from starting the inevitable seduction process—something which felt uncomfortably like the fierce stab of his conscience. For a moment he fought it, resenting its intrusion on what should have been a straightforward conclusion to the evening. He knew how much she still wanted him. It was obvious from the way she looked at him—even if he hadn't felt her nipples hardening against his chest or heard the faltering quality of her words, as if she was having difficulty breathing. Just as he knew that his desire for her was greater than anything he'd felt for any other woman. The words he'd spoken while they'd been dancing were true.

But his duty lay elsewhere and he had no right to lose himself in her soft and curvy body. No right to taste her sweetness one last time, because what good would it do—other than trigger a frustration which might take weeks to settle? It wasn't fair to the woman who was intended as his wife, even though it had been twelve months since he'd even seen her. And it wasn't fair to Lisa either.

He remembered that yearning look on her face when she'd spoken about her sister's child—a look which indicated a certain broodiness, as women of her age were programmed to be broody. He needed to let her go to find her own destiny, one which was certainly not linked to his.

Reluctantly, he drew away from her and it was as though he had flicked a switch inside himself. Self-discipline swamped desire as it had done for the past two years, and, now that sex was off the agenda, he noticed again the pallor of her complexion and faint shadows beneath her eyes. Suddenly, Luc was appalled at his thoughtlessness and ruthlessness. Had he really been planning to satisfy himself with her and then simply walk away and marry another woman?

Yes, he had.

His mouth twisted. *What kind of a man was he?*

'Let's go,' he said abruptly.

'Go?' She looked up at him in bewilderment. 'But it's still early.'

'You're tired,' he said tightly. 'Aren't you?'

She shrugged her shoulders. 'I guess so.'

'And you've probably done all the sales pitching you can for tonight. The party will really get going in a minute and I doubt whether anyone will be asking you how long your turnaround times are or whether you can make them a dress in time for their birthday party. So let's just slip away without a big fuss.'

Aware that she was in no position to object, Lisa nodded but her mood was strangely deflated as they walked towards Luc's waiting car and the sounds of music and laughter grew fainter. For a while back then it had felt so magical and so *familiar* being in his arms again. She'd felt warm and sexy as he'd held her close and his hard body had tensed against hers in silent acknowledgement of the powerful attraction which still pulsed between them. She hadn't thought beyond the dance but had thought they might stay like that for most of the evening. But now, with the moon barely beginning to rise and a trip back to her grotty home in London on the horizon—she felt strangely *cheated*. And embarrassed. As if she had been somehow presumptuous. Because hadn't she wondered if they might end up in bed together? Hadn't that been the one thought which had *really* been on her mind?

Once in the car, she accelerated her Cinderella mood by kicking off the high-heeled shoes and folding herself into one corner of the wide back seat, as if she could simply disappear if she made herself small enough. But Luc didn't react. He simply took out his cell phone and began to read from the screen. It was as if he had retreated from her. As if she were just part of the fixtures and fittings—as inconsequential as the soft leather seat on which they sat.

So don't show him you care, she told herself— even though she could feel the unfamiliar pricking of tears behind her eyes. Had she arrogantly thought he wouldn't be able to keep his hands off her? That he still found her as irresistible as she found him? She closed her eyes and leaned back against the soft leather, wondering if she had misread the whole situation.

Luc stared unseeingly at the screen of his phone until the regular sound of Lisa's breathing told him she was sleeping. It was torture to sit beside her without touching her—when all he wanted to do was to slip his hand beneath her dress and make her wet for him.

He was silent throughout the journey and it was only as they began to edge towards London that he glanced out of the window and began to notice his surroundings. The city was still buzzy as he leaned forward and quietly told the driver to go to Lisa's address.

'You want me to drop you off on the way, boss?' asked the driver.

Luc glanced at his watch. Tempting to call it a night and get away from the enticement she presented, but he owed her more than waking up alone in an empty car. She didn't deserve that. The frown at his brow deepened. She'd never given him any trouble. She hadn't tried to sell her story to the press or to capitalise on her royal connections, had she?

'No,' he said. 'Let's take her home first.'

But he was surprised when the car changed direction and entered the badly lit streets of an unfamiliar neighbourhood, where rubbish fluttered on the pavement and a group of surly-looking youths stood sucking on cigarettes beneath a lamp post. Luc frowned as he remembered the ordinary but very respectable apartment she'd had before. What the hell was she doing living somewhere like this?

As the car slid to a smooth halt, he reached out and gently shook her awake.

'Wake up, Lisa,' he said. 'You're home.'

Lisa didn't want to leave the dream—the one where she was still locked in Luc's arms and he was about to kiss her. But the voice in her ear was too insistent to ignore and her eyes fluttered open to see the Prince leaning over her, his face shadowed.

Feeling disorientated, she sat up and looked around. She was home—and she didn't want to be. Still befuddled, she bent to cram her feet back into her shoes and picked up her silver clutch bag. 'Thanks,' she said.

'This is where you live?'

She heard the puzzled note in his voice and understood it instantly. She bet he'd never been somewhere like this in his privileged life. For a split second she was tempted to tell him that she was just staying here while her own home was being redecorated, but she quickly swallowed the lie. Why be ashamed of what she was and who she'd become?

'Yes,' she said, her voice still muzzy from sleep. 'This is where I live.'

'You've moved?' he demanded. 'Why?'

'I told you that Brittany had a baby and the three of them were cramped in a too-small apartment. So...' She shrugged. 'We just did a swap. It made sense. I'm planning to get myself something better when—'

'When business picks up?' he questioned astutely.

'When I get around to it,' she said quickly. Too quickly. 'Anyway, thanks for taking me to the party. Hopefully, I'll have drummed up some new business and it...well, it was good to catch up.'

'Yeah.' Their eyes met. 'I'll see you to the door.'

'Honestly, there's no need.' She flashed him a smile. 'I'm a big girl now, Luc.'

'The subject isn't up for debate,' he said coolly. 'I'll see you to your door.'

The night air was still warm on her bare arms yet Lisa shivered as Luc fell into step beside her. But it wasn't shame about him seeing her home which was bothering her—it was the sudden sense of inevitability which was washing over her. The realisation that this really was goodbye. Fishing the key from her bag, she fumbled with the lock before turning back to face him, unprepared for the painful clench of her heart and an aching sense of loss. She would never see him again, she realised. Never know that great rush of adrenaline whenever he was close, or the pleasurable ache of her body whenever he touched her. For a split second she found herself wondering why she'd been stupid enough to finish with him, instead of eking out every available second until her royal lover had ended the relationship himself. She'd done it to protect herself from potential heartache, but what price was that protection now?

Sliding her arms around his neck, she reached up on tiptoe and brushed her lips over his. 'Be happy,' she whispered. 'Goodnight, Luc.'

Luc froze as the touch of her lips ignited all his re-pressed fantasies. He felt it ripple over his skin like the tide lapping over dry sand as he tried to hold back. He told himself that kissing a man was predatory and he didn't like predatory women. He was the master—in charge of every aspect of his life—and he'd already decided that no good could come from a brief sexual encounter.

Yet his throat dried and his groin hardened as the warmth of her body drew him in, because this was dif-ferent. This was Lisa and her kiss was all the things it shouldn't be. Soft yet evocative—and full of passionate promise. It reminded him of just how hot she'd been in his bed and yet how cool the next morning.

And it was over.

It had to be over.

So why wasn't he disentangling her arms and walk-ing back towards his purring limousine? Why was he pushing her through her door and slamming it shut behind them? A low moan of hunger erupted from somewhere deep inside him as he pushed her up against the wall and drove his mouth down on hers.

CHAPTER THREE

Luc was aware of little other than a fierce sexual need pumping through his veins as he crushed his lips down on Lisa's. He barely noticed the cramped hallway as he levered her up against the peeling wallpaper, or the faint chill of damp in the air as her arms closed around him. He was aware of nothing other than her soft flesh and the hard jerk of the erection which throbbed insistently at his groin.

He kissed her until she cried out his name. Until she circled her hips over his with a familiar restlessness which made him slide his hand underneath the hem of her silver dress. His heart pounded. Her legs were bare and her thighs were cool and he could hear the silent scream of his conscience as his fingertips began their inevitable ascent. He thought about all the reasons why this shouldn't happen, but he was too hot to heed caution and this was too easy. As easy as breathing. He swallowed. With her it always had been that way.

She gave a shuddering little moan as he reached her panties and the sound only fuelled his own hunger.

'Luc,' she gasped.

But he didn't answer. He was too busy sliding the panties aside to provide access for his finger. Too busy reacquainting himself with her moist and eager flesh. He teased her clitoris until she bucked with pleasure and he could smell the earthy scent of sex in the air.

'Hell, you're responsive,' he ground out.

'Are you surprised when you touch me like...*that*?'

Her hands were reaching blindly for his zip and Luc held his breath as she eased it down. His trousers concertinaed to the ground like those of a schoolboy in an alley, and her dextrous hands were now dealing with his boxer shorts—peeling them down until his buttocks were bare. She was cupping his balls and scraping her fingernails gently over their soft swell and in response he reached down and tore her panties apart with a savage rip of the delicate material. Her low laugh reminded him of how much she liked to be dominated in the bedroom and, although his conscience made one last attempt to tell him this was wrong, ruthlessly, he erased it from his mind. Halting her just long enough to remove a condom from his pocket, he tore open the foil with unsteady fingers before sheathing himself.

And then it was happening and there didn't seem to be a damned thing he could do about it. It was as if he were on a speeding train with no idea how to stop. He cupped her bottom so that she could wrap her legs around his hips. Her lips were parted against his cheek and her breasts were flattened against his chest.

'Are you sure you want this?' he whispered, his tip grazing provocatively against her slick flesh.

Her words came out as gasps. 'Are you?'

'I'll give you three guesses,' he murmured and drove deep into her.

His thrusts were urgent and her cries so loud that he had to kiss them silent. It was mindless and passionate and it was over very quickly. She came almost instantly and so did he, hot seed spurting into the rubber and making his body convulse helplessly. He pressed his head against her neck and, as one of her curls attached itself to his lips, he wished it hadn't been so brief. Why the hell hadn't he taken his time? Undressed her slowly and tantalised them both, while demonstrating his legendary control?

He cupped his hand over her pulsating mound, feeling the damp curls tangling in his fingers and enjoying the last few spasms as they died away. Already he could feel himself growing hard and knew from experience that Lisa would like nothing better than to do it all over again. But he couldn't stay for a repeat performance. No way. He needed to get out of there, and fast. To forget this had ever happened and put it to the back of his mind. To get on with his future instead of stupidly allowing himself to be dragged back into the past. He bent down and tugged his trousers back up, struggling to slide the zip over his growing erection, before glancing around the cramped hallway.

'Bedroom?' he questioned succinctly.

She swallowed. 'Third door along.'

It wasn't difficult to find in such a small apartment, and he thought the room was unremarkable except for the rich fabric which covered a sagging armchair and a small vase of fragrant purple flowers on the windowsill. Luc drew the curtains and snapped on a small lamp, intending just to see her safely in bed. To kiss her goodbye and tell her she was lovely—maybe even cover her up with a duvet and suggest she get some sleep. But somehow it didn't quite work out that way. Because once inside her bedroom it seemed a crime not to pull the quicksilver dress over her head and feast his eyes on her body. And an even bigger crime not to enjoy the visual fantasy of her lying on top of the duvet, wearing nothing but an emerald-green bra and a pair of sexy high-heeled shoes.

'Lisa,' he said, thinking how hollow his voice sounded.

In the soft lamplight he could see the bright gleam of her eyes.

She wriggled a little, her thighs parting fractionally in invitation. 'Mmm…?'

Luc knew she was teasing him and that this was even more dangerous. He told himself he didn't want to get back into that special shorthand of lovers or re-mind himself how good this part of their relationship had always been. Yet somehow his body was refusing to heed the voice of reason as he took her hand and guided her fingers to the rocky hardness at his groin.

'Seems like I want you again,' he drawled.

She laughed as her fingers dipped beneath the waistband and circled his aroused flesh. 'No kidding?'

'What do you think we ought to do about it?' he questioned silkily.

Her voice grew husky as she mimicked his voice. 'I'll give you three guesses.'

His mouth was dry as he undressed them both, impatiently pushing their discarded clothing onto the floor as he reacquainted himself with her curves. He groaned as she caressed the tense muscles of his thighs with those beautiful long fingers. Her curls tickled him as she bent to slide her tongue down over the hollow of his belly. But when she reached the tip of his aching shaft, he grabbed a thick rope of curls.

'No,' he said unsteadily.

'But you like—'

'I like everything you do to me, Lisa, I always did. But this time I want to take it a bit more slowly.' He groaned as he pushed her back against the mattress and leaned over her, his eyes suddenly narrowing. 'But you do realise that this changes nothing? I'm still not in a position to offer you any kind of future.'

Her smile was brittle. 'Don't make this all about you, Luc,' she said. 'It's supposed to be about mutual pleasure.'

A spear of jealousy ran through him. 'And have you had many other lovers?' he questioned. 'A stream of men lying just like this on your bed?''

'You have no right to ask me something like that.'

'Is that a yes?'

She shook her head but now her voice was shaking with indignation.

'If you must know, there's been nobody since you,' she declared. 'And before you start reading anything into that—don't bother. There hasn't been time for sex, that's all. I've been juggling too many balls and trying to keep my business afloat.'

But Lisa knew she wasn't being completely honest as she heard his low laugh of triumph. Of *course* there hadn't been anybody else—because who could compare to the arrogant Prince? Who else could make her feel all the stuff that Luc did? But he didn't want feelings—he wasn't in the market for that and he never had been. Hadn't he just emphasised that very fact? So pretend you don't care. Show him you're independent and liberated and not building stupid fantasies which are never going to happen.

'And just to put your mind at rest, yes—I do realise you're not in the market for a wedding ring,' she added drily.

For a moment she felt him grow tense—as if he was going to say something—and she looked up at him expectantly. But the moment passed and instead he bent his head to kiss her—a kiss that was long and slow and achingly provocative. It made her remember with painful clarity just what she'd been missing. The intimate slide of his fingertips over her skin. The way he could play her body as if he were playing a violin. He grazed his mouth over her swollen breasts, teasing each nipple with his teeth as her hands clutched at the bedclothes beneath her.

She realised she was still wearing her shoes and that the high heels were in danger of ripping through the cotton duvet. She bent one knee to unfasten the buckle but he forestalled her with an emphatic shake of his head.

'No,' he growled as he straddled her, his finger

reaching down to caress the leather as if it were an extension of her own skin. 'The shoes stay.'

She could feel the weight of his body and his erection pressing against her belly. He put his hand between her thighs and started to stroke her and Lisa wondered how she could have lived without this for so long.

'Luc,' she breathed as a thousand delicious sensations began to ripple over her.

His thumb stilled. 'You want more?'

She wanted him to hold her tightly and tell her how much he'd missed her, but she was never going to get that. So concentrate on what he can give you.

'Much more,' she said, coiling her arms around his neck. 'I want to feel you inside me again.'

He made her wait, eking out each delicious touch until she was almost weeping with frustration. She could feel the wetness between her thighs as he pushed them apart at last and heard his soft words of French as he entered her.

There was triumph as well as pleasure in his smile as he started to thrust his pelvis and suddenly Lisa wanted to snatch some of the control back. With insistent hands she pushed at his chest and, their bodies still locked, rolled him onto his back so that she was now on top. She saw the light of pleasure which danced in his eyes as she cupped her breasts and began to play with them, tipping her head backwards so that her curls bounced all the way down her back.

'Lisa!' Now it was his turn to gasp as he clamped his hands over her hips, anchoring her to him as their movements became more urgent. He pulled her head down so that he could kiss her, the movement of his tongue mimicking the more intimate thrusts he was making deep inside her.

Lisa shuddered because it felt so real. So *primitive*. This was the most alive she'd felt in a long time. Maybe ever.

She found herself wanting to rake her fingernails over his flesh—even though he'd always been so insistent she shouldn't mark him. But suddenly the desire to do just that was too strong to resist. Caught in a moment made bittersweet by the knowledge that it would never be repeated, she felt the first waves of her orgasm as she touched her lips to his shoulder. The first ripple of pleasure hit her and just before it took her under, she bit him. Bit him and sucked at his flesh like some rookie vampire, and the salty taste of his sweat and his blood on her lips only seemed to intensify her pleasure. His too, judging by the ragged cry he gave as he bucked inside her.

Afterwards she lay there, slumped against his damp body—not wanting to move or speak or to do anything which might destroy the delicious sense of *completeness* which enveloped her.

Go to sleep, she urged him silently as she listened to the muffled pounding of his heart. Go to sleep and let's pretend we're two normal people one last time. I can make you toast and coffee in the morning, and we can sit on stools in my tiny kitchen and forget that you're a prince and I'm a commoner before you walk out of my life for good.

But he was wide awake. She could tell from the tension in his body and the way he suddenly eased himself out of her body. Without a word, he pushed back the sheet and got out of bed.

'Luc?' she questioned, but he had switched on the main light and was walking over to the oval mirror which hung on the wall.

The harsh light emphasised just how cheap the room must look to a man used to palaces—throwing into relief the threadbare rug and the chipped paintwork which she hadn't yet got around to restoring. Tipping his head back, he narrowed his eyes as he studied the bite on his neck, which was already turning a deep magenta colour.

'Bathroom?' he snapped.

'J-just along the corridor,' she stumbled.

He was back some minutes later, having obviously splashed his face with water and raked his fingers through his ruffled black hair in an attempt to tame it. And then her heart clenched with disbelief as he bent down to pick up his clothes and began pulling them on. Surely he wasn't planning on leaving straight away? She'd known it was only ever going to be a one-off but she'd hoped he'd at least sleep with her.

'Is something wrong?' she asked.

'You mean, apart from the fact that you've bitten my neck, like some teenage girl on a first date?' He paused in the act of buttoning up his shirt, his lips tight with anger as he turned to look at her. 'What was the point of that, Lisa? Did you want to make sure you left a trophy mark behind?'

'I know. I know. I shouldn't have done it.' She gave

a helpless shrug. 'But you were just too delicious to resist.'

But he didn't smile back. In the glaring light she could see how stony his sapphire eyes looked. He finished dressing and slipped on his shoes. 'I have to go,' he said, giving a quick glance at his watch. 'I shouldn't even be here.'

'Oh?' Her voice was very quiet as she looked at him. 'Have you suddenly decided that my new downmarket accommodation is a little too basic for His Royal Highness? Can't wait to get away now you've had what you came for?'

'Please don't, Lisa,' he said. 'Don't make this any more difficult than it already is. This should never have happened. We both know that.'

She sat up in bed then, her hair falling over her shoulders as she grabbed at the rumpled sheet to cover her breasts, shielding them from the automatic darkening of his eyes as they jiggled free. 'But you were the one who came into my shop!' she protested furiously. 'The one who practically bribed me into going to that wedding party with you—'

'And you were the one who came onto me on your doorstep when I had already decided to resist you.'

'I didn't hear you objecting at the time!'

'No, you're right. I didn't.' He gave a bitter laugh. 'Maybe I was just too damned weak.'

'Okay. So we were both weak. We wanted each other.' She stared at him. 'But what's the big deal? Why start regretting it now? I mean, it's not as if we're hurting anyone, is it?'

Luc let out a low hiss of air. He didn't want to tell her, but maybe telling her was the only option. The only way she might get the message that this really was the last time and it could never happen again. Yet he wouldn't have been human if he hadn't experienced a sense of regret. His heart clenched in his chest as he looked at her—at the golden-brown curls tumbling down over her milky skin. He stared into the spiky-lashed green-gold of her eyes and felt another unwanted jerk of lust. Another deep desire to go over there and kiss her until there was no breath left in her lungs—until she was parting her thighs and pulling him deep inside her again. And judging from the hunger in her eyes, she was feeling exactly the same.

He wondered if she was aware of just how irresistible he still found her. Perhaps she thought there might be more episodes like this in the future. Maybe she was labouring under the illusion that he would start making regular trips to see her, which would all end up with this seemingly inevitable conclusion. And didn't part of him long for such a delicious scenario?

Yet his sexual hunger was tempered by a deep sense of guilt at what had just happened, because hadn't he just betrayed the woman who had been waiting so patiently for him on the island of Isolaverde? Hadn't he broken his self-imposed celibacy—big time—and with the very last woman he should have chosen?

'I'm afraid it is a big deal,' he said slowly.

She looked at him and grew completely still, as if sensing from the sudden harshening of his voice that she was about to hear something she would prefer not to.

'I don't understand.'

'There's someone else.'

The words hung in the air between them and for a moment they were met with nothing other than a disbelieving silence before her shoulders stiffened in shock.

'Someone else?' she repeated blankly.

'Yes.'

'You mean…?' she managed at last, her green-gold eyes icing over. 'You mean you're sleeping with two women at the same time? Or is that a little conservative of me? Maybe there are more than two—are you operating some sort of outdated harem?'

'Of course I'm not!' he gritted back. 'And it isn't that simple. Or that easy.'

'Oh, Luc. Your tortured face is a picture. You poor thing! My heart bleeds for you.'

'I have been betrothed to a princess since she was a child,' he said heavily.

'Betrothed?' Lisa gave a brittle little laugh, as if sarcasm could protect her from the pain which was lancing through her heart. As if it would blind her to the fact that she had misjudged him. Worse, she had trusted him. She hadn't asked him for the stars but she had expected him to behave with some sort of integrity towards her. *But why should she expect integrity when she knew how ruthless men could be?* 'This is the twenty-first century, Luc. We don't use words like *betrothed* any more.'

'Where I come from, we do. It's the way things work in my country.' He picked up one of his gold cufflinks which were lying next to the vase of purple flowers. 'The way they've always worked, ever since—'

'Please! I don't want a damned lesson in Mardovian history!' she hissed. 'I want you to tell me how you've just had sex with me if there's…someone else.'

He clipped first one cufflink and then the other, before lifting his eyes to hers. 'I'm sorry.'

'You *bastard*.'

'I made it very clear from the beginning that there could never be any future between us. I always knew that my destiny was to marry Sophie.'

Sophie. Somehow knowing her name made it even worse and Lisa started to tremble.

'But you didn't think to tell me that at the time.'

'At the time there was no reason to tell you, for she and I had an agreement that we should both lead independent lives until the time of the wedding approached.'

'And now it has.'

'Now it has,' he agreed, and his voice was almost gentle. Like a doctor trying to find the kindliest way of delivering a deadly diagnosis. 'This was my last foreign trip before setting the matrimonial plans in motion.'

'And you thought you'd have one final fling—with the woman who would probably ask the least questions?'

'It wasn't like that!' he said hotly.

'No? What, you just *happened* to come into my shop last week?'

'I wanted to tie off some of the loose ends in my life.'

There was a pause. Lisa had never imagined herself being described as a *loose end* and something told herself to kick him out. To get his cheating face out of her line of vision and then start trying to forget him. But she didn't. Some masochistic instinct made her go right ahead and ask the question. 'What's she like? *Sophie.*'

He winced, as if she had committed some sort of crime by saying the Princess's name out loud while she sat amid sheets still redolent with the scent of sex.

'You don't want to know,' he said roughly.

'Oh, but that's where you're wrong, Luc. I do. Indulge me that, at least. I'm curious.'

There was a brief pause before he answered. 'She is young,' he said. 'Younger even than you. And she is a princess.'

Lisa closed her eyes as suddenly she wished this night had never happened. Because if he hadn't come back she would never have known about Sophie. Luc would have existed in her imagination as the perfect lover she'd had the strength to walk away from and not as the duplicitous cheat he really was. 'And how does she feel, knowing just what her precious fiancé is up to the moment her back is turned?' she questioned in a shaking voice. 'Or doesn't she mind sharing you with another woman?'

'I have never been intimate with Sophie!' he bit out. 'Since tradition dictates she will come to me as a virgin on our wedding night.' He paused as he surveyed her from between his lashes, his expression suddenly sombre. 'Because that is my destiny and the duty which has been laid down for me since the moment of my birth. And a prince must always put duty, Lisa, above all else. That has always been my guiding principle.'

She shook her head, terrified she was going to do something stupid, like picking up the vase of purple flowers and hurling it at him. Or bursting into useless tears. 'You wouldn't know the meaning of the word *principle* if it was staring out of a dictionary at you!'

His voice tensed, but he forged on—sounding as if someone had written him a script and he was reading from it. 'And once my ring is on her finger, I will stray no more.'

Lisa closed her eyes. So that was all she was to him. Someone to 'stray' with. Like a stray cat—lost and hungry and taken in by the first person to offer it a decent meal. What a stupid mistake she'd made. She'd let herself down. She'd tarnished the past and muddied the present. And all because of one little kiss. Because she'd reached up and brushed her lips over his and the whole damned thing had got out of hand.

So show some dignity. Don't scream and rage. Don't let his last memory of you be of some woman on the rampage because he's passing you over for someone else. Because she had never given him access to her emotions and she wasn't about to start now. Bitterness and vitriol were luxuries she couldn't afford, because she might not have much—but she still had her pride. She opened her eyes and met the sapphire glint of his, only now she barely noticed their soft blaze—just as she no longer saw the beauty in his olive-skinned features. All she saw was duplicity and deceit.

'Just go, Luc,' she said.

He hesitated and for a moment she thought he might be about to come over to the bed and kiss her good-bye, and she tried to tell herself that she would slap his cheating face if he attempted *that*—because how was it possible to want something and to fear it, all at the same time? But he didn't. He just turned and walked out of the bedroom and Lisa slumped back on the pillows and lay there, listening to the sounds of his leaving. The front door clicked shut and she heard the thud of his footsteps on the pavement before a door slammed and his powerful car pulled away.

She lay there until she needed to go to the bathroom and then padded across the room to where her discarded green panties lay and beside them a small, cream-coloured card, which must have fallen from his trouser pocket.

She picked it up and stared at it and a feeling of self-disgust rippled over her shivering skin. She'd thought it wasn't possible to feel any worse than she already did but she was wrong. Oh, Luc, she thought. How *could* you? He had taken her to a party and had sex with her afterwards—but had still managed to bag himself a calling card from the beautiful Hollywood actress she'd seen at the wedding.

Compressing her lips together to stop them from trembling, Lisa crushed the card between her fingers and dropped it into the bin.

CHAPTER FOUR

'JASON THINKS YOU'RE PREGNANT.'

Lisa almost dropped the toddler-sized dress she had been in the process of folding and slowly turned her head to stare at her sister. They were sitting side by side on the carpet as they sorted out Tamsin's clothes, deciding which ones would still fit her for the cold winter months ahead. But now the tiny dress dangled forgotten from her fingers as she looked into green-gold eyes so like her own. 'What…did you say?'

Brittany appeared to be choosing her words with care. 'Jason says you've got the same look I had when I was carrying Tamsin. And I've noticed that you've stopped wearing your own dresses, which struck me as kind of strange.' Brittany gave a little wriggle of her shoulders. 'Since you've always told me that wearing your own dresses was your best advertisement. And you've never been the kind of woman to slop around in jeans and a loose shirt before.'

Lisa didn't answer as she put the dress down and picked up a tiny pair of dungarees, knowing she was playing for time but not caring. She didn't owe Brittany an explanation. Or Jason, for that matter. Especially not Jason—who was so fond of judging other people but who never seemed to take the time to look at his own grasping behaviour.

But Jason's scrounging was irrelevant right now, because somehow he had unwittingly hit on the truth and passed it on to her sister—and the hard fact remained that she *was* starting to show. At just over sixteen weeks Lisa guessed that was inevitable. Unless she was still in that horrified state of denial which had settled over her at the beginning, when the countless pregnancy tests she'd taken had all yielded the same terrifying results—but at least they'd explained why she'd felt so peculiar. Why her breasts had started aching in a way which was really uncomfortable. Eventually, she had taken herself off to the doctor, who had pronounced her fit and healthy and then smilingly congratulated her on first-time motherhood. And if Lisa's response had been fabricated rather than genuine, surely that wasn't surprising. Because how could she feel happy about carrying the child of a man who no longer wanted her? A man who was about to marry another woman?

'So who's the father?' questioned Brittany.

'Nobody you know,' said Lisa quickly.

There was a pause. 'Not that bloke you used to go out with?'

Lisa stiffened. 'Which bloke?'

'The one you were so cagey about. The one you never wanted anyone to meet.' Brittany sniffed. 'Almost as if you felt we weren't good enough for him.'

Lisa bit her lip. It was true she'd never introduced

Brittany or Jason to the Prince—and not just that she had been worried that Jason might attempt to 'borrow' money from the wealthy royal without any intention of ever paying it back. She'd known there was no future in the relationship and therefore no point of merging their two very different lives.

And she didn't want to bring Luc into the conversation now. If she told her sister that she was expecting the child of a wealthy prince, Brittany would inevitably tell Jason and she wouldn't put it past him to go hawking the story to the highest bidder. 'I'd rather not discuss the father,' she said.

'Right.' Brittany paused. 'So what are you going to do?'

'Do?' Lisa sat back on her heels and looked at her sister blankly. 'What do you mean, *do*?'

'About the *baby*, of course! Does he know?'

No, he didn't know—though she'd done her best to try to contact him. Lisa chewed on her lip. Even that had been another stark lesson in humiliation. She had tried to ring him on the precious number she still had stored in her phone—but the number was no longer in service. Of course it wasn't. So she'd summoned up all her courage to telephone the palace in Mardovia, somehow managing to get through to one of his aides— a formidable-sounding woman called Eleonora. But Eleonora had stonewalled all her attempts to speak to the Prince and, short of blurting out her momentous news on the phone, Lisa had eventually given up—because how could she possibly disclose something like that to a member of Luc's staff?

And if she was being totally honest, she had been slightly relieved, thinking perhaps it was better this way. He was due to marry another woman. Someone called Princess Sophie—a woman who had never done *her* any harm. How could she ruin her life by announcing that an impulsive one-night stand had resulted in another woman carrying his baby? Damn Luc Leonidas, Lisa thought viciously. Damn him for not bothering to tell her about his impending marriage *before* he'd jumped into bed with her.

'No,' Lisa said, steeling herself against the curiosity in her sister's eyes. 'He doesn't know and he isn't going to. He doesn't want to see me again and he certainly doesn't want to be a father to my child. So I'm going to bring this baby up on my own and it's going to be a happy and well-cared-for baby.'

'But, Lisa—'

'No, please. Don't.' Lisa shook her head, feeling little beads of sweat at the back of her neck and so she scooped up the great curtain of curls and waved it around to let the air refresh her skin. She looked pointedly at her sister, her gaze intended to remind her of the harsh truth known to both of them. That a child brought up in a home with a resentful man was not a happy home. 'I'm not asking your opinion on this, Brittany,' she said quietly. 'I'm just telling you how it's going to be.'

There was a pause. 'Is he married?'

Not yet.

'No comment. Like I said, the discussion is over.'

Lisa gave a grimace of a smile as she rose to her feet. 'But you've given me an idea.'

'*I* have?' Brittany looked momentarily puzzled.

'Yes. I keep saying that you're much cleverer than you give yourself credit for.' Lisa narrowed her eyes, her mind suddenly going into overdrive. 'And if I'm going to spend the next few months getting even bigger, I might as well do it in style.'

Brittany's green-gold eyes narrowed. 'What's that supposed to mean?'

'It means that although I've had a few extra orders since I went to that fancy wedding back in August, it hasn't been enough to take the business forward as I'd hoped. What I need is a completely new direction—and I think I've just found one.' Lisa sucked in a deep breath as she patted her expanding stomach. 'Think about it. There aren't many really fashionable maternity dresses on the market right now—especially ones in natural fabrics, which "breathe". I can work in more fabrics than just my trademark silk. Cotton and linen and wool. There's an opportunity here staring me right in the face, and it seems I'm the perfect person to model my new collection.'

'But…won't that get publicity?'

Lisa smiled and it felt like the first genuine smile she'd given in a long time. 'I sincerely hope so.'

'You aren't afraid that the father will hear about it and come to find you?'

Lisa shook her head. No. That was one thing she *wasn't* worried about. Luc certainly wouldn't be trawling the pages of fashion magazines now that he'd turned his back on his playboy life and locked himself away on his Mediterranean principality. Luc had made his position very clear.

'No,' she said quietly. 'He won't find out.'

She sat back on her heels and as a rush of something like hope flooded through her, so did a new resolve. She needed to be strong for her baby and that wasn't going to happen if she sat around wailing at the unfairness of it all. She was young, fit and hard-working and she had more than enough love to give this innocent new life which was growing inside her.

Her baby *would* be happy and well cared for, she vowed fiercely. No matter what it took.

Luc sat at his desk feeling as if he had just opened Pandora's box. The blood pounded inside his head and his skin grew clammy. There must be some kind of mistake. There *must* be. He had been bored. Why else would he have tapped Lisa's name into the search engine of his computer? Yet wasn't the truth something a little more unpalatable? That he couldn't get her out of his head, no matter how hard he tried.

Nearly six months had passed since he'd seen her and he had been eaten up with guilt about what had happened just before he'd left London. He had broken his self-imposed celibacy with his ex-lover, instead of the woman he was due to marry. But he was over that now and the date for his wedding to Sophie was due to be announced next week. It was the end of an era and the beginning of a new one, and he intended to embrace it wholeheartedly. And that was why he had typed Lisa's name into the search engine—as a kind of careless test to see whether he could now look on her with indifference.

A muscle at his temple flickered as once again he stared with disbelief at the screen. He was no stranger to shock. He had lost his mother in the most shocking of circumstances—and in some ways he had lost his father at the same time. He had thought nothing would ever rock him like that again, but a faint echo of that disbelief reverberated through him now. He stared at the image in front of him and his mouth dried. A picture of Lisa at a fashion show. Her lustrous caramel curls were pulled away from her face and her eyes and skin seemed to glow with a new vitality—but it hadn't been that which had made his blood run cold.

He stared at her swollen belly. At the hand which lay across her curving shape in that gently protective way which pregnant women always seemed to adopt. Features hardening into a frown, he read the accompanying text.

DESIGNER LAUNCHES SWELL NEW LINE!
Lisa Bailey, famous for the understated dresses which captivated a generation of 'Ladies Who Lunch', last night launched her new range of maternity wear. And stunning Lisa just happened to be modelling one of her own designs!

Coyly refusing to name the baby's father, the six-months-pregnant St Martin's graduate would say only that, 'Women have successfully been

bringing up children on their own for centuries.
It's hardly ground-breaking stuff.'

Ms Bailey's collection is available to buy from
her Belgravia shop.

Luc sat back in his chair.

Lisa, *pregnant*? He felt the ice move from his veins to his heart. It couldn't be his. Definitely not his. He shook his head as if his denial would make it true, but memories had started to crowd into his mind which would not be silenced. Her heated claim that there had been no other lover than him since they'd been apart—and he had *believed* her, because he knew Lisa well enough to realise she wouldn't lie about something like that. Six months pregnant. He sat back in his chair, his heart pounding as he raked a strand of hair away from his heated face. Of *course* it was his.

Lisa Bailey was carrying his baby.

His baby.

Disbelief gave way to anger as he shut down the computer. Why the hell hadn't she told him? Why had she left him to find out in such a way—and, just as importantly, who else knew?

He reached out for the phone, but withdrew his hand again. He needed to think carefully and not act on impulse, for this was as delicate a negotiation as any he had ever handled. Using the phone would be unsatisfactory and there was no guarantee the call wouldn't be overheard by someone at her end. Or his. It occurred to him that she might refuse to speak to him—in fact, the more he thought about it, the more likely a scenario that seemed, for she could be as stubborn as hell.

Leaning forward, he pressed the buzzer on his desk and Eleonora appeared almost immediately.

'Come in and close the door.' Luc paused for a moment before he spoke. 'I want you to cancel everything in my diary for the next few days.'

Her darkly beautiful face remained impassive. 'That might present some difficulties, Your Royal Highness.'

Luc regarded her sternly. 'And? Is that not what I pay you for—to handle the tricky stuff and smooth over any difficulties?'

'Indeed.' Eleonora inclined her dark head. 'And does Your Royal Highness wish me to make any alternative arrangements to fill the unexpected spaces in your diary?'

Luc's mouth flattened as he nodded. 'I need to fly to Isolaverde and afterwards I want the plane on standby, ready to take me to London.'

'And am I allowed to ask why, Your Royal Highness?'

'Not yet, you're not.'

Eleonora bit her lip but said nothing more and Luc waited until she had left the office before slowly turning to stare out of the window at the palace gardens. Already the days hinted at the warm weather ahead, yet his heart felt as wintry as if it had been covered with layers of ice. He couldn't bear to sit here and think about the unthinkable. He wanted to go to England now. To go to Lisa Bailey and…and…

And what? His default mechanism had always been

one of action, but it was vital he did nothing impulsive. He must think this through carefully and consider every possibility which lay open to him.

The following morning he flew to Isolaverde for the meeting he was dreading and from there his jet took him straight to London—but by the time he was sitting in his limousine outside Lisa's shop, his feelings of disbelief and anger had turned into a clear focus of determination.

The evening was cold and a persistent drizzle had left the pavements shining wet, with a sickly orange hue which glowed down from the streetlights. In the window of Lisa's shop was a pregnant mannequin wearing a silk dress, her hand on her belly and a prettily arranged heap of wooden toys at her feet. Luc had sat and watched a procession of well-heeled women being dropped off by car or by taxi, sheltered from the rain by their chauffeurs' umbrellas as they walked into the shop. Business must be booming, he thought grimly.

He forced himself to wait until the shop closed and a couple of women who were clearly staff had left the building. As Luc waited, a passing police officer tapped on the window of the limousine, discreetly overlooking the fact that it was parked on double yellow lines once he was made aware of the owner's identity.

He waited until the lights in the shop had been dimmed and he could see only the gleaming curls of the woman sitting behind a small desk—and then he walked across the street and opened the door to the sound of a tinkly bell.

Lisa glanced up as the bell rang, wondering if a

customer had left their phone behind or changed their mind about an order—but it was nothing as simple as that. It felt like a case of history repeating itself as Luc walked into her shop, only this time there wasn't a look of curiosity on his face which failed to conceal the spark of hunger in his eyes. This time she saw nothing but fury in their sapphire depths—though when she stopped to think about it, could she really blame him?

Yet she had stupidly convinced herself that this scenario would never happen—as if some unknown guardian angel were protecting her from the wrath of the man who stood in front of her, his features dark with rage. She was glad to be sitting down, because she thought her knees might have buckled from the shock of seeing him standing there—trying to control his ragged breathing. He didn't have to say a word for her to know why he was here; it was as obvious as the swell of her belly, which he was staring at like a man who had just seen a ghost.

Don't be rash, she reasoned, telling herself this was much too important to indulge her own feelings. She had to think about the baby and only the baby.

'Luc,' she said. 'I wasn't expecting you.'

He lifted his gaze from her stomach to her face as their eyes met in a silent clash. 'Weren't you?' he said grimly. 'What's the matter, Lisa? Surely you must have known I would turn up sooner or later?'

She licked her suddenly dry lips. 'I tried not to think about it.'

'You tried not to think about it?' he repeated. 'Is

that why I was left to discover via social media that you're pregnant?'

'I didn't mean—'

'I don't care what you did or didn't mean because you're going to have a baby.' Ruthlessly, he cut across her words. But for the first and only time since she'd known him, he seemed to be struggling with the rest of the sentence, because when finally he spoke, he sounded choked. '*My* baby.'

Lisa could feel the blood draining from her face and thought how wrong this all seemed. A miracle of life which should—and did—fill her with joy and yet the air around them throbbed with accusation and tension. Her hands were unsteady and she felt almost dizzy, and all she could think was that this kind of emotion couldn't be good for the baby. 'Yes,' she breathed at last, staring down at the tight curve of her belly as if to remind herself. 'Yes, I'm having your baby.'

There was an ominous silence before he spoke again. A moment when he followed the direction of her gaze, staring again at her new shape as if he couldn't believe it.

'Yet you didn't tell me,' he accused. 'You kept it secret. As if it was your news alone and nobody else's. As if I had no right to know.'

'I did try to tell you!' she protested. 'I tried phoning you but your number had changed.'

'I change my number every six months,' he informed her coldly. 'It's a security thing.'

Lisa pushed a handful of hair away from her hot

face. 'And then I phoned the palace and got through to one of your aides. Eleonora, I think her name was.'

Luc's head jerked back. 'You spoke to Eleonora?'

'Yes. And she told me that you weren't available. Actually, it went further than that. She said I wasn't on your list of telephone contacts. If you must know she made me feel like some pestering little groupie who needed to be kept away from the precious Prince at all costs.'

Luc let out a long sigh. Of course she had. Eleonora was one of his most fiercely loyal subjects, and part of her role had always been to act as his gatekeeper, and never more so than when he'd returned to Mardovia following his illicit night with Lisa. When he'd been full of remorse for what he'd done but unable to shake off the erotic memories which had clung to his skin like the soft touch of her fingers. He had thrown himself into his work, undertaking a punishing schedule which had taken him to every town and city on the island. And he had instructed his fiercely loyal aide not to bother him unless absolutely necessary.

'You could have written,' he said.

'What, sent you a postcard, or a letter which was bound to be opened by a member of your staff? Saying what? *Dear Prince Luciano, I'm having your baby*?' Her gaze was very steady. 'You told me you were going to marry another woman. You made it very clear you never wished to see me again. And after you'd gone, I found a card on my bedroom floor—a card from some Hollywood actress you must have met at the wedding. My lowly place in the pecking order was confirmed there and then.'

'I could tell you that I took the card simply as a politeness with no intention of contacting her again, but that is irrelevant,' he gritted out. 'Because the bottom line is that you're pregnant, and we're going to have to deal with that.'

She shook her head. 'But there's nothing to deal with. You don't have to worry. I have no wish to upset your fiancée or your plans for the future. And lots of women have children without the support of men!' she finished brightly.

'So you said in your recent interview,' he agreed witheringly.

'And it doesn't matter what you say.' She looked at him defiantly, because defiance made her feel strong. It stopped her from crumpling to the ground and just opening her mouth and *howling*. It stopped her from wishing he would cradle her in his arms, like any normal father-to-be—his face full of wonder and tenderness. She licked her lips. 'Because when it boils down to it, this is just a baby like any other.'

'But that's where you're wrong, Lisa,' he negated softly. 'It *is* different. This is not *just a baby*. The child you carry has royal blood running through its veins. Royal Mardovian blood. Do you have any idea of the significance of that?' His face hardened. 'Unless that was the calculated risk you took all along?'

She stared at him in confusion. 'I'm not sure I understand.'

'No?' The words began to bubble up inside him, demanding to be spoken and, although years of professional diplomacy urged Luc to use caution, the shock of this unexpected discovery was making him want to throw that caution to the wind. 'Maybe this is what you hoped for all along,' he accused. 'I saw your face at the wedding when you started talking about your niece. That dreamy look which suggested you longed to become a mother yourself. I believe women often become broody when they're around other people's children. When their body clock is ticking away as yours so obviously is. Is that what happened to you, Lisa? Only instead of saddling yourself with a troublesome partner as your sister seems to have done—maybe you decided to go it alone.'

'You're *insane*,' she breathed. 'Completely insane.'

'Am I? Don't they say that children are the new accessories for the modern career woman? Was that why you threw yourself at me that night, when I was trying to do the honourable thing of resisting you?' He gave a bitter laugh. 'Was that why you made love to me so energetically—riding me like some rodeo rider on a bucking bronco? Perhaps hoping to test the strength of the condom we used—because you wanted my seed inside you. It is not unknown.'

She stared at him in disbelief as his words flooded over her in a bitter stream. 'Or maybe I went even further?' she declared. 'Perhaps you think I was so desperate to have your child that I went into the bathroom after you'd gone and performed some sort of amateur DIY insemination? That's not beyond the realms of possibility either!'

'Don't be so disgusting!' he snapped.

'Me?' She stared at him. 'That's rich. You're the

one who came in here making all kinds of bizarre suggestions when all I wanted was to try to do the decent thing—for everyone concerned. You're going to marry Sophie and...' She stood up then, needing to move around, needing to bring back some blood to her cramped limbs. Leaving behind the clutter of her desk, she walked over to a rail of the new maternity dresses which she'd worked so hard on—pretty dresses which discreetly factored in the extra material needed at the front. She'd been feeling so proud of her new collection. She'd taken lots of new orders after the show and had allowed herself the tentative hope that she could carry on supporting Brittany and Tamsin and still make a good life for herself and her own baby. Yet now, in the face of Luc's angry remarks—her will was beginning to waver.

She straightened a shimmery turquoise dress before forcing herself to meet his gaze. 'Don't you understand that I'm letting you off the hook? I don't want to mess up your plans by lumbering you with a baby you never intended to have. A commoner's baby. You're going to be married to someone else. A princess.' The hurt she'd managed so successfully to hide started to creep up, but she forced herself to push it away. To ask the question she needed to ask and to try to do it without her voice trembling, which suddenly seemed like one of the hardest things she'd ever had to do. 'Because how the hell do you think Princess Sophie is going to feel when you tell her you're going to be a father?'

CHAPTER FIVE

'SHE KNOWS,' SAID LUC, the words leaving his mouth as if they were poison. 'Princess Sophie knows about the baby and it's over between us.'

He watched Lisa grow still, like an animal walking through the darkened undergrowth suddenly scenting danger. Her green-gold eyes narrowed as she looked at him and her voice was an uncertain tremble.

'B-but you said—'

'I know what I said,' he agreed. 'But that was then. This is now. Or did you really think I was going to take another woman as my wife when you are pregnant with my child? This changes everything, Lisa.' There was a heartbeat of a pause. 'Which is why I went to see the Princess before I came to England.'

She winced, closing her eyes briefly—as if she was experiencing her own, private pain. 'And what…what did she say?'

Luc picked his words carefully, still trying to come to terms with the capriciousness of women. He didn't understand them and sometimes he thought he never would. And when he stopped to think about it—why should he, when the only role models he'd known had all been paid for out of the palace purse?

He had been expecting a show of hurt and contempt from his young fiancée. He had steeled himself against her expected insults as he had been summoned into the glorious throne room of her palace on Isolaverde, where shortly afterwards she had appeared—an elegant figure in a gown of palest blue which had floated around her. But the vitriol he deserved hadn't been forthcoming.

'She told me she was relieved.'

'Relieved?'

'She said that a wedding planned when the bride-to-be was still in infancy was completely outdated and my news had allowed her to look at her life with renewed clarity. She told me that she didn't actually *want* to get married—and certainly not to a man she didn't really know, for the sake of our nations.' He didn't mention the way she had turned on him and told him that she didn't approve of his reputation. That the things she'd heard and read in the past—exploits which some of his ex-lovers had managed to slip to the press—had appalled her. She had looked at him very proudly and announced that maybe fate was doing her a favour by freeing her from her commitment to such a man. And what could he do but agree with her, when he was in no position to deny her accusations? 'So I am now a free man,' he finished heavily.

Lisa's response to this was total silence. He watched her walk over to the desk and pour herself a glass of water and drink it down very quickly before turning back to face him. 'How very convenient for you,' she said.

'And for you, of course.'

Abruptly, she put the glass down. 'Me?' The wariness in her green-gold eyes had been replaced by a glint of anger. 'I'm sorry—you've lost me. What does the breaking off of your engagement have to do with me? We had a one-night stand with unwanted consequences, that's all. Two people who planned never to see one another again. Nothing has changed.'

Luc studied her defensive posture, knowing there were better methods of conveying what he needed to say and certainly more suitable environments in which to do so than the shop in which she worked. But he didn't have the luxury of time on his side—for all kinds of reasons. His people would be delighted by news that his royal bloodline would be continued, but he doubted they'd be overjoyed to hear that the royal mother was an unknown commoner and not their beloved Princess Sophie. He would have to ask the Princess to issue a dignified announcement before introducing Lisa as his bride, for that would surely lessen the impact. And he would get his office to start working on image control—on how best to minimise the potential for negative repercussions for him and for Mardovia.

'Everything has changed,' he said. 'For I am now free to marry you.'

Lisa's heart missed a beat, but even in the midst of her shock she reflected what cruel tricks life could play. Because once Luc's words would have affected her very differently. When she'd been starting to care

for him…really care. When she'd been standing on the
edge of that terrifying precipice called love. Just before she'd pulled back and walked away from him—
she would have given everything she possessed to hear
Luc ask her to marry him.

And now?

Now she accepted that the words were as empty as
a politician's sound bites. The mists had cleared and
she saw him for who he really was. A powerful man
who shifted women around in his life like pawns in a
game of chess. Why, even his brides were interchange-
able! Princess Sophie had been heading for the altar,
only to be cast aside with barely a second thought because a pregnant commoner counted for more than a
virgin princess. And now *she* was expected to step in
and take her place as his bride. Poor Sophie. And poor
her, if she didn't grow a backbone.

She drew in a deep breath. 'You really think I'd
marry you, Luc?'

The arrogant smile which curved his mouth made
it clear he thought her protest a token one.

'I agree it isn't the most conventional of unions,'
he said. 'But given the circumstances, you'd be crazy
not to.'

Lisa could feel herself growing angry. Almost as
angry as when she'd looked down at her dead mother's
face and thought how wasted her life had been. She
remembered walking away from the funeral parlour
hoping that she had found peace at last.

She'd been angry too when Brittany had dropped
out of her hard-fought-for place at one of England's top

universities because Jason had wanted her to have his baby, and nothing Lisa had said could talk her sister out of it, or make her wait. Another woman who had allowed herself to be manipulated by a man.

But maybe she no longer had a right to play judge and jury when now she found herself in a situation which was wrong from just about every angle. She stared into Luc's face but saw no affection on his rugged features—nothing but a grim determination to have things on *his* terms, the way he always did. And she couldn't afford to let him—because if she gave him the slightest leeway, he would swamp her with the sheer force of his royal power.

'I think we'll have to disagree on the level of my craziness,' she said quietly. 'Because you must realise I can't possibly marry you, Luc, no matter what you say—or how many inducements you make.'

His sudden stillness indicated that her reply had surprised him.

'I don't really think you have a choice, Lisa,' he said.

'Oh, but that's where you're wrong. There is always a choice. And mine was to have this child alone and to love it with all my heart. It still is.'

'But I am the father.'

'I know you are. And now that it's all out in the open you must realise that I shan't deny you access to your child.' She smiled up at him. 'We'll keep emotion out of it and try to come to some satisfactory arrangement for all of us.'

He didn't smile back.

'You seem to forget that you carry a prince or princess,' he said softly. 'And it is vital they should grow up on the island they will one day inherit.'

She met his gaze. 'I didn't realise illegitimate offspring were entitled to inherit.'

A muscle began to flicker at Luc's temple because this conversation wasn't going according to plan. His marriage proposal had been intended to pacify her and possibly to thrill her. To have her eating out of his hand—because women had been trying to push him towards the altar most of his adult life and deep down he had imagined Lisa would be no different. He'd thought she would be picturing herself walking down the wide aisle of Mardovia's famous cathedral—a glittering tiara in her curly hair. Yet all she was doing was surveying him with a proud look and he felt the slow burn of indignation. Who the *hell* did she think she was—turning down his offer of marriage without even a moment's consideration?

For a split second he felt powerless—an unwelcome sensation to someone whose power had always been his lifeblood. He wanted to tell her that she *would* do exactly as he demanded and she might as well resign herself to that fact right now. But the belligerent expression on her face told him he had better proceed with caution.

His gaze drifted over her, but for once the riot of curls and green-gold eyes were not the focus of his attention. He noted how much fuller her breasts were and how the swell of her belly completely dwarfed her tiny frame. *And inside that belly was his child.* His throat thickened.

She looked like a tiny boat in full sail, yet she was no less enticing for all that. He still wanted her and if circumstances had been different he might have pulled her in his arms and started to kiss her. He could have lulled her into compliance and taken her into one of those changing rooms. Drawn the velvet curtains away from prying eyes and had her gasping her approval to whatever it was he asked of her.

But she was heavy with child. Glowing like a pomegranate in the thin winter sun—and because of that he couldn't use sex as a bargaining tool.

'Get your coat,' he said. 'And I'll take you home.'

'I haven't finished what I was doing.'

'I'll wait.'

'There's no need. Honestly, I can get a cab.'

'I said, I'll wait. Don't fight me on this, Lisa—because I'm not going anywhere.' And with this he positioned himself on one of the velvet and gilt chairs, stretching his long legs in front of him.

Lisa wanted to protest, but what was the point? She couldn't deny they needed to talk, but not now and not like this—when she was still flustered by his sudden appearance and the announcement that he'd called off his wedding. She needed to have her wits about her but her brain currently felt as if it were clouded in mist, leaving her unable to think properly. And that was dangerous.

He had taken out his cell phone and was flicking through his emails and giving them his full attention, and she found herself almost envying him. If only she were capable of such detachment of thought! The figures in front of her were a jumble and in the end she gave up trying to make sense of them. How could she possibly concentrate on her work with Luc distracting her like this?

She shut down her computer and gave him a cool look. 'Okay. I'm ready,' she said.

She sensed he was exerting considerable restraint to remain patient as she carried the jug and water glass out into the kitchen, set the burglar alarm, turned off the lights and locked the door. Outside, the drizzle was coming down a little heavier now and his driver leapt from the car to run over and position a huge umbrella over her head. She wanted to push the monstrous black thing away—uncaring that the soft rain would turn her hair into a mass of frizz—but she stopped just in time. She needed to be calm and *reasonable* because she suspected that she and Luc were coming at this pregnancy from completely different angles. And if she allowed her fluctuating hormones to make her all volatile, he would probably get some awful Mardovian judge to pronounce her unfit to be a mother!

She sat in frozen silence on the way to her apartment and a feeling of frustration built up inside her when he made no attempt to talk to her. Was he playing mind games? Trying to see which of them would buckle first? Well, he had better realise that this wasn't a game—not for her. She was strong and resolute and knew exactly what she wanted.

But when they drew up outside her humble block, he surprised her with his words.

'Have dinner with me tomorrow night.'

'Dinner?'

'Why not?' he said. 'We need to discuss what we're going to do and there's nothing in the rulebook which says we can't do it in a civilised manner.'

In the dim light Lisa blinked. She thought about the two of them making an entrance in the kind of fancy restaurant he would no doubt frequent—the handsome Prince and the heavily pregnant woman.

'But if we're seen out together,' she said slowly, 'that would be making a fairly unequivocal statement, wouldn't it? A prince would never appear alone in public with a woman in my condition unless he was willing to be compromised. Is that what you want, Luc?'

His eyes glittered as he leaned towards her. 'Yes,' he said. 'That's exactly what I want. I *want* the world to know that I am the father. You have my child in your belly, Lisa. Do you really think I intend to relinquish my claim on my own flesh and blood?'

The words sounded almost *primitive* and they were filled with a sense of possession. They reminded Lisa of the full force of his power and the fact that he had grown up with very different values from her. 'Of course I don't!' she said. 'We can meet with a lawyer and have a legal agreement drawn up. You can see your child any time you like—within reason. Surely you can have no objection to that?'

His eyes were cold and so was his voice. 'I think you are missing the point, *chérie*. I intend to marry you.'

'I'm sorry, Luc.' She gave a slight shake of her head as she reached for the door handle. 'I'm afraid that's just not going to happen.'

But he leaned across the seat and placed his hand over her forearm, and Lisa hated the instant ripple of recognition which whispered over her skin the moment he touched her. Did he feel it, too—was that why he slid his thumb down to her wrist as if to count the beats of the rocketing pulse beneath?

'Let me see you to your door,' he said.

The set of his jaw told her that objection would be a waste of time and so she shrugged. 'Suit yourself. But you're not coming in.'

Luc made no comment as he accompanied her to her front door as he'd done what now seemed a lifetime ago. But this time there was no warmth and light gilding the summer evening into a golden blur which matched their shared desire. This time there was only the cold bite of a rainy night and a barely restrained sense of hostility. But she was pregnant, he reminded himself. *Inside her beat the tiny heart of his own flesh and blood. And that changed everything.*

Luc was not a sentimental man and emotion had been schooled out of him from an early age, but now he became aware of something much bigger than himself. He stared at her swollen frame with the realisation that here lay something more precious than all the riches in his entire principality. And he was shaken by just how badly he wanted it.

'I don't want to have to fight you to get what I want, Lisa,' he said softly as they reached her door. 'But if you force my hand then I'm afraid that's what's going to happen. Perhaps I should warn you now that it is better not to defy me.'

Her eyes narrowed like those of a cornered cat. 'If only you could hear yourself!' she retorted, unlocking her front door and pushing it open. 'I can defy you all I like! I'm a free spirit—not your possession or your subject. This is the twenty-first century, Luc, and you can't make me do something I don't want to—so why don't we resume this discussion in the cold light of day when you're ready to see sense?'

His powerful body grew still and for one hopeful moment Lisa thought he was about to take her advice. But she was wrong. He lifted his hand to rake his fingers back through his rain-spangled hair and she hated the sudden erotic recall which that simple gesture provoked.

'Your backer is a man called Martin Lawrence,' he said slowly.

She didn't ask how he knew. She didn't show her surprise or foreboding as she raised her eyebrows. 'And?'

'And yesterday afternoon he sold all his interest in your business to me.'

It took her a few seconds to process this and once the significance hit her, she shook her head. 'I don't believe you,' she said. 'Martin wouldn't do that. He wouldn't. Not without telling me.'

'I'm afraid he did.' A cynical smile tugged at the corners of his mouth. 'The lure of money is usually enough to eclipse even the most worthy of principles and I offered him a price he couldn't refuse.'

'You…bastard,' she said, walking like a robot into her hallway, too dazed to object when he followed her and snapped on the harsh overhead light. But this time there were no frantic kisses. No barely controlled hunger as they tore at each other's clothes. There was nothing but a simmering mistrust as Lisa stared into his unyielding blue eyes. 'So what are you planning to do?' she questioned. 'Dramatically cut my funds? Or slowly bleed me dry so that you can force me into closure?'

'I'm hoping it won't come to that,' he said. 'My acquisition of your business was simply a back-up. An insurance policy, if you like, in case you proved to be stubborn as I anticipated, which is exactly what has happened. But I have no desire to be ruthless unless you make me, Lisa. I won't interfere with your business if you return to Mardovia with me as my wife.'

She shook her head. 'I can't do that, Luc,' she breathed. 'You know I can't.'

'Why not?' His gazed bored into her. 'Is it because I'm the wrong man? Are you holding out for Mr Right? Is that what this is all about?'

She gave a short laugh. 'Mr Right is a fictional character created by women who still believe in fairy tales. And I don't.'

'Well, isn't that just perfect, because neither do I. Which means that neither of us have any illusions which can be shattered.'

But his declaration gave Lisa little comfort. Her back was aching and her feet felt swollen. She walked into the tiny sitting room and slumped into one of the overstuffed armchairs without even bothering to put the light on. But Luc took control of this, too, following her and snapping on a lamp before drawing the curtains against the darkness outside. She found herself thinking that his servants must usually do this kind of thing for him and wondered what it must be like, to live his privileged life.

'We don't have to go through with a sham marriage,' she said wearily. 'I told you. We can do this the modern way and share custody. Lots of people do. And given all the wealth at your disposal, it will be easier for us to achieve than for most people.' From somewhere she conjured up a hopeful smile. 'I mean, it's not like we're going to be worried about whether we can afford to run two households, is it?'

But he didn't respond to her feeble attempt at humour.

'You're missing the point,' he said. 'I have a duty to my people and the land I was born to rule. Mardovia's stability has been threatened in the past and the principality was almost destroyed as a result. It cannot be allowed to happen again and I will not let it. This child is the future of my country—'

'What? Even if it's a girl?'

He went very still. 'Do you *know* the sex of the baby?' he questioned.

Lisa thought about lying. Of saying she was going to have a girl in the hope that the macho rules which seemed to define him would make him reconsider his demand that she marry him. But she couldn't do that. It would be a cheap move to use their baby as a pawn in their battle, and she sensed it wouldn't make any difference.

She shook her head. 'No. I told the sonographer

I didn't want to know. I didn't like the idea of going through a long labour without even the promise of a surprise at the end. A bit like getting your Christmas presents and discovering that nobody had bothered to wrap them.'

He smiled at this and, inexplicably, Lisa felt herself softening. As if nature had programmed her to melt whenever the father of her child dished out some scrap of affection. *And she couldn't afford to melt.*

'Whatever the sex of the baby, there's no reason why the act of succession cannot be re-examined some time in the future,' he said and walked across the room towards her, towering over her, his muscular body completely dominating her line of vision. 'I am doing my very best to be reasonable here and I will do everything in my power to accommodate your desires, Lisa. And before you start glowering at me like that, I wasn't referring just to physical desires, though I'm more than happy to take those into account.'

Lisa could feel her face growing hot and her breasts beginning to prickle. And the most infuriating thing of all was that right then she wanted him to touch them again. To cup and fondle them and flicker his tongue over them. She wanted him to put his hand between her legs and to ease the aching there. Was it *normal* for a pregnant woman to feel such a powerful sense of desire?

'I can't do that,' she said in a low voice. 'My life is here. I can't leave my little niece, or my sister.'

'Why not?'

'Because I...help them.'

'What do you mean, you help them?'

She shrugged. 'They have no regular income.'

'Your sister is a single parent?'

'Sort of. She's with Jason, only they're not married and he's rather work-shy.'

'Then it's about time he changed his attitude,' he said. 'Your sister and child will receive all the support they require because I will be able to help with that, too. And soon you will have a family of your own to think about.'

'And my business?' she demanded, levering herself into a sitting-up position and trying to summon the energy to glare at him. 'What about that? I've worked for years to establish myself and yet now I'm expected to drop everything—as if my work was nothing but some disposable little hobby.'

'I am willing to compromise on that and I don't intend to deprive you of your career,' he said softly. 'You have people who work for you. Let them run the shop in your absence while you design from the palace.'

And Lisa knew that whatever objection she raised Luc would override her. Because he could. He didn't care that she was close to her little niece and terrified that everything she'd worked for would simply slip away if she wasn't there to oversee it. He didn't care about her—he never had. All he cared about was what *he* wanted. And he wanted this baby.

'You don't understand.' She raised her hands in a gesture of appeal, but the answering look in his eyes was stony.

'I understand more than you might think,' he said.

'I shall accommodate your wishes as much as possible. I don't intend to be a cruel husband. But be very clear about one thing, Lisa—that this topic is not open for debate. That if it comes to it, I will drag you screaming and kicking to the altar, because you *will* be my wife and my child *will* be born on Mardovian soil.'

There was a pause as she bit her lip before looking up at the grim determination which made his blue eyes look so cold. 'If…if I agree to this forced marriage, I want some form of compensation.'

'Compensation?' he echoed incredulously, as if she was insulting him—which in a way she guessed she was. Unless you counted what she wanted as some old-fashioned kind of dowry.

'Yes,' she said quietly. 'I want you to buy my sister a house of her own and provide her with a regular income which will free her from the clutches of her sponging partner.'

His mouth twisted. 'And that is the price for your consent?'

Lisa nodded. 'That is my price,' she said heavily.

CHAPTER SIX

LUC LOOKED AROUND the room—a relatively small room but the one where his wedding to Lisa Tiffany Bailey was about to take place. It was decked out with garlands of flowers, their heavy fragrance perfuming the air, and over the marble fireplace was the crimson and gold of the Mardovian flag. Everything around him was as exquisitely presented as you would expect in the embassy of a country which had a reputation for excellence—and the staff had pulled out all the stops for the unexpected wedding of their ruler to his English bride. But when it boiled down to it, it was just a room.

His face tightening with tension, he thought about the many generations of his family who had married in the august surroundings of the famous cathedral in Mardovia's capital. Grand weddings attended by other royals, by world leaders, politicians and aristocracy. Huge, glittering affairs which had been months in the planning and talked about for years afterwards.

But there would be no such wedding for him.

Because how could he marry in front of his traditionally conservative people with such a visibly pregnant bride in tow? Wouldn't it flaunt his own questionable behaviour, as well as risking offending Princess Sophie—a woman adored by his subjects? This was to be a small and discreet ceremony, with a woman who did not want to take part in it.

He allowed himself a quick glance at the chairs on which her small family sat. The sister who looked so like her, and her boyfriend Jason, who Lisa clearly didn't trust. *Just as she didn't trust him.* Luc watched the casually dressed man with the slightly too long hair glance around the ornate room, unable to hide his covetous expression as he eyed up the lavish fixtures and fittings. He sensed Lisa was disappointed that the new house and income which had been given to her sister had failed to remove Jason from the equation. It seemed that her sister's love for him ran deep…

But her dysfunctional family wasn't the reason he was here today and Luc tensed as the Mardovian national anthem began to play. Slowly, he turned his head to watch as Lisa made her entrance, his heart pounding as she started to walk towards him and he was unprepared—and surprised—by the powerful surge of feeling which ran through him as she approached.

His mouth dried to dust as he stared at his bride, thinking how *beautiful* she looked, and he felt the inexplicable twist of his heart. More beautiful than he could ever have imagined.

She had left her hair spilling free—a glossy cascade broken only by the addition of white flowers which had been carefully woven into the honeyed locks. To some extent, the glorious spectacle of her curls drew the eye away from her rounded stomach, but her dressmaker's eye for detail had also played a part in that—for her gown was cleverly designed to minimise the appearance of her pregnancy. Heavy cream satin fell to her knee and the matching shoes showcased shapely legs which, again, distracted attention from her full figure. And, of course, the gleaming tiara of diamonds and pearls worn by all Mardovian brides drew and dazzled the eye. Beside her, with one chubby little hand clinging on tightly, walked the toddling shape of her little niece—her only bridesmaid.

And then Luc looked into Lisa's face. At the unsmiling lips and shuttered eyes, and a sense of disappointment whispered over him. She certainly wasn't feigning a joy she clearly didn't feel! Her expression was more suited to someone about to attend their own execution rather than their wedding.

Yet could he blame her? She had never sought closeness—other than the purely physical variety. This must be the last thing in the world she wanted. His jaw tightened. And what about him? He had never intended for this to happen either. Yet it *had* happened. Fate had presented him with a very different kind of destiny from the one mapped out for him, and there wasn't a damned thing he could do about it. He stared at her as a powerful sense of certainty washed over him. Except vow to be the best father and husband he could possibly be.

Could he do that?

'Are you okay?' he questioned as she reached his side.

Okay? Chewing on her lip, Lisa bent to direct her little niece over to the ornate golden chair to sit beside her mother. No, she was *not* okay. She felt like a puppet. Like a *thing*. She was being dragged into matrimony like some medieval bride who had just been bought by her powerful master.

But if she was being forced to go through with this marriage, maybe she ought to do it with at least the *appearance* of acceptance. Wouldn't it be better not to feed the prejudices of his staff when she sensed they already resented his commoner bride? So she forced a smile as she stepped up beside Luc's towering figure.

'Ecstatic,' she murmured and met the answering glint in his eyes.

The ceremony passed in a blur and afterwards there was a small reception. But an overexcited Tamsin started running around and ground some wedding cake into an antique rug, and Lisa didn't like the way Jason seemed to be hovering over a collection of precious golden artefacts sitting on top of a beautiful inlaid table.

It was Luc who smoothly but firmly brought the proceedings to an end—and Lisa had to swallow down the sudden tears which sprang to her eyes as she hugged her little niece goodbye, before clinging tightly to her sister.

'I'm going to miss you, Britt,' she said fiercely.

And Brittany's voice wobbled as she hugged her back. 'But you'll be back, won't you, Lisa? My lovely new house is certainly big enough to accommodate my princess sister,' she whispered. 'Or we can come out and stay with you in Mardovia. We'll still see each other, won't we?'

Lisa met her sister's eyes. How did you tell your closest relative you were terrified of being swallowed up by an alien new life which would shut out the old one for good? With a deep breath, she composed herself. You didn't. You just got on with things and made the best of them, the way she'd done all her life. 'Of course we will,' she said.

'Are you ready, Lisa?' came Luc's voice from behind her and she nodded, glad that confetti was banned on the surrounding fancy London streets—because she honestly didn't think she could smile like some happy hypocrite as she walked through a floating cloud of rose petals.

A car whisked them to the airfield, where they were surrounded by officials. Someone from the Aviation Authority insisted on presenting Lisa with a bouquet, which only added to her feelings of confusion because she wasn't used to people curtseying to her. It wasn't until they were high in the sky over France that she found herself alone with Luc at last, and instantly she was subjected to a very different kind of confusion— a sensual tug-of-war which had become apparent the moment the aircraft doors had closed and they were alone together.

He had changed from his Mardovian naval uniform and was wearing a dark suit which hugged his powerful frame, and his olive skin looked golden and glowing. His long legs were spread out in front of him and, distractingly, she couldn't stop remembering their muscular power and the way he had shuddered with pleasure as she had coiled her fingertips around them. Her mouth dried and she wondered if he knew how uncomfortable she was feeling as his sapphire gaze rested thoughtfully on her.

'Now, as weddings go...' he elevated his black brows in a laconic question '...was that really so bad?'

She shrugged. 'That depends what you're comparing it with. Better than being adrift at sea for three days with no water, I suppose—though probably on a par with being locked up for life and having the key thrown away.'

'Oh, Lisa.' The brief glint of amusement which had entered his eyes was suddenly replaced with a distinct sense of purpose. 'Your independent attitude is something I've always enjoyed but this marriage isn't going to work if you're going to spend the whole time being obstructive.'

'And what did you think I was going to do?' she questioned, her voice low because she was aware that although the officials were out of sight, they were still very much present. 'Fall ecstatically into your arms the moment you slid the ring on my finger?'

'Why not? You wouldn't hear any objection from me and it's pretty obvious that the attraction between us is as powerful as it ever was—something which was demonstrated on the night our baby was conceived. And now we're man and wife,' he said, sliding his hand over her thigh and leaving it to rest there, 'isn't that what's supposed to happen? Isn't it a pity to let all this frustrated desire go to waste?'

Lisa stared down at the fingers which were outlined against the grey silk jersey of her 'going away' dress and thought how right they felt. As if they had every right to be there—ready to creep beneath the hem of her dress. Ready to slip inside her panties, which were already growing damp with excitement. She thought about the pleasure he was capable of giving her. Instant pleasure which could be hers any time she liked.

But something told her that she shouldn't slip into intimacy with him—no matter how tempting the prospect—because to do so would be to lose sight of his essential ruthlessness. He had brought her here like some kind of *possession*. An old-fashioned chattel who carried his child. He had married her despite all her protestations, and there hadn't been a thing she could do about it. She was trapped. The deal had been sealed. She had made her bed and now she must lie in it.

She just didn't intend sharing it with him.

That was the only thing she was certain of—that she wasn't going to complicate things by having sex with a man who had blackmailed her to the altar. Her resistance would be the key to her freedom, because a man with Luc's legendary libido would never endure a sexless marriage. Inevitably, he would be driven into the arms of other women and she would be able to divorce him on grounds of infidelity. She pushed his hand away, telling herself it was better this way. Better never to start something which could only end in heartache. But that didn't stop her body from missing that brief caress of his fingers, from wishing that she could close her eyes and pretend not to care when they slipped beneath her dress and began to pleasure her...

'We may be married,' she said. 'But it's going to be in name only.'

'Do I take that to mean you're imposing a sex ban?' he questioned gravely.

She smoothed down the ruffled silk jersey, which still bore the imprint of his hand, and waited until her heart had stopped racing quite so much. 'A ban would imply that something was ongoing, which is definitely not the case. We had one night together—and not even a whole night because you couldn't wait to get away from me, could you, Luc? So please don't try suggesting that I'm withdrawing something which never really got off the ground.'

Luc frowned, unused to having his advances rejected, or for a woman to look at him with such determination in her eyes. His power and status had always worked in his favour—but it was his natural *charisma* which had always guaranteed him a hundred per cent success rate with the opposite sex. Yet he could sense that this time was different. Because *Lisa* was different. She always had been. He remembered the silent vow he had taken as she'd walked towards him in all her wedding finery. A vow to be the best husband he could. She was a newly crowned princess and she was *pregnant*—so shouldn't he cut her a little slack?

'I hear what you say,' he said. 'But the past is done, Lisa. All we have is the present. And the future, of course.'

'And I need you to hear this,' she answered, in a

low and fervent voice. 'Which is that I will perform my role as your princess, at least until after the birth. But I will be your wife in name only. I meant what I said and I will not share a bed with you, Luc. I don't intend to have sex with you. Be very clear about that.'

'And is there any particular reason why?' His eyes mocked her, his gaze lingering with a certain insolence on the swell of her breasts. 'Because you want me, Lisa. You want me very badly. We both know that.'

There was silence for a moment as Lisa willed her nipples to stop tingling in response to his lazy scrutiny. She swallowed. 'Because sex can weaken women. It can blind them to the truth, so that they end up making stupid mistakes.'

'And you have experience of this, do you?'

She shrugged. 'Indirectly.'

His voice was cool. 'Are you going to tell me about it? We need something to do if we aren't going to celebrate our union in the more conventional manner.'

Lisa hesitated. As usual, his words sounded more like an order than a question and her instinct was to keep things bottled up inside her, just as she'd always done. He'd never been interested in this kind of thing in the past, but she guessed things were different now. And maybe Luc needed to know why she meant what she said. To realise that the stuff she'd experienced went bone deep and she wasn't about to change. She didn't *dare* change. She needed to stay exactly as she was—in control. So that nobody could get near to her and nobody could ever hurt her. 'Oh, it's a knock-on effect from my scarred childhood,' she said flippantly.

Pillowing his hands behind his dark head, he leaned back in the aircraft seat and studied her. 'What happened in your childhood?'

It took a tense few moments before the words came out and that was when she realised she'd never talked about it before. Not even with Britt. She'd buried it all away. She'd shut it all out and put that mask on. But suddenly she was tired of wearing a mask all the time—and she certainly had no need to impress Luc. Why, if she gave him a glimpse into her dysfunctional background, maybe he might do them both a favour and finish the marriage before it really started.

'My father died when my sister and I were little,' she said. 'I was too young to remember much about him and Britt was just a baby. He was much older than my mother and he was rich. Very rich.' She met his sapphire gaze and said it before he could. 'I think that was the reason she married him.'

'Some women crave security,' he observed with a shrug.

She had expected condemnation, not understanding, and slowly she let out the breath she hadn't even realised she'd been holding. 'She was brought up in poverty,' she said slowly. 'Not the being-broke-before-payday kind, but the genuine never knowing where your next meal is coming from. She once told me that if you'd ever experienced hunger—*real* hunger—then you never forgot it. And marrying my father ensured that hunger became a thing of the past. When he died she became a very wealthy woman…'

'And?' he prompted as her voice trailed off, his eyes blue and luminous.

'And…' Lisa hesitated. She had tried to understand her mother's behaviour and some of it she could. But not all. She compressed her lips to stop them wobbling. 'She found herself in the grip of lust for the first time in her life and decided to reverse her earlier trend by marrying a man much younger than herself. A toy boy,' she finished defiantly. 'Although I don't believe the word was even invented then.'

'A man more interested in her money than in a widow with two young children to care for?'

She gazed at him suspiciously. 'How did you know that?'

'Something in your tone told me that might be the case, but I am a pragmatist, not a romantic, Lisa,' he said drily. 'And all relationships usually involve some sort of barter.'

'Like ours, you mean?' she said.

'I think you know the answer to that question,' he answered lightly.

She stared down at the silk-covered bump of her belly before lifting her gaze to his again. 'He wasn't a good choice of partner. My stepfather was an extremely good-looking man who didn't know the meaning of the word fidelity. He used to screw around with girls his own age—and every time he was unfaithful, it broke my mother just a little bit more.'

'And that affected you?'

'Of course it affected me!' she hit back. 'It affected me *and* my sister. There was always so much *tension* in the house! One never-ending drama. I used to get home from school and my mother would just be sitting there gazing out of the window, her face all red and blotchy from crying. I used to tidy up and cook tea for me and Britt, but all Mum cared about was whether or not *he* would come home that night. Only by then he'd also discovered the lure of gambling and the fact that she was weak enough to bankroll it for him, so it doesn't take much imagination to work out what happened next.'

His dark lashes shuttered his eyes. 'He worked his way through her money?'

Lisa stared at him, trying not to be affected by the understanding gleam in his eyes and the way they were burning into her. But she *was* affected.

'Lisa? What happened? Did he leave you broke?'

She thought she could detect compassion in his voice, but she didn't want it. Because what if she grew to like it and started relying on it? She might start wanting all those things which women longed for. Things like love and fidelity. Things which eluded them and ended up breaking their hearts. She forced herself to remember Luc's own behaviour. The way he'd coldly left her in bed on the night their child had been conceived. The way he'd focussed only on the mark she'd left on his neck instead of the fact that he had *used* her. And that there was some poor princess waiting patiently in her palace for him to return to marry her. Kind Princess Sophie who had been generous enough to send them a wedding gift, despite everything which had happened.

So don't let on that it was a stark lesson in how a man could ruin the life of the women around him. Let him think it was all about the money. He would understand that because he was a rich man and rich men were arrogant about their wealth. Lisa swallowed. He'd shown no scruples about buying out her business and exerting such powerful control over her life, had he? So tell him what he expects to hear. Make him think you're a heartless bitch who only cares about the money.

'Yeah,' she said flippantly. 'The ballet lessons had to stop and so did the winter holidays. I tell you, it was hell.'

She saw the answering tightening of his lips and knew her remark had hit home. And even though she told herself she didn't *care* about his good opinion, it hurt to see the sudden distaste on his face. Quickly, she turned her head towards the window and looked out at the bright blue sea as they began their descent into Mardovia.

CHAPTER SEVEN

'AND THIS,' SAID LUC, 'is Eleonora.'

Lisa nodded, trying to take it all in. The beautiful green island. The white and golden palace. The child kicking frantically beneath her heart. And now this beautiful woman who was staring at her with an expression of disbelief—as if she couldn't quite believe who Luc had married.

'Eleonora has been my aide for a number of years,' Luc continued. 'But I have now assigned her to look after you. Anything you want or need to know—just ask Eleonora. She's the expert. She knows pretty much everything about Mardovia.'

Lisa tried to portray a calm she was far from feeling as she extended her hand in greeting. She felt alone and displaced. She was tired after the flight and her face felt sticky. She wanted to turn to her new husband and howl out her fears in a messy display of emotion which was not her usual style. She wanted to feel his strong arms wrapped protectively around her back, which would be the biggest mistake of all. So instead she just fixed a smile to her lips as she returned Eleonora's cool gaze.

She wondered if she was imagining the unfriendly glint in the eyes of the beautiful aide. Did Eleonora realise that Lisa had been feeling completely out of her depth from the moment she'd arrived on the island and her attitude wasn't helping? The aide was so terrifying elegant—with not a sleek black hair out of place and looking a picture of sophistication in a slim-fitting cream dress, which made Lisa feel like a barrel in comparison. Was she looking at her and wondering how such a pale-faced intruder had managed to become Princess of Mardovia? She glanced down at her bulky tum. It was pretty obvious how.

Lisa sucked in a deep breath. Maybe she was just being paranoid. After all, she couldn't keep blaming Eleonora for not putting her in touch with Luc that time she'd telephoned. She hadn't known Lisa was newly pregnant because Lisa hadn't told her, had she? She'd only been doing her job, which was presumably to protect the Prince from disgruntled ex-lovers like her.

So she smiled as widely as she could. 'It's lovely to meet you, Eleonora,' she said.

'Likewise, Your Royal Highness,' said Eleonora, her coral lips curving.

Luc glanced from one woman to the other. 'Then I shall leave you both to become better acquainted.' He turned towards Lisa. 'I have a lot of catching up to do so I'll see you at dinner. But for now I will leave you in Eleonora's capable hands.'

Lisa nodded, because what could she say? *Please don't go. Stay with me and protect me from this woman with the unsmiling eyes.* She and Luc didn't have that kind of relationship, she reminded herself, and she was supposed to be an independent woman. So why this sudden paralysing fear which was making her feel positively *clingy*? Was it the see-sawing of her wretched hormones playing up again?

In silence Lisa watched him go, the sunlight glinting off his raven hair and the powerful set of his shoulders emphasising his proud bearing. Suddenly the room felt empty without him and the reality of her situation finally hit home. She was no longer ordinary Lisa Bailey, with a failing shop, a mortgage and a little sister who was being dominated by a feckless man. She was now a princess, married to a prince adored by all his people—and all the curtseying and bowing was something she was going to have to get used to.

And despite all her misgivings, she couldn't help but be entranced by the sun-drenched island. During the drive to Luc's palace, she had seen rainbows of wild flowers growing along the banks of the roads and beautiful trees she hadn't recognised. They had passed through unspoiled villages where old men sat on benches and watched the world go by in scenes which had seemed as old as time itself. Yet as they had rounded a curve in one of the mountain roads she had looked down into a sparkling bay, where state-of-the-art white yachts had dazzled like toys in an oversized bathtub. It had been at that point that Lisa had realised that she was now wife to one of the most eligible men in the world.

'You would like me to show you around the palace?' questioned Eleonora in her faultless English.

Lisa nodded. What she would have liked most would have been for Luc to give her a guided tour around his palatial home, but maybe that was asking too much. She could hardly tell him she had no intention of be-having like a *real* wife and then expect him to play the role of devoted husband. And mightn't it be a good idea to make an ally out of his devoted aide? To show a bit of genuine sisterhood? She smiled. 'I should like that very much.'

'You will find it confusing at first,' said Eleonora, her patent court shoes clipping loudly on the marble floors as they set off down a long corridor. 'People are always taken aback by the dimensions of the royal household.'

'Were you?' questioned Lisa as she peeped into a formal banqueting room where a vast table was adorned with golden plates and glittering crystal gob-lets. 'A bit shell-shocked when you first came here?'

'Me?' Eleonora's pace slowed and that coral-lipped smile appeared again. 'Oh, no. Not at all. My father was an aide to Luc's father and I grew up in one of the staff apartments on the other side of the complex. Why, the palace is the only home I've ever really known! I know every single nook and cranny of the place.'

Lisa absorbed this piece of information in silence, wondering if she was supposed to feel intimidated by it. But she wasn't going to *let* herself be intimidated. She had been upfront with Luc and maybe she should be just as upfront with his aide—and confront the enor-mous elephant which was currently dominating the palatial corridor.

'I know that Luc was supposed to marry Princess Sophie,' she said quietly. 'And I'm guessing that a lot of people are disappointed she isn't going to be Luc's bride.'

It was a moment before Eleonora answered and when she did, her voice was fierce. 'Very disappointed,' she said bluntly. 'For it was his father's greatest wish that the Princess should marry Luc. And the Princess is as loved by the people of Mardovia as she is by her own subjects on Isolaverde.'

'I'm sure she is,' said Lisa. 'And...' Her voice tailed off. How could she possibly apologise for having ruined the plans for joining the two royal dynasties? She couldn't even say she would do her best to make up for it by being the best wife she possibly could. Not when she had every intention of withholding sex and ending the marriage just as soon as their baby was born.

So she said very little as she followed Eleonora from room to room, trying to take in the sheer scale of the place. She was shown the throne room and several reception rooms of varying degrees of splendour. There was a billiards room and a huge sports complex, with its fully equipped gym and Olympic-sized swimming pool. She peered through the arched entrance to the palace gardens and the closed door to Luc's study. *'He doesn't like anyone to disturb him in there. Only I am permitted access.'* Last of all they came to a long gallery lined with beautiful paintings, and Lisa was filled with a reluctant awe as she looked around, because this could rival some of the smaller art galleries she sometimes visited in London.

There were portraits of princes who were clearly Luc's ancestors, for they bore the same startling sapphire eyes and raven tumble of hair. There were a couple of early French Impressionists and a sombre picture of tiny matchstick men, which Lisa recognised as a Lowry. But the paintings which captured her attention were a pair hanging together in their own small section of the gallery. Luminously beautiful, both pictures depicted the same person—a woman with bobbed blonde hair. In one, she was wearing a nineteen-twenties flapper outfit with a silver headband gleaming in her pale hair, and Lisa couldn't work out if she was in fancy-dress costume or not. In the other she was flushed and smiling in a riding jacket—the tip of her crop just visible.

'Who is this?' Lisa questioned suddenly.

Eleonora's voice was cool. 'This is the Englishwoman who married one of your husband's ancestors.'

It was a curious reply to make but the coral lips were now clamped firmly closed and Lisa realised that the aide had no intention of saying any more. She sensed the guided tour was over, yet it had thrown up more questions than answers. Suddenly, the enormity of her situation hit her—the realisation of how *alien* this new world was—and for the first time since their private jet had touched down, a wave of exhaustion washed over her.

'I think I'd like to go to my room now,' she said.

'Of course. If you would like to follow me, I will show you a shortcut.'

Alone at last in the vast marital apartment, Lisa

pulled off her clothes and stood beneath the luxury shower in one of the two dazzling bathrooms. Bundling her thick curls into the plastic cap she took with her everywhere, she let the powerful jets of water splash over her sticky skin and wash away some of the day's tension. Afterwards she wrapped herself in a fluffy white robe which was hanging on the bathroom door and began to explore the suite of rooms. She found an airy study, a small dining room—and floor-to-ceiling windows in the main reception room, which overlooked a garden of breathtaking beauty.

For a moment Lisa stared out at the emerald lawns and the sparkling surface of a distant lake—reflecting that it was worlds away from her home in England. Inside this vaulted room, the scent of freshly cut flowers wafted through the air and antique furniture stood on faded and exquisite silken rugs. Peeping into one of the dressing rooms, she saw that all her clothes had been neatly hung up in one of the wardrobes.

The bedroom was her last port of call and she hovered uncertainly on the threshold before going in, complicated feelings of dread and hunger washing over her as she stared at the vast bed covered with a richly embroidered throw. She didn't hear the door open or close, only realising she was no longer alone when she heard a soft sound behind her—like someone drawing in an unsteady breath—and when she turned round she saw Luc standing there.

Instantly, her mouth dried with lust and there wasn't a thing she could do about it. His hair was so black and his eyes so blue. How was it possible to want a man who had essentially trapped her here, like a prisoner? He looked so strong and powerful as he came into the bedroom that her heart began to pound in a way she wished it wouldn't, and as her breasts began to ache distractingly she said the first thing which came into her head.

'I told you I wasn't going to share a bed with you.'

He shrugged as he pulled off his jacket and draped it over the back of a gilt chair. 'It's a big bed.'

She swallowed, acutely aware of the ripple of muscle beneath his fine silk shirt. 'That's not the point.'

'No?' He tugged off his tie and tossed it on top of the jacket. 'What's the problem? You think I won't be able to refrain from touching you—or is it the other way round? Worried that you won't be able to keep your hands off me, *chérie*? Mmm…? Is that it? From the hungry look in your eyes, I'm guessing you'd like me to come right over there and get you naked.'

'In your dreams!' she spat back. 'Because even if you force me to share your bed, I shan't have sex with you, Luc, so you'd better get…get…' Her words died away as he began to undo his shirt and his glorious golden torso was laid bare, button by button. 'What… what do you think you're doing?'

'I'm undressing. What does it look like? I want to take a shower before dinner, just like you.'

'But you can't—'

'Can't what, Lisa?' The shirt had fluttered to the ground and his blue eyes gleamed as he kicked off his shoes and socks. She was rendered completely speechless by the sight of all that honed and bronzed torso before his fingers strayed suggestively to his belt. 'Does the sight of my naked body bother you?'

She told herself to look away. To look somewhere—anywhere—except at the magnificent physique which was slowly being revealed. But the trouble was that she couldn't. She was like a starving dog confronted by a large, meaty bone, which was actually the worst kind of comparison to make in the circumstances. She couldn't seem to tear her eyes away from him. He was *magnificent*, she thought as he stepped out of his trousers and she was confronted with the rock-hard reality of his powerful, hair-roughened thighs. His hips were narrow and there was an unmistakably hard ridge pushing insistently against his navy blue silk boxers—and, oh, how she longed to see the complete reveal. But she didn't dare. With a flush of embarrassment mixed with a potent sense of desire, she somehow found the courage to turn her back on him before walking over to the bed.

Heaving herself down onto the soft mattress—her progress made slightly laborious by her swollen belly—she shut her eyes tightly but she was unable to block out the sound of Luc's mocking laughter as he headed towards the bathroom.

'Don't worry, you're quite safe from me, *chérie*,' he said softly. 'I've never found shower caps a particular turn-on.'

To Lisa's horror she realised that her curls were still squashed beneath the unflattering plastic cap, and as she heard the bathroom door close behind him she wrenched it free, shaking out her hair and lying back down on the bed again. For a while she stared up at the ceiling—at the lavish chandelier which dripped like diamonds—wishing it could be different.

But how?

Luc had married her out of duty and brought her to a place where the woman she'd usurped was infinitely more loved. How could she possibly make that right?

She must have slept, because she awoke to the smell of mint and, disorientated, opened her eyes to see Luc putting a steaming cup of tea on the table beside the bed. He had brought her *tea*?

'Feeling better?' he said.

His kindness disarmed her and she struggled to sit up, trying to ignore the ache of her breasts and the fact that he was fully dressed while she was still wearing the bathrobe which had become looser while she slept. She pulled the belt a tiny bit tighter but that only emphasised the ballooning shape of her baby bump and she silently cursed herself for caring what she looked like. At least the sight of her was unlikely to fill him with an uncontrollable lust, she reflected. It wasn't just the shower cap which wasn't a turn-on, it was everything about her...

She cleared her throat. 'Much better, thanks,' she lied. 'What time is dinner?'

Luc walked over to the window and watched as she began to sip at her tea. With her face all flushed and her hair mussed, she looked strangely vulnerable—as if she was too sleepy to have remembered to wear her familiar mask of defiance. Right then it would have been so easy to take her into his arms and kiss away some of the unmistakable tension which made her body look so brittle. But she'd made her desires clear—or, rather, the lack of them. She didn't want intimacy and, although right now he sensed she might be open to *persuasion*, it wouldn't work in his favour if he put her in a position which afterwards she regretted. And she was *pregnant*, he reminded himself. She was carrying his baby and therefore she deserved his consideration and protection.

'Dinner is whenever you want it to be.'

She put the cup back down on the saucer, looking a little uncomfortable. 'Will it be served in that huge room with all the golden plates?'

'You mean the formal banqueting room which we use for state functions? I don't tend to eat most meals in there,' he added drily. 'There are smaller and less intimidating rooms we can use.' He paused. 'Or I could always have them bring you something here, on a tray.'

'Seriously? You mean like a TV dinner?' Her green-gold eyes widened. 'Won't people think it odd if we don't go down?'

'I am the Prince and you are my wife and we can do whatever we damned well like,' he said arrogantly. 'What would you like to eat?'

'I know it probably sounds stupid, but I'd love… well, what I'd like more than anything is an egg sandwich.' She looked up at him from between her lashes. 'Do you think that's possible?'

He gave a short laugh. When she looked at him like that, he felt as if anything were possible. But how ironic that the only woman in a position to ask for anything should have demanded something so fundamentally *humble*. 'I think that can be arranged.'

A uniformed servant answered his summons, soon reappearing with the sandwich she'd wanted—most of which she devoured with an uninhibited hunger which Luc found curiously sensual. Or maybe it was the fact that she was ignoring him which had stirred his senses—because he wasn't used to *that* either.

After she'd finished and put her napkin down, she looked up at him, her face suddenly serious.

'Eleonora showed me the gallery today,' she said.

'Good. I wanted you to see as much of the palace as possible.'

She traced a figure of eight on the linen tablecloth with the tip of her finger before looking up.

'I noticed two paintings of the same woman. Beautiful paintings—in a specially lit section of the gallery.'

He nodded. 'Yes. Two of Kristjan Wheeler's finest works. Conall Devlin acquired one of them for me.'

'Yes, I knew he was an art dealer as well as a property tycoon,' she said. 'But what I was wondering was…'

He set down his glass of red wine as her voice tailed off. 'What?' he questioned coolly.

She wriggled her shoulders and her hazelnut curls shimmered. 'Why Eleonora seemed so *cagey* when I asked about the paintings.'

He shrugged. 'Eleonora has always been the most loyal of all my aides.'

'How lovely for you,' she said politely. 'But surely as your wife I am expected to know—'

'Who she is? The woman in the paintings?' he finished as he picked up his glass and swirled the burgundy liquid around the bowl-like shape of the glass. 'She was an Englishwoman called Louisa De Lacy, who holidayed here during the early part of the last century. She was an unconventional woman—an adventuress was how she liked to style herself. A crack shot who smoked cheroots and wore dresses designed to shock.'

'And is that relevant? She sounds fun.'

'Very relevant. Mardovia was under the rule of one of my ancestors and he fell madly in love with her. The trouble was that Miss De Lacy wasn't deemed suitable on any grounds, even if she'd wanted to be a princess, which she didn't. Despite increasing opposition, he refused to give her up and eventually he was forced to renounce the throne and was exiled from Mardovia. After his abdication his younger brother took the crown—my great-great-grandfather—and that is how it came to be passed down to me.'

'And was that a problem?' she questioned curiously.

He shrugged. 'Not for me. Not even for my father—because we were born knowing we must rule—but for my great-great-grandfather, yes. He had never wanted to govern and was married to a woman who was painfully shy. The burden of the crown contributed to his early death, for which his wife never forgave Louisa De Lacy, and in the meantime…'

'In the meantime, what?' she whispered as his voice trailed off.

'Unfortunately the exiled Prince was killed in a riding accident before he could marry Louisa, who by then had given birth to his child.'

Her head jerked up. 'You mean...'

Luc's temper suddenly shortened. Maybe it was because he was tired and frustrated. Because she was sitting there with that cascade of curls flowing down over her engorged breasts and he wanted to make love to her. He wanted to explore her luscious body with fingers which were on the verge of trembling with frustration, not to have to sit here recounting his family history. Because this was not the wedding night he had anticipated.

'I mean that somewhere out there a child was born out of wedlock—a child of royal Mardovian blood who was never seen again—and they say that there is none so dangerous as a dispossessed prince.' His voice grew hard. 'And I was not prepared for history to repeat itself. Because I have no brothers, Lisa. No one else to pass on the reins to, should I fail to produce an heir. Succession is vital to me, and to my land.'

'So that's why you forced me to marry you,' she breathed.

He nodded. It was not the whole truth, but it was part of it—because he was slowly coming to realise that there were worse fates than having a woman like Lisa by his side. Duty, yes—he would not shirk from that—but couldn't duty be clothed in pleasure?

Wasn't she aware that now he had her here, he had no intention of letting her or the child go? If she accepted that with a good grace then so much the better, but accept it she would. His will was stronger than hers and he would win because he *always* won.

And then something else occurred to him—a fact which he had pushed to the back of his mind because the sheer logistics of getting her here had consumed all his thoughts. But it was something he needed to address sooner rather than later. He tensed as he realised that until they consummated the marriage, their union was not legal. His heart missed a beat. He realised that, but did she?

He remembered her defiant words on the plane—a variation on what she'd said just now, when she'd announced she had no intention of sharing a bed with him. He didn't doubt her resolve, not for a moment, for Lisa was a strong and proud woman. Yet women were capricious creatures who could have their minds changed for them. But only if you played them carefully. He had learnt his first lessons in female manipulation from the governesses who'd been employed to look after him after his mother's death. Run after a woman and it gave her power. Act like you didn't care and she would be yours for the taking.

Duty clothed in pleasure.

He had vowed to be a good husband as well as a good father, so surely one of his responsibilities was making sure his wife received an adequate share of sexual satisfaction? He looked at her green-gold eyes and as he detected the glint of sexual hunger she could not disguise, he smiled.

His for the taking.

CHAPTER EIGHT

THE NEXT FEW weeks were so full with being a new wife, a new princess *and* mother-to-be that Lisa had barely any time to get homesick. Eleonora introduced her to most of the palace staff, to her own personal driver and the two protection officers who would accompany her whenever she left the palace. She was given her own special servant—Almeera—a quiet, dark-eyed beauty who chattered excitedly about how much she loved babies. She met the royal dressmaker who said she'd happily make up Lisa's own designs for the duration of her pregnancy, or they could send to Paris or London for any couture requirements the Princess might have.

She also had her first appointment with the palace obstetrician, Dr Gautier, who came to examine her in her royal apartments, accompanied by a midwife. At least Eleonora made herself scarce for that particular appointment, although Lisa was surprised when Luc made a sudden appearance just before the consultation began.

Her heart began to pound as he walked into the room, nodding to the doctor and midwife who had stood up to bow, before coming to sit beside her and giving her hand a reassuring squeeze. And even though she knew the gesture was mainly for the benefit of the watching medics, she stupidly *felt* reassured. Could he feel the thunder of her pulse? Was he aware that her breasts started to ache whenever he was close? She wondered if they looked like any other newly-wed couple from the outside and what the doctor would say if he realised they hadn't had sex since the night their child was conceived. And she wondered what Luc would say if he knew how at night she lay there, wide-eyed in the dark—unable to sleep because her body was craving his expert touch…

Dr Gautier flicked through the file which lay on the desk before him before fixing his eyes firmly on Luc.

'I am assuming that Your Royal Highness already knows the sex of the baby?' he questioned.

Did Luc hear Lisa's intake of breath? All he had to do was to ask the doctor what he wanted to know and it would be done. The fact would be out there. Lisa swallowed. Some people might think she was being awkward in not wanting this particular piece of information, but it was important to her. It felt like her last remnant of independence and the only control she had left over her life.

'My wife doesn't wish to know,' said Luc, meeting her eyes with a faintly mocking expression. 'She wants it to be a surprise on the day.'

'Very sensible,' said the doctor, turning to ask Lisa if there was anything she wanted to know.

The questions she wanted to ask were not for the

obstetrician's ears. Nor for the ears of the husband sitting beside her.

How soon can I return to England after the birth?

When will Luc let me leave him?

Or the most troubling of all.

Will I ever stop wanting a man who sees me only as the vessel which carries his child?

But some of Lisa's fears left her that day and she wasn't sure why. Was it Luc's simple courtesy in not demanding to know the sex of their baby? Or that meaningless little squeeze of her hand which had made her relax her defences a little? Afterwards, when they were back in their suite, she turned to him to thank him and the baby chose that moment to deliver a hefty kick just beneath her ribs. Automatically, she winced before smiling as she clutched her stomach and when she looked into Luc's face, she was surprised by the sudden *longing* she read in his eyes.

She asked the question because she knew she had to, pushing aside the thought that it was a somehow dangerous thing to do—to invite him to touch her. 'Would you like to…to feel the baby kick?'

'May I?'

She nodded, holding her breath as he laid his hand over her belly and they waited for the inevitable propulsion of one tiny foot. She heard him laugh in disbelief as a tiny heel connected with his palm and, once the movement had subsided, she wondered if he would now do what her body was longing for him to do—and continue touching her in a very different way. She thought how easy it would be. He could move his hand upwards to cup a painfully engorged breast and slowly caress her nipple with the pad of his thumb. Or downwards, to slide his fingers between her legs and find how hot and hungry she was for him.

But he didn't.

He removed his hand from her belly and although she silently cursed and wanted to draw him back to her, she was in no position to do so. She wondered if she had been too hasty in rejecting him, particularly when she hadn't realised he could be so *kind*. And she was fast discovering that kindness could be as seductive as any kiss.

Maybe that was the turning point for Lisa. The discovery that as the days passed the palace stopped feeling like a prison. Or maybe it was a direct result of Luc's sudden announcement that he had a surprise for her. One morning after breakfast, he led her through the endless maze of corridors to a part of the palace she hadn't seen before, where he opened a set of double doors, before beckoning her inside.

'Come and take a look at this,' he said. 'And tell me what you think.'

Lisa was momentarily lost for words as she walked into an airy studio overlooking the palace gardens. She glanced around, trying to take it all in—because in it was everything a dress designer could ever desire. On a big desk were pencils and paints and big pads of sketch paper. There was a computer, a sophisticated music system, a tiny kitchen and even a TV.

'For when you get bored,' Luc drawled. 'I wasn't sure if artwork on the walls would inspire you or distract you—but if you'd like some paintings, then speak to Eleonora and she'll arrange for you to have something from the palace collection.' He searched her face with quizzical eyes. 'I hope this meets with your satisfaction?'

It was a long time since anyone had done something so thoughtful. Something just for *her* and Lisa felt overwhelmed—a feeling compounded by the way Luc was looking at her. His skin was glowing and his black hair was still ruffled from the horse ride he liked to take before breakfast each morning. Which she guessed explained why he was never there when she woke up. Why on more than one occasion she'd found herself rolling over to encounter nothing but a cool space where his warm body should have been.

Because he had spoken the truth. It *was* a big bed. Big enough for two people to share it without touching. For them to lie side by side like two strangers. For her to be acutely aware of his nakedness, even though she couldn't actually see it. Yet as the dark minutes of the night ticked by—punctuated only by the rhythmical sounds of Luc's steady breathing—Lisa was furious with herself for *wanting* him to make love to her. Wondering why hadn't he even *tried* to change her mind? Was her swollen belly putting him off? More than once she had wondered what he would do if she silently moved to his side of the bed. She could put her hand between his legs and start to caress him in that way he liked. She swallowed. Actually, she had a pretty good idea what he'd do...

'I love it,' she said softly, cheeks flushing with embarrassment at her erotic thoughts as she lifted her gaze from the pencils lined up with military precision. 'Thank you.'

There was a pause as their eyes met. An infinitesimal pause when Lisa thought she saw his mouth relax. A moment when his eyes hinted at that flinty look they used to get just before he kissed her. She held her breath. Hoping. No, praying. Thinking—to hell with all her supposedly noble intentions. He was her husband, wasn't he? He was her husband and right then she wanted him with a hunger which was tearing through her body like wildfire. He could make love to her right now—she was sure he would be gentle with her. She felt the molten ache of frustration as she imagined him touching her where she was crying out to be touched.

But just like always, he moved away from her. Only by a fraction, but it might as well have been a mile. She found her cheeks growing even pinker; she walked over to one of the pristine drawing pads in an effort to distract herself. 'I'll start work on my next collection right away,' she said.

He turned to leave but at the door, he paused. 'Has Eleonora told you about the May Ball?'

Lisa shook her head. No. That was something Eleonora must have missed during daily conversations, which usually managed to convey how matey Princess Sophie's father had been with Luc's father, and about the blissful holidays the two families used to enjoy on the island of Isolaverde.

'No,' she said slowly. 'I don't believe she did. Anyway, shouldn't it have been you who told me?'

He raised his eyebrows. 'I'm telling you now,' he said, with a trace of his customary arrogance. 'It's something of a palace tradition. The weather is always fine and the gardens are at their loveliest. It will be the perfect opportunity for you to meet the great and the good. Oh, and you might want to wear some jewels from the royal collection. Speak to Eleonora and she'll show you.'

Lisa forced a smile. She seemed to do nothing but *speak to Eleonora*, but she nodded her head in agreement. And after Luc had gone, she emailed her sister and asked for some new photos of Tamsin, before taking herself off into the palace grounds for a walk.

The gardens were exquisite. Not just the rose section or the intricate maze which led onto the biggest herb garden she'd ever seen, but there were also high-hedged walkways where you could suddenly turn a corner and find some gorgeous marble statue hidden away. Yet today Lisa had to work hard to focus on the beauty of her surroundings because all she could think about was Luc's attitude towards her. He could do something immensely kind and thoughtful like surprising her with a new studio or bring her tea in bed, but he seemed content to keep her at arm's length and push her in the direction of his ever-loyal Eleonora.

But that was what she had wanted.

Only now she was beginning to realise she didn't want it any more. She didn't want to lie chastely by his side while he slept and her body hungered for him. She wanted him to take her in his arms and kiss her. If not to love her—then at least to *make* love to her.

Suddenly, withholding sex as a kind of bargaining tool seemed not only stupid, but self-sacrificing. Maybe she had misjudged the whole situation. She wanted the freedom to be able to return to England but she recognised that she needed Luc's blessing in order to do so. Wouldn't he be more amenable to reason if he was physically satisfied?

And wouldn't she?

He had told her about the ball and he wanted her to wear some of the royal jewels. Couldn't she embrace her new role as his princess and appear comfortable in it? Wouldn't he be pleasantly pleased—maybe even proud of her—giving her the perfect opportunity to seduce him? And since Luc showed no sign of coming on to *her*, she was going to have to be proactive. If she wanted him, then she must show him how much…

She felt the baby stirring inside her, almost as if it were giving her the proverbial thumbs-up, and Lisa felt a sudden warmth creep through her veins. Fired up by a new resolve, she made her way back towards the palace, sunlight streaming onto her bare head. Going straight to her studio, she rang for Eleonora and the aide arrived almost immediately, a questioning look on her smooth face.

Lisa drew a deep breath. 'Luc told me about the ball. He suggested I might wear some of the crown jewels for the occasion.'

Eleonora gave a bland smile. 'Indeed. He has already mentioned it to me.'

Lisa didn't miss a beat, squashing down her indignation. Didn't matter that he confided in Eleonora, because soon he would be in *her* arms and confiding in *her*. 'Could we go and take a look at them, please? Now? Because I think I'd like to design my outfit around the jewels.'

'Of course.'

The collection was housed in a section of the palace not far from the art gallery, and Lisa was momentarily startled when she walked into the spotlighted room, where priceless gems sparkled against inky backdrops of black velvet. Her eyes widened at the sheer opulence of the pieces on display. There were glittering waterfalls of diamonds—white ones and pink ones and even citrusy yellow ones, some with matching drop earrings and bracelets. There were sapphires as blue as Luc's eyes and mysterious milky opals, shot through with rainbows. Lisa was just about to choose a choker of square-cut emeralds when Eleonora indicated a set of drawers at the far end of the room.

'How about these?' Eleonora suggested softly, pulling open one of the drawers and beckoning for Lisa to take a closer look.

Lisa blinked. Inside was a flamboyant ruby necklace with glittering stones as big as gulls' eggs—their claret colour highlighted by the white fire of surrounding diamonds.

'Oh, my word,' she breathed. 'That is the most exquisite thing I've ever seen.'

'Isn't it just?' agreed Eleonora softly as she carefully removed the necklace. 'It hasn't been worn for a long time and is probably the most valuable piece in our entire collection. Why not surprise your husband with it?'

The jewels spilled like rich wine over Lisa's fingers as she took them from the aide, and she could picture exactly the kind of dress to wear with them.

It became a labour of love. Something to work towards. Making her dress for the ball became her secret and she decided it would be her gift to Luc. An olive branch handed to him to make him realise she was prepared to do things differently from now on. That the current situation was far from satisfactory and she'd like to change it. She wanted to be his lover as well as his wife.

'You are looking very pleased with yourself of late,' he observed one evening as they walked down the wide marble corridor towards the dining room.

'Am I?'

'Mmm.' His gaze roved over her as a servant opened the doors for them. 'Actually, you look…*blooming*.'

'Thank you.' She smiled at him. 'I think that's how pregnant women are supposed to look.'

Luc inclined his head in agreement, waiting until she'd sat down before taking his seat opposite and observing her remarkable transformation. When she'd first arrived she had looked strung out and her expression had been pinched—something which had not been improved by their unsatisfactory sleeping arrangements. He had briefly considered moving into his old bachelor rooms to give her the peace she so obviously needed. To make her realise that the only thing worse than sharing a bed with him was *not* sharing a bed with him.

But then some miraculous thaw had occurred. Suddenly, she seemed almost…contented. He heard her humming as she brushed her teeth before bed. He noticed that she'd started reading the Mardovian history book he had given her on the plane. Hungrily, he had watched the luscious thrust of her breasts as she walked into the bedroom with a silken nightdress clinging to every ripe curve of her body, and realised he had nobody but himself to blame for his frustration. He could feel himself growing hard beneath the sheets and had to quickly lie on his belly, willing his huge erection to go away, and he wondered if now was the time to make a move on her. Because his experience with women told him that she would welcome him with open arms…

'You are excited about the ball?' he questioned one evening when they were finishing dinner.

'I'm…looking forward to it.'

His eyes flicked over her. 'You have something to wear?'

'You mean…' on the opposite side of the table she smoothed her hand down over the curve of her belly '…something which will fit over my ever-expanding girth? It's not very attractive, is it?'

'If you really want to know, I find it very attractive,' he said huskily.

She stilled, her hand remaining exactly where it was. 'You don't have to say that just to make me feel better.'

'I never say anything I don't mean.' He touched the tip of his tongue to his lips to help ease their aching dryness and wished it were as simple to relieve the aching in his groin. 'So why don't you go and put on your dress? Show me what you'll be wearing.'

She hesitated. 'It's a secret.'

For some reason her words jarred, or maybe it was his apparent misreading of the situation. The idea that she was softening towards him a little—only to be met with that same old brick wall of resistance.

'So many secrets,' he mocked.

At this her smile died.

'That's a bit rich, coming from the master of secrecy,' she said. 'There's so much about yourself that you keep locked away, Luc. And, of course, there's the biggest concealment of all. If you hadn't kept your fiancée such a big *secret*, we wouldn't have found ourselves in this situation, would we?'

'And doubtless you would have preferred that?'

'Wouldn't you?'

Her challenge fell between them like a stone dropped into a well but Luc told himself he would not allow himself to be trapped into answering hypothetical questions. Instead, he deflected her anger with a careless question. 'What is it about the hidden me you would like revealed, my princess?'

She put down the pearl-handled knife with which she had been peeling an apple and he wondered how deeply she would pry. Whether she would want him to divulge the dark night of his soul to her—and if he did, would that make her understand why he could never really be the man she needed?

'What was it like for you, growing up here?'

It was an innocent enough query but Luc realised too late that all questions were a form of entrapment. That if you gave someone an answer, it paved the way for more questions and more exposure. He gave a bland smile, the type he had used countless times in diplomatic debate. He would not lie to her. No. He would be… What was it that accountants sometimes said? Ah, yes. He would be economical with the truth.

'I imagine it was the same for me as for many other princes born into palaces and surrounded by unimaginable riches,' he said. 'There is always someone to do your bidding and I never wanted for anything.'

Except love, of course.

'Whatever I asked for, I was given.'

But never real companionship.

'I was schooled with other Mardovian aristocrats until the age of eighteen, when I went to school in Paris.'

Where he had tasted freedom for the first time in his life and found it irresistible. But the truth was that nothing had ever been able to fill the emptiness at the very core of him.

'And what about your mum and dad?'

Luc flinched. He had never heard his royal parents described quite so informally, and his first instinct was to correct her and ask her to refer to them by their titles. But he slapped his instinct down, because a lesson in palace protocol would not serve him well at this moment. Not when she was looking at him with that unblinking gaze which was making his heart clench with something he didn't recognise.

'Like you, my mother died when I was very young.'

'I'm sorry for your loss,' she said instantly and there was a pause. 'Did your father remarry?'

He shook his head. 'No.' His father had been locked in his own private world of grief—oblivious to the fact that a small boy was hurting and desperately missing his mother. Unable to look at the child who so resembled his dead wife, he had channelled that grief into duty—pouring all his broken-hearted passion into serving his country. And leaving the care of his son to the stream of governesses employed to look after him.

'I don't think he considered anyone could ever take the place of my mother,' he continued slowly and he felt a twist of pain. Because hadn't he witnessed his father's emotional dependence on the woman who had died—and hadn't it scared him to see such a powerful person diminished by the bitterness of heartbreak?

'How old were you?'

'Four,' he said flatly.

'So who looked after you?'

'Governesses.' Even the sound of the word sent shivers down his spine as he thought of those fierce women, so devoted to his father—who had put duty to the throne above everything else. They had taught him never to cry. Never to show weakness, or fear. They had taught him that a prince must sublimate his own desires in order to best serve his country.

'What were they like?'

He considered Lisa's question—about how many countless variations there were on the word *cold*. 'Efficient,' he said eventually.

She smiled a little. 'That doesn't tell me very much.'

'Maybe it wasn't supposed to.'

But still she persisted. 'And did they show you lots of affection?'

And this, he realised, was an impossible question to answer except with the baldness of truth. 'None whatsoever,' he said slowly. 'There were several of them on some sort of rotation and I think it must have been agreed that they should treat me politely and carefully. I don't think it was intended for any of them to become a mother substitute, or for me to attach myself to anyone in particular. I suspect there was a certain amount of competitiveness between them and they were unwilling to tolerate me having a favourite.'

'Oh, Luc.' Did she notice his faint frown, intended to discourage further questioning? Was that why she deliberately brightened her tone?

'You were lucky,' she added. 'At least you didn't have the proverbial wicked stepmother to deal with.'

He looked into her eyes. Was he? Was anyone ever really 'lucky'? You worked with what you had and fashioned fate to suit you.

He sensed she was softening towards him and that filled him with satisfaction. He had played his part with his restraint—now let her play hers. Let her admit that she wanted him. He gave a grim smile.

Because you made your own luck in life.

CHAPTER NINE

THE MAY BALL was the biggest event in the palace calendar, and Lisa planned her first formal introduction
to the people of Mardovia with the precision of a military campaign. She ordered a bolt of crimson silk satin
and made a gown specially designed to showcase the
ruby and diamond necklace from the royal collection.

For hours she worked to the familiar and comforting sound of the sewing machine, painstakingly finishing off the gown with some careful hand stitching.
She would surprise Luc with her dress, yes. Her pulse
began to race. And not just at the ball. Her self-imposed sex ban had gone on for long enough and now
she wanted him in her arms again. He had heeded her
words and treated her with respect. Night after night he
had lain beside her without attempting to touch her—
even though there had been times when she'd wished
he would. When that slow heat would build low in her
belly, making her want to squirm with frustration as
he slept beside her.

She finished the dress to her satisfaction but as she
got ready for the ball she felt shot with nerves—be-

cause what if Luc had decided he no longer wanted her? What if their stand-off had killed his desire for her? Smoothing down the full-length skirt, she stared at her reflected image in the mirror. He *had* to want her.

She thought back to how she'd felt when she had first arrived here, when she'd married him under duress and had been apprehensive about what lay ahead. But he had respected her wishes and not touched her. And as he had gradually opened up to her, so had her fears about the future diminished. For fear had no place in the heart of a mother-to-be and neither did selfishness. The life she had been prepared to embrace now seemed all wrong. She'd thought a lot about Luc's lonely childhood and the repercussions of that. And she knew she couldn't subject this baby to single parenthood without first giving her husband the chance to be a full-time father. *And a full-time husband.*

Her heart began thundering with an emotion she could no longer deny. Because when tonight's ball was ended, she was going to take her husband in her arms and tell him she wanted them to start over. Tell him she was willing to try to create the kind of family unit which neither of them had ever had before. And then she was going to seduce him…

The woman in the mirror looked back at her with hope shining from her eyes and Lisa allowed herself a small smile. Years of working in the fashion industry had taught her to be impartial—especially about her own appearance. She knew that her already curvy body was swollen with child but she was also aware that never had she looked quite so radiant as she did tonight. Her hair was glossy and her skin was glowing. Her handmade dress was fitted tightly on the bodice and cleverly pleated at the front, so that it fell to the ground in a flattering silhouette. And the stark, square neckline provided the perfect setting for the real star of the show—the royal rubies which blazed like fire against her pale skin.

'Lisa!'

She heard Luc calling and, picking up the full-length black velvet cloak lined with matching crimson satin, she slipped it around her shoulders. Luc would see her at the same time as all his subjects and friends, she thought happily. Tonight she was going to *do him proud.*

'Nervous?' he questioned as she walked alongside him through the flame-lit corridors in a rustle of velvet and silk.

'A little,' she admitted.

He glanced down at the dramatic fall of black velvet which covered her entire body. 'Aren't you going to show me this dress you've been working on so furiously?'

'I will when we get there.'

'Are you hiding your bump until the last minute? Is that it?'

'Partly.' Lisa felt the heavy necklace brushing against her throat and shivered a little as she pulled the cloak closer. 'And I'm a little cold.'

But it wasn't just nerves which were making her skin prickle with little goosebumps, because the fine weather which traditionally characterised the May Ball hadn't materialised. As soon as Lisa had opened her eyes that morning, she'd realised something was different. For the first time since she'd been on the island, the sun wasn't shining and the air was laced with an unseasonable chill. According to the servant who had served her breakfast, the temperamental wind they called Il Serpente was threatening to wreak havoc on the Mediterranean island.

But although the predinner drinks had now been moved inside, the palace looked more magnificent than Lisa had ever seen it. Dark roses threaded into ivy were woven around the tall ballroom pillars, giving the place a distinctly gothic feel, and more crimson roses decorated the long table where the meal would be served. The string section of the Mardovian orchestra was playing softly, but as soon as the trumpets announced her and Luc's arrival they burst into the national anthem. As the stirring tune drew to a close, Lisa slipped the velvet cloak from her shoulders.

She was not expecting such an OTT reaction as the collective gasps from the guests who had assembled to greet the royal guests of honour. Nor for her to glance up into Luc's face to find herself startled by the dark look stamped onto his features which seemed to echo the growing storm outside. Was her dress a mistake? Did the vibrant colour draw attention to the swell of her body, reminding the Prince and all his subjects of the real reason she was here?

'Is something…wrong?'

Luc's cold gaze was fixed on the blaze of jewels at her throat, but he must have been aware that everyone around them was listening because he curved his lips into a smile which did not meet his eyes. 'Wrong?' he questioned smoothly. 'Why should there be anything wrong? You look exquisite. Utterly exquisite, *ma chérie.*'

But Lisa didn't feel exquisite as she sat down to dinner, in front of all that shiny golden cutlery. She felt *tawdry*. As if she'd broken a fundamental rule which nobody had bothered to tell her about. What on earth was the matter? And then she glanced down the table and met Eleonora's eyes and wondered if she was imagining the brief look of triumph which passed over the aide's face.

Somehow she managed to get through the lavish meal, perversely relieved that protocol meant she wasn't sitting next to her husband, because no way could she have eaten a thing if she'd been forced to endure another second of his inexplicable rage. She had lost her appetite anyway and merely picked at her food as she tried to respond to the Sultan of Qurhah's amusing observations, when all she could think about was Luc's forbidding posture. But it wasn't until the dancing started and he came over to lead her imperiously onto the ballroom floor for the first dance that she found herself alone with him at last.

'Something *is* wrong,' she hissed as he slid his arms around her waist, but instead of it being a warm embrace, it felt as if she were locked inside a powerful vice. 'Isn't it? You've been glaring at me all evening. Luc, what's the matter? What am I supposed to have *done*?'

'Not here,' he bit out. 'I'm not having this discussion here.'

'Then why are you bothering to dance with me?'

'Because you are my wife and I must be *seen* to dance with you.' His words were like ice. 'To paint the illusion of marital bliss for my idealistic subjects. That is why.'

Distress welled up inside her and Lisa wanted to push him away from her. To flounce from the ballroom with her head held high so that nobody could see the glimmer of tears which were pricking at the backs of her eyes. But pride wouldn't let her. She mustn't give anyone the opportunity to brand her as some kind of hysteric. That would be a convenient category for a woman like her, wouldn't it?

So she closed her eyes to avoid having to look at her husband and as she danced woodenly in his arms, she wondered how she could have been so stupid. Had she really thought that some silent truce had been declared between them? That they had reached a cautious kind of harmony?

Stupid Lisa, she thought bitterly. She had let it happen all over again. Despite everything she knew to be true, she had allowed herself to trust him. She had started to imagine a marriage they might be able to work at. A marriage which might just succeed.

Behind her tightly shut eyelids she willed away her tears and finished her dance with Luc, and afterwards she danced with the Sultan and then the cousin of the Sheikh of Jazratan. Somehow she managed to play the part expected of her, even though her smile felt as if it had been plastered to her lips like concrete.

But at least her late pregnancy gave her a solid reason to excuse herself early. She slipped away from the ballroom and had one of the servants bring her cloak, which she wrapped tightly around herself as she made her way back along the deserted corridors to their apartments.

Once inside the suite, she didn't bother putting the lights on. She stood at the window and watched as the storm split open the skies. Forked lightning streaked like an angry silver weapon against the menacing clouds and the sound of thunder was almost deafening. But after a while she didn't even see the elemental raging outside because the tears which were streaming down her face made her vision blurry. She dashed them away with an impatient hand, unsure of what to do next. Should she get ready for bed? Yet wouldn't lying on that monstrous mattress in her nightgown make her even more vulnerable than she already felt?

So she rang for some camomile tea and had just finished drinking it when the doors were flung open and the silhouetted form of her husband stood on the threshold. He was breathing heavily and his body was hard and tense as he stared inside the room. She could tell that he was trying to adjust his vision to the dim light, but when he reached out to put on one of the lamps, she snapped out a single word.

'Don't.'

'You like sitting in the dark?'

'There's nothing I particularly *like* right now, Luc.

But somewhere near the top of my dislikes is having you try to control the situation yet again. If anyone's going to put the light on, it's going to be me. Understand?' She snapped on the nearest lamp, steeling herself against the sight of his powerful body in the immaculate dress suit as he shut the door behind him with a shaking hand. And even though she felt the betraying stir of her senses, her anger was far more powerful than her desire. 'Do you want to tell me what I've done wrong?' she demanded. 'What heinous crime I'm supposed to have committed?'

She could see the tension in his body increase and when he spoke, his words sounded as if they had been chipped from a block of ice. 'Why the hell did you wear that necklace without running it past me first?'

For a moment she blinked in surprise. Because he'd told her to choose some jewels from the royal collection. Because Eleonora had drawn her attention to the undoubted star of the collection and quietly suggested that she 'surprise' her husband. Lisa opened her mouth to tell him that, but suddenly her curiosity was piqued. 'I didn't realise I had to *run it past* you first. You made no mention of any kind of *vetting* procedure. What was wrong with me wearing it?'

There was a pause as his face became shuttered and still his words were icy-cold. 'That necklace was given to my mother by Princess Sophie's mother. My mother wore it on her wedding day. It was—'

'It was supposed to be worn by Sophie on the day of her marriage to you,' finished Lisa dully, her heart clenching. 'Only you never married her, like you were supposed to do. You married a stranger. A commoner. A woman heavy with your child who appeared at the ball tonight looking like some spectre at the feast. The wrong woman wearing the jewels.'

Her remarks were greeted by silence, but what could he possibly say? He could hardly deny the truth. Lisa ran her tongue over her lips. She supposed she could tell him it had been Eleonora's subtle lead which had made her choose the rubies, but what good would that do? She would be like a child in the classroom, telling tales to the teacher. And it wouldn't change the facts, would it? That she was like a cuckoo in the nest with no real place here. An outsider who would always be just that. The human incubator who carried the royal heir. Reaching up, she unclipped the necklace and pulled it from her neck, dropping it down onto a bureau so that it fell there in a spooling clatter of gems.

But as her anger bubbled up, so did something else—a powerful wave of frustration, fuelled by the sudden violent see-sawing of her hormones. For weeks now she'd been trying her best to fit in with this strange new life of hers. Night after night she had lain by his side, staring up at the ceiling while he had fallen into a deep sleep. She had been polite to the servants and tried to learn everything she could about Mardovia— only now he was treating her with all the contempt he might have reserved for some passing tramp who had stumbled uninvited into his royal apartment. How dared he? How *dared* he?

'Well, damn you, Luc Leonidas!' she cried, and she launched herself across the room and began to batter her fists hard against his chest. 'Damn you to high heaven!"

At first he tried to halt her by imprisoning her wrists, but that only made her kick even harder at his shins and he uttered something soft and eloquent in French—before swooping his mouth down on hers.

His kiss was hard—and *angry*—but his probing tongue met no resistance from her. On the contrary, it made her give a shuddering little moan of something like recognition—because she could do anger, too. So she kissed him back just as hard, even though he was now trying to pull away from her, something impossible to achieve when he was still holding her wrists. And then his grip on her loosened and she took that opportunity to stroke her fingertip down his cheek and then over the rasp of his chin. And although he shook his head when she continued down over his chest, he didn't stop her—not until her hand reached his groin, where he was so hard for her that her body stiffened in anticipation.

'Lisa, no,' he warned unsteadily as she slid her palm over the rocky ridge beneath his trousers.

'Luc, *yes*,' she mimicked as she began to slide down the protesting zip.

After that there was no turning back. Nothing but urgent and hungry kissing as she freed his erection and gazed down at it with wide-eyed pleasure. But when she began to slide her finger and thumb up and down over the silken shaft, he batted her hand away then picked her up and carried her over to the bed. He set her down beside it, his eyes flicking over the long line of hooks which went all the way down the back of her dress, and his hands were shaking as he reached for the first.

'No,' she said, wriggling away from him as she pushed him down onto the bed. 'It will take too long and I'm done with waiting. I'm not going to wait a second longer for this.' With an air of determination, she began to tug off his trousers and boxer shorts, before slithering out of her panties and climbing on top of him, uncaring of her bulkiness. Not caring that this was wrong—because the powerful hunger which was pulsing through her body was blotting out everything but desire.

'Lisa…' His words sounded slurred and husky as her bare flesh brushed against his. He swallowed. 'We can't…we can't do this.'

'Oh, but we can. There are many things we can't do, but this isn't one of them.' The red silk dress ballooned around her as she positioned herself over him, and she saw his eyes grow smoky as the tip of him began to push insistently against her wet heat.

'But you're…pregnant,' he breathed.

'You think I don't know that?' She gave a hollow laugh. 'You think pregnant women don't have sex? Then I put it to you that you, Luc Leonidas, with all your supposed experience of the female body, are very wrong.' Slowly she lowered herself down onto his steely shaft, biting out a gasp as that first rush of pleasure hit her.

He lay there perfectly still as she began to rock forward and back and she could see the almost helpless look of desire on his face as her bulky body accustomed itself to the movements. And she *liked* seeing him like that. Powerful Prince Luc at *her* mercy. But her sense of victory only lasted until the first shimmerings of pleasure began to ripple over her body and then, of course, he took over. His hands anchored to her hips, he angled his own to increase the level of penetration while leaning forward to whisper soft little kisses over her satin-covered belly. And it was that which was her undoing. That which made her heart melt. His stupid show of tenderness which *didn't mean a thing*.

Not a thing.

All it did was make her long for the impossible. For Luc to love her and want her and need her. And that was never going to happen.

But she could do nothing to stop the orgasm which caught her up and dragged her under, and as her body began to convulse around him she heard his own ragged groan. His arms tightened as he held her against him, his lips buried in the hard swell of her stomach as he kissed it, over and over again. For a while there was nothing but contentment as Lisa clung to him, listening to the muffled pounding of her heart.

But not for long. Once the pleasure began to ebb away, she forced herself to pull away from him, collapsing back against the pile of pillows and deliberately turning her face to the wall as a deep sense of shame washed over her. How could she? How *could* she have done that? Climbed on top of him with that out-of-control and wanton desire?

'Lisa?'

She felt the warmth of his hand as he placed it over one tense shoulder and some illogical part of her wanted to sink back into his embrace and stay there. Because when he touched her it felt as if all the things she didn't believe in had come true. It felt like love. *And she couldn't afford to think that way because love was nothing but an illusion.* Especially with Luc.

She closed her eyes as she pushed his hand away, because she was through with illusions. With going back on everything she knew to be true and allowing herself to get sucked into fantasy. He was a man, wasn't he? And no man could really be trusted. Did she need someone to carve it on a metal disc for her, so she could wear it around her neck? She needed to be strong enough to resist him and, for that, she needed him to go.

'Lisa?' Luc said again and his ragged sigh ruffled the curls at the back of her neck. 'Look, I know I over-reacted about the necklace and I'm sorry.'

She pulled away. 'It doesn't matter.'

'It *does* matter.'

But she wasn't in the mood to listen. She made herself yawn as she curled up into a ball—well, as much of a ball as her heavily pregnant state would allow. 'I just want to go to sleep,' she mumbled. 'And I'd prefer to do it alone.'

CHAPTER TEN

'LISA, WE HAVE to talk about this. We can't keep pretending nothing has happened.'

Lisa closed her eyes as Luc's voice washed over her skin, its rich tone setting her senses tingling the way it always did. It made her think of things she was trying to forget. Things she *needed* to forget. She swallowed. Like the night of the ball when she'd let her raging hormones get the better of her and had ended up on the bed with him. When passion and anger had fused in an explosive sexual cocktail and, for a short and surreal period, she had found herself yearning for the impossible.

And now?

She turned away from the window, where the palace gardens looked like a blurred kaleidoscope before her unseeing eyes.

Now she felt nothing but a deep sense of sadness as she met his piercing sapphire gaze.

'What is there left to say?' she questioned tiredly. 'I thought we'd said it all on the night of the ball. Considering what happened, I thought we'd adapted to a bad situation rather well.'

'You think so?' His eyebrows arched. 'With me occupying my former bachelor apartments while you sleep alone in the marital suite?'

'What's the matter, Luc? It can't be the sex you're missing. I mean, it isn't as if we were at it like rabbits before all this blew up, is it?'

'There's no need to be crude,' he snapped.

If they'd been a normal couple Lisa might have made a wry joke about that remark, but they weren't. They were about as far from normal as you could get— two strangers living in a huge palace which somehow felt as claustrophobic as if they were stuck in some tenement apartment.

'Are you worried what people are saying?' she demanded. 'Is that it? Afraid the servants will gossip about the Prince and Princess leading separate lives?' She pushed a handful of curls away from her hot face and fixed him with a steady look. 'Don't you think that's something they should get used to?'

Luc clenched the fists which were stuffed deep in the pockets of his trousers and tried very hard not to react to his wife's angry taunts. If he'd been worried about gossip he would never have brought her back here. He would never have… He closed his eyes in a moment of frustration. How far back did he have to go to think about all the things he *wouldn't* do with her— and why couldn't he shake off the feeling that somehow all his good intentions were meaningless, because he felt *powerless* when it came to Lisa?

He shook his head. 'No. I'm not worried about what people are saying.'

'Maybe you're still regretting the other night?' she said softly. 'Wishing you hadn't had sex with me?'

Luc swallowed as her words conjured up a series of mental images he'd tried to keep off limits but now they hurtled into his mind in vivid and disturbing technicolour. Lisa pushing him back onto the bed. Lisa on top of him in the billowing crimson dress, her face flushed with passion as she rode him. His mouth dried. He *wanted* to regret what had happened, but how could he when it had been one of the most erotic encounters of his life? He had felt like her puppet. Her slave. And hadn't that turned him on even more? Dazed and confused, he had left their suite afterwards and stumbled to the library to discover that what she'd said had been true—that pregnant women *did* have sex. It seemed his wife had been right and there were some things he *didn't* know about women.

Especially about her.

'No, I'm not regretting that.'

'What, then?'

His gaze bored into her. 'Why didn't you tell me that Eleonora persuaded you to wear the necklace?'

'Why bother shooting the messenger?' she answered. 'Eleonora might have had her own agenda but she wasn't the one who made you react like that. You did that all by yourself.' She glanced at him from between her lashes. 'Did she tell you?'

'No,' he said grimly. 'I overheard her saying something about it to one of the other aides and asked to see her.'

'Gosh. That must have been a fun discussion,' she

said flippantly. 'Did she persuade you that it had been a perfectly innocent gesture on her part? Flutter those big eyes at you and tell you that you'd be better off with her beloved Princess Sophie?'

'I wasn't in the mood for any kind of *explanation*,' he bit out angrily. 'And neither was I in the mood for her hysterical response when I sacked her.'

Lisa blinked. 'You…*sacked* her?'

'Of course I did.' He fixed her with a cool stare. 'Do you really think I would tolerate that kind of subversive attitude in my palace? Or have an aide actively trying to make trouble for my wife?'

Lisa didn't know what to think. She'd been stupid and gullible in agreeing to Eleonora's suggestion that she 'surprise' Luc, but she shouldn't allow herself to forget why she had embraced the idea so eagerly in the first place. She had wanted to impress him. To show him she was willing to be a good wife and a good princess. And if she was being brutally honest—hadn't she been secretly longing for some kind of answering epiphany in him? Hoping that the emotional tide might be about to turn with her first public presentation?

But it hadn't and it never would. If anything, the situation was a million times worse. The sex had awoken her sleeping senses but highlighted the great gulf which lay between them. And wouldn't she be the world's biggest fool if she started demanding something from a man who was incapable of delivering it?

She stared at him. 'So what do you want to talk about?'

Repressing another frustrated sigh, Luc met her

gaze, knowing there was no such thing as an easy solution. But had he expected any different? She was the most complicated and frustrating woman he'd ever met. He gave a bitter smile. And never had he wanted anyone more.

When she had walked towards him at the Mardovian Embassy in her subdued wedding finery, he had made a silent vow to be the best husband and father he possibly could be, and he had meant it. Yet now he could see that it might have been a challenge too far. *Because he didn't know how to be those things.* And for a woman who was naturally suspicious of men— He suspected that he and Lisa were the worst possible combination.

So did he have the strength to do what he needed to do? To set her free from her palace prison? To release her from a relationship which had been doomed from the start? It wasn't a question of choice, he realised— but one of necessity. He had to do it. A lump rose in his throat. He could do it for her.

'Do you want to go back to England?' he questioned quietly. 'Not straight away, of course. But once the baby is born.'

Lisa jerked back her head and looked at him with suspicious eyes. 'You mean you'll let me go?'

'Yes, Lisa.' He gave a mocking smile. 'I'll release you from your prison.'

'And you're prepared to discuss shared custody?' Now she was blinking her eyes very hard. 'That's very...civilised of you, Luc.'

His mouth twisted. 'None of this sounds remotely

civilised to me—but it's clearly what you want. And I am not so much of a tyrant to keep you here against your will.'

She lifted her clear gaze to him. 'Thank you,' she said.

He walked away from her, increasing the distance between them, removing himself from the tantalising danger of her proximity. But once he had reached the imposing marble fireplace, he halted, his face grave. 'I guess we should look on the bright side. At least now we've had sex, it means that our marriage has been legitimised and our child will be born as the true heir to Mardovia.'

She stiffened, her lips parting as she stared at him. '*What* did you say?'

'I was just stating facts,' he answered coolly. 'Up until the other night our marriage wasn't legal because we hadn't consummated it.'

'Was that why you did it? Why you let me make love to you?' she whispered, her face blanching. 'Just to make our marriage *legal*?'

'Please don't insult me, Lisa. We both know why I had sex with you that night and it had nothing to do with legality.' He met her gaze for a long moment before turning away from her. 'And now, if you'll excuse me—I have a meeting with my ministers, which I really can't delay any longer.'

Lisa watched him go but it wasn't until he had closed the door behind him that she collapsed on the nearest chair as the significance of his words began to sink in. He was letting her go. After the baby was born, he was going to let her leave the island. She would no longer be forced to stay in this farce of a marriage with a cold man who could only ever express himself in bed. He would probably give her a house, just as he had given one to her sister, and she would be free to live her life on *her* terms.

So why did she feel as if someone had twisted her up in tight knots?

She forced herself to be logical. To think with her head instead of her heart. As Luc's estranged wife, she would never again have financial worries. And she would work hard at forging an amicable relationship with Luc. That would be a priority. They wouldn't become one of those bitter divorced couples who made their child's life a misery by their constant warring.

But Lisa couldn't shake off her sudden sense of emptiness as she went to her studio and looked at her sketches she'd been making for her next collection. Maybe she should make some more. Because what else was she going to do during the days leading up to the birth? Prowl around the palace like a bulky shadow, staring at all the beauty and storing it away in her memory to pull out on lonely days back in England— as if to remind herself that this hadn't all been some surreal dream.

For the next few days she immersed herself completely in her work. She began drawing with a sudden intensity—her designs taking on clean new lines as she liaised with her workshop back in London about an overall vision for the new collection. She worked long sessions from dawn to dusk—punctuated only by brisk walks in the gardens, where sometimes she would sit on a stone bench and watch the sunlight cast glittering patterns on the sapphire sea far below—and tried not to wonder what her husband was doing.

Mostly he left her alone, but one evening he came to her studio, walking in after a brief knock, to find her bent over a swatch of fabrics.

'Don't you think you're overdoing the work ethic a little?' he observed, with a frown. 'One of the servants told me you've been here since sunrise.'

'I couldn't sleep. And I'm nearly finished. I just want to get this last bit done.'

'You're looking tired,' he said critically. 'You need to rest.'

But this single concerned intervention had been the exception, because mostly she only saw him at mealtimes. Perhaps he was already withdrawing from her and preparing for the reality of their separation. And in truth, it was better this way. She spent a lot of time convincing herself of that. It was how it was going to be and she had better get used to it.

Dr Gautier visited daily, pronouncing himself quietly satisfied at her progress—and if he wondered why Luc no longer attended any of the appointments, he made no mention of it. That was yet another of the advantages of being royal, Lisa realised. People just accepted what you did and never dared challenge you—and that couldn't be a good thing. It would make you grow up thinking that you could fashion the world according to whim. Wasn't that what Luc had done by bringing her here and forcing her to marry him?

She was over a week away from her due date when the first pain came in the middle of the night, waking her up with a start. A ring of steel clamped itself around her suddenly rock-hard belly and Lisa clutched her arms around it in the darkness, trying to remember the midwife's instructions. It was the early hours of the morning and the contractions were very irregular—she had plenty of time before she needed to let anyone know.

But as they got stronger and more painful, she rang for Almeera, whose eyes widened when she saw her mistress sitting on the edge of the bed, rocking forward and back.

'Fetch the Prince,' said Lisa, closing her eyes as she felt the onset of another fierce contraction. 'Tell him I'm in labour.'

Luc arrived almost immediately, looking as if he'd just thrown his clothes on and not bothered to tidy his hair. His cell phone was pressed to his ear as he walked into the room, his gaze raking over her.

'Dr Gautier wants to know how often the contractions are coming,' he said.

'Every...' She gasped as she glanced at the golden clock on the mantelpiece. 'Every five minutes.'

He relayed this information, slipping naturally into French before cutting the connection. 'The ambulance is on its way and so is Dr Gautier.'

She gazed up at him. 'My...my waters have broken,' she stumbled.

He smiled. 'Well, that is normal, isn't it, *chérie*?'

His soft tone disarmed her and so did his confidence.

It made her forget about the distance between them. And suddenly Lisa wanted more than his support—she needed some of his strength. And comfort. 'Luc?' she said brokenly as another contraction came—surely far sooner than it was supposed to.

He was by her side in an instant, taking her hand and not flinching when her fingernails bit into his flesh as another contraction powered over her. 'I'm here,' he said.

'I'm supposed to have the baby in the hospital,' she whispered.

'It doesn't matter where you have the baby,' he said. 'We have everything here you need. You're going to be fine.'

And somehow she believed him, even when Dr Gautier arrived with another doctor and two midwives and said there was no time to go anywhere. All the things she'd read about were starting to happen, only now they were happening to *her*. At first she was scared and then it all became too intense to be anything but focussed. She tried to concentrate on her breathing, aware of the immense pressure building up inside her and Luc smoothing back her sweat-tangled curls. The medical staff were speaking to each other very quickly—sometimes in French—but Luc was murmuring to her in English. Telling her that she was brave and strong. Telling her that she could do this. She could do anything.

And then it was happening. The urge to push and being told she couldn't push, and then being unable to do anything *but* push. Still gripping Luc's hand,

Lisa gritted her teeth and tried to pant the way she'd been taught—and just as she thought the contractions couldn't get any more intense, her baby was delivered into the hands of the waiting doctor and a loud and penetrating wail filled the air.

'*C'est une fille!*' exclaimed Dr Gautier.

'A girl?' said Lisa, looking up into Luc's eyes.

He nodded. 'A beautiful baby girl,' he said unsteadily, his eyes suddenly very bright.

Lisa slumped back against the pillows as a sense of quiet and purposeful activity took over. The intensity of the birth had morphed into an air of serenity as the doctor finished his examinations, and, now cocooned in soft white cashmere, the baby was handed to her.

She felt so light, thought Lisa as a shaft of something fierce and protective shot through her. So light and yet so strong. With unfamiliar fingers, she guided her daughter to her breast, where she immediately began to suckle. Dimly, she became aware that Luc had left the room and, once the baby had finished feeding, the midwives helped her wash and gave her a clean silk nightgown. And when she next looked up, Luc was back and it was just the three of them.

She felt strangely shy as he dragged up a gilt chair and sat beside her, his elbows on his knees, his palms cupping his chin as he watched her intently. Their eyes met over the baby's head and Lisa suddenly felt a powerful sense of longing, wishing he would reach out and touch her. But they didn't have that kind of relationship, she reminded herself. They'd gone too far in the wrong direction and there was no turning back.

'We need to discuss names,' she said.

'Names?' he echoed blankly.

'We can't keep calling her "the baby". Are you still happy with Rose and then both our mothers' names?'

'Rose Maria Elizabeth,' he said, his slow gaze taking in every centimetre of the baby's face. 'They are perfect. Just like her.'

'Rose,' Lisa echoed softly, before holding out the snowy bundle towards him. 'Would you like to hold her?'

Luc's hesitation was brief as he reached out but his heart maintained its powerful pounding as he held his baby for the first time. He had never known real fear before, but he knew it now. Fear that he would prove inadequate to care for this tiny bundle of humanity. Fear that he might say the wrong thing to the woman who had just blown him away by giving birth to her.

As he cradled his sleeping daughter and marvelled at her sheer tininess, he felt the thick layer of ice around his heart begin to fracture. He could feel the welling up of unknown emotion—a whole great storm of it—packed down so deeply inside him that he hadn't even realised it was there. It felt raw and it felt painful, but it felt *real*—this sudden rush of devotion and a determination to protect his child for as long as he lived.

'Thank you,' he said softly, glancing up to meet Lisa's eyes.

'You're welcome.'

He saw the cloud which crossed like a shadow over her beautiful face but there was no need to ask what had caused it. For although their child had been born safely and mother and daughter were healthy, none of their other problems had gone away. They were still estranged. Still leading separate lives, with Lisa no doubt counting down the days until she could return to England. Concentrating only on her shadowed eyes, he stood up, carrying Rose over to her crib and laying her gently down before looking at Lisa's pinched face.

'You're exhausted,' he said. 'Shall I phone your sister and tell her the news and you can speak to her yourself later?'

She folded her lips together as if she didn't trust herself to speak, and nodded.

Resisting the desire to go over and drop a grateful kiss onto her beautiful lips, he took one last look at her before walking over to the door. 'Go to sleep now, Lisa,' he said unevenly. 'Just go to sleep.'

CHAPTER ELEVEN

IT WAS LIKE living in a bubble.

A shining golden bubble.

Lisa woke up every morning feeling as if she weren't part of the outside world any more. As if her experience was nothing like that of other women in her situation—and she supposed that much was true. Most new mothers didn't live in a beautiful palace with servants falling over themselves to make her life easier. And most new mothers didn't have a husband who was barely able to look at them without a dark and sombre expression on his face.

She told herself to be grateful that Luc clearly adored their daughter, and she was. It made a lump stick in her throat to see how gentle he was with their baby. It was humbling to see such a powerful man being reduced to putty by the starfish hands of his daughter, which would curl themselves tightly around his fingers as she gazed up at him with blue eyes so like his own.

Lisa would sit watching him play with Rose, but the calm expression she wore didn't reflect the turmoil she was feeling inside. Did Luc feel just as conflicted? she wondered. She didn't know because they didn't talk about it. They discussed the fact that their daughter had the bluest eyes in the world and the sweetest nature, but *they didn't talk about anything which mattered.*

Before the birth he'd promised Lisa she could return to England, and she knew she had to broach the subject some time. But something was stopping her and that something was the voice of her conscience. She had started to wonder how she could possibly take Rose away from here, denying Luc the daily parenting he so clearly enjoyed.

Because Lisa had never had that kind of hands-on fathering. When her own father had died she'd been too young to remember if he cuddled her or read her stories at night. And she'd never really had the chance to ask her mother because she had remarried so quickly. All evidence of the man who had died had been ruthlessly eradicated from the house. Her new stepfather had been so intolerant of her and Brittany that the two little girls had walked around on eggshells, terrified of stirring up a rage which had never been far from the surface. They'd learnt never to speak unless spoken to and they'd learnt never to demand any of their mother's time. Lisa had watched helplessly as he had whittled away at their fortune—and she wondered if it had been that which had made her so fiercely independent. Was the lack of love in their childhood the reason why Brittany had jettisoned her university course and fallen straight into the arms of the first man to show her some affection?

All Lisa knew was that she couldn't contemplate bringing Rose up without love. At the moment things were tolerable because it was all so new. She was getting used to motherhood and Luc was getting used to fatherhood. But the atmosphere between the two of them was at best polite. They were like two people stuck together in a broken-down lift, saying only as much as they needed to—but it wouldn't stay like that, would it? Once they were out of the baby-shock phase, things would return to 'normal'. But she and Luc had no 'normal'. Sooner or later they were going to start wanting different things.

She decided to speak to him about it after dinner one evening—a meal they still took together, mainly, she suspected, to maintain some sort of charade in front of the staff.

Leaving Almeera with Rose, Lisa washed her hair before slipping into a long, silk tunic which disguised the extra heaviness of her breasts and tummy. She even put on a little make-up, wondering why she was going to so much trouble. *Because I want to look in control. I want to show him that I mean business.*

But when she popped her head in to check on Rose before going down for dinner, it was to find Luc standing by the crib, his fingers touching the baby's soft black hair as he murmured to her softly.

'Oh,' she said. 'You're here.'

He glanced over at Almeera, who was fiddling with the intricate mobile which hung over the crib. 'I wonder if you'd mind leaving us for a moment, Almeera,' he said.

The servant nodded and slipped away and Lisa looked at Luc, feeling suddenly disorientated.

'I thought we were having dinner,' she said.

He raised his eyebrows. 'I think we're able to apply a little flexibility about the time we eat, don't you?' he said drily. 'Unless you're especially hungry.'

Lisa shrugged, wondering why tonight he was looking at her more intently than he had done for weeks. Automatically, she skated a palm down over the curve of one hip without considering the wisdom of such an action. 'I ought to be cutting back on food,' she said.

'Don't be ridiculous,' he said, his voice growing a little impatient before it gentled. 'You look beautiful, if you really want to know. Luscious and ripe and womanly.'

Actually, she didn't want to know and she didn't want his voice dipping into a sensual caress like that, making her long for something which definitely *wasn't* on the menu. She took an unsteady breath. 'We have to discuss the future,' she said.

There was a pause. 'I know we do.'

Luc looked into the questioning face of his wife and wondered afterwards if it was the sense of a looming ultimatum and dread which made him drop his guard so completely. He stared at her shiny hazelnut curls and the fleshy curves of her body and he felt his throat dry to dust as he forced himself to confront the truth.

Because in a sudden flash of insight he realised that the feelings he had were not just for their child, but for the woman who had given birth to her. A woman he'd brought here as a hostage, but who had tried to reach out to him all the same. He could recognise it now but he'd been too blind to see at the time. Because once her initial opposition to being his wife had faded, he realised that she'd tried to make the best of her life here. She had studied the history of his country and quietly gone about her own career without making undue demands on his time.

But despite the silent vow he'd made on their wedding day, he had continued to keep her at arm's length, hadn't he? He had kept himself at a physical distance even though he'd sensed that she'd wanted him. He had deliberately not laid a finger on her, knowing that such a move was calculated to make her desire for him grow. To *frustrate* her. And deep down, his disapproval had never been far from the surface. If he was being honest, hadn't he experienced a certain *relief* that he'd been able to chastise her over the damned necklace? As if he had needed something to justify why he could never allow himself to get close to her. The truth was that he had treated Lisa as an object rather than a person. *Because he hadn't known how to do it any other way.*

But suddenly he did—or at least, he thought he did. Was Rose responsible for opening the floodgates? Emotion flooded over him like a warm tide as he looked down at his daughter. Tentatively, she opened her eyes, and as he gazed into a sapphire hue so like his own he felt his heart clench. He lifted his head to meet Lisa's watchful gaze, the dryness in his throat making the thought of speech seem impossible, but that was no excuse. Because this was something he could not turn away from. Something he could no longer deny.

'I love her, Lisa,' he said simply.

For a moment there was silence before she nodded. 'I know. Me, too. It's funny, isn't it?' She gave a little laugh, as if she was embarrassed to hear him say the words out loud. 'How you can feel it so instantly and completely.'

Luc drew in a deep breath as he met her eyes. He thought about the first time he'd met her and that rare glint of shared understanding which had passed between them. The way he hadn't been able to get her out of his head in all the months which had followed. When he'd seen her again, the chemistry between them was as explosive as it had ever been—but what he felt now was about more than sex. Much more. Because somehow he'd come to realise that his spunky designer with the clear green-gold gaze treated him as nobody else had ever done.

She treated him like a man and not a prince.

So tell her. Take courage and tell her the words you never imagined you'd say.

'And I love you, too, Lisa,' he said. 'More than I'd ever realised.'

At first Lisa thought she must be dreaming, because surely Luc hadn't just told her that he loved her? She blinked. But he had. Even if the words hadn't still been resonating on the air, she knew she hadn't misheard them from the look on his face, which seemed to be savage yet silky, all at the same time. She felt a shiver whispering its way over her skin as she tried to ignore the sensual softening of his lips and to concentrate on facts, not dreams. Be careful what you wish for—that was what people said, wasn't it? And suddenly she understood why.

Luc had let his cold mask slip for a moment. Or rather, it hadn't *slipped*—he had just replaced it with a different mask. A loving mask which was far more suitable for ensuring he got what he wanted.

His baby.

Yet she wouldn't have been human if her first response hadn't been a fierce burst of hope. If she hadn't pictured the tumultuous scene which could follow, if she let it. Of her nodding her head and letting all the tears which were gathering force spill from her eyes before telling him shakily that yes, she loved him, too.

And, oh, the exquisite irony of that—even if it happened to be true. Admitting she loved a man who was cold-bloodedly trying to manipulate her emotions by saying something he didn't mean. What about all the lessons she was supposed to have learnt?

He was looking at her from between narrowed lashes and she knew she had to strike now. Before she had the chance to change her mind and cling to him and beg him to never let her go.

'Do you think I'm stupid?' she questioned quietly, her voice low and unsteady. 'Because I would have to be pretty stupid not to realise why you just told me you loved me. You don't *love* me, Luc. You've fallen in love with your daughter, yes—and I'm over the moon about that. But this isn't like going to the supermarket— which you've probably never done. We don't come as a two-for-one deal! And you can't smooth-talk me into staying on Mardovia just because you've trotted out the conditional emotional clause which most women are brainless enough to fall for!'

He went very still, his powerful body seeming to become the whole dark focus of the room. 'You think I told you I loved you because I have an ulterior motive?' he questioned slowly.

'I don't think it—I *know* it!'

He flinched and nodded his head. 'I had no idea you thought quite so badly of me, Lisa.'

Something in the quiet dignity of his words made Lisa's heart contract with pain, but she couldn't retract her accusation now—and why should she? He was trying to manipulate her in every which way and she wouldn't let him. She couldn't *afford* to let him. Because she'd crumble if he hurt her, and she never crumbled.

'I don't think badly of you,' she said. 'I think you're a great dad and that's what's making you say all this stuff. But you don't have to pretend in order to make things work. I want things to be…amicable between us, Luc.'

'Amicable?' he bit out before slowly nodding his head, and in that moment Lisa saw a cold acceptance settle over his features. 'Very well. If that's what you want, then that's what you'll get.' There was a pause. 'When *exactly* do you want to leave?'

Lisa and Rose's journey was scheduled for the end of the week. She was to fly back to London with Rose and Almeera and two protection officers, who would move into a section of Luc's large London house, which would now be her home. The idea of two of Luc's henchmen spying on her filled her with dread and Lisa tried to assert her independence.

'I don't need two protection officers,' she told Luc.

'You may not, but my daughter does.'

Lisa licked her lips. 'So I'm trapped any which way?'

He shrugged. 'Trapped or protected—it all depends how you look at it. And now, if you've quite finished, there are things I'd like to do while Rose is still in residence, and today I'd like to take her into Vallemar to meet some friends.'

Lisa told herself she didn't want to be parted from her baby and that was why she asked the question. 'Can't I come?'

'Why?' he questioned coolly. 'These are people you are unlikely to see in the future—so why bother getting to know them? No point in complicating an already complicated situation.'

So Lisa was forced to watch as Luc, Rose and Almeera were driven away in one of the palace limousines while she stayed put. She paced the gardens, unable to settle until they returned—with an exquisite selection of tiny Parisian couture dresses for Rose, from someone called Michele—and Lisa could do nothing about the sudden jealous pounding of her heart. But she didn't dare ask Luc who Michele was. Even she could recognise that she didn't have the right to do that.

At last, after a final sleepless night, it was time to leave. Lisa stood awkwardly in the main entrance of the palace, feeling small and very isolated as she prepared to say goodbye to Luc. Already in the car with Almeera, Rose was buckled into her baby seat—but now there was nothing but a terrible sense of impending doom as Lisa looked up into the stony features of her royal husband.

'Well,' she said, her bright voice sounding cracked. 'I guess this is it. And you'll…you'll be over to London next week?'

'I'll be over whenever I damned well please and I shall come and go as I please,' he said, his blue eyes glittering out a warning. 'So don't think you can move some freeloader into my house while I'm away, because I will not tolerate it.'

Don't rise to it, thought Lisa. Don't leave with the memory of angry words between you. She nodded instead. 'I have no intention of doing that, which I suspect you already know. So…goodbye, Luc. I'll… I'll be seeing you.'

And suddenly his cold mask seemed to dissolve to reveal the etching of anger and pain which lay behind. Did he realise she had witnessed it? Was that why he reached out and gripped her arms, his fingers pressing into the soft flesh, as if wanting to reassert the control he had momentarily lost?

'Better have something other than a tame goodbye to remember me by, dear wife,' he said. 'Don't you agree?'

And before she could raise any objection, his lips were pressing down on hers in a punishing kiss which was all about possession and nothing whatsoever to do with affection. But it worked. Oh, how quickly it worked. It had her opening her lips beneath the seeking pressure of his and gasping softly as she felt the tip of his tongue sliding over hers. She swayed slightly and as his big hands steadied her she could feel the clamour of her suddenly hungry body as it demanded more. Touch me, she thought silently, wishing that they were somewhere less public, though pretty sure none of the servants were around. Just *touch* me.

But just as suddenly he terminated the kiss—stepping away from her, the triumph darkening his eyes not quite managing to hide his contempt, so that she could hardly bear to look at him. As she stumbled out of the door towards the car she could feel his gaze burning into her back.

Rose was sleeping and Almeera was sitting in the front beside the driver as the car headed towards the airfield, and all Lisa could think about was Luc. Raw pain ripped through her. She found herself wishing that it could all have been different. Wishing he'd meant it when he told her that he loved her.

They were almost at the airfield when her thoughts jarred and then jammed—the way CDs used to get stuck if there was a fault on the disc and started repeating the same piece of music over and over again. She creased her brow as she tried to work out what it was which was bothering her.

She found herself remembering what he'd told her about his upbringing and the women paid to look after him after his mother's death. His words had moved her, despite the flat and matter-of-fact way in which he'd delivered them—as if he were reading from the minutes of a boring meeting. But you would have needed a heart of stone not to be affected by the thought of the lonely little boy growing up alone in a palace, with nobody but a grieving father and a series of strict governesses for company.

Had those governesses ever told him they loved him? Held him tightly in their arms and hugged him and kissed his little head? She bit her lip. Of course not—because that hadn't been in their job description. They had been there to serve. To drum in his duty to his country. A duty he must be reminded of whenever he saw the Wheeler portraits of Louisa De Lacy, whose love affair with his ancestor had almost destroyed the Mardovian dynasty. But it had not. The principality had survived and today it was strong—and powerful.

Yet despite all his wealth and power, Luc had not fought her for his daughter's custody, had he? With his access to the world's finest lawyers she sensed he had the ability to do that—and to win—so why hadn't he?

What did that say about him as a man? That he could be understanding, yes. Magnanimous, compassionate and kind. Or even that he cared more about her happiness and Rose's than about his own.

That he *loved* her?

She stared out of the car window and thought about how closed up he could seem. About the courage it must have taken for him to come out and say something like that. The way his voice had cracked with emotion as he'd spoken—and she knew then that he would never have said it if he didn't mean it. He had even told her that, once. Yet she had just batted his words back to him as if they'd been of no consequence, hadn't she? She had turned away from him, too frightened and so entrenched in her own prejudices to believe him.

For how could either of them know about the giving and receiving of love if neither of them had ever witnessed it?

'Stop the car!' she yelled, before recovering herself slightly and leaning forward to speak to the driver. 'Please. Can you take us back to the palace?'

Lisa's heart was racing during a drive back which seemed to take much longer than the outward journey, and she couldn't stop thinking that maybe it was already too late. What if he'd gone out, or refused to see her, or…?

But there were a million variations on 'what if' and she tried to push them from her mind as they drove up the mountain road with the beautiful blue bay glittering far below.

Leaving Almeera to bring Rose inside, Lisa went rushing into the palace, knowing that she should be walking calmly in a manner befitting a princess—even if she was an estranged one—but she couldn't seem to stop herself. She was about to ask one of the footmen where she could find the Prince when she saw Luc's rather terrifying new aide, Serge, coming from the direction of one of the smaller anterooms.

'I need to see the Prince,' she blurted out.

Serge's face remained impassive. 'The Prince has left strict instructions that under no circumstances is he to be disturbed.'

Had her departure already robbed her of any small

vestige of power her royal status might once have given her? Stubbornly, Lisa shook her head and sped noiselessly in the direction she'd seen Serge walking from.

With shaking fingers she opened doors. The first room was empty, as was the second, but in the third Luc stood alone by the window, his body tense and his shoulders hunched as he stared out.

Behind her Lisa could hear rapid footsteps and she turned round to see that the Russian had almost caught her up.

'Your Highness…' Serge began.

'Leave us, Serge,' said Luc, without turning round.

Lisa's heart was pounding but she waited until the aide had retreated and closed the door behind him before she risked saying anything.

'Luc,' she said breathlessly, but all the things she'd been meaning to say just died in her throat as nerves overcame her.

He turned around then, very slowly, and she was shocked by the ravaged expression on his face—at the deep sense of sorrow which seemed to envelop him, like a dark cloud. His sapphire eyes were icy-cold and she'd never seen someone look quite so unwelcoming.

'Where's Rose?' he demanded.

'Almeera's just bringing her in. I needed…' she swallowed '…to speak to you.'

'Haven't we said everything which needs to be said, Lisa? Haven't we completely exhausted the subject?'

'No,' she said, knowing that she needed the courage to reach into her frightened heart, despite the forbidding look on his face. 'We haven't.'

But clearly he wasn't about to help her. 'What do you want?' he questioned impatiently, as if she were a servant who had neglected to remove one of the plates.

'I want to tell you,' she whispered, before drawing in a deep breath, 'how very stupid I've been. And to try to tell you why.'

'I'm not interested in your explanations,' he snapped.

'I want to explain,' she continued, with a sudden feeling of calm and certainty, which she sensed was her only lifeline, 'that I was scared when you told me you loved me. Scared you didn't mean it. Scared I'd get hurt—'

'And you've spent your whole life avoiding getting hurt, haven't you, Lisa?' he finished slowly, as if he had just worked it out for himself. 'You learnt a bitter lesson at your mother's knee that love could destroy you.'

'Yes. *Yes!* Those feelings aren't always logical, but that doesn't make them any less valid. That's why I finished with you the first time.' She stared down at her shiny gold wedding band, before lifting her gaze to his. 'Oh, I knew there was no future in it—you told me that right from the start—but that wasn't why. Because who wouldn't have wanted to prolong every wonderful second of what we had? It was because I had started to fall in love with you and I knew that was a mistake. You didn't want love. Not from me. You told me you didn't want anything from me. I tried to forget you—I tried so very hard—and then when you walked into the shop that day, I realised nothing had changed.' She shrugged. 'Not a single thing. I still wanted you.'

'And I still wanted you,' he said. 'Even though everything about it was wrong and even though I tried to resist you, in the end I couldn't.'

'Maybe you just can't resist sex when it's offered to you on a plate.'

'Oh, but I can,' he assured her softly. 'I hadn't— haven't—had sex with anyone else since my relationship with you first ended.'

She stared at him in disbelief. 'Nobody?'

'Nobody.'

'But why? I mean, why not? There must have been plenty of opportunities to bed all kinds of women.'

Luc rubbed his thumb over his lips, realising that you could say words of love and mean them, but that was only the beginning. Because you needed to go deeper than that. To be prepared to show another person every part of you—to draw aside the curtain of mystique and admit that inside even *he* could be vulnerable.

'Initially I convinced myself that I needed a time of celibacy before settling down with Sophie, but that wasn't the real reason.' He shook his head and shrugged. 'Because the truth was that I just didn't want anyone else but you, Lisa. I don't know how and I don't know why—but you're the woman who has made me feel stuff I didn't even realise existed. The only one. And I want—'

'No,' she rushed in, as if eager to show him her own vulnerability. 'Let me tell you what I want, Luc. I want to be a real wife to you, in every sense of the word. I want to live here or anywhere, just so long as it's with you and Rose. I'd like to have more children, if you would. And I'd like to be the best princess I can possibly be. I want time to love you and to show you all the stuff I've never dared show you before. So what have you got to say to that, Luciano Gabriel Leonidas? Will you take me on?'

He could feel the powerful beat of his heart as he pulled her into his arms, but for the first time in his adult life he realised that his cheeks were wet with tears. And so were hers. He dried them with his lips and then bent his head so his mouth met hers. 'I'll take you on any time you like,' he said unsteadily, just before he kissed her. 'Because I love you.'

EPILOGUE

'IS SHE ASLEEP?'

'Flat out.' Lisa walked into their bedroom, pulling the elastic band from her hair and letting her curls tumble free. Luc was lying on top of the bed, reading. His eyes slitted as he watched her and he put the book down and smiled.

Lisa smiled back as her heart gave an unsteady thunder as she looked at her beloved husband. The light from the sunset was bathing everything in rose gold as it flooded in through the open windows—turning his naked body into a gilded statue. He really was magnificent, she thought hungrily, enjoying the way that the glowing light highlighted the hard muscle and silken flesh of his physique. She looked into his eyes, thinking how very quickly time passed and how important it was to treasure every single moment.

Sometimes it was hard to believe that their daughter was already two years old and probably the most sophisticated little jet-setter of all her peers. But everyone said that Princess Rose had the sweetest and sunniest nature in the world and her besotted parents tended to agree with them.

She wiped her still-damp hands down over her dress. 'Your daughter seems to think that bath time was made for fun,' she observed, with a smile.

'Just like her mother.' Luc's eyes gleamed. 'I think you and I might share a shower in a little while, but I have other plans for you first.'

'Oh? What plans?'

'Well, you are looking a little overdressed compared to me.' A lazy gesture of his hand lingered fractionally over his hardening body and he slanted her a complicit smile. 'So why don't you take off your dress and come over here?'

'That sounds like a very sensible idea to me,' she murmured, shivering a little with anticipation as she pulled the dress over her head and joined him on the bed.

He unclipped the rose-black lace of her bra and bent his mouth to the puckered point of her nipple, giving it a luxurious lick, before raising his eyes to hers. 'Looking forward to tomorrow?'

'I can't wait.'

He smiled. 'Then I guess we'd better do something to help pass the time as satisfactorily as possible. Don't you?'

Lisa stroked her toes against his foot as he slithered her panties down. Tomorrow the three of them were joining Brittany, Jason and Tamsin for a week-long break on the quieter southwestern shores of Mardovia—a sprawling idyll of a royal retreat, well away from all the servants and protocol of the main palace. It was one of the few places where they could be totally free, but Lisa accepted that the occasional loss of freedom was the price to be paid for the honour of ruling this ancient island alongside her husband. And she was happy to pay it, because she had worked hard to ensure her smooth transition into palace life and all its expectations.

Early on she'd recognised that maintaining a business in England while trying to settle into her new role was probably not sustainable in the long term—though Luc had told her that if she wanted to continue, then somehow they would make it happen. But being a full-time designer did not fit in with being a full-time princess and mother—and a part-time designer was never going to make waves. So she sold the label and the few pangs of regret she experienced soon passed.

Luc had invested in and commandeered the building of a new Art and Fashion School, which was named after her, and she had been taken aback and humbled by this gesture of his love. She was proud and honoured to be the patron of the state-of-the-art institution and planned to give monthly lectures on design, as well as making sure Mardovia became a hub for fashion innovation. There was a lot of young talent on this island, she realised—and she was going to make sure that every Mardovian child's talent would be fulfilled.

She had tried very hard to understand Eleonora's behaviour towards her. Lisa soon recognised that it had been an overdeveloped sense of patriotism and rather warped sense of devotion towards Luc which had made the aide resent the new commoner princess so much. But, as Lisa whispered to Luc one evening, she didn't want to start out her royal life with enemies, and forgiveness was good for the soul. So she had given Eleonora a key administrative role in the new Art School, and Eleonora had rewarded her with genuine loyalty ever since.

She and Luc had done everything in the wrong order, Lisa reflected ruefully as her panties fluttered to the floor. Her pregnancy had come before the wedding and there hadn't been a honeymoon for many months—not until Rose had been settled enough to leave with Almeera.

The other big change was with Jason. Brittany's new-found independence had given her the strength to tell Jason that there was no future for them until he got himself a job. And she'd meant it. Jason had found himself a job in a warehouse and had put in the hours and the backbone. It wasn't the most glamorous job in the world, but it proved something to them all—that Tamsin's father did have grit and commitment somewhere inside him. Six months later he and Britt were married and Luc offered him a role with his security facility at the Mardovian Embassy in London.

'What are you smiling to yourself for?' Luc's deep voice interrupted her reverie—as did the finger drifting over her ribcage—and Lisa looked into the sapphire gleam of her husband's eyes.

'I'm just thinking how perfect my life is.'

'I'm pleased to hear it. Perhaps I can think of a way to make it even more perfect.'

She batted her eyelashes. 'Really?'

'Really.' A smoky look entered his eyes as he

brushed his lips over hers. 'I intend making love to you until the moon is high in the sky, *chérie*—but first there is something I need to do.'

She lifted her hand to his face, resting it tenderly against the angled contours of his cheek. 'Which is?' she whispered, though she knew what was coming for it was something of a daily ritual for them—a glorious reaffirming of the vows they had once made under duress. At times they had each felt this particular emotion, but neither of them had dared say it, but now the words could be spoken freely and spoken from the heart. And they said them just as often as they could, as if to remind themselves of their good fortune.

'I love you,' he said softly.

Was it crazy that tears had begun to prick at the backs of her eyes? Lisa didn't care because she no longer shied away from showing emotion. And when something felt this good, you just had to let it all come rushing out.

'I love you, too, my darling Luc,' she whispered back. 'Now and for ever.'

And she drew his dark head towards her so that she could kiss him, in a room gilded rose gold by the glorious Mardovian sunset.

* * * * *

THE ICE PRINCE

SANDRA MARTON

CHAPTER ONE

THE first time he noticed her was in the Air Italy VIP lounge.

Noticed? Later, that would strike him as a bad joke. How could he not have noticed her?

The fact was, she burst into his life with all the subtlety of a lit string of firecrackers. The only difference? Firecrackers would have been less dangerous.

Draco was sitting in a leather chair near the windows, doing his best imitation of a man reading through a file on his laptop when the truth was he was too sleep-deprived, too jet-lagged, too wound up to do more than try to focus his eyes on the screen.

As if all that weren't enough, he had one hell of a headache.

Six hours from Maui to Los Angeles. A two-hour layover there, followed by six hours more to New York and now another two-hour layover that was stretching toward three.

He couldn't imagine anyone who would be happy at such an endless trip, but for a man accustomed to flying in his own luxurious 737, the journey was rapidly becoming intolerable.

Circumstances had given him no choice.

His plane was down for scheduled maintenance, and with

the short notice he'd had of the urgent need to return to Rome, there'd been no time to make other arrangements.

Not even Draco Valenti—*Prince* Draco Marcellus Valenti, because he was certain his ever-efficient PA had resorted to the use of his full, if foolish, title in her attempts to make more suitable arrangements—could come up with a rented aircraft fit for intercontinental flight at the last minute.

He had flown coach from Maui to L.A., packed in a center seat between a man who oozed over the armrest that barely separated them and an obscenely cheerful middle-aged woman who had talked nonstop as they flew over the Pacific. Draco had gone from polite *mmms* and *uh-huhs* to silence, but that had not stopped her from telling him her life story.

He had done better on the cross-country flight to Kennedy Airport, managing to snag a suddenly available first-class seat, but again the person next to him had wanted to talk, and not even Draco's stony silence had shut him up.

For this last leg of his journey, the almost four thousand miles that would finally take him home, he had at the last minute gone to the gate and, miracle of miracles, snagged two first-class seats—one for himself, the other to ensure he would make the trip alone.

Then he'd headed here, to the lounge, comforted by the hope that he might be able to nap, to calm down, if nothing else, before the confrontation that lay ahead.

It would not be easy, but nothing would be gained by losing control. If life had taught him one great lesson, that was it. And just as he was silently repeating that mantra, trying to focus on ways to contain the anger inside him, the door to the all but empty first-class lounge swung open so hard it banged against the wall.

Cristo!

Just what he needed, he thought grimly as the pain in his temple jumped a notch.

Glowering, he looked up.

And saw the woman.

He disliked her on sight.

At first glance, she was attractive. Tall. Slender. Blond hair. But there was more to see and judge than that.

She wore a dark gray suit, Armani or some similar label. Her hair was pulled back in a low, no-nonsense ponytail. A carry-on the size of a small trunk dangled from one shoulder, a bulging briefcase from the other.

And then there were the shoes.

Black pumps. Practical enough—except for the spiked, sky-high heels.

Draco's eyes narrowed.

He'd seen the combination endless times before. The severe hairstyle. The businesslike suit. And then the stilettos. It was a look favored by women who wanted all the benefits of being female while demanding they be treated like men.

Typical. And if that was a sexist opinion, so be it.

He watched as her gaze swept across the lounge. There were only three people in it at this late hour. An elderly couple, seated on a small sofa, their heads drooping, and him. Her eyes moved over the sleeping couple. Found him.

And held.

An unreadable expression crossed her face. It was, he had to admit, a good face. Wide set eyes. High cheekbones. A full mouth and a determined chin. He waited; he had the feeling she was about to say something...and then she looked away and he thought, *Bene*.

He was not in the mood for making small talk; he was not in the mood for being hit on by a woman. He was not in the mood for any damned thing except being left alone, returning to Rome and dealing with the potential mess that threatened him there, and he turned his attention back to his

computer as her heels tap-tapped across the marble floor to
the momentarily deserted reception desk.

"Hello?" Impatience colored her voice. "Hello?" she said
again. "Is anyone here?"

Draco lifted his head. Wonderful. She was not just impatient but irritable, and she was peering over the desk as if she
hoped to find someone crouched behind it.

"Damn," she said, and Draco's lips thinned with distaste.

Impatient. Irritable. And American. The bearing, the voice,
the *me-über-alles* attitude—she might as well have had her
passport plastered to her forehead. He dealt with Americans
all the time—his main offices were in San Francisco—and
while he admired the forthrightness of the men, he disliked
the lack of femininity in some of the women.

They tended to be good-looking, all right, but he liked
his women warm. Soft. Completely female. Like his current
mistress.

"Draco," she'd breathed last night after he'd joined her in
the shower of the beachfront mansion he'd rented on Maui,
lifted her into his arms and taken her while the water beat
down on them both. "Oh, Draco, I just adore a man who takes
charge."

No one would ever take charge of the woman at the reception desk, now tapping one stiletto-clad foot with annoyance,
but then, what man would be fool enough to want to try?

As if she'd read his thoughts, she swung around and stared
around the room again.

Stared at him.

It lasted only a couple of seconds, not as long as when
they'd made eye contact before, but the look she gave him
was intense.

So intense that, despite himself, he felt a stir of interest.

"So sorry to have kept you waiting," a breathless voice said.

It was the lounge hostess, hurrying toward the reception desk. "How may I help you, miss?"

The American turned toward the clerk. "I have a serious problem," Draco heard her say, and then she lowered her voice, leaned toward the other woman and began what was clearly a rushed speech.

Draco let out a breath and dropped his eyes to his computer screen. That he should, even for a heartbeat, have responded to the woman only proved how jet-lagged he was.

And he had to be in full gear by the time he reached Rome and the situation that awaited him.

He was accustomed to dealing with difficult situations. In fact, he enjoyed resolving them.

But this one threatened to turn into a public mess, and he did not countenance public anythings, much to the media's chagrin. He did not like publicity and never sought it.

He had built a financial empire from the ruins of the one his father and grandfather and countless great-great-grandfathers had systematically plundered and ultimately almost destroyed over the course of five centuries.

And he had done it alone.

No stockholders. No outsiders. Not just in his financial existence. In his world. His very private world.

Life's great lesson *numero due*.

Trusting others was for fools.

That was why he'd left Maui after a middle-of-the-night call from his PA had dragged him out of a warm bed made even warmer by the lush, naked body of his mistress.

Draco had listened. And listened. Then he'd cursed, risen from the bed and paced out the bedroom door, onto the moon-kissed sand.

"Fax me the letter," he'd snapped. "And everything we have in that damned file."

His PA had obliged. Dressed in shorts and a T-shirt, Draco

had read through it all until the pink light of dawn glittered on the sea.

By then he'd known what he had to do. Give up the cooling trade winds of Hawaii for the oppressive summer heat of Rome, and a confrontation with the representative of a man and a way of life he despised.

The worst of it was that he'd thought he'd finished with this weeks ago. That initial ridiculous letter from someone named Cesare Orsini. Another letter, when he ignored the first, followed by a third, at which point he'd marched into the office of one of his assistants.

"I want everything you can find on an American named Cesare Orsini," he'd ordered.

The information had come quickly.

Cesare Orsini had been born in Sicily. He had immigrated to America more than half a century ago with his wife; he had become an American citizen.

And he had repaid the generosity of his adopted homeland by becoming a hoodlum, a mobster, a gangster with nothing to recommend him except money, muscle and now a determination to acquire something that had, for centuries, belonged to the House of Valenti and now to him, Prince Draco Marcellus Valenti, of Sicily and Rome.

That ridiculous title.

Draco didn't often use it or even think it. He found it officious, even foolish in today's world. But, just as his PA would have resorted to using it in her search for a way to get him from Hawaii to Italy, he had deliberately used it in his reply to the American don, couching his letter in cool, formal tones but absolutely permitting the truth—*Do you know who you're dealing with? Get the hell off my back, old man*—to shine through.

So much for that, Draco had thought.

Wrong.

The don had just countered with a threat.

Not a physical one. Too bad. Draco, whose early years had not been spent in royal privilege, would have welcomed dealing with that.

Orsini's threat had been more cunning.

I am sending my representative to meet with you, Your Highness, he had written. *Should you and my lawyer fail to reach a compromise, I see no recourse other than to have our dispute adjudicated in a court of law.*

A lawsuit? A public airing of a nonsensical claim?

In theory, it could not even happen. Orsini had no true claims to make. But in the ancient land that was *la Sicilia,* old grudges never ended.

And the media would turn it into an international circus—

"Excuse me."

Draco blinked. Looked up. The American and the lounge hostess were standing next to his chair. The American had a determined glint in her eyes. The hostess had a look in hers that could only be described as desperate.

"Sir," she said, "sir, I'm really sorry but the lady—"

"You have something I need," the American said.

Her voice was rushed. Husky. Draco raised one dark eyebrow.

"Do I, indeed?"

A wave of pink swept into her face. And well it might. The intonation in his words had been deliberate. He wasn't sure why he'd put that little twist on them, perhaps because he was tired and bored and the blonde with the in-your-face attitude was, to use a perfectly definitive American phrase, clearly being a total pain in the ass.

"Yes. You have two seats on flight 630 to Rome. Two first-class seats."

Draco's eyes narrowed. He closed his computer and rose

slowly to his feet. The woman was tall, especially in those ridiculous heels, but at six foot three, he was taller still. It pleased him that she had to tilt her head to look at him.

"And?"

"And," she said, "I absolutely must have one of them!"

Draco let the seconds tick by. Then he looked at the hostess.

"Is it the airline's habit," he said coldly, "to discuss its passengers' flying arrangements with anyone who inquires?"

The girl flushed.

"No, sir. Certainly not. I don't—I don't even know how the lady found out that you—"

"I was checking in," the woman said. "I asked for an upgrade. The clerk said there were none, and one word led to another and then she pointed to you—you were walking away by then—and she said, 'That gentlemen just got the last two first-class seats.' I couldn't see anybody with you and the clerk said no, you were flying alone, so I followed you here but I figured I should confirm that you were the man she'd meant before I—"

Draco raised his hand and stopped the hurried words.

"Let me be sure I understand this," he said evenly. "You badgered the ticket agent."

"I did not badger her. I merely asked—"

"You badgered the hostess here, in the lounge."

The woman's eyes snapped with irritation.

"I did not badger anyone! I just made it clear that I need one of those seats."

"You mean you made it clear that you want one."

"Want, need, what does it matter? You have two seats. You can't sit in both."

She was so sure of herself, felt so entitled to whatever she wanted. Had she never learned that in this life no one was entitled to anything?

"And you need the seat because…?" he said, almost pleasantly.

"Only first class seats have computer access."

"Ah." Another little smile. "And you have a computer with you."

Her eyes flashed. He could almost see her lip curl.

"Obviously."

He nodded. "And, what? You are addicted to Solitaire?"

"Addicted to…?"

"Solitaire," he said calmly. "You know. The card game."

She looked at him as if he were stupid or worse; it made him want to laugh. A good thing, considering that he had not felt like laughing since that damned middle-of-the-night phone call.

"No," she said coldly. "I am not addicted to Solitaire."

"To Hearts, then?"

The hostess, wise soul, took a step back. The woman took a step forward. She was only inches away from him now, close enough that he could see that her eyes were a deep shade of blue.

"I am," she said haughtily, "on a business trip. A last-minute business trip. First class was sold out. And I have an important meeting to attend."

This time it was her intonation that was interesting.

He had not bothered shaving; he had taken time only to shower and dress in faded jeans and a pale blue shirt with the sleeves rolled to his elbows, the top button undone. He wore an old, eminently comfortable pair of mocs and, on his wrist, the first thing he'd bought himself after he'd made his first million euros—a Patek Phillipe watch for no better reason than the first own he'd owned he had stolen and, in a fit of teenage guilt, had a day later tossed into the Tiber.

In other words he was casually but expensively dressed. A woman wearing an Armani suit would know that. He'd reserved two costly seats, not one. Add everything together and she would peg him as a man with lots of money, lots of time on his hands and no real purpose in life, while she was a captain of industry, or whatever was the female equivalent.

"Do you see why the seat is so important to me?"

Draco nodded. "Fully," he said with a tight smile. "It's important to you because you want it."

The woman rolled her eyes. "My God, what's the difference? The seat is empty."

"It isn't empty."

"Damnit, will someone be sitting in it or not?"

"Or not," he said, and waited.

She hesitated. It was the first time she had done so since she'd approached him. It made her seem suddenly vulnerable, more like a woman than an automaton.

Draco felt himself hesitate, too.

He had booked two seats for privacy. No one to disturb his thoughts as he worked through how to handle what lay ahead. No one with whom he'd have to go through the usual *Hello, how are you, don't you hate night flights like this one?*

He was not in the mood for any of it; if truth be told, he was rarely in the mood for sharing his space with others.

Still, he could manage.

He didn't like the woman, but so what? She had a problem. He had the solution. He could say, *Va bene, signorina. You may have the seat beside mine.*

"You know," she said, her voice low and filled with rage, "there's something really disgusting about a man who thinks he's better than everyone else."

The hostess, by now standing almost a foot away, made a sound that was close to a moan.

Draco felt every muscle in his body tighten. *If only you were a man,* he thought, and for one quick moment imagined the pleasure of a punch straight to that uptilted chin....

But she wasn't a man, and so he did the only thing he could, which was to get the hell out of there before he did something he would regret.

Carefully he bent to the table where his laptop lay, turned it off, put it in its case, zipped the case closed, slung the strap over his shoulder. Then he took a step forward; the woman took a step back. Her face had gone pale.

She was afraid of him now. She'd realized she had gone too far.

Good, he thought grimly, even though part of him knew this was overkill.

"You could have approached me quietly," he said in a tone of voice that had brought business opponents to their knees. "You could have said, 'I have a problem and I would be grateful for your help.'"

The color in her face came back, sweeping over her high cheekbones like crimson flags.

"That's exactly what I did."

"No. You did not. You told me what you wanted. Then you told me what *I* was going to do about it." His mouth thinned. "Unfortunately for you, *signorina,* that was the wrong approach. I don't give a damn what you want, and you will not sit in that seat."

Her mouth dropped open.

Hell. Why wouldn't it? Had he really just said something so foolish and petty? Had she reduced him to that?

Get moving, Valenti, he told himself, and he would have...

But she laughed. Laughed! Her fear had given way to laughter.

His face burned with humiliation.

There was only one way to retaliate and he took it.

He closed the last inch of space between them. She must have seen something bright and icy-hot glowing in his eyes, because she stopped laughing and took another quick step back.

Too late.

Draco reached out. Ran the tip of one finger over her lips.

"Perhaps," he said softly, "perhaps if you had offered me something interesting in trade…"

He put his arms around her, lifted her into the leanly muscled length of his body and took her mouth as if it were his to take, as if he were a Roman prince in a century when Rome ruled the world.

He heard the woman's muffled cry. Heard the hostess gasp.

Then he heard nothing but the thunder of his blood as it coursed through his veins, tasted nothing but her mouth, her mouth, her sweet, hot mouth…

She hit him. Hard. A surprisingly solid blow to the ribs. The sting of her small fist was worth the rage he saw in her eyes when he lifted his head.

"Have a pleasant flight, *signorina*," he said, and he brushed past her, leaving Anna Orsini standing right where he'd left her, staring at the lounge door as it swung shut behind him while she wished to hell she'd had the brains to slug the sexist bastard not in the side but right where he lived.

Where all men lived, she thought grimly as she snatched up her carry-on and briefcase that had somehow ended up on the floor.

In the balls.

CHAPTER TWO

ANNA stalked through the crowded terminal, so furious she could hardly see straight.

That insufferable pig! That supermacho idiot!

Punching him hadn't been enough.

She should have called the cops. Had him arrested. Charged him with—with sexual assault....

Okay.

A kiss was not sexual assault. It was a kiss. Unwanted, which could maybe make it a misdemeanor...

Not that anyone would call what had landed on her lips *just* a kiss.

That firm, warm mouth. That hard, long body. That arm, taut with muscle, wrapped around her as if she were something to be claimed...

Or branded.

A little shudder of rage went through her. It *was* rage, wasn't it?

Damned right it was.

Absolutely, she should have done something more than slug him.

Where was the gate? Her shoulders ached from the weight of her carry-on and briefcase. Her feet hurt from the stilettos. Why in hell hadn't she had the sense to change to flats? She'd worn the stilettos to court. Deliberately. It had become her uniform. The tailored suit coupled with the spike heels. It was a look she'd learned worked against some of the high and mighty prosecutors who obviously thought a female defense counsel, especially one named Orsini, would be easy to read.

Nothing about her was easy to read, thank you very much, and Anna wanted to keep it that way.

But the shoes were wrong for hurrying through an airport. Where on earth was that gate?

Back in the other direction, was where.

Anna groaned, turned and ran.

By the time she reached the right gate, the plane was already boarding. She fell in at the end of the line of passengers shuffling slowly forward. Her hair had come mostly out of the tortoiseshell clip that held it; wild strands hung in her face and clung to her sweat-dampened skin.

Anna shifted her carry-on, dug into its front pocket, took out her boarding pass. Her seat was far back in the plane and, according to the annoyingly perky voice coming over the loudspeaker, that section had already boarded.

Perfect.

She was late enough so that the most convenient overhead bins would surely be full by the time she reached them.

Thank you, Mr. Macho.

The line, and Anna, moved forward at the speed of cold molasses dripping from a spoon.

He, of course, would have no such problem. First-class passengers had lots of overhead storage room. By now he probably had a glass of wine in his hand, brought by an attentive flight attendant who'd do everything but drool over her good-looking passenger, because there were lots of women who'd drool over a man who looked like that.

Tall. Dark. Thickly lashed dark eyes. A strong jaw. A face, a body that might have belonged to a Roman emperor.

And the attitude to go with it.

That was why he would have access to a computer outlet, and she would not….

Anna took a breath. No. Absolutely not. She was not going there!

Concentrate, she told herself. Try to remember what it said on those yellowed, zillion-year-old documents her father had given her.

Hey, it wasn't as if she hadn't read them….

Okay. She hadn't read them. Not exactly. She'd looked through them prior to scanning them into her computer, but the oldest ones were mostly handwritten. In Italian. And her Italian was pretty much confined to *ciao, va bene* and a handful of words she'd learned as a kid that wouldn't get you very far in polite company.

The endless queue drew nearer to the gate.

If only she'd had more time, not just to read those notes but to arrange for this flight. She'd have flown first class instead of coach, let her father pay for her ticket because Cesare was the only reason she was on this fool's errand.

Cesare could afford whatever ridiculous amount of money first class cost.

She certainly couldn't. You didn't fly in comfort on what you earned representing mostly indigent clients.

And comfort was what first class was all about. She'd flown that way once, after she'd passed her bar exams and her brothers had given her a two-week trip to Paris as a gift.

"You're all crazy," she'd said, blubbering happily as she bestowed tears and kisses on Rafe and Dante, Falco and Nicolo.

Plus, she'd flown on the private jet her brothers owned. Man, talk about flying in comfort…

"Boarding pass, please."

Anna handed hers over.

"Thank you," the gate attendant said. In, naturally, a perky voice.

Anna glowered.

Seven hours jammed into an aluminum can like an anchovy was not something to be perky about.

Not that she disliked flying coach. It was what real people did, and she had spent her life, all twenty-six years of it, being as real as possible.

Which wasn't easy, when your old man was a *la famiglia* don.

It was just that coach had its drawbacks, she thought as she trudged down the ramp toward the plane. No computer outlets, sure, but other things, too.

Like that flight to D.C. when the guy next to her must have bathed in garlic. Or the one to Chicago, when she'd been sandwiched between a mom with a screaming infant on one side and a dad with a screaming two-year-old on the other.

"You guys want to sit next to each other?" Anna had chirruped helpfully.

No. They didn't. They weren't together, it turned out, and why would any sane human being want to double the pleasure of screaming kids trying their best to drive everyone within earshot to infanticide?

One of the flight attendants had taken pity on her and switched her to a vacant seat. To the *only* vacant seat.

Unfortunately, it was right near the lavatories.

By the time the plane touched down, Anna had smelled like whatever it was they piped into those coffin-sized closets.

Or maybe worse.

In essence, flying coach was like life. It wasn't always pretty, but you did what you had to do.

And what she had to do right now, Anna told herself briskly, was find a way to review her notes in whatever time her cranky old laptop would give her.

At last. The door to the plane was just ahead. She stepped through and somehow managed not to snarl when a flight attendant greeted her with a smiling *"Buona notte."*

It wasn't the girl's fault she looked as if she'd just stepped out of a magazine ad. Anna, on the other hand, knew she looked as if she had not slept or fixed her hair or her makeup in days.

Come to think of it, she hadn't.

Her father had dumped his problem on her twenty-four hours ago and she had not slowed her pace since then. A long-scheduled speech to a class of would-be lawyers at Columbia University, her alma mater. Two endless meetings. A court appearance, a desperate juggling of her schedule followed by a taxi ride to the airport through rush-hour Manhattan traffic, only to learn that her flight was delayed and that no, she could not upgrade her seat even though she'd realized during the taxi ride that she had to do so if she wasn't going to walk into the meeting in Rome without a useful idea in her head.

And on top of everything, that—that inane confrontation with that man...

There he was.

The plane was an older one, which meant the peasants had to shuffle through first and business class to get to coach. It gave her the wonderful opportunity to see him in seat 5A—all, what, six foot two, six foot three of him sitting in 5A, arms folded, long legs outstretched, with 5B conspicuously, infuriatingly empty.

Her jaw knotted.

She wanted to say something to him. Something that would show him what she thought of him, of men like him who thought they owned the world, thought women were meant to fall at their feet along with everybody else, but she'd already tried that and look where it had gotten her.

And, almost as if he'd heard her thoughts, he turned his head and looked right at her.

His eyes darkened. The thick lashes fell. Rose. His eyes got even darker. Darker, and focused on her face.

On her mouth.

His lips curved in a slow, knowing smile. *Remember me?* that smile said. *Remember that kiss?*

Anna felt her cheeks turn hot.

His smile tilted, became an arrogant, blatantly male grin.

She wanted to wipe it from his face.

But she wouldn't.

She wouldn't.

She wouldn't, she told herself, and she tore her gaze from his and marched past him, through first class, through business class, into the confines of coach where the queue ground to a halt as people ahead searched for space in the crowded overhead bins and stepped on toes as they shoehorned themselves into their designated seats.

"Excuse me," Anna said, "sorry, coming through, if I could just get past you, sir..."

At last she found her row and found, too, with no great surprise, that there was no room in the overhead bin for her carry-on. Which was worse? That she had to go four more seats to the rear before she found a place where she could jam it into a bin, or that she had to fight her way back like a salmon swimming upstream?

Or that the guy in the window seat bore a scary resemblance to Hannibal the cannibal, and the woman on the aisle was humming. No discernible melody. Just a steady, low humming. Like a bee.

Anna took a deep breath.

"Excuse me," she said brightly, and she squeezed past the hummer's knees, tried not to notice that part of Hannibal's thigh was going to be sharing her space, shoved her bulging briefcase under the seat in front of her and folded her hands in her lap.

It was going to be a very long night.

At 30,000 feet, after the usual announcement that it was okay to use electronic devices, she hoisted the briefcase into her lap, opened it, took out her laptop, put down the foldout tray, plunked the machine on it and tapped the power button.

The computer hummed.

Or maybe it was the woman on the aisle. It was hard to tell.

The computer booted. The screen came alive. Wasting no time, Anna searched for and found the file she needed. Clicked on it and, hallelujah, there it was, the most recent document, a letter from Prince Draco Marcellus Valenti to her father.

The name made her snort.

So did the letter.

It was as stiffly formal as that ridiculous name and title, wreathed in the kind of hyperbole that would have made a seventeenth-century scribe proud.

One reading, and she knew what the prince would be like.

Old. Not just old. Ancient. White hair growing from a pink scalp. Probably growing out of his ears, too. She could almost envision his liver-spotted hands clutching an elaborate cane. No, not a cane. He'd never call it that. A walking stick.

In other words, a man out of touch with life, with reality, with the modern world.

Anna smiled. This might turn out to be interesting. Anna Versus the Aristocrat. Heck, it sounded like a movie—

Blip.

Her computer screen went dark.

"No," she whispered, "no…"

"Yup," Hannibal said cheerfully. "You're outta juice, little lady."

Hell. Little lady? Anna glared at him. What she was, was out of patience with the male of the species…but Hannibal was only stating the obvious.

Why dump her anger on him?

Sure, she was ticked off by what had happened in the lounge, but her mood had been sour even before that.

It had all started on Sunday, after dinner at the Orsini mansion in Little Italy. Anna's mother had phoned the previous week to invite her.

"I can't come, Mom," Anna had said. "I have an appointment."

"You have not been here in weeks." Sofia's tone of reprimand had taken Anna straight back to childhood. "Always, you have an excuse."

It was true. So Anna had sighed and agreed to show up. After the meal her father had insisted on walking her to the front door, but when they were about to pass his study, he'd stopped, jerked his head to indicate that Freddo, his *capo* and ever-present shadow, should step aside.

"A word with you alone, *mia figlia*," he'd said to Anna.

Reluctantly she'd let Cesare lead her into the study. He'd sat down behind his massive oak desk, motioned her to take a seat, looked at her for a long moment and then cleared his throat.

"I need a favor of you, Anna."

"What kind of favor?" she'd said warily.

"A very important one."

Anna had stared at him. A favor? For the father she pretended to respect for the sake of her mother but, in reality, despised? He was a crime boss. Don of the feared East Coast *famiglia*.

Cesare had no idea she knew that about him, that she and her sister, Isabella, had figured it out when Izzy was thirteen and Anna was a year older.

Neither could remember exactly how it had happened. Maybe they'd read a newspaper article. Maybe the whispers of the girls at school had suddenly started to make sense.

Or maybe it was their realization that their big brothers, Rafe, Dante, Falco and Nick, had struck out on their own as soon as they could and treated Cesare with cold disdain whenever they visited the mansion and thought the girls and their mother were out of earshot.

Anna and Izzy only knew that one day they'd suddenly realized their father was not the head of a waste management company.

He was a crook.

Because of their mother, they hadn't let on that they knew the truth. Lately, though, that was becoming more and more difficult. Anna, especially, was finding it hard to pretend her father's hands were not dirty, even bloody.

Do a favor, for a man like him?

No, she'd thought. No, she wouldn't do it.

"I'm afraid I'm incredibly busy, Father. I have a lot on my plate just now, and—"

He'd cut her off with an imperious wave of his hand.

"Let us be honest for once, Anna. I know what you think of me. I have known it for a very long time. You can fool your mama and your brothers, but not me."

Anna had risen to her feet.

"Then you also know," she'd said coolly, "that you're asking the wrong person for a favor."

Her father had shaken his head.

"I am asking the right person. The only person. You are my daughter. You are more like me than you would care to admit."

"I am nothing like you! I believe in the law. In justice. In doing what is right, no matter what it takes!"

"As do I," Cesare had said. "It is only that we approach such things differently."

Anna had laughed.

"Goodbye, Father. Don't think this hasn't been interesting."

"Anna. Listen to me, *per favore*."

The *per favore* did it. Anna sat back and folded her arms.

"I need to see justice done, *mia figlia*. Done your way. The law's way. Not mine. And you are a lawyer, *mia figlia,* are you not? A lawyer, one who carries my blood in her veins."

"I can't do anything about being your daughter," Anna said coldly. "And if you need an attorney, you probably have half a dozen on your payroll."

"This is a personal matter. It is about family. *Our* family," her father said. "Your mother, your brothers, your sister and you."

Not interested, Anna wanted to say, but the truth was Cesare had piqued her curiosity.

What her father was now calling "our family" had never seemed as important to him as his crime family. How could that have changed?

"You have five minutes," she said after a glance at her watch. "Then I'm out of here."

Cesare pulled a folder of documents from a drawer and dumped them on the shiny surface of his desk. Most were yellowed with age.

Anna's curiosity rose another notch.

"Letters, writs, deeds," he said. "They go back years. Centuries. They belong to your mother. To her family."

"Wait a minute. My mother? This is about her?"

"*Sì*. It is about her, and what by right belongs to her."

"I'm listening," Anna said, folding her arms.

Her father told her a story of kings and cowards, invaders and peasants. He spoke of centuries-old intrigue, of lies on top of lies, of land that had belonged to her mother's people until a prince of the House of Valenti stole it from them.

"When?"

Cesare shrugged. "Who knows? I told you, these things go back centuries."

"When did you get involved?"

"As soon as I learned what had happened."

"Which was what, exactly?

"The current prince intends to build on your mother's land."

"And you learned this how?"

Cesare shrugged again. "I have many contacts in Sicily, Anna."

Yes. Anna was quite sure he did.

"So what did you do?"

"I contacted him. I told him he has no legal right to do such a thing. He claims that he does."

"It's difficult to prove something that happened so long ago."

"It is difficult to prove something when a prince refuses to admit to it."

Anna nodded.

"I'm sure you're right. And it's an interesting story, Father, but I don't see how it involves me. You need to contact an Italian law firm. A Sicilian firm. And—"

Her father smiled grimly.

"They are all afraid of the prince. Draco Valenti has enormous wealth and power."

"And you're just a poor peasant," Anna said with a cool smile.

Her father's gaze was unflinching.

"You joke, Anna, but it is the truth. No matter what worldly goods I have accumulated, no matter my power, that is exactly what I am, what I shall always be, when measured against a man like the prince."

Anna shrugged. "Then that's that. Game, set, match."

"No. Not yet. You see, I have one thing the prince does not have."

"Blood on your hands?" Anna said with an even cooler smile than before.

"No more than on his, I promise you that." Cesare leaned forward. "What I have is you."

Anna laughed. Her father raised his eyebrows.

"You think I am joking? I am not. His attorneys are shrewd, clever men. They are paid well. But you, *mia figlia…* You are a believer."

She blinked. "Excuse me?"

"You graduated first in your class. You edited the *Law Review.* You turned down offers from the best legal firms in Manhattan to join one that takes on cases others turn away. Why? Because you believe," Cesare said, answering his own question. "You believe in justice. In the rights of all men, not only those born as kings and princes."

His words moved her. He was right—she did believe in those things.

And though it shamed her to admit it, even to herself, it warmed her heart to hear of his paternal pride in her.

Maybe that was why she brought her hands together in slow, insulting applause.

"Quite a performance, Father," she said as she rose and started for the door. "You want to give up crime, you might consider a career on—"

"Anna."

"Dear Lord," she said wearily, "what is it now?"

"I have not been the father you wanted or the one you

deserved, but I have always loved you. Is there not some part of you that still loves me?"

Such simple words, but they had changed everything. The shameful truth was that he was right. Somewhere deep in her heart she was still a sweet, innocent fourteen-year-old who loved the father she had once believed him to be.

So she'd gone back to his desk. Sat across from him. Listened while he told her that he had been fighting to claim the land. He had sent Prince Valenti letters that the prince had ignored. He had contacted lawyers, in Sicily where the disputed land lay and in Rome, where the prince lived. None would touch the problem.

"We cannot permit a man like Valenti to ride roughshod over us simply because he believes our blood is not the equal of his," Cesare said. "Surely you must see that, Anna."

She did. Absolutely, she did. The haves and the have-nots had always been at war, and there was always fierce joy in showing the haves that they could not always win.

"Do not do this for me," Cesare had said. "Do it because it is right. And for your mother."

Now, hurtling through the skies at 600 miles an hour, Anna asked herself for what was surely the tenth time if she'd been had.

She sighed.

The thing was, she knew the answer.

Her father was right about her. She hated to see the rich and powerful walk over the poor and powerless. Okay, her father was hardly poor or powerless, but her mother's family had surely been both when the House of Valenti stole the land.

Besides, she'd given her word that she'd meet with this Italian prince, and she would.

Too bad she wasn't the slightest bit prepared for the meeting, but her father was right—she was a good lawyer, an excellent negotiator. She could handle this even if she didn't know all the details and facts.

What did any of that matter? This was the privileged prince against the poor peasant and, okay, her father wasn't poor or a peasant, but the principle was the same.

This prince, this Draco Marcellus Valenti, was an anachronism. He lived in an elegant past with no idea the rest of the world was living in the twenty-first century.

Like that guy in the VIP lounge who thought he owned the world, owned people...

And any woman he wanted.

He probably could.

Women, idiots that they were for good looks, undoubtedly fawned all over him.

But not her.

Not her, no matter how his mouth felt on hers, how his arms felt around her, how alive that one kiss had made her feel...

Ridiculous.

He'd kissed her for a purpose. To show her that he was male, and powerful, and sexy.

But did that impress her? *Ha,* Anna thought, and she put her head back and closed her eyes.

What was sexy about a man with a low, deep voice? With darkly lashed eyes that were neither brown nor gold, and a face that might have been carved by an ancient Roman sculptor? With a body so leanly muscular she'd felt fragile in his arms, and that was saying a lot for a woman who stood five foot eight in her bare feet.

What could possibly be sexy about being kissed like that, as if an absolute stranger had the power to possess her? To put his mark on her, as if she were his woman?

Anna shifted in her seat.

What if instead of slugging him, she'd wound her arms

around his neck? Opened her mouth to his? What would he have done?

Would he have said to her, *Forget that plane. That flight. Come with me. We'll go somewhere dark and private, somewhere where I can undress you, whisper things to you. Do things to you...*

A tiny sound vibrated in her throat.

She could almost feel it happening. The kisses. The caresses. And then, finally, he'd take her. She'd been with men. Sex was as much a woman's pleasure as a man's, but this would be—it would be different.

He would make her moan, make her writhe, make her cry out...

"Signorina?"

Make her cry out...

"Signorina. Forgive me for disturbing your sleep."

Anna's eyes flew open.

It was him. The man from the lounge. The man who had kissed her.

The man whose kiss she could still feel on her lips.

He was standing in the aisle, looking down at her. And the little smile on his beautiful mouth stole her breath away.

CHAPTER THREE

DRACO watched as the woman's eyes flew open.

Blue, just as he recalled, but to say only that was like saying that the seas that surrounded Sicily were blue.

Not so.

The colors of the Ionian Sea, the Tyrrhenian Sea, the Mediterranean were more than blue. And so were her eyes.

Not pale. Not dark. The shade reminded him of forget-me-nots blooming under the kiss of the noon sun along the Sicilian cliffs where he was reconstructing a place that he was sure had once been as magnificent as the view those cliffs commanded.

His gaze fell to her mouth. Her lips were parted in surprise. It was a very nice mouth. Pink. Soft. Enticing.

Draco frowned.

So what? The color of her mouth, of her eyes, was unimportant. She could look like the witch in *Hansel and Gretel*, for all it mattered to him.

He'd made his decision based on what was right and what was wrong, not on anything else.

A man who could not see past his own ego was not a man deserving of life's riches. That had been another lesson of his childhood, learned by watching how men with power, with wealth, with overinflated ideas of their own importance thought nothing of trampling on others.

At the announcement that it was now permissible to use electronic devices, he'd put aside his glass of more-than-acceptable burgundy, thanked the flight attendant for handing him the dinner menu, plugged in his computer…

And thought, suddenly and unexpectedly, of the woman.

Yes, she had infuriated him, that arrogant, the-world-is-mine-if-only-you'd-get-out-of-my-way attitude…

But was his any better?

Half an hour or so of soul-searching—remarkable, really, when you considered that many of those who knew him would have insisted Draco Valenti had no soul to search—and he'd decided he might have overreacted.

After all, first-class flying was comfortable. Not as comfortable as his own jet would have been but still, it was acceptable. Yes, his legs were long, his shoulders broad but still, the seat accommodated him.

You could have made do with the one seat, he'd found himself thinking.

As for not wanting someone next to him who would jabber away the entire time… That wouldn't be a problem. The reason the blonde wanted that vacant seat was that she had work to do.

In other words, she would keep to herself.

He would keep to himself.

No problem in that at all.

The bottom line? He'd been tired, grumpy and bad tempered. She'd been desperate, overeager and short-fused. Not a good combination under any circumstances, and in these particular circumstances, it had led to her being insulting and him being no better.

It was, he'd decided, an honest assessment and once he'd made it, he'd risen to his feet and headed toward the rear of the plane.

"Something I can do for you, Your Highness?" the eager

flight attendant had said as soon as she saw the direction he was taking.

"Yes," Draco had said crisply. "You can stop calling me 'Your Highness.'"

He'd softened the words with a quick smile as he moved past her. Then he'd walked and walked and walked, going from first-class luxury to business-class efficiency and, finally, through what he'd tried not to think of as a sardine tin until he'd figured he might just end up in Oz.

And then, at last, he'd spotted her. Her sun-kissed hair was like a beacon. And when her eyes opened, her lips parted, he almost smiled, imagining how delighted she would be at the sight of him....

Maybe not.

She was staring at him as if he were an apparition. If he'd given it any thought, and he hadn't, he'd have known his sudden appearance would take her by surprise.

Well, it had.

But the look on her face, the shock and amazement, told him that she was a woman people rarely took by surprise.

That he'd done so was a bonus.

He could see her struggling for words. That was nice to see, too. She certainly hadn't been at a loss for words earlier... except when he'd kissed her....

And that kiss had as little to do with this as the color of her eyes. This was a matter of human decency. Nothing more and nothing less.

"Sorry to have awakened you," he said politely.

She sat up straight and tugged down her skirt, which had ridden halfway up her thighs.

They were good thighs.

Actually, they were great.

Firm. Smooth. Lightly tanned to a sort of gilded bronze. Was she that color all over? Her hips. Her belly. Her breasts...

Damnit, he thought, and when he spoke again his tone had gone from polite to brusque.

"I said I'm sorry to have—"

"I wasn't asleep."

Probably not. Who could sleep, jammed between a woman who looked like a ticking time bomb's worth of neuroses and a guy with a look about him that reminded Draco of some movie character he couldn't place.

"And what are you doing here?"

Draco cleared his throat. This wasn't going quite the way he'd anticipated.

"I, ah, I've changed my mind."

"About what?"

Dio, was she going to make this difficult?

"About the seat. If you want it, it's yours."

Her eyes narrowed. "Why?"

Her tone was flat. Sarcastic. Was she playing to their audience? The guy to her right and the woman to her left were both watching him with the intensity of people viewing an accident on a highway.

So much for doing the right thing, Draco thought grimly, and met her slitted stare with one of his own.

"Why?" he snapped. "Because, fool that I am, I thought you might still prefer a first-class seat to—to this!"

"What's wrong with this?" the woman next to her demanded, and Draco threw up his hands and started back up the aisle.

"Wait!"

The cry carried after him. It was her, the blonde with more attitude than any one person, male or female, could possibly need.

A smart man would have kept walking, but Draco had already proved to himself that he wasn't being terribly smart tonight, so he stopped, folded his arms, turned…

And saw her hurrying toward him, that ridiculously lumpy briefcase swinging from one shoulder.

Despite himself, his mouth twitched.

What had become of all her crisp American efficiency?

The heavy case had tugged her suit jacket askew in a way he suspected Giorgio Armani would never approve; her golden hair had slipped free of its clasp. A shoe dangled from her fingers. In her rush to go after him, she'd apparently lost one of those high heels, which she'd managed to retrieve.

Those incredibly sexy high heels.

The thought marked the end of any desire to laugh. Instead, his eyes grew even more narrow. It was an indicator of his mood, and would have made any of his business opponents shudder.

"Well? What is it?"

"I—I—"

His gaze, as cold as frost on a January morning, raked over her.

"You what?"

It was, Anna thought, an excellent question. How did you admit you'd made a mistake? Not in judging this man. He was as cold, as self-centered, as insolent as ever—but that wasn't any reason to have rejected his offer.

Never mind that she couldn't think of a reason he'd made it, or that sitting next to him all the way to Rome would be the equivalent of choking down more humble pie than any one human being should have to consume.

Only an idiot would refuse gaining access to a spot where she could plug in her computer…and, okay, incidentally combine that with a seat that lacked the psycho bookends.

"I am waiting," he growled, that accent of his growing more pronounced by the minute.

Anna swallowed. Hard. The first bite of crow did not go down easily.

"I—I accept your apology."

He laughed. Laughed, damn him! So did someone else. Anna looked around, felt her face blaze when she realized their little drama was proving more interesting than books or magazines to what looked like this entire section of the plane.

"I did not apologize. I will not apologize."

She drew closer. He was inches away. Once again she had to tilt her head to look up at him, the same as she'd had to in the lounge an eternity ago. It was just as disconcerting now as it had been then, and suddenly she thought, *He's going to kiss me again, and if he does—if he does…*

"What I did was offer you the empty seat beside mine." His mouth twisted. "The one you groveled for a little while ago."

"I did not grovel. I would never grovel. I—I—"

Anna fell silent. She didn't know where to look. There was nowhere that was safe, given the choice between his dark, hard eyes and the attentive faces of their audience.

"Jeez, lady, are you nuts? You tell him you'll take the seat or I will," a male voice said, and somebody snickered. "Yes or no, lady? Last chance."

Anna glared. It was a toss-up who she despised more—her father for putting her in this untenable position or this…this arrogant idiot for putting her in this situation.

"You are," she said, her voice shaking, "a horrible, hideous man."

His eyelids flickered. "I take it that's a yes," he said, and he swung away from her and headed briskly up the aisle.

Anna did the only thing that made sense.

She fell in behind him and followed him to the front of the plane.

* * *

An hour later Anna turned off her computer, closed it and put it away.

So much for going through the document file.

She'd read and read, switched screens and made notes, and she still didn't have a true grasp of what was happening.

No.

She had a grasp, all right.

She was about to step into a pile of doggy-doo, two centuries old and a mile high.

There was a piece of land somewhere in Sicily that either belonged to her mother or belonged to a prince. None of the papers Anna had seen proved ownership; none even hinted at it.

Unless the papers written in Italian said something different, the documents Cesare had given her proved nothing beside the fact that her father had sent several letters to the prince.

The prince had sent only one that really mattered.

It was a note written by one of his lackeys on a sheet of vellum that weighed almost much as her computer, and it took half a dozen paragraphs to say, basically, "Go away."

The one certainty was her father's insistence that the royal House of Valenti had stolen the land in question. And how could that be possible? Anna asked herself tiredly. She didn't know much about what her father called the old country, but she knew enough to be certain that peasants didn't argue with princes.

For all she'd learned, she might as well still be back in coach, without access to her computer.

And without access to the man seated on the aisle seat beside her.

Anna gave him a covert glance.

Access was the wrong word to use. He had not looked at her or spoken to her since they'd sat down. He had a computer on his lap, too, and it was the only thing that claimed his attention.

That was fine.

The hell it was.

Calmer now, she could look at him and admit that he was a beautiful sight. That chiseled, masculine face. That hard body. Those strong-looking hands, one lightly wrapped around his computer, the other working its touch pad...

She knew what his hands felt like.

Back in the lounge, he'd grasped her shoulder. Here, he'd put his palm lightly on the small of her back, guiding her into the window seat. His touch had been impersonal then.

What if he touched her differently?

Not that automatic, you-first thing men did, but a stroke of those long, tanned fingers. A caress of that powerful hand.

Anna frowned, shifted in her seat.

Such nonsense!

He wasn't her type and she wasn't his. He'd like girlie women. Pliable in nature, eager to please, the kind who'd do whatever it took to make a man happy.

She was none of that.

"Prickly," a guy she'd dated a couple of times had called her.

"Difficult," another had claimed.

"Tough as nails," her brothers said, with pride.

Yes, she was.

How else did a woman get to make it in a world dominated by men, or endure growing up in a household where your mother walked two paces behind your father? Metaphorically, of course, but still...

Back to peasants and princes. And the man next to her. And the simple fact that in this situation he was the prince. Not because of their different seating arrangements but because he'd done something gracious and she...

She had not.

Would a simple *thank you* have killed her?

No. It would not have.

Was it too late to say the words now? *It's never too late to say something nice,* she could almost hear her sister, Izzy, saying. Okay. She wasn't sweet like Iz—she never would be—but she could try.

"Finished already?"

She blinked. He was looking at her, a hint of a smile on his lips.

Anna cleared her throat. "Yes."

"Didn't find what you wanted on your computer?"

She shook her head. "I only wish."

"Same here." He closed the cover of his and put it away. "I'm going to a meeting that will almost surely be a complete waste of time."

"Sounds like my story." She gave a little laugh. "Don't you just hate that kind of thing?"

"I despise it," he said, nodding in agreement. "There's nothing worse than having to sit across the table from a guy who can't figure out he's absolutely not going to accomplish anything."

"Exactly. It's so useless." Anna sighed. "Actually, what I'd like to do is walk into my meeting and say, 'Okay, this is pointless. I'm going to turn around and go home and if you have half a brain, so will you.'"

He chuckled. "Yes, but if the idiot really had half a brain, he wouldn't be there, eating up your time in the first place."

Anna grinned. "Exactly."

"That's life, isn't it? Things don't always work out as one expects."

"No, they don't." She hesitated. It was the perfect segue, and she took it. "Which brings me to offering my thanks for this seat. I should have said it sooner, but—"

"Yes," he said, "you should have."

"Now, wait a minute…"

He laughed. "Just teasing. This was my fault, too. I over-reacted when you first asked for the seat. How about we call it even? I'll apologize if you will."

Anna laughed, too. "You're not a lawyer, are you?"

He gave a mock shudder. "*Dio,* no. Why do you ask?"

"Because you have a way with words."

"It's what I do," he said, smiling. "I'm a negotiator." What better way to describe fashioning deals that made him millions and millions of dollars and euros? "So, do we have a truce?"

He held out his hand. Anna took it—and jerked back. An electric current seemed to flow from his fingers to hers.

"Static electricity," she said quickly. "Or something."

"Or something," he said, and all at once his voice was low and husky.

Their eyes met. His were dark, deep, fathomless. Anna felt her heartbeat stutter. *I'm tired,* she thought quickly. *I must be terribly tired or everything wouldn't seem so—so—*

"Would you like to see the wine list?"

It was the flight attendant, her smile perfect, her voice bright and bubbly, though Anna had to give her credit for not having reacted to the sight of a refugee from coach slipping into the cabin an hour or so before.

"Champagne," said the man still holding her hand, his gaze never leaving hers. "Unless you'd rather have something else?"

"No," Anna said quickly. "No, champagne would be lovely."

"Lovely," he said, and Anna wondered why she'd ever thought him cold or arrogant.

They drank champagne. In flutes. Glass flutes, not plastic. Switched to red wine, also in glasses, when dinner was served—served on china, with real flatware and real linen napkins.

Being in first class wasn't bad.

Neither was being with such a gorgeous stranger.

He ordered for them both. Normally Anna would have bristled at a man assuming he could order for her, but tonight it seemed right.

Everything seemed right, she thought as they ate and talked. Conversation flowed easily, not about anything important, just about the weather they'd left behind in New York, how it would compare to the weather they'd find in Rome, about where he lived—in San Francisco, overlooking the bay, he said. And where she lived—in Manhattan, on the lower east side.

For all of that, they didn't exchange names.

That seemed right, too.

There was something exciting about hurtling through the night at six hundred plus miles an hour, laughing and talking and having dinner with a man she didn't know and would never see again.

Anything was possible, Anna thought after their dishes had been whisked away and the cabin lights were dimmed. Absolutely anything, she thought, looking at him, and a faint tremor went through her.

"Are you cold?"

"No," she said quickly. "I'm fine."

"Tired, then."

"No. Really…"

"Of course you're tired. I'm sure your day has been as long as mine. In fact, I'm going to put my seat back. You'll do the same."

That tone of easy command made Anna laugh. "Do you ever ask a woman what she wants, or do you simply tell her?"

Their eyes met. Her heart did a little stutter step.

"There are times when there is no need to ask," he said softly.

Heat swept through her. *Get up,* she thought. *Get up and go back to your own seat in the rear of the plane.*

But she didn't.

He reached out. Leaned across her. She caught her breath as he pressed the button that eased her seat all the way back.

"Close your eyes, *bellissima,*" he whispered. "Get some sleep."

She nodded. Closing her eyes, pretending to sleep was probably a good plan. No reason to tell him that she never, ever was able to sleep on a plane....

When she woke, the cabin was almost completely dark.

And she was cocooned in warmth.

Male warmth.

Somehow she was lying in the stranger's arms, both of them covered by a soft blanket. Her head was on his shoulder, her face buried in the curve where his neck met his shoulder.

He was asleep. She could tell by the deep, slow exhalations of his breath.

Move, she told herself. *Anna, for heaven's sake, shift away from him.*

Instead, she shifted closer. Closer. Drew his scent—masculine, musky, clean—deep into her lungs.

Her hand rose. By itself, surely. No way would she have deliberately lifted it, placed it against his jaw, rubbed her fingers lightly over the sexy stubble.

The sound of his breathing changed. Quickened. Her heartbeat quickened, too.

"Hello," he whispered.

Anna touched the tip of her tongue to her lips. "Hello," she whispered back.

His arms tightened around her. He turned his face, brought his lips against her palm in a soft kiss.

She heard a sound. Low, urgent...

The sound had come from her.

"I dreamed I was holding you," he said. His teeth fastened lightly in the tender flesh at the base of her thumb. "And then I awoke, and you were in my arms."

A tremor went through her. Or perhaps through him. She couldn't tell. And it didn't matter. The excitement growing within her was growing within him, too. His heartbeat had quickened. And when she shifted her weight, when she shifted her weight...

Yes. Oh, yes.

He was hard. Fully aroused. And she—dear God, she was, too. She could feel her breasts lift, her nipples bud. And she was wet. So wet...

He kissed her mouth. Her lips parted against his. He groaned; his teeth fastened lightly in the tender flesh of her bottom lip, his tongue stroked across the tiny, exquisite wound and Anna gave a soft, pleading cry.

He murmured something in Italian. She didn't understand the words but she'd have had to be a fool not to understand their meaning.

His fingers tangled in her hair. Drew her head back. She could barely see his face in the dim light, but what she could see thrilled her—those dark eyes, the bones etched hard and harsh beneath his skin.

"You are playing with fire, *cara*," he said thickly.

Anna cupped her hand around the back of his head. "I like fire," she whispered.

"So do I." His voice was low, rough, as hot as his skin.

She brought his head down to hers, brushed her lips over his.

"I wanted you long before this," he said. "I wanted you hours ago, back in that lounge."

Anna trembled. Ran her fingers into his hair. It had been the same for her. That was why she'd argued with him. Fought with him. Because she had wanted him. Wanted this. His heat. His embrace. His strength...

She cried out as his hand slipped under her suit jacket. Under her blouse. Found her breast, cupped it over her silky bra, and she would have cried out again but he captured her lips with his, shaped her lips with his, slipped his tongue inside her mouth and claimed her with a slow, deep, kiss.

His thumb swept over her nipple.

She gasped, arched against him, felt her nipple bead and press blindly against his hand.

Please, Anna thought, *please...*

Draco gave a low growl.

He shifted the woman against him, raised her leg, brought it over his hip and pressed his aroused flesh against her.

Now, he thought, now...

The cabin lights winked on.

"Ladies and gentlemen, we'll be serving breakfast in just a few minutes...."

The woman in his arms froze. Her eyes flew open, blurred with passion and then with shock.

Cristo, he was having difficulty grasping the facts himself. What had happened—what had *almost* happened...

Impossible.

He'd had sex on planes before. That was one of the perks of owning a private jet, but sex, or the closest thing to it, in a plane filled with people?

It was crazy.

How could he have done such a thing? It was an unacceptable, inexplicable loss of control, and he was not a man given to losses of control or, for that matter, to doing things that were either inexplicable or unacceptable.

"Let go of me," the woman snapped.

Draco looked at her. She was as white as paper, and trembling.

"Easy," he started to say, but she cut him short.

"Are you deaf? Let go!"

"Look, *bella,* I know you're upset—"

"Damnit, let go!"

His mouth thinned. Was she going to try to label him the villain in this little drama?

"With pleasure, once I'm convinced you're in control of your senses." He waited, watched her face. "Are you?"

"You'd better believe I am."

There was no panic in her voice now, only razor-sharp warning. A muscle knotted in Draco's jaw. Then, with elaborate care, he took his hands from her.

In a flash she tossed off the blanket, pushed the button that brought her seat upright, shot to her feet. He did the same, if a split second later.

"Listen to me," he said...

Too late.

She had already turned and fled.

CHAPTER FOUR

DRACO exited Fiumicino Airport, his cell phone at his ear.

"Just tell your boss that I am not, repeat, *not* going to meet his representative an hour from now. Two hours from now. That's the best I'll do. You don't know if you can get in touch with his rep?" Draco took the phone from his ear and glared at it. "That is not my problem—it is yours."

One good thing about old-fashioned desk phones, he thought grimly as he ended the call. In moments like this, you could slam the thing down and get some satisfaction out of it.

"Il mio principe!"

Heads swiveled. Glowering, Draco eyeballed his Maserati and his driver and strode toward them.

The man beamed. *"Buon giorno, il mio principe. Come è stato il vostro volo?"*

"My flight was a nightmare," Draco snarled, "and must you announce my title to the world?"

Merda. The driver's face fell. The man had been with him only a couple of weeks; he was just trying to be pleasant.

Draco took a deep breath, forced a smile he hoped was not a grimace to his lips.

"Mi dispiace. I'm sorry. I'm just jet-lagged."

"You must not apologize to me, sir! It is my fault, surely."

The driver clapped his heels together, lifted Draco's carry-on, and reached for the handle of the rear door just as Draco did the same. Their hands and arms collided.

Cristo! Could the man's face get any longer?

"Scusi," the driver said in tones of hushed horror, *"Dio, signore, scusi..."*

"Benno. That is your name, is it not?"

"Sì. It is, sir, and I offer my deepest—"

"No. No apologies." Draco smiled again. At least, he pulled his lips back from his teeth. "Suppose we start over. You say 'Hello, how was your flight?' And I'll say—"

"Scusi?"

"I'll say," Draco said quickly, "it was fine. How's that?"

His driver looked bewildered. "As you wish, sir."

"Excellent," Draco replied, and he got into the backseat of the Maserati and sank into its leather embrace.

He was going to have to be careful.

He had put off the impending meeting with the Sicilian's man. That would, at least, give him time to shower, change his clothes, make some small attempt at getting his head on straight, but he was tired, not just jet-lagged but jet-fatigued.

Only that could explain what had happened on the plane.

"Il mio principe? Do you wish to go to your office or to your home?"

"Home, *per favore,* as quickly as possible, *sì?"*

"Sì, il mio principe."

Draco sat back as the Maserati eased from the curb.

How could jet fatigue possibly be the reason for the incident on the plane? And what a hell of a way to describe that thing with the woman. What was that all about?

Draco frowned.

Well, he knew what it was all about.

He'd made love to her. And she'd made love to him, until

those cursed lights went on, though he couldn't call what they'd been doing "making love."

It had been sex.

Mind-blowing, incredible sex.

Those few moments had been as exciting as any he'd ever spent with a woman.

He'd forgotten everything. Their surroundings, the fact that there were other people only a few feet away. All he'd known was her. Her taste. Her scent. Her heat.

There was a logical explanation, of course. There always was. For everything. In this case, the rush had come from having sex with a beautiful stranger in a place where anyone might have stumbled across them.

She'd been as out of control as he.

And then the lights had come on and she'd tried to lay it all on him.

No way, Draco thought, folding his arms over his chest.

All he'd done was watch her fall asleep, then drawn the blanket over her. All right. It had been his blanket, not hers, but her blanket had been half-tucked under her.

It had been logical to use his.

How was he to know she would sigh and fling her arm across his chest? That she'd lay her head on his shoulder? He was a man, not a machine; she'd all but moved into his embrace. Was he supposed to push her away? And when she'd lifted her dark lashes and looked up at him, her eyes as blue as the sea, when she'd caressed his cheek…

Everything after that had been unplanned. Unstoppable. The kiss. The way she'd opened her mouth to his. The way she'd moaned when he cupped her breast, the way her heart had raced when he put his hand under her blouse…

Damnit, he was hard, just remembering.

Enough.

He'd made a mistake, and the sole value of a mistake was learning not to make it again.

No danger of that, he thought grimly. He would never see the woman again.

Besides, it was time to turn his mind elsewhere, to the meeting that would take place in just a couple of hours with the sleazy representative of a sleazy hoodlum. An hour wasted was what it would be, but at least he'd have the satisfaction of knowing he'd sent the Orsini stooge home to the States with his tail between his legs.

His phone rang.

Draco took it from his pocket. *"Pronto,"* he said brusquely. He listened, listened some more and then he snarled a word princes surely did not use and jammed the phone back into his pocket.

His attorney couldn't make the meeting. "Forgive me, sir," the man had said. "Reschedule it for whenever you like…"

Draco scowled.

The hell he would.

He had not flown all this distance to reschedule a meeting. It would go on as planned.

The day he couldn't handle a Sicilian's errand boy had not yet dawned.

His home was a villa in the parkland that surrounded the Via Appia Antica, ocher in color in keeping with its ancient Roman roots, set far back from the road and protected by massive iron gates.

He'd been drawn to the place the first time he saw it, though what the draw had been was anybody's guess. The villa had been a disaster, part of it in total disrepair, the rest of it in desperate need of work.

Still, something about it had appealed to him. The history,

he'd thought, the realization of what the house must have seen over the centuries.

Foolish, of course; a man with demanding responsibilities did not give in to sentimental drivel. He'd taken an acquaintance to see it. An architect. His report was not encouraging.

Draco, he'd said, *you want to do this, we'll do it. But the place is an ugly pile of rubble. Why spend millions on it when you already own a magnificent palazzo on the Tiber?*

It was an amazingly honest assessment. Draco told himself the man was right. Why not rebuild the Valenti palace? Once, a long time ago, he had promised himself that he would. His ancestors, his father, even his mother had stripped it of almost everything that could bring in cash and then neglected it to a state of near collapse, but he had the money to change all that.

So he had done it. Restored the palazzo to medieval grandeur. Everyone had pronounced it exquisite. Draco's choice of adjectives was far less flattering, though he kept his thoughts to himself.

You could breathe new life into a building, but you could not rewrite the memories it held.

He had gone back to the realtor who'd shown him the villa. He bought it that same day, restored it and moved in. There was an honesty to its rooms and gardens. Best of all, its ghosts wore togas.

The memories the villa held had nothing to do with him.

The Maserati came to a purring stop at the top of the driveway. The driver sprang from behind the wheel, but Draco was already out of the car and striding up the curved marble steps that led to the villa's massive wooden doors, which opened before he could touch them.

"Buon giorno, signore," his smiling housekeeper said, wel-

coming him home. Did he want something to eat? Breakfast? Some fruit and cheese, perhaps?

Coffee, Draco said. Not morning coffee. Espresso. A large pot, *per favore,* and he would have it in the sitting room in the master suite.

His rooms were warm; he suspected the windows had not been opened since he'd left for his San Francisco office three weeks ago. Now he flung them open, toed off his mocs, stripped off shirt, jeans, all his clothes, left them as part of a long trail that led to his bathroom.

He could hardly wait to shower away the endless hours of travel.

One of the first things he'd seen to when he'd arranged for the restoration of the villa was the master bath. He wanted a deep marble Jacuzzi, marble vanities and the room's centerpiece: a huge, glass-enclosed steam shower with multiple sprays.

His architect had raised an eyebrow. Draco had grinned. Life in America, he'd said, with all those oversize bathrooms, had spoiled him.

Perhaps it had.

His California duplex had a huge bathroom with a shower stall the size of a small bedroom. There were times, at the end of a long day, that he stood inside that stall and could almost feel the downpouring water easing the tension from him.

Now, standing in the shower at Villa Appia, Draco waited for that to happen.

Instead, an image suddenly filled his mind.

The blonde, here with him. Her hair undone, streaming like sunlight over her creamy shoulders, over her breasts, the pale apricot nipples uptilted, awaiting him.

He imagined his lips closed on those silken pearls, drawing them deep into his mouth.

His hand between her thighs.

Her hand on his erection.

Draco groaned.

He would back her against the glass, lift her in his arms, take her mouth as he brought her down, down, down on his hard, eager length….

Another groan, more guttural than the first, burst from his throat. His body shuddered, did what it had not done since he'd had his first woman at the age of seventeen.

Her fault, he thought in sudden fury. The blonde. She had made a fool of him yet another time.

He wished he could see her again, and make her pay.

Draco shut his eyes. Raised his face to the spray. Let the water wash everything from his body and his mind. He had to be alert for the meeting that loomed ahead.

The land in Sicily was his. He'd been in Palermo on business, gone for a drive to relax and passed through the town of Taormina, where something had drawn him to a narrow road, a hairpin curve, a heart-quickening view of the sea…

And a stretch of land that seemed unaccountably familiar.

He had taken the necessary steps to ensure his possession of it, brought in an architect… And suddenly received a letter from a man he'd never heard of, Cesare Orsini, who had made claims that were not only nonsense, they were lies.

The land was his. And it would remain his, despite the best efforts of a thug to claim it.

Draco had learned a very long time ago never to give in to bullies.

It was a lesson that had changed his life, one he would never, ever forget.

Anna's hotel was old.

Under some circumstances, that would have been fine. After all, Rome was old. And magnificent.

The same could not be said about her hotel.

She'd made the reservation herself, online at something called BidCheap.com. Bidding cheap was where it was at; if only she'd had the common sense to demand her father hand over a credit card…

Never mind.

She'd traveled on the cheap before, after university and during spring breaks in law school. How bad could a place be?

Bad, she thought as she followed a shriveled bellman into a room the size of a postage stamp.

Water stains on the ceiling, heaven only knew what kinds of stains on the carpet, a sagging club chair in front of a window with a rousing view of…

An airshaft.

All the way to Rome so she could overlook an airshaft.

Well, so what?

She wouldn't be here long enough for it to matter. Besides, right now she felt as if she were walking in her sleep. She'd done that a couple of times, when she was little. Once she'd awakened in the kitchen, standing in front of the open fridge.

The next time, she'd been halfway out the conservatory door into the garden when she'd walked into one of her brothers. Falco, or maybe Rafe. Whichever, he'd startled her into wakefulness; she'd shocked him into a muffled oath.

"What are you—" they'd both said, and then they'd shushed each other and laughed, and agreed to keep quiet about the whole thing, because he'd obviously been sneaking back into the sleeping house and she'd just as obviously been sneaking out of it.

Anyway, she still remembered the feeling when her eyes had blinked open. She'd been awake, but not really. Her feet had seemed to be inches off the floor, her eyes had felt gritty, her body had felt…the only word that described it was *floaty*.

That was exactly how she felt now as she waited patiently for the bellman to finish showing her how to adjust the thermostat, how to open and close the drapes, how to use the minibar.

She yawned. Maybe he'd take the hint.

No way.

Now he was at the desk, opening drawers, snapping them shut, moving to the TV, turning it on and off, and, oh my God, now he was showing her how to set the clock radio…

Anna gave herself a mental slap on the forehead. Duh. He was waiting for a tip.

She opened her purse, dug inside, took out a couple of euros and, less than graciously, shoved them at him.

"Thank you," she said. "*Grazie*. You've been very helpful."

Her form would probably have earned demerits from Sister Margaret, who'd taught tenth grade deportment, but it satisfied the bellman, who smiled broadly, wished her a good day and exited, stage left.

"Thank God," Anna said, and fell facedown on the bed.

Everything ached.

Her arms from keeping her elbows tucked to her sides the last couple of hours of the flight. Her shoulders from hunching them. Her butt from pretty much doing the same kind of thing to keep her thighs and hips from coming into contact with Hannibal and the Hummer.

Her head hurt, too. A baby a couple of rows back had decided to scream in protest at the unfairness of life. Anna couldn't blame the kid; she'd have screamed, too, if it would have done any good.

But it wouldn't.

She had done something awful, and being packed into the

middle seat would never be sufficient to expiate her total, complete, hideous feelings of embarrassment.

Anna groaned.

Embarrassment didn't even come close. Humiliation was an improvement, but horror was better. Much better. She was totally, completely, mind-numbingly horrified at what she'd done. What she'd almost done.

Okay, what she had done and what she had been on the way to doing…

His fault. The stranger's. All of it, his fault.

First, driving her temper into the stratosphere, then confusing her, then charming her.

An overstatement.

He had not charmed her. He could never be the charming type. He'd simply lulled her into thinking he was human. And maybe just a little bit interesting.

Pleasant conversation. A couple of smiles. His looks had been part of it, too. She had to admit, he was nice-looking.

A hunk, was more like it.

And then to wake up and find him all over her…

Anna sprang to her feet. Unzipped her carry-on.

"The bastard," she hissed as she tore through the contents in search of toothpaste, toothbrush, cosmetics.

Who gave a damn about his looks? He'd pawed her. Attacked her.

She groaned again and sank onto the edge of the bed.

"Liar," she whispered.

She was blaming everything on him when the truth was, whatever he had done, she had encouraged.

"How could you?" she whispered. "My God, Anna, how *could* you?"

The question was pointless. She didn't have an answer. And she was not a child.

You opened your mouth to a man's kisses, you moaned

*under his touch, you draped your leg over him... What could
you call all that, if not encouragement?*

The stranger hadn't done anything she hadn't wanted him
to do.

Anna closed her eyes.

And, oh my, he had done it magnificently.

That wonderful, knowing mouth. That hard, long body.
Those big hands on her breasts...

"Enough," she said briskly, and got to her feet.

She had things to do before the meeting. And, thankfully,
miraculously, an hour in which to do them. Her father's *capo*
had called on her cell. The prince had delayed the meeting
by an hour.

Excellent news.

Not that she'd let the prince know it, Anna thought as she
dumped the contents of her carry-on on the bed. On the contrary. She'd tell him that his change of plans—his unilaterally
made change of plans—was an inconvenience. She would tell
him of her flight, of how she had spent the entire time in the
air diligently bent over her computer, studying the documents
that proved, irrefutably, her mother's ownership of the land
in—in whatever the name of that town in Sicily was. Torminia.
Tarminia. Taormina, and she had less than an hour to at least
get that much into her weary brain.

A shower. A change of clothes. A quick look at the file that
had, thus far, proven useless.

Yes, but she'd gone into court with less information before
and come out the winner.

She was one hell of a fine attorney.

The prince's attorney would probably be top grade, but so
what? She could handle that. And she could definitely handle
a fawned-upon, effeminate blue blood of a prince.

She was an American, after all.

Quickly she laid out fresh clothes. Another suit. Charcoal-gray, this time. Another blouse. Ivory silk, of course. A change of shoes. Stilettos. Black and glossy, with—for kicks—peep toes. Underwear. Silk. Sexy.

People could see the stilettos. The undies were just for her. She liked knowing that under the uniform she was all female.

The stranger would probably have liked it, too.

He was the kind of man who'd know how to strip a woman of a sexy half bra, a sexy thong. There were times she'd thought, fleetingly, that what she'd worn under her clothes had been wasted on a lover.

It would not be wasted on him.

His hands would be sure and exciting as he took off her bra, his fingers just brushing across her nipples. They'd be steady as he hooked his thumbs into the edges of her thong and slid it down her hips, his eyes never leaving hers even as her breathing quickened, as she felt herself getting wet and hot and…and…

"Damnit!" she said. What was with her today?

She liked men. Liked sex. But this, wanting a man whose name she didn't even know, a man she'd never see again, not only wanting him but going into his arms in a place where anyone could have seen them…

Anna yanked her cell phone from her purse, hit a speed-dial digit. Her sister answered on the first ring.

"Anna?"

Oh, the wonders of caller ID.

"Izzy. I have something to ask you."

"Anna, where are you? I called your office and your secretary said—"

"Isabella," Anna said briskly, "how many times must I remind you? There are no more secretaries. She's a PA. A personal assistant. Got it?"

"Got it—but where are you? Your sec—your PA said you

were in Italy, and I said that wasn't possible because you never told me that—"

"I'm in Italy, Iz. I never told you because I never had the chance. The old man cornered me Sunday—which, by the way, he could not have done if you'd shown up for dinner the way you were supposed to."

"I wasn't. I mean, nobody asked me to show up. And what's that got to do with you being in—"

"Later," Anna said impatiently. "Right now, just answer a question, okay?"

"What's the question?"

"It's…it's…" Anna cleared her throat. "You took psych, right?"

"Huh?"

"Izzy, I said—"

"I heard you. Sure. I took psych 101. So did you."

"Yeah. Well, remember that section on, ah, on sexual fantasies?"

"Anna," Isabella said carefully, "what's going on?"

"Wasn't there something about, ah, about fantasizing sex with a stranger?"

"A dark, dangerous stranger."

Anna put her fingers to her forehead, gave her temple a little rub.

"Right. And—and wasn't there something else about sex in public places? Where there was a risk of being caught?"

"Anna," Izzy said firmly, "what's going on?"

"Nothing. Nothing, I swear. I just—I just wanted to clarify something, is all."

"About risk? About sex with dangerous strangers? In public places? Hey, big sister, this is me, remember? What have you done?"

"I told you, nothing. I, ah, I read a magazine article on the plane. It was about sex. Risky sex. Hey, it's jet lag, you know? Makes you think strange things."

"Think them," Izzy said firmly. "Don't do them. I mean, you're not contemplating sex in a public place with a dangerous stranger, are you?"

Isabella lightened her question with a laugh. After a second, Anna laughed, too.

"Not even I would do something so crazy," she said, and then she said she had to run, that she'd phone when she had more time, kiss-kiss, talk to you soon…

And ended the call.

Silly to have called Isabella. The truth was, she'd intended to ask her if she'd ever wanted hot, fast sex with a stranger, and what would sweet Izzy know about sex, hot or otherwise?

Anna sighed. Undressed. Headed into the ancient bathroom, stepped into a rust-stained tub, tried not to bang her skull on the showerhead and turned a squeaking handle that wheezed out a thin stream of lukewarm water.

Forget the plane. The unintelligible files. Most of all, forget the man and what had happened. Correction. What had *almost* happened, because, thank goodness, she'd come to her senses in time.

What she had to concentrate on was the forthcoming meeting. The farcical concept of a prince in this, the twenty-first century. On making it crystal clear that no one, not even a doddering old stooge with a pretend crown on his balding pate and, for all she knew, a roomful of lawyers, could steal her mother's land and get away with it.

It was a good plan.

An excellent one.

It might have taken Anna far had she not, seventy-five minutes later, rushed through the doors of an elegant building just off the Via Condotti and paused at a reception desk only long enough to tell a receptionist elegant enough to grace the elegant building that she had an appointment with Prince Draco Valenti.

"And you are…?" the receptionist said, peering at Anna down her—what else could it have been?—Roman nose.

"I," Anna said, knowing it was time to marshal her resources, "I am counsel for Signore Cesare Orsini."

The receptionist nodded and reached for a telephone.

"Fourth floor, take a right, end of the corridor."

The elevator was elegant, too.

So was the man waiting for her. One man, not the legal team she'd anticipated. One man, standing at a window overlooking the street, his back to her.

Even so, he gave an immediate impression of…what?

Power, she thought. Power and strength, masculinity and youth. The tall, leanly muscled body evident within the stylish gray Armani suit; the broad shoulders; the long legs. He stood with those legs slightly apart; she could tell his arms were folded. His posture signaled irritation and arrogance.

Strange. There was something familiar about him…

Anna's heart leaped into her throat. *No,* she thought, *no!*

She made a sound, something between a choked gasp and a low moan. The man heard it.

"I do not appreciate being kept waiting," he said coldly as he swung toward her…

"You," Draco Valenti, *il Principe* Draco Marcellus Valenti of Rome and Sicily said, and the only good thing about this awful, terrible moment was that Anna knew the surprise and shock on his cold, classically beautiful face had to mirror hers.

CHAPTER FIVE

DRACO stared at the figure in the doorway.

No. No! It was not possible!

Lots of women had golden hair. Eyes the color of the Tyrrhenian Sea. A soft-looking, tender-pink mouth…

Dio, who was he trying to fool?

It was she. It was her. And what the hell did the intricacies of English grammar matter right now? He hadn't worried about his command of English in years, not since he'd taken the small financial company he'd started on equal parts bluff, brains and balls and turned it into an empire.

That a woman—that *this* woman—should turn his life so upside down proved that his brain was scrambled…

And, yes, impossible or not, it was the same woman. No question, no doubt. The unforgettable face, the curvaceous body demurely hidden within a dressed-for-success suit, the long legs set off by nothing-demure-about-them stiletto heels…

This was the woman he'd almost initiated into the Mile High club. Although *initiated* might be the wrong word. The way she'd come awake in his arms, the way she'd responded to his kisses…

For all he knew, she was a charter member.

Or wasn't.

She'd gone from hot to cold in the blink of an eye, and—

And who cared about that?

What was she doing here? She could be in Rome, yes. But she most assuredly could not be Cesare Orsini's representative.

Had she come looking for him? Maybe she hadn't been able to forget what had happened and now she wanted to finish that long, exciting slide into sexual oblivion...

Forget that.

His receptionist had buzzed him. *Cesare Orsini's representative is here, sir,* she'd said. And his receptionist had been with him a long time. No one could get past her without proper ID. So this had to be—it had to be—

The woman stopped in the doorway, face white.

"Ohmygod," she said. "Ohmygod!"

Draco's last, faint hope that this was a mistake vanished.

"You?" The woman reached for the doorjamb, curved her hand around it as if that might keep her from fainting. Her voice rose an octave. "You're Draco Valenti?"

Draco took a deep breath. "And you are...?"

She laughed, but it was not a real laugh. It was the kind of sound someone might make when what was really called for was an anguished wail of despair.

"The Orsini attorney."

Draco had always heard that hope died hard. Now he discovered that it didn't simply die—it crashed to earth in flames.

"Small world," he said drily.

She nodded. "Small, indeed." All at once the look of shock vanished. "Wait a minute," she said slowly, letting go of the jamb, straightening to her full height. Her eyes narrowed. "It was all deliberate!"

"I beg your pardon?"

Color suffused her face. "I cannot believe anyone would resort to such a thing."

"Perhaps you'd like to enlighten me, Miss—Miss—"

She stalked toward him menacingly, a cat approaching its prey.

"You set me up!"

"What?"

"You—you sneaky, slimy—"

"Watch what you say to me," Draco said sharply.

"You played me for a patsy!"

What did that mean? This woman was playing havoc in his head.

"You tried to take advantage of me!"

Draco gave a mirthless laugh.

"Are we back to that?" Slowly he let his gaze travel over her, from head to toe and back again. "Believe me, if I could erase that momentary behavioral aberration, I would."

A momentary behavioral aberration? Was that what he called what had happened—what had almost happened? And that chill in his eyes. In his voice. How could he speak so—so clinically of what had taken place on the plane?

Anna narrowed her eyes until they were slits.

"That behavioral aberration," she said, somehow making the words sound as if they consisted of four letters each, "was a clever ploy. At least, that's what you intended it to be. But it didn't work, did it? It didn't work because I'm not one of your—your women."

Draco raised an eyebrow. Looked over his shoulder. Stared into the corners of the elegant room.

"My women?" he purred.

She tossed her head.

"You know damned well what I mean. A man like you thinks he can snap his fingers and the entire female population of the planet will fall at his feet!"

"An interesting abuse of the laws of physics," he said coldly. "And what has it to do with you and me and that airplane?"

"You thought you could compromise my position."

"Was that the position you took when your leg was draped over mine?" Draco said with chilling politeness.

Her face turned an angry shade of crimson.

"You're despicable!"

"And you are wasting my time."

"You knew who I was all the time, Valenti!"

"You will address me as 'prince' or 'sir,'" Draco heard himself say, and tried not to wince at the idiocy of it, but what better way to deal with the representative of a smarmy Sicilian gangster than to play on the ancient, if ridiculous, elements of class distinction?

"That's why you invited me to sit with you."

"I hope you know what you're talking about, madam, because I most assuredly do not!"

She strode forward, came to a stop inches from him. The scent of her rose to him, something as feminine, delicate and sexy as her stiletto heels.

He recalled the scent from those moments she'd lain in his arms on the plane.

He recalled more than that.

The feel of her, pressed against him. The softness of her breasts against his chest. The heat of her body. The swift race of her heart against his, the sigh of her breath…

Draco frowned.

His body was remembering, too. Damnit, that was the wrong thing to have happen right now.

"You offered me that seat for a reason!"

"I offered it out of the goodness of my heart and the graciousness of my soul."

"Ha!"

She tossed her head again. A couple of golden curls slipped free of whatever it was women called those silly things they used to catch their hair and keep it from falling free, as nature had intended.

"How pathetic! That you'd stoop to such measures."

Her mouth was curled with contempt. Yes, he thought, but he could uncurl it in a heartbeat, kiss that mouth until it softened and sweetened under his.

"You—knew—who—I—was," she said hotly, punctuating the words by jabbing her index finger into the center of his chest. "And don't bother trying to deny it!"

Had he missed something? Had he been so busy remembering the taste of her, the feel of her, that he'd lost track of the conversation?

The realization made him even angrier.

"Deny what?" he demanded. "And stop doing that," he growled, clasping her hand and folding his fingers around hers.

"What happened on the plane. What you did."

"Excuse me?"

"Kissing me. It was all for a purpose."

He laughed. He couldn't help it. What man wouldn't laugh at such an accusation?

Her eyes flashed with anger. "You think this is amusing?"

"Let me be sure I understand this. You're accusing me of kissing you on purpose?"

"Absolutely."

"Well, that's a relief. I mean, I'd hate to have you accuse me of kissing you without any purpose."

Anna blinked. How could he do this? Twist her words so they came out wrong. Take her accusations and turn them into jokes.

Most of all, how could he be so damnably arrogant and officious and clever and still be so incredibly easy on the eyes? How could the feel of his fingers wrapped around her wrist make her remember the feel of his body against hers? The feel of his mouth? The taste of his kisses?

"Don't play dumb," she said. "You thought if you seduced me it would be impossible for me to represent Cesare Orsini's interests."

He gave her a long, steady look. Then, curse the man, he laughed. Again.

"*Dio,* am I clever!"

"What you are is a bast—"

"I hate to rewrite your script, madam, but you've got it all wrong. I had no idea who you were. The only thing I knew about you was that you had one hell of a quick temper."

"What I have, oh your worshipful highness, is no tolerance for bull."

"A quick temper. A sharp tongue." Suddenly his voice turned low and rough. "And you fell asleep in my arms and came awake wanting me as much as I wanted you."

Anna's heart banged against her ribs.

"I was half-asleep. You took advantage. You wanted to compromise me."

He gave a soft, sexy laugh.

"*Compromise* is not the word to describe what I wanted of you." His arms went around her. "What we wanted of each other."

"Let go," Anna said.

"That's what you said on the plane."

"Exactly. And I'm saying it again. Let—"

"You said it only after the lights came on." His arms tightened around her; she could feel every inch of him against her. "Until then, you were as turned on as I was."

"That isn't true! I wasn't—"

His gaze dropped to her lips. She could almost feel the warmth of his mouth on hers, taste those remembered kisses.

"The hell you weren't."

His voice was husky. Hot with masculine warning. He was aroused. The hard ridge of his erection was against her belly.

Desire, urgent and primitive, shot through her blood. He was the enemy. He was everything she despised, a damnable aristocrat, a man who obviously thought he could treat a woman as if he owned her. He was her father's and her mother's enemy, for heaven's sake...

But what did that matter when her body throbbed with need?

They could finish what had started hours ago.

Alone. Here, with no prying eyes to see them, no one to interrupt a joining of eager bodies.

Anna shuddered. A whisper of sound sighed from her mouth. Her lashes fell, veiled her eyes as she rose toward him...

His arms opened, dropped to his sides.

She blinked. Looked up. Saw that his face was stony, his mouth cruel.

"Now," he said calmly as he took a step back, "now, *signorina,* you have been compromised."

Her hand balled into a fist at her side. She wanted to hit him. Hard. Leave an imprint on that smug, cold, handsome face.

"You did that once," he said coldly. "I would advise you not to do it again."

Anna took a steadying breath. And laughed, though it took everything she possessed to choke out the sound.

"You're so easy, Your Highness. Oh, sorry. Does the news come as a shock? Do you honestly believe one look from you turns my knees to water?"

Draco narrowed his gaze.

What he believed was that she was lying. To him. To herself.

If he wanted her, he could have her. Now. Here. But he didn't. Damnit, he didn't. What he wanted was to get everything to do with Cesare Orsini out of his life.

"Enough of these games," he growled. "What is your name? And what do you want?"

"I want you to face facts." Anna's voice was steady. Amazing, because her pulse was ragged. "No matter what you claim, I can make an excellent case for you knowing my identity all along." She smiled brightly. "So if you want to talk about compromising one's legal position…"

"An excellent speech. Unfortunately, it's also meaningless. I didn't know your name on that plane. I still don't."

Anna gave a negligent shrug. "He said, she said. Stuff like that is bread and butter in courts of law."

"Which brings me to the second reason your little speech is meaningless." He smiled. "This would never get adjudicated in a court of law."

"I'm an attorney."

Another quick smile, this one pure venom. "Not in Italy."

Damnit, he was quick, and he was right. She had no legal standing here. She'd tried telling that to her father. *You want a lawyer, find one who's Italian,* she'd said, but Cesare had been adamant. This was a family matter. A personal matter. He didn't need a stranger to speak for him, for Sofia. He needed her.

"So," the Prince of All He Surveyed said, "we have a—what would you call it? A situation. I am the rightful owner of land your client would like to claim is his."

"The land in question belongs to my client's wife. *She* is the rightful owner."

Draco shrugged, walked to his impressive desk, hitched a hip onto its edge.

"I agreed to meet with Cesàre Orsini's representative as a courtesy."

"You agreed," Anna said coolly, "because you know you have a problem on your hands."

She wasn't wrong. There were those in the judiciary who would be more than happy to see a Valenti prince trapped in endless legal wrangling over a mess like this. The land was indisputably his, but thanks to the way things worked in Sicily, it could take years to put the case to rest.

Assuming there was a case, and there wouldn't be.

He knew enough about Cesàre Orsini and men like him to understand they had only two methods of settling debts.

One involved blood.

The other…

Draco sighed. His plane was back in service; his pilot was already en route to Rome so he could fly him back to Hawaii, the sea, the sun and the warm bed of his mistress—a woman who would not play hot then cold, as this one did.

"Very well." He went behind the desk, sat down in a chair, pulled open a drawer, took out a gold pen and a leather checkbook. "How much?"

"I beg your pardon? How much what?"

"Didn't you hear what I said? I'm tired of playing games. How much does Orsini want?"

"To buy his land?"

A muscle knotted in Draco's jaw. "The land is not his to sell."

The woman gave him a smile that would have sent a diabetic to the hospital. She was going to drive him crazy!

"I am not offering to buy it, I am offering—"

"A payoff?"

"Compensation. What does your client want to end this insane charade?"

Anna tossed her briefcase on a chair and strolled to the

enormous desk. It was probably very old, and obviously hand carved. Mythological griffins dove on falcons, falcons dove on rabbits, wolves sank their fangs into the hindquarters of stags and brought them to their knees.

The history of the landed gentry, she thought coldly. She knew a lot about that history. She'd made a point of studying it when she'd first realized her father's true profession, hoping against hope that understanding the old Sicilian antagonisms would help her understand him.

What she'd ended up understanding was that the world could be a brutally unfair place, but the world of her father was more than brutal.

Right now, though, what she was seeing firsthand went a long way toward validating her opinion of princes who thought they could take whatever they wanted from mere mortals, and get away with it.

"Well?"

She looked up. The prince, gold pen poised, was watching her much as the wolves carved into his desk had surely watched the creatures they hunted. He looked intent. Determined. Coldly analytical, and certain of how the chase would end.

Not so fast, big boy, she thought, and she took a long breath.

"Well, what?"

"You're pushing your luck," Draco said softly.

"And you're making foolish assumptions if you think you can buy your way out of this." Anna jerked her chin toward the checkbook. "You can put that thing away."

Draco said nothing for a long minute. A muscle knotted and unknotted in his jaw. Then he dropped the pen and checkbook back into the drawer and slammed it shut with enough force to send the sound bouncing around the room.

"Let's get down to basics," he snapped. "If you don't want money, what do you want?"

"You know what I want. The land, of course."

"That's impossible. The land is mine. I have the deed to it. No court in Sicily will—"

"Perhaps not."

"Then, how—"

Anna gave him her best look of wide-eyed innocence.

"Roman Aristocrat Steals Land from Helpless Grandmother," she said sweetly, and batted her lashes. "Maybe they can work the words *puppies* and *kittens* into that headline, too."

"You left something out. *Sicilian Citizen Protects Land from Theft by American Hoodlum.*" Draco flashed a smug smile. "Or don't you like that wording?"

"You're no more Sicilian than I am!"

"My ancestors settled in Sicily five hundred years ago."

"You mean they invaded it five hundred years ago. The Orsinis were already there."

"I asked you a question. What do you want?"

"And I answered it. I want the land. If you think my client will run from a newspaper calling him a gangster…" Anna showed her teeth in a brilliant smile. "Trust me, Valenti. It won't be the first time."

"Do not address me that way," Draco said, hating himself for sounding ridiculous, hating the woman for pushing him to it. "As for headlines…" He shrugged. "They come and go."

She smiled. It was the kind of smile that made him want to shoot to his feet and toss her out of his office…

Or take her in his arms and remind her of just how easily he could change her cold contempt to hot desire.

"The thing is, oh powerful prince, we love that kind of stuff in the States. We give it all our attention. Page Six of the *Post. People. US. The Star.* All those juicy tabloids, the even juicier internet blogs. The cable news channels."

"You're pushing your luck again," he said in a soft voice.

She knew she was, but it was too late to back down now.

"Even the real newspapers—the *New York Times,* the *San Francisco Chronicle,* the *Washington Post*—will love this." Anna leaned closer. "See, one of the few things I had time to do was look you up on Google. I know you're not just a prince, stealing money from the peasants—"

"A gangster's legal mouthpiece calling me a thief?" Draco leaned back in his chair, folded his arms over his chest and laughed.

"You also control a huge financial empire."

His laughter ended. A look of cold determination took its place as he rose to his feet

"If you have a point, get to it."

"Oh, I do," Anna said. She paused for effect, as if this were a grungy New York City courtroom instead of an elegant office. "How do you think a company like yours would stand up to such a scandal in today's financial climate?"

His face darkened.

"How dare you threaten me? Who the hell are you?"

Anna dug into her pocket, took out a small leather case and extracted a business card. Nonchalantly she plucked a pen from his desk, scribbled the name of her hotel on the back, then flipped the card at him. He caught it, read the black engraving and looked at her through narrowed eyes.

"Anna Orsini," he said softly. "Well, well, well."

"That's me," Anna said cheerfully. "Anna Orsini. Cesare's daughter." Her voice became cold and flat. "In other words, a full-blooded member of the Orsini *famiglia*. I urge you to keep that in mind."

It seemed the right line, the closing line, especially when your enemy looked as if he might spring across the desk and throttle you...

Especially when your own heart was banging so hard you were afraid it might leap from your chest.

Anna pivoted on her heel, picked up her briefcase and walked out.

CHAPTER SIX

DRACO watched Anna Orsini march to the door.

Head up, shoulders back, spine straight, her long-legged stride on those amazing stilettos clearly sending a to-hell-with-you message.

Almost.

The shoes changed her walk, ever so slightly. Balancing on them made her hips sway, changing what she surely meant to be a brisk march into something feminine and damned near feline.

Golden-haired seductress. Cold-blooded *consigliere*. Which was the real Anna Orsini?

For a dangerous couple of seconds Draco came close to demanding the answer.

He would go after her, swing her toward him, look down into those blue eyes and say, *Hell, woman, how dare you threaten me! Are you fool enough to think I can be brought to heel by you and your hoodlum father?*

Or he'd say nothing at all.

He'd pull her into his arms, lower his head to hers and kiss her hard and deep until she forgot about being her father's mouthpiece and became the woman he'd known on the plane, the one who'd come within a heartbeat of giving herself up to him.

Instead, he stood his ground. He didn't even breathe until she slammed the door hard enough to make it rattle.

He had to move carefully. No rash decisions. No letting the emotions within him overtake logic.

Draco went to his desk and sat in the massive chair behind it.

No question, he had a problem. Anna's threat had teeth.

Teeth?

Hell, it had fangs, fangs that could sink into his throat and destroy him. There were some businesses that sought publicity, that thrived on it.

Not Valenti Investments.

Even being mentioned in the same breath as a crook like Cesare Orsini could mean the end of everything he had worked for. Not just money, although the amount he might lose, for himself and for his clients, was staggering.

But there was more at stake than money. If Anna forced a public confrontation, Draco would lose that which mattered most to him.

The honor of his name. The respect it once again carried.

A muscle jumped in his cheek.

To think he'd almost had sex with her. With Cesare Orsini's *consigliere.*

Cristo, he wanted to laugh!

Not that this was a laughing matter, Draco thought grimly as he took the gangster's letters from his briefcase and stacked them on the desk in front of him. Nothing about the situation was even remotely amusing.

If only he'd known who she was last night, he'd never have let things go so far.

Actually, the more he thought about it, the less he understood why he had become involved with her at all.

Her name could be Jane Doe, and he wouldn't want her.

She wasn't his type. She was too tall, too blonde, too slender. His tastes ran to petite women. Brunettes, with voluptuous bodies.

And that attitude of hers, that feminist chip she carried on her shoulder…

What man in his right mind would be attracted to a woman who argued over everything?

Calmer now, he could see that it had been the situation, not the woman, that had turned him on. The hushed darkness. The isolation that came of being five miles above the earth. The added rush of knowing you were in a public setting.

Draco sat back in his chair.

Given all that, what man would not want to take things to their natural conclusion when he awoke with a woman draped over him like a blanket?

In a way, he owed Anna Orsini his thanks. Men thought with parts of their anatomy that had nothing to do with their brains. She had saved them both from making an embarrassing mistake.

Imagine if he'd actually had sex with the Orsini *consigliere*…

Draco did laugh this time.

There was a solution to the problem. There always was. And he would find it—something he could do to get the Orsinis, father and daughter, out of his life.

He was, above all else, a logical man. A pragmatist. And pragmatism, not emotion, would save the day. Control over your emotions was everything.

His father and those before him had never understood that.

They drank to excess. Gambled with money they didn't have. They went from woman to woman, losing themselves in the kind of passion and intensity that could only lead to trouble.

The Valenti family history was a minefield of greed, infidelity, abandonment and divorce.

Absolutely, a man had to learn to curb his emotions. And Draco had learned early how to curb his.

His boyhood had been filled with scenes that still made him grimace. His mother had taken a string of lovers who helped themselves to what little remained of the family's money. Still, she'd apparently found her life boring and abandoned her husband and Draco when he was a toddler.

His father might as well have done the same. He was too busy whoring and gambling to pay attention to his son. Draco's early memories were of big, silent rooms, most of them stripped of what had once been elegant furnishings. The few servants who remained, overworked and underpaid, ignored him.

He had been a solitary and lonely child; it had never occurred to him other children might have had different existences from his.

One winter, his father stayed sober long enough to figure out that the last of what he'd still referred to as his staff had abandoned ship, leaving nine-year-old Draco to fend for himself.

The prince had given his young son orders to bathe and dress in his best clothes. Then he'd taken him to a school run by nuns.

The Mother Superior, who was also the principal, had eyed Draco and wrinkled her nose, as if he gave off a bad smell. She'd tested him in math. In science. In French and English.

Draco had known the answers to all her questions. He was a bright boy. An omnivorous reader. From age five he'd sought solace by immersing himself in the few remaining volumes in the once-proud Valenti library.

But he'd been struck speechless.

The nun's voice had been sharp; he'd been able to see his own reflection in her eyeglasses, and that was somehow disorienting. Her coif had made her round face with its pointed nose look like an owl's.

She had been, in his eyes, an alien creature, and he'd been terrified.

"Answer the Mother Superior," his father had hissed.

Draco had opened his mouth, then shut it. The nun glared at his father, then at him.

"The boy is retarded," she'd said. Her fingers had clamped hard on Draco's shoulder. "Leave him with us, Prince Valenti. We will, if nothing else, teach him to fear his God."

That was the theology he'd received at the hands of the sisters.

The other boys had taught him more earthly things to fear.

Beatings, on what was supposed to be the playground. Beatings at night, in the sour-smelling dormitory rooms. Humiliation after humiliation.

It had been the equivalent of tossing a puppy into a cage of hungry wolves.

Draco had been skinny and pale. His clothes were threadbare, but their style had marked him as a member of a despised upper class, as had the way in which he spoke. He was quiet, shy and bookish, with the formal manners of a boy who had never before dealt with other children.

It had been a recipe for disaster, either unnoticed or ignored by the sisters until one day, almost a year later, when Draco had decided he could not take any more.

It was lunchtime, and everyone had been on the playground. Draco saw one of his tormenters closing in.

All the hurt, the fear, the emotions he'd kept bottled inside him burst free.

He'd sprung at the other boy. The fight had turned ugly, but when it was over, the other kid was on the ground, sobbing. Draco, bloodied and bruised but victorious, had stood over him.

His reputation was made. And if keeping it meant stepping up to the challenge of other boys from time to time, beating them and, occasionally, being beaten in return, so be it.

The Mother Superior had said she'd always known he would come to no good.

The day he turned seventeen, one of the senior boys decided to give him a very special gift. He'd come to Draco during the night while he slept, slapped a hand over his mouth and yanked down his pajama bottoms.

Draco was no longer small or skinny. He had grown into manhood; he was six foot three inches of fight-hardened muscle.

With a roar, he'd shot up in bed, grabbed his attacker by the throat and if the other boys hadn't pulled him off, he might have killed him.

The Mother Superior asked no questions.

"You are," she told Draco, "a monster. You will never amount to anything. And you are unwanted here."

He hadn't argued. As far as he knew, she was right on all counts.

She'd expelled him, told him to be gone the next morning, and he'd thought, *So be it.*

That night he'd jimmied the lock on the door to her office and taken four hundred euros from her desk. Going home was not an option. He had no home, not really. The castle was in a state of near disaster and his father, who had visited him once the first year and then never again, meant nothing to him.

The next day he'd flown to New York with the clothes on his back, a determination to make something of himself, and a philosophy by which to live.

Never show weakness.

Never show emotion.

Trust no one but yourself.

New York was big, brash and unforgiving. It was also a place where anything was possible. For Draco, that "anything" meant finding a way to make sure he'd seen the last of hunger, poverty and humiliation.

He'd found jobs. In construction. As a waiter. A cab driver. He'd worked his royal ass off—not that anybody knew he was a royal. And in the dark of night, in a roach-infested room in a part of Brooklyn that was beyond any hope of gentrification, he'd lie awake and admit to himself that he was going nowhere.

A man needed a goal. A purpose. He'd had neither.

Until, purely by accident, he'd learned that his father had died.

Prince Mario Valenti, a one-inch item buried in the *New York Post* said, *died yesterday in a shooting accident involving former movie star...*

The details didn't matter. His father had died a shameful death, broke and in debt. And in that moment Draco had known what he would do with his life.

He would redeem the Valenti name.

That meant paying off his father's debts. Restoring the castle. Making the family name, even the accursedly ridiculous title, stand for something again.

He'd wanted a new start. To get it, he'd worked his way across the vast expanse of the United States. He liked Los Angeles, but San Francisco struck him as not just beautiful but the kind of place that rewarded individuality. He'd talked himself into San Francisco State University, chosen classes in mathematics and finance because he found them interesting. Writing a term paper, he'd stumbled upon an idea. An investment plan. It worked in theory but would it in real life?

Only one way to find out.

Draco took everything he'd set aside for the next year's tuition and sank it in the stock market.

His money doubled. Tripled. Quadrupled. He quit school, devoted himself to investing.

And parlayed what he had into a not-so-small fortune.

"Draco Valenti," the *Wall Street Journal* said the first time it mentioned him, "a new investor on the scene, who plays the market with icy skill."

Was there any other way to play the market or, in fact, to play the game of life?

Eventually he founded his own company. Valenti Investments. He made mistakes, but mostly he made choices that led to dazzling successes.

He knew the dot com ride would not last forever, and acted accordingly. He thought packaged mortgages sold by banks made no sense and he bet his money, instead, on their eventual failure. He found small tech firms with big ideas and invested in them.

He made more money than seemed humanly possible, enough to buy the San Francisco condo, the Roman villa. Enough to restore the Valenti castle.

And enough to fund a school for poor kids in Rome and others in Sicily, New York and San Francisco, though he kept those endeavors strictly private.

He was tough, he was hard, he was not sentimental. The schools were simply a practical way of using up some of his money, and he'd be damned if he'd let anybody try to put a different spin on it.

Draco shoved aside the Orsini documents and swung his chair toward the window behind him.

There had to be a way around the Orsini problem.

Valenti Investments could not, must not, go under. He could live through the financial loss—hell, life was, at best, an uphill battle—but to tarnish the Valenti name…

He could not bear the thought of that happening again.

He turned from the window.

There was a solution, and he would find it, but not by concentrating on it. He would, instead, do what he always did at moments of stress. He would think about anything but the problem at hand. He would think logically. Rid his thoughts of emotion.

Draco rang the intercom. His PA answered.

"I have some letters to dictate," he said.

But, damnit, Anna Orsini would not stay in the mental file drawer in which he'd placed her. She kept appearing in his mind, front and center.

Ridiculous, because she was not really the problem. Her father was.

Then why did he keep seeing her face, that sleepy, sexy look in her eyes when she'd lain in his arms last night?

Why did he keep remembering the way she dressed, the conservative suit, the do-me stilettos?

What did she have on under that suit? Was it the equivalent of banker's gray? Or was it silk and lace, as sexy as the shoes?

"Sir?" his PA said.

Draco blinked.

"Sorry," he said briskly. "Uh, where was I?"

"The Tolland merger," his PA said, and Draco nodded and picked up where he'd left off in his dictation.

Five minutes later, he gave up.

"That's all for now, Sylvana," he said.

His PA left the room. Draco rose to his feet, grabbed his suit coat and went to lunch. He followed that with a long, hard workout at his gym.

He still had not come up with a way to handle the Orsini situation.

Worse, Anna Orsini was still in his head.

At five, he called for his car.

"Where to, sir?" his driver said.

Draco thought of the various answers he could give.

He could go out to dinner. He had no reservations any-where, but that would not matter. There was not a *ristorante* in Rome that would not give him its best table if he showed up at the door.

He could take out his BlackBerry, phone one of a dozen beautiful women. There wasn't one in Rome who would deny him anything he might ask of her, even at the last minute.

That made him think of his mistress, waiting for him in Hawaii.

Cristo, he had not thought of her once the entire day.

"Take me home," he told his driver, and while the big car made its way through the crushing end-of-day traffic, Draco put through a call to her.

"Hello?" she said in a sleepy voice.

What time was it in Hawaii, anyway? No way was he going to ask.

"It's me," he said. "How are you?"

"Draco," she said. He could picture the look on her face. Sultry, sexy, pouty. "I thought you'd forgotten me."

Draco rubbed his temple with his free hand.

"How did you spend your day?" he said, because he knew he had to say something.

She laughed.

"I spent it shopping, darling. Well, window-shopping. I have a whole bunch of gorgeous things picked out for you to buy me when you get back."

Draco closed his eyes and imagined the hours she'd expect him to spend in a dozen different boutiques.

"When *will* you be back, Draco?" Her voice turned husky. "I miss you."

The truth was she missed the status that came of being seen

with him. The knowledge that he would buy her whatever she'd shopped for today. She missed his title, his status, his money.

And, yes, his looks, and his expertise in bed.

It would be foolish to deny that women liked both.

"Darling? When will you be back?"

He wouldn't be.

The realization was sudden, and so was its full meaning.

Draco cleared his throat.

"Something's come up," he said. "So, ah, so here's what I suggest. Stay on a few more days. Do some shopping—tell the shops to phone my office and they'll okay the charges. Take your time. Enjoy yourself. When we're both back on the coast, I'll give you a call."

Silence. Then she said, "And when, exactly, will that be?"

Her tone was cool. She was not a stupid woman, not when it came to men and the ways of the world. Their two-month relationship was over; Draco had not even realized it until this minute.

"I don't know," he said with brutal honesty. "But I do know that I wish you only the best."

He disconnected, put his BlackBerry in his pocket as the car pulled through the gates that led to his villa.

He had not planned on ending things just now. Soon, yes. But why now?

An image flashed into his mind.

Anna Orsini.

Naked this time, her golden hair loose on his pillows, her arms raised to him...

"Signore?"

The car had stopped at the foot of the steps to the villa. His driver stood beside the open rear door. Draco climbed out, told him he was free for the rest of the evening, went into the house and told his housekeeper the same thing.

She had left a salad for him. He ate it, had a cold beer and went to his rooms, where he undressed and stepped into the big steam shower.

Maybe the hot water would work the tension from his shoulders and neck.

Maybe it would wash away the image of Anna, naked, hot and silken under the stroke of his hand.

Draco cursed, stepped from the shower, wrapped a towel around his hips.

She had accused him of playing her, but he was the one being played!

An entire day wasted. And for what? He had money. Power. He could take on the entire Orsini *famiglia* and break it.

Why had he been so civilized when she showed up at his office? He should have told her to get the hell out. Of his office, of his life, of Rome.

And that exit she'd made. Gloating. Egotistical. As if she were the royal and he was the commoner—and wasn't it pathetic she had him thinking such crap?

Anna Orsini needed to be put in her place. Reminded that she was a woman, not *consigliere* to a gangster.

And he could have reminded her. In the most basic way possible. Gone after her, slapped his hand on the door to keep her from opening it. Locked the damned thing, then finished what had begun somewhere high over the Atlantic, because that was what this was all about, not land, not her father, not anything but a man and a woman and frustrated desire.

He could see her in his mind's eye, stripped to her soft skin, that mass of golden hair unbound, drifting over her shoulders, over her breasts. He'd put his mouth to the pebbled tips, his hand between her thighs, his fingers searching out her hot, wet heat because she *would* be hot and wet, eager, *Dio,* hungry for him, only for him.

Draco's instant erection pushed hard against the towel draped around his hips. He said a word that came straight from the schoolyard of his childhood, but the urgency that accompanied it was solely that of a man.

Basta! Enough.

He had met Anna Orsini only last night, but she had already turned his life upside down. He could think about nothing but her.

And he had let her do this to him. He had permitted it.

Quickly, he tossed the towel aside, pulled on boxers, a pair of age-softened jeans, a black T-shirt, a pair of mocs.

His wallet, with her business card in it, was on a small table near the front door, where he'd left it. He yanked the card out and looked at it. He had never heard of her hotel, but he knew the location.

It would take him half an hour to get there.

He could have phoned her, but that wouldn't be half as satisfying as confronting her.

Do your worst, he'd say. *Go to the media. Spread whatever story you like, write it across the sky.*

He would withstand the ugly publicity. Hell, he'd turn it in his favor. A hoodlum and his daughter, threatening Prince Draco Valenti?

Draco gave an ugly laugh.

He had money. Power. Far more of both than Cesare Orsini could ever hope to have. And he would use them both.

By the time he was done with the old man and his daughter, they would wish to God they'd never even heard of him.

There were three cars, and the keys to them, in his garage. The big Maserati limo, a red Lamborghini and a black Ferrari. He got behind the wheel of the Ferrari.

The car was fast and powerful and it suited the rage boiling within him.

He made the drive in fifteen minutes, his foot to the floor, cutting off whatever vehicle was in his way, ignoring the bleat of horns and raised fingers of the drivers he sped past.

The car's tires squealed as he brought it to a stop in the hotel's driveway. A uniformed doorman approached, hand raised, to tell him he couldn't park there. Draco tossed him a hundred-euro note and moved quickly through the front door.

The desk clerk looked up at his approach.

"May I help you," he started to say, but Draco cut him short.

"Anna Orsini. What room?"

"I am sorry, *signore,* but I cannot—"

Draco reached across the desk, grabbed the clerk by the tie and hauled him forward.

"What room?" he growled.

"Three—three fourteen," the clerk sputtered.

Draco nodded, dropped another hundred-euro note on the counter.

There were two elevators, one in use, one with an out-of-order sign taped to its door. He waited a couple of seconds for the one that was supposedly operating and then he took the stairs instead.

Room 314 was at the end of a dark hall. He strode along a frayed carpet runner until he reached it and then he hit the door once, with his fist.

It opened instantly.

"Wow," Anna said, "that's the quickest room service I ever—"

"Anna."

She was barefoot, swaddled in a voluminous white terry-cloth robe, her face bare of makeup and as beautiful as any ever sculpted by Michelangelo. Her hair was a damp tumble of golden curls; her eyes were wide with shock and as blue as the deepest part of the sea.

"Draco?" she whispered.

He stepped into the room. Shut the door behind him without once looking away from her.

"I am not room service," he said in a low voice. "And I am not a man you can toy with." He paused. He could feel the rage in him changing to something dark and hot and far more dangerous.

"Anna," he said roughly, "goddamnit, Anna…"

"Goddamnit, Draco," Anna said, "what took you so long?"

And then…

Then she was in his arms.

CHAPTER SEVEN

ANNA was on her toes, her body tight against Draco's, her arms wound around his neck.

His mouth was on hers, open, demanding and merciless. His hands were under her robe, hard and hot on her skin, cupping her bottom and lifting her into him. His erection pressed urgently against her belly, the masculine power surging against his closed fly, sent hot shudders of excitement racing through her.

She had had lovers before. Anticipating the moment, the first electric shimmer of desire, was always thrilling.

But never like this.

She was trembling, breathless, almost dizzy with need.

Draco said something, the words rushed and urgent. She couldn't understand them; he spoke in the kind of elegant, upper-class Italian that was nothing like the Sicilian dialect she'd heard as a child, but she didn't have to make sense of the words to know their meaning.

Draco wanted her.

Right now. Right here.

It was what she wanted, too.

He untied her robe, shoved it back on her shoulders. His hands swept over her, down her spine, kneading her hips, then rising up her torso to cup her breasts.

His thumbs moved over her nipples and a cry broke from

her throat. Anna caught his black T-shirt in her fists and tugged it free of his jeans. She put her palms flat against his naked chest, and he groaned.

She answered his groan with one of her own.

The feel of his body!

His skin was hot, hair-roughened. He was all muscle, and when she ran her hands down his belly, to the jeans he wore low on his hips, her fingers marveled over the ridged, perfect abs.

"Draco," she whispered.

He growled her name, pushed her robe away and it fell to her feet. The air felt cool on her overheated flesh; he bent his head, kissed her throat, the slope of one breast, drew its beaded tip deep into his mouth.

Anna cried out; her head fell back and a curl of flame swept from low in her belly directly to where Draco's mouth worked its magic.

He raised his head, kissed her deeply, thrust his fingers into her hair and took her mouth again and again.

Now his hands were on her. All over her. His caresses were not gentle, but gentle wasn't what she wanted.

Not now.

What she wanted was this. Draco's lips at her throat. His fingers on her nipples. His denim-clad knee between her thighs.

And then his hand. Oh, his hand, cupping her. His fingers parting her.

"Hot," he said thickly. "So hot and wet…"

She sobbed his name, felt her body weeping with hunger against his palm.

"Oh God, hurry!" she said. "Oh, hurry!"

He made a sound deep in his throat as he unzipped his fly. Anna pushed his hand aside, reached for his straining flesh. Her heart pounded as his erection sprang free. Her breath hissed as she closed her fingers around the silk-over-steel power of his hardened flesh.

He was big. Incredibly big, and she gasped as she wrapped her hand around him.

"Anna," he said, only that, but the single word was so filled with urgency that she rose on her toes and nipped at his bottom lip.

"Yes," she said against his mouth, "please, please…"

It was the soft, desperate plea that was his final undoing.

Draco scooped her into his arms, swung around and pushed her back against the closed door. She wrapped her legs around his hips. He grunted and drove into her.

Her scream was everything a man could want, the cry of a woman swept away by passion.

He thrust into her again. And again. Harder and harder as she cried out in ecstasy.

"Draco," she sobbed, "oh, sweet heaven, Draco…"

He shifted her weight, one powerful arm around her buttocks, one angled against her back, his hand in her hair so that his mouth could plunder hers.

He was relentless. Kissing her. Thrusting into her. She was panting, sobbing, riding him and riding him and he was going to come, *Dio,* he was going to come….

Anna screamed.

And Draco exploded deep, deep inside her.

The world stood still.

After a very long time Anna drew a ragged breath. Her head fell forward onto Draco's shoulder, and she buried her face against his throat.

Her heart felt as if it were trying to pound its way out of her chest, or was that racing beat his?

She sighed and closed her eyes.

He held her tight, and she all but purred.

"Wow," she said in a shaky whisper. "That was—it was…"

Draco laughed softly. "*Sì*. It certainly was." He hesitated. "It was not too quick?"

Anna lifted her head.

"You just want to hear me say 'wow' again."

He grinned. "Perhaps. But I was too fast."

"No. You weren't. And if you keep apologizing, I won't let you do this again." Her lips curved in a wickedly sexy smile. "At least, I won't let you do it more than another two or three dozen times."

Laughter rumbled in his chest.

"Is that all?" he teased, and he swung her into his arms, carried her to the bed, tumbled onto it with her. "Sorry, Orsini. Twenty or thirty times isn't going to be enough."

Anna looped her arms around his neck.

"You're right," she said softly. "It won't be."

Draco kissed her, his mouth moving slowly over hers. Then he drew back a little and looked at her.

Her hair, a beautiful tangle of gold, was spread over the pillow, just as he had imagined it. Her eyes were deep pools of violet-blue.

Her face glowed.

It pleased him to know that he, his lovemaking, was the reason for that glow.

"Bellissima," he murmured, but she was more than beautiful. There was a wildness to her. She was exotic. Untamed. A feral cat that would purr only at the stroke of a special hand.

His hand.

"Draco. What are you thinking?"

"I'm thinking that you are an amazing woman, Anna Orsini." He gathered her into his arms, brushed his lips lightly over hers. "And I'm very glad I came here tonight."

"So am I. Very glad you came here." She hesitated. "Not

that I realized it until I opened the door and found you standing outside it, glowering at me."

He laughed softly.

"Glowering, huh?"

"Like a thundercloud."

"Well, I came here because I was angry."

"I know. I was, too."

"But then you opened the door and I saw you."

"All dressed up," Anna said, fluttering her lashes. "That designer robe. My hair in my eyes. And you couldn't resist me."

Draco grinned. Then his smile faded.

"And I knew I'd been lying to myself. That I'd come because I wanted you. I was just too thickheaded to see it."

"Too proud, you mean."

"No," he said quickly. Then he shrugged. "Maybe. Hell, not maybe. Yes. You're right." He kissed her, luxuriating in the sweetness of her mouth. "And you figured this out because…?"

"Because I can be the same sometimes. Proud. And a little arrogant." She sighed. "Which adds up to sometimes refusing to admit the truth to myself. See, you were supposed to be a chicken sandwich and a pot of tea."

"I am shocked, *bellissima*," he said sternly, "shocked to learn that you were waiting for a chicken sandwich and not for me."

Anna laughed. "You aren't my type at all, you know."

"Well, you aren't mine. You're too beautiful, too sexy, too—"

"I'm serious."

She was. He could see it in her eyes.

"Because?"

"Because I'm not into arrogant, 'me Tarzan, you Jane' guys."

"Me? Arrogant?"

"You, Prince Valenti. Impossibly, egotistically arrogant." Her voice fell to a husky whisper. "And overdressed."

"Over...?" Draco laughed. She was right. She lay naked beneath him, but he was still wearing all his clothes. "You're right. But that's an easy problem to solve."

He rose to his feet, toed off his mocs, stripped off his clothes, watched her eyes darken when she saw that he was hard and erect again.

"Better now?" he said as he came down to her and gathered her in his arms.

"Much better. Much, much..."

He stopped her with a kiss. And then another kiss. He kissed his way down her throat, to her breasts, heard her breath catch as he sucked her nipples.

"Draco," she whispered, and he wrapped his fingers lightly around her wrists, lifted her hands to the bed's headboard, to its pale oak latticework.

"Hold on to that," he said gruffly, and he grasped her thighs and spread them wide. He looked at her for long seconds and then he gave a soft groan. "Such a perfect flower," he whispered, and he put his mouth to her and kissed her.

Anna cried out and jerked against the kiss, against the stroke of his tongue, and he slipped his hands beneath her, lifted her to him, sucked the sweet pink bud until she moaned with pleasure.

Yes, he thought. *Yes.* This was why he had come here tonight...

For her. For what she was, a woman with the heart and passion of a tigress.

For what she was, not who she was.

For her.

"Anna," he said, rising above her. "Anna," he demanded, "look at me."

Her eyes, dark and filled with a woman's mysteries, met his. When they did, he entered her. One long, hard thrust and he was deep inside her.

Together they set a rhythm as urgent as their need. Anna, sobbing, moved with him, moaning, her arms and legs wrapped around him.

"Draco," she said, "Draco…"

She felt her muscles begin to contract and she arched upward as she cried out.

His groan of release seemed to come from the depths of his soul.

She was weeping when he collapsed on top of her, tears of joy that he kissed away before rolling onto his back, taking her with him and holding her tightly against his heart.

Anna slept.

At least she thought she'd slept, because she opened her eyes and saw that the room was dark.

Someone had shut off the light. Drawn up the duvet that had been left, folded, at the foot of the bed.

No. Not "someone." Draco. She was in his arms, draped over him, skin to skin, her face against his throat, her hand splayed over his chest.

She could feel his heart beating slowly, steadily against hers.

Amazing, that she had fallen asleep in his arms. Amazing, that she had fallen asleep at all. She never slept after sex.

Well, yes. Of course she did, but never in a lover's arms.

After sex she liked to lie quietly with her lover for a while. They might talk or cuddle, and then she'd say that it was getting late and she had a busy day tomorrow, or whatever it took to remind the man it was time to leave her bed.

At least she'd stayed true to form for that. This was a hotel bed, but it was hers for tonight. And when a relationship reached the point where having sex was part of it, she wanted it to be in her own bed.

Not the man's.

It wasn't a rule or anything—it was just the way it was.

You brought a man into your bed, you remained in charge. You could tell him when it was time to go; you didn't have to suffer the ignominy of walking past a doorman, of getting into a taxi at eight in the morning wearing what you'd worn the night before.

And you avoided the kind of situation that might lead to a lover thinking you wanted the forevermore thing.

Anna had seen the forevermore thing, close up. Her father dominating her mother's very existence. Her mother living the life of a second-class citizen.

Start to finish, you were the one in control when the bed you slept in belonged to you.

Men had an intuitive understanding of that basic fact.

She'd once overheard her brothers talking as they lazed around in the conservatory of the Orsini mansion, drinking beer and BS-ing with an eye on the clock after some family occasion none of them had wanted to attend.

They were guys, and not married back then, so the conversation eventually got around to women.

Anna, hidden in the depths of an oversize wing chair, had started to stand up and tell them they might want to curtail the chatter until she was out of earshot, but before she could, Rafe had said he'd been thinking.

"Thinking," Dante had said. "You?"

"About, you know, what would be the perfect woman," Rafe had said, ignoring the dig. "Like, if she stayed the night, she wouldn't help herself to my razor to shave her legs."

There'd been murmurs of agreement all around.

"Right," Nick had said, "and she'd carry her own toothbrush in her purse."

"And she wouldn't want conversation in the morning," Dante had added.

That had elicited a grunt from Falco, Anna remembered wryly.

"What you guys mean is that the perfect woman would appear in your bed when you needed her, and disappear like Tinker Bell when you didn't."

The others had laughed like loons, which was the only reason Anna had risen from her chair.

"Whoa," Nick had said, and Anna had said that *whoa* was exactly right, that what men really wanted were real-life versions of those vinyl blow-up dolls.

All her brothers had turned beet-red, and after she'd had a good laugh at the sight, she'd told them that she had a big surprise for them.

"Women want the same thing," she'd said. "A guy who'd show up in bed when you needed him and then vanish."

If there was a shade that went past beet-red, her brothers had achieved it.

"You're just trying to embarrass us," the usually non-embarrassable Falco had sputtered.

Well, no.

She hadn't been trying to do that—she'd simply been speaking honestly.

Women liked sex, too. At least, most of them did.

It was just that women were brought up to think that good girls never admitted it or, at the very least, good girls wrapped sex with pink ribbons.

Not her.

She didn't believe in sleeping around—talk about misnomers!—but that didn't mean you couldn't be honest about what you wanted. And what you didn't want.

And what Anna didn't want, ever, was one man, one woman, that whole foolish thing called forevermore…

Which brought her back to basics.

It was time to wake Draco, tell him this had been wonderful but it was late, she had a full day ahead of her tomorrow and it was time he went home.

Of course, that wouldn't be news to him. The full-day-tomorrow part. He knew it, because he was going to be part of that day.

Great sex or not, they hadn't settled anything. He still owned land she'd come here to claim.

Anna nearly groaned.

How could she have forgotten that? Since when did she let emotion get in the way of logic?

What she'd told Draco was true. She'd been attracted to him from the start, even though she'd denied it until tonight. Seeing him at her door had forced her to face the truth, that even while she'd said she despised him, she'd wanted to go to bed with him.

Okay. Desire was one thing, but violating her ethical role in this situation was very much another issue.

She was an attorney, and attorneys didn't get involved with the respondents in their cases. Assuming there would be a case to be involved in.

Okay. She'd made a mistake, a big one, but there was no sense in dwelling on it. What mattered was that it would not happen again.

The sex had been good, but she'd had good sex before…

"Hey."

Startled, Anna raised her head and looked at Draco, who gave her a slow, sexy smile.

"You're up," she said brightly. "Good. I mean, I was just going to wake you."

He shifted his weight, rolled her onto her back and framed her face with his hands.

"And just how were you planning on doing that?"

The sound of his voice sent a tremor dancing along her spine.

"Draco," she said, "listen to me."

"This was a mistake."

"Yes. Yes, it was. I'm glad you understand—"

He kissed her, his lips moving against hers with slow, heart-stopping deliberation. She wanted to return the kiss, wrap herself in his heat, but she knew better than to give in.

"Please listen, Draco. I'm trying to tell you that—"

"We're on opposite sides of what might become a lawsuit."

"Exactly. And—"

"That makes us enemies."

Anna sighed with relief. "Yes. This was…it was nice, but—"

"Nice?" he said, his voice a low growl.

"More than nice. It was—"

He kissed her again, deeper, more intensely. She felt him harden against her, felt that hot, electric jolt racing from her belly to her breasts.

Oh no, she thought, no, this wasn't just good sex, it was something much more. She'd never felt this way before, as if she were standing at the edge of forever.

Draco slid into her. Her breath caught. Helpless, drowning in pleasure, she cried out as she rose toward him.

"Tell me to stop," he said thickly, "and I will."

She stared up into his dark eyes.

"All you have to do is say the words, Anna."

"All right." She ran the tip of her tongue over her lips. "I want—I want—"

Anna moaned, tunneled her fingers into his hair and brought Draco's mouth to hers.

* * *

A long time later she stirred, rolled to her side and nestled back against him.

"I meant to tell you," she said drowsily, "you don't have to worry. I'm on the pill."

"Bene." He curved his arm around her, his hand cupping her breast. "Otherwise, I would have to leave you and go in search of a pharmacy." He nipped the nape of her neck. "And that would be a pitiful sight, *bellissima,* a grown man crawling on his hands and knees through the nighttime streets of Rome."

Anna laughed.

And tumbled into the dark cavern of sleep.

CHAPTER EIGHT

REALITY came back in the blurred rush of gray morning light seeping through the sheer drapes, the soft patter of rain…

And the pressure of a man's muscular arm curved around Anna's waist.

Disoriented, she closed her eyes, concentrated….

And remembered everything.

Draco. The thrill of opening her door and finding him there. The shimmering flash of excitement at what she saw in his face, the realization that she had wanted him all along, that half her anger at him was really anger at herself for wanting a man like him.

The night had been… What word could possibly sum it up? Incredible. Fantastic. Electric with passion so powerful it had turned her brain to jelly.

How else to explain why he was still in her bed?

She could make sense of having fallen asleep in his arms that first time. Combine exhaustion with the out-of-body feeling she always got from jet lag, and anything was possible.

She'd gone through that list of explanations hours ago.

But she'd done it again. Gone to sleep in his arms so soundly that she couldn't even recall it happening.

Surprise number one, for sure.

And added to that, surprise number two.

Why had he stayed? He could have left any time during

the night. From what she knew of men, given a choice, that was the way they preferred it.

No man wanted the morning-after thing, that series of dance steps that could be far more complicated than the dance a man and woman had just performed in bed a couple of hours before.

Stilted chitchat. The "after you, no, that's fine, after you" shower routine. A guy's unattractive early-morning stubble, a woman's totally unappealing bed-head hairstyle.

Hers was, for sure. Lots of curls, no sleek smoothness, just unruly locks that were wild and, without question, awful looking.

The entire morning-after scenario was enough to ruin romance as a concept, for lack of a better phrase. The truth was, good sex didn't have anything much to do with romance. It had to do with physical attraction. And hormones. A certain look in a man's eyes, a certain way he touched you.

If he was right and the time was right, that was all you needed. Given those basics, a woman was ready.

Anna shifted her weight just a little.

Draco felt so good spooned against her.

And she'd been ready. Hell, ready and waiting even when she hadn't known what she'd been ready and waiting for.

Draco Valenti was one gorgeous hunk.

And as it turned out, he was spectacular in bed. He knew what to touch and how to touch it; he knew when to whisper and when to keep silent; he knew when to take charge—yes, he certainly did—and when to let a woman take the lead.

And she was turning herself on.

Ridiculous, because one of the other reasons she didn't like sleeping with a man all night was that men always wanted morning sex as part of The Morning Thing, and Anna had never been a morning-sex fan.

Bottom line? Good sex was, well, it was good sex. Yes,

she had to like a guy to have sex with him. Had to enjoy his company, but sex was sex. Women who didn't understand that were in for trouble.

They fell in love.

They got married.

And, surprise surprise, they ended up hurt.

Anna, fortunately, was not, would never be, one of those women.

She and Isabella had talked about it just a few months ago.

They'd met for lunch at a place they both liked in midtown, poking at salads and drinking Diet Cokes, playing catch-up because they hadn't seen each other in a couple of weeks. Izzy had asked about a guy Anna had been seeing, if maybe she was serious about him, and Anna had rolled her eyes and said what was there to be serious about?

He was fun, he was interesting, he was good in bed.

"End of story," she'd told Iz. "Why would I want to spoil things?"

Izzy had put down her fork and heaved one of her Izzy sighs, the kind you could imagine a fairy princess giving while she waited for her Prince Charming to appear.

"That's such a sad attitude, Anna. What about love?"

"What about it?" Anna had replied, spearing a grape tomato and popping it into her mouth. "You have to stop reading all those women's magazines stuffed with that June, moon, forever-after bull."

Izzy had sighed again. "Honestly, Anna, I don't know what you're trying to prove."

"Nothing. Women don't need to prove anything. Well, maybe only that we're women, not idiots. You don't really think only men are entitled to be realistic about these things? About sex?"

Iz had shaken her head and Anna had smiled benignly, and

they'd gone on to safer ground—Anna's defense of a woman who'd shoplifted a winter jacket for her little boy because she didn't have the money to buy one, and Izzy's plans for the garden she was designing for a friend.

The thing was, Izzy's lovely head was in the clouds.

Anna's was right here, squarely on her shoulders.

She liked her space the same way men liked theirs, which brought her straight back to the fact that Draco was still in her bed and she was still in his arms and—

"Buon giorno, bellissima."

She tried to think of some clever reply, but she couldn't come up with anything. "Good morning" was deliciously sexy in his husky Italian, but it was only "good morning" in American English.

"How did you sleep?"

Deeply. Soundly. Who wouldn't sleep that way after what had happened that last time they'd made—that last time they'd had sex?

All she remembered were Draco's kisses, his caresses, his hard length deep, deep inside her and a rush of exquisite sensation, a breathless moment when the world spun out of control—and then the feel of him drawing her back into the warm, secure cradle of his body...

"Anna."

Draco's voice was low and rough. Just the sound of it made her skin tingle. And when he slid his hand up her side and cupped her breast...

Physiology, she told herself, that was what it was. He was a wonderful lover. Any woman would react to his touch even when she knew it was time to put the night in perspective.

"Anna," he said again, and turned her toward him.

Her heartbeat stuttered. He was gorgeous. Why had she ever thought early-morning stubble unattractive? It was perfect, the absolutely proper accent note to his square jaw, that magnificent Roman nose, the dark, dark eyes.

He smiled.

Anna almost flinched.

Why wouldn't he smile? She probably looked like a wild woman.

"Beautiful Anna," he said softly, and he threaded his fingers through her awful, scrunched-up hair and brought his mouth to hers.

The kiss was long. And tender.

It wasn't at all what she expected.

Her couple of experiences of The Morning Thing involved one kind of kiss.

A kiss that was a prelude to morning sex.

Which, as she had already established, was not her thing at all.

But this kiss was.

It was soft. Undemanding. A sweet meeting of lips, of tongues...

"Stop analyzing," Draco whispered.

Anna jerked back.

"What do you mean? I am not analy—"

"*Sì, Signorina Avocato.* You are." He drew her to him, his lips curved in a smile. "You're being an attorney, trying to decide what to say. What to do. And you're struggling for answers to questions. Why did we make love? Why did he spend the night? Why did I permit it?" He kissed her again. "This is not a courtroom, Anna."

Anna couldn't help smiling. "And a good thing it isn't."

"I agree, for if it were a courtroom..." Draco rolled her onto her back. "If it were, I could not do this."

"Oh. Oh..."

"Or this."

Her lashes drooped to her cheeks. "Draco," she whispered, "Draco, wait…"

He kissed her, and this kiss was not tender or soft—it was hot and urgent. So was the play of his fingers on her breast. And when he parted her thighs, brought his mouth to her core, Anna cried out, reached for her lover, rose to him and impaled herself on his rigid flesh.

It turned out that there was no problem with bed-head hair.

"Don't look at me," Anna said a long time later when Draco wanted to do exactly that. "I'm a mess."

His dark eyebrows rose.

"You think so?" he said, and when she nodded, he scooped her into his arms, carried her to the bathroom and stood her before the full-length mirror. "Look," he said, and when Anna groaned and tried to turn away, he wouldn't let her. "Look," he demanded in a tone she'd learned meant he wouldn't take no for an answer.

So she looked—and saw herself, her hair a tousled mass of gold curls, her mouth pink and gently swollen, her breasts still rosy from her last orgasm.

She saw the faint blue bruises on her thighs where Draco had nipped her flesh, then soothed it with kisses; saw a matching mark on her throat…

Saw him standing behind her, his arms cradling her.

God, how beautiful he was. How incredibly masculine. How big and powerful and…

Her breath caught as he cupped her breasts, played with her nipples as his eyes grew dark as the night.

Watching him, watching herself, was the most erotic thing Anna had ever done.

He bent his head, nuzzled aside the curls from the nape of her neck and kissed her skin, then kissed the juncture of her neck and shoulder. She moaned, reached between them and encircled as much as she could of his rigid, straining erection.

A growl rose in his throat; his teeth sank into her flesh and she cried out in passion.

"Hold on to the vanity, *bellissima*," he said thickly, his hands clasping her hips. "*Sì*. Just like that..."

She sobbed his name, came apart the instant he entered her. She heard his cry, felt him shudder and the world shattered again.

Draco's arms swept around her. She fell back against his hard body, trembling, her legs boneless. He held her as their heartbeats steadied, his face buried in her hair, and then he turned her to him, enfolded her in his embrace, held her close as his big hands stroked up and down her spine.

"Are you all right?" he whispered.

Anna nodded. He lifted her face to his, brushed his lips lightly over hers. Then he scooped her off her feet and carried her into the shower.

He washed her. She washed him. It was a game at first; how could it have been anything else after what had just happened?

But their hands moved more and more slowly, found more and more places to soap and gently, carefully wash until Draco groaned, leaned his forehead against Anna's and said, "I hope the maid has a strong heart."

Anna looked up at him. "Why?"

"When she finds us in here, waterlogged... Well, you and I will have died happy, but I doubt if she will."

Anna laughed. Draco grinned, turned off the shower, grabbed a bath sheet and wrapped her in it.

"You think that's funny, Orsini?" he said, trying his damnedest to sound stern. He didn't feel stern, not even jokingly so. He felt...he felt happy, and though he'd felt a lot of different things after sex, *happy* wasn't a word he'd have used to describe any of them.

"You have to admit," Anna said, "it's an, um, an interesting image."

"What is?" he said, and then he remembered what he'd said about the housekeeper and he laughed and tipped her chin up. "Where's your compassion?"

"Where's yours?" she said, teasing him right back. "A compassionate man would have phoned down for coffee by now."

"You're right," he said solemnly as he spun her toward the door, then patted her lightly on the backside. "Get into your robe while I order breakfast."

Anna looked at him. "Was that an order, Valenti? Because you need to know I don't follow orders."

Her tone was still teasing, but there was a quick flash of fire in her eyes. *Dio,* Draco thought, this was one hell of a woman.

"No?"

"No."

"We'll see about that," he said huskily, and he took her mouth in another long, deep kiss.

Breakfast arrived.

And somewhere between the fresh fruit and the coffee, reality once again began its inevitable claim.

I don't follow orders, she'd said.

And Draco had answered, *We'll see about that.*

Meaningless banter… Or was it?

Those were not the words you wanted to hear from your adversary.

That was who Draco Valenti was. Her adversary. She'd come to Rome to deal with him. Instead, she'd slept with him.

She'd even told him to order breakfast.

It was such a silly mental segue that Anna almost laughed….
But she didn't. This was her room. She should have phoned
down for the meal. Why let a man do what she could and
should do for herself?

She looked at Draco, sprawled back against the pillows in
a matching hotel robe, his dark-as-midnight hair still damp,
his skin tanned and golden against the white linens.

Was this what came of letting your lover spend the entire
night in your bed?

Actually, he wasn't her lover. They had no relationship
apart from what had happened last night and this morning.

What she'd let happen.

Okay. So she'd broken a rule. Let him spend the night.
Well, no. She'd broken two rules. She shouldn't have had sex
with him in the first place. This was no different than being
in a courtroom.

Would she sleep with the prosecutor? And hadn't she had
the discussion with herself already? She had. Then how had
this happened? How had she let this man make her forget such
basic principles?

"A penny," Draco said in that low, husky voice of his. Anna
raised her eyebrows and played dumb. He smiled. "For your
thoughts."

He had an amazing smile.

Tender. Sexy. Masculine. She felt its effects straight down
to her toes. Even looking at him looking at her made her feel…
well, it made her feel strange.

As if she'd lost her equilibrium. Or something.

It was unsettling. She didn't like it. Or maybe she liked it
too much, and what in heck was that supposed to mean?

"Anna?" He put his coffee cup on the nightstand and sat
up straight. "What is it?"

Anna cleared her throat.

"Nothing. I mean—I mean, I was just thinking…. Perhaps this would be a good time to agree on what happens next."

He grinned. It made her pulse stutter.

"An excellent suggestion, *cara*." He took her cup from her hands and set it beside his. His fingers brushed hers. She fought the sudden urge to fling herself into his arms.

What in the world is wrong with you, Orsini? Are you losing your mind?

"I suspect we can think of something," he said.

"No." Her voice was breathy, the kind of old-fashioned I'm-just-a-girl-and-you're-such-a-sexy-stud thing she despised in women. "No," she said, briskly this time, and drew back her hand. "I didn't mean it that way."

His eyes focused on hers. "What way did you mean it?"

Anna wished she were not wearing a robe, not sitting on a bed rumpled from a night of sex, not facing a man who looked as if he had just stepped out of *GQ*.

"I meant…well, I was thinking that—that I hope you understand, this was, uh, it was fine."

His eyes narrowed to obsidian slits.

"Fine?" he said softly, and Anna winced.

"It was great."

"Great," he said even more softly.

She was digging herself into a hole. She took a breath, forced what she hoped was a brilliant smile.

"You know what I mean. It was—it was—"

"What was, Anna? Breakfast? The coffee?" A muscle knotted in his jaw. "Or are you speaking of what happened between us in this bed?"

Now she was blushing. She knew it. And what was there to blush about?

He folded his arms over his chest.

"Let me save you the trouble. You were thinking that the sex had nothing to do with our situation."

"Yes," she said quickly. "I'm glad you understand. We're still adversaries."

He said nothing. Perhaps he hadn't understood her. His English seemed flawless but, as an attorney, especially one who worked with the poor, she often dealt with people who seemed to speak excellent English and yet still struggled with words that had a particular subtlety to them.

"You know," she said carefully. "The land."

He went on looking at her, saying nothing. A muscle ticked in his jaw; she saw it and she stood up to gain whatever advantage it might give her.

"Look, I'm simply trying to set things straight. We slept together."

"Such a charming phrase."

"Why? Because it comes from a woman?"

Draco's lips drew back from his teeth. "It comes from the Orsini *consigliere*."

Anna's chin came up. "You're twisting my words."

"Then let me untwist them. You're telling me that we had sex. And I should not assume the event was a turning point in our little legal drama."

His voice was more than flat; it was as cold as winter. Anna moistened her lips with the tip of her tongue.

"I wouldn't have put it quite so—so—"

"Bluntly?" He stood up, and she lost whatever pathetic advantage in height she'd had.

"Well, yes. I mean—"

"You mean," he said with a quick, sharp smile, "I should not think that by sleeping with me, you've given up your right to try and take from me that which is mine."

There it was again, all that upper-class arrogance. That I-am-rich-and-you-are-not rubbish that had driven her parents from Sicily, that she saw every day in her work.

"The land is not yours, and you damned well know it!"

"It is mine, it has always been mine, and no Sicilian thug is going to change that by sending his daughter to do his dirty work in her bed."

"You—you aristocratic bastard!"

"Tell me, Anna. Whose idea was it to sleep with the enemy? Yours? Or your father's?"

Anna's hand flew through the air and cracked against Draco's jaw. He caught her by the wrist, twisted her arm behind her, brought her to her toes.

"Did you really think I would tell you that I changed my mind? That I would be happy to let you have the land in exchange for me having had you?"

"That's disgusting!"

"What is disgusting," he said in a low voice, "is that I should have forgotten, even for a moment, that the blood of thieves and thugs runs in your veins."

"Get out," she snapped. "Get the hell out of my room!"

His hand fell from hers. "With pleasure," he said, turning his back and reaching for his clothes.

"Just get this straight," Anna said, her voice shaking with anger. "The Orsinis will see to it that you'll never be able to use that land, not if I have to stay here for the next hundred years."

He turned toward her just as his robe fell open.

Her heartbeat stuttered.

Naked, he was as dangerous looking as he was beautiful. The wide shoulders, leanly muscled torso and long legs. And the part of him that was male, that she knew so intimately, knew was almost frighteningly potent…

The air in the room seemed to turn thick and still.

Anna's gaze flew to Draco's face. She could hear the pulse of her blood beating in her ears. Neither of them moved until, at last, he gave a harsh laugh.

"You flatter yourself, *bellissima*. I have had my fill of what you so generously offered." Slowly, confidently he dressed, then strolled to the door. "I'll return for you in an hour. Be ready. I don't like to be kept waiting."

"Ready for what?"

"Ready to deal with our mutual problem so that we can see the last of each other."

Anna moved toward him. "Just tell me where to meet you. I absolutely forbid you to—"

"Was that an order, Orsini?" His smile was as thin as the blade of a knife. "Because you have to know I don't follow orders."

"Listen, Valenti—"

"No," he snarled, "*you* listen! I will be back in an hour, *il mio consigliere*. And if you have anything in your luggage besides those lady lawyer suits and ridiculous stilettos, I suggest you wear them."

"You're despicable," Anna said. "Absolutely des—"

Draco caught her by the wrist, hauled her to him and stopped the angry flow of words with a merciless kiss.

Then he was gone.

CHAPTER NINE

THE hotel doorman was not the same one as last night.

He looked shocked when Draco asked for his Ferrari.

A Ferrari? Here? No. That was impossible. Surely the *signore* could see that this was not a hotel at which anyone would leave such an automobile.

True enough.

The place was clean, but that was about it. Apparently, Cesare Orsini didn't believe in providing his *consigliere* with a decent expense account.

Draco, fighting an anger he knew was meant for that *consigliere* and not for the pudgy fool dressed like an extra in a bad operetta, agreed.

The hotel was not the place for a Ferrari.

Nonetheless, he said, he had left *his* Ferrari here, at the curb, last evening. And as he said it, he took a hundred-euro note from his wallet and handed it over.

Ah, the doorman said, palming the bill, how could he have forgotten? He snapped his fingers, pointed at a pimply-faced kid wearing what Draco figured was a bellman's costume, and sent the boy running. Seconds later the car was at the curb. Draco tipped the kid and got behind the wheel, burning rubber as he peeled away.

The intersection ahead was a typical snarl of traffic, cars and taxis and motorcycles growling like jungle beasts in anticipation of the green light and the chance to cut each other off.

Draco floored the gas, steered between a truck and a taxi, skidded around a motorcycle, got to the front of the pack just as the light changed and kept going. It won him a chorus of angry-sounding horns. A joke, considering that obeying traffic laws was pretty much against Roman law.

Too bad one of the drivers didn't feel like making something of it. That big guy on the black Augusta motorcycle, for example. Hell, if he was looking for trouble…

Dio.

Draco was the one looking for trouble, and for what reason? A woman he'd slept with had said something that had angered him. If he had a hundred euros for every female who'd ever said anything that had irritated him…

But this had gone beyond irritation. Anna's suggestion, hell, her assumption that he'd figure the night they'd spent had changed the fact that they had a dispute to settle was insulting.

He had to put it out of his head.

Draco stepped down harder on the gas. The mood he was in, driving fast was safer than thinking, but how could a man stop thinking?

His head felt as if it might explode.

Damn Anna Orsini. Damn himself, too. How could he have forgotten that old saw about never mixing business with pleasure?

That he had just didn't make sense.

Anna was attractive. So what? He knew dozens, scores of attractive women. Why be modest at a moment like this? Attractive women, beautiful women were his for the taking.

Hadn't he just left one behind in Hawaii? In fact, he thought coldly, if you wanted to be blunt about it, Giselle was the better looking of the two.

Maybe not.

Maybe she was just more interested in pleasing him than Anna was.

Giselle was always perfumed, every hair in place, her face carefully made-up even when he knew she'd spent who knew how long making sure she didn't look made-up. He'd been with her for, what, two months? In all that time he'd never seen her looking disheveled unless it was artfully so.

Sometimes he suspected she slipped from bed so she could tiptoe into the bathroom to fix her hair and face before he woke and saw her.

Anna certainly hadn't bothered to do that.

By morning her hair had been a wild tangle, her lipstick a memory. She had not looked even remotely perfect.

Draco's hands tightened on the steering wheel.

She'd looked like a woman who had enjoyed every moment she'd spent in her lover's arms, but if that were true, would she even have thought of pointing out that their dispute was not settled just because they'd had sex?

Was there nothing on her mind but that cursed land in Sicily?

Probably not.

A woman with so much attitude... *Dio,* she was impossible. She had an opinion on everything. She was stubborn and defiant, and she argued at the drop of a hat.

He had to have been out of his mind to have slept with her.

Not that he preferred his women to be compliant.

He was not a male chauvinist—he was just a man who understood that men were men and women were women, and a little show of deference to the dominant sex, goddamnit, could be a very nice thing.

He was still driving too fast, but the traffic had lessened.

That was one of the benefits of living off the Via Appia Antica. A handful of villas, lots of parkland, lots of space.

And space, metaphorically speaking, was what he needed right now.

Unbelievable that Anna would think of the land first and the hours they'd spent making love a distant second.

Correction again.

They hadn't made love.

They'd had sex. Anna had been very clear about that, and rightly so. That ability to see sex as a man saw it was definitely one thing he liked about her.

Making love was a woman's phrase, a female way of twisting words to turn something basic and honest into something they could do without having to admit they had the same appetites as men.

Men spoke of making love, but the truth was that as far as they were concerned, "making love" was a euphemism for a four-letter word or, in polite company, a three-letter one.

S-e-x.

It was what men and women did in bed. It was what he and Anna had done. In bed, and out of it. Against the wall, with her legs wrapped around him. Against the vanity, with his hands on her hips. In the shower, with the soap turning their skin slick…

Was he insane? He had to be, or why would he be driving along at a zillion miles an hour and turning himself on with hot images of a woman he was sorry he'd ever met?

The gates to his villa loomed ahead. Draco slowed the Ferrari, depressed a button and the gates swung slowly open.

The point was they'd had sex. And then she'd brought them both down to earth by accusing him of figuring the night they'd spent together might have been a *quid pro quo*.

What it had been, he thought grimly as he pulled up before

the villa and killed the engine, what it had been was pure, raw hunger.

It had filled him, nearly consumed him, though he'd refused to admit it, even to himself, until Anna had opened the hotel door, looking beautiful without makeup, with her hair a sexy tumble of untamed curls; looking delicate and strong—and no way was he going to try to figure out how a woman could seem strong and fragile at the same time.

Anna did, that was all.

She was too complex for her own good and certainly for his, and knowing that, he'd still wanted her.

And she had wanted him just as intensely, just as passionately, even though he was supposed to be her enemy.

She had an honest, open attitude toward sex. He liked that about her, too. And damnit, it was ridiculous to fault her for putting into words what a man might well have thought—that maybe being intimate had put an end to their legal dispute.

Only a man would think that way. Or, at least, speak so bluntly.

Was that what this was all about?

Was he angry because Anna Orsini was a gorgeous, desirable woman, never mind all that nonsense about her simply being attractive, who spoke a man's thoughts and expressed a man's hunger? He'd never dealt with a woman like her before.

Did it make him uncomfortable?

Or did it go beyond that?

Was it because in some deep, dark foolish part of him, he wanted to know if she was like this with other men? Was she as ready, as hot, as wet for them as she had been for him?

Not that he gave a damn...

Draco slapped his hands against the steering wheel.

There was no logic to it. There could not be any logic to it. He'd made a mistake, and that was that.

He should never have permitted the controversy with Cesare Orsini to go this far. He should have ignored that last letter. Failing that, he should not have gone ahead and met with Orsini's representative without his own lawyer present.

But he had, and now he'd compounded the mess by sleeping with Anna.

He was tired of the nonsense. Of all of it. A thug who had spent his life stealing from others and thought he could go on doing it. A woman who thought he might see sex as a bargaining tool...

Draco narrowed his eyes.

Was that the real purpose of that little speech? Had she hoped that he truly had seen the night as a kind of trade? She'd given him a night to remember; he would give her the land?

Hold on, a voice inside him said, *she never even suggested that. It was you, dummy. You haven't just leaped to a conclusion, you arrived in that fantasyland all by yourself. And you didn't just arrive there, you landed with both feet. Remember what you said about her doing her father's dirty work in her bed?*

A mess. At total, stinking mess.

Draco got out of the car and slammed the door behind him.

Who cared who had done what? He'd had enough of the Orsinis, father and daughter.

By nightfall he'd be rid of them both.

Anna had packed lightly for her trip to Rome.

Two suits. Four white silk blouses. Three pairs of heels, and what had that full-of-himself fool meant by calling her stilettos 'ridiculous'?

"You try going without lunch for four months to buy a pair," she muttered as she pawed through the clothes she'd brought with her.

Better still, let him try wearing them.

The picture that leaped into her head, Draco attempting to stuff his big feet into her size sevens, might have made her laugh if she'd been in a laughing mood. But she wasn't, not even over the Cinderella story told in reverse.

Besides, no matter how you turned things around, Prince Valenti was no Prince Charming.

He was an aristocratic, autocratic idiot, she thought grimly. And if she owed him for anything, it was that he'd gone out of his way to remind her of it.

Such an overreaction to her simple statement about them still being adversaries. How could you insult a man by telling him the truth?

Or maybe that was the problem. Maybe the truth was that he'd figured he was so good in bed that he'd dazzled her into giving up what had brought her to Rome in the first place.

Anna rolled her eyes as she searched through her clothes.

That would never work with her. She wasn't a girlish fool who'd lose her girlish heart over him just because she'd slept with him, and what was with the silly euphemism?

They hadn't slept together—they'd had sex. That's what it always was to a man, and to any woman with a functional brain.

One of the things Anna loved about the law was that it had the right words to describe whatever needed describing.

Sex was like that.

Why pretend? Why give the act fanciful names that had to do with sleeping or, even worse, with romance? Why make it sound as if the heart was involved in a strictly biological act?

As for her pointing out that a night of sex had not changed the bottom line… The almighty prince might not like hearing the truth, but people traded sex for what they really wanted all the time. Her professional life was full of examples. Sad-eyed women staying with men who beat them, just so they could have roofs over their heads. Gorgeous models married grotesque old men so they could wallow in money and jewels.

Anna's mouth thinned.

There were other kinds of trades, too. Look at the one her own mother had made.

Sofia Orsini stayed with her gangster husband so that she wouldn't have to face the disgrace that went with an old-fashioned Sicilian woman asking for a divorce. What other explanation could there possibly be?

Anna slapped her hands on her hips and blew a curl off her forehead.

Well, she wasn't like that.

She didn't need a man to keep her housed, clothed and fed. She didn't want jewels or anything she couldn't afford to buy for herself. And she sure as hell would divorce a bastard who deserved divorce, except she'd never have to.

Marriage, a lifetime commitment, was absolutely not on her agenda.

She liked men, liked spending time with them, liked having sex on occasion, but all on her own straightforward terms. No trading. No promises. No lies.

Love was an illusion. Sex was sex, and what did any of that have to do with the ugly little scene here a few minutes ago?

She'd made a candid statement. How had Draco managed to make it sound, well, cheap? It wasn't. It had been honest, that was all.

The prince didn't like honesty? Too bad.

And she wasn't going to forget that accusation he'd hurled at her. Suggesting she'd gone to bed with him to change his mind about the land…

That had hurt. Because making love with him… No. Having sex with him had been, it had been…

"Damnit," Anna said, her voice shaking.

Never mind thinking about what had happened.

It was time to look forward.

And where were the jeans, the T, the sneakers she knew she'd packed? She always brought along stuff like that. Getting snowed in at an airport in upstate New York on a ski trip her senior year in law school had taught her two things.

One, she hated skiing.

Two, when you flew anywhere, you always had to pack something comfortable to wear.

And there were the things she'd been looking for, tucked on a shelf in the tiny hotel-room closet. Old jeans. Older sneakers. An ancient T-shirt that she positively adored.

Who wouldn't?

This was not any T, it was the one Isabella had given her on her last birthday. It was vintage, from the 1970s. Isabella said she'd found it in a little shop in Soho. The shirt was gray and slightly faded, but the words that marched across the front of it read loud and clear.

A Woman Needs a Man Like a Fish Needs a Bicycle.

Truer words had never graced a T-shirt.

Anna took off the robe, pulled on a bra and panties, stepped into the jeans, zipped them up and tugged the shirt over her head.

The jeans rode low on her hips; the shirt was a little short.

She looked in the mirror. Her belly button showed. Maybe she'd get it pierced when she got home.

Too bad she hadn't done it sooner. Then she'd be wearing the perfect outfit for Draco's stuffy office because, of course, that was where he was taking her.

Did he think the formal setting would intimidate her?

The hell it would.

Neither would whatever he intended to say.

She wasn't finished with this fight. There were courts here, just as there were back home, and Cesare had all the money she'd need for translators, lawyers, the works.

Plus, just as she'd warned Draco, there was the ever-voracious press. He was right—her father would not want the publicity. But who cared what Cesare wanted? He'd sent her here. How she handled things was her business.

Anna grabbed her purse.

Forget going home tomorrow. She would stay in Rome as long as it took to recoup her mother's land.

She didn't know how she'd pull it off, not yet, but she would.

After that, Prince Draco Marcellus Valenti could go straight to hell.

CHAPTER TEN

DRACO saw Anna the minute he pulled his car to the curb outside the hotel.

She was standing a few feet away, highlighted by the watery sun that had appeared after the rain, and he could see that she'd taken his advice.

No lady lawyer suit. No killer heels. She wore jeans, sneakers, a T-shirt. What did the shirt say? He squinted, read it…and knew he was in for a long day.

At least she looked like an average woman.

The hell she did.

There was nothing average about her. It was all pure Anna, from the straight-as-an-arrow posture to the defiant set of her chin, from the tips of those well-worn and, he was sure, definitely unfashionable sneakers to the gold curls that were already trying to spring free of whatever it was she'd used to tie them back.

What was it he'd thought before? Delicate but strong—and so what?

He wanted her gone, and by tomorrow she would be.

The guy in the Gilbert and Sullivan get-up spotted him, saw Anna begin marching toward him and rushed past her, his obvious goal to score points by reaching the car before she did.

Anna offered a stony glare and a dismissive wave of her hand.

All she had to add was a thumbs-down gesture and a lion would surely have appeared to sink its fangs into the poor guy and drag him away.

And then there was that T-shirt. Never mind the way her breasts thrust against the thin cotton, or the way it clung to her skin. It was the message written across it that got him, that woman-bicycle-fish thing.

For some crazy reason it made him want to drag her into the car and kiss her until she wound her arms around his neck and begged him to make love to her—except it wasn't love, it was, just as she'd pointed out, sex.

"You find this amusing?" she demanded.

Draco turned what threatened to be a grin into a scowl.

"Nothing about you is amusing, Orsini." He leaned across the front seat and pushed the door open. "Get in."

"Perhaps you didn't get my message. I don't need you to open doors. I am perfectly capable of doing things for myself."

Her voice rang with icy scorn. Draco narrowed his eyes. The lady needed some lessons in manners, and for the few hours she'd still be annoyingly at his side he was damned well going to be the one teaching them to her.

"Forgive me," he said, his voice as chilly as hers. "For a moment I forgot how you feel about good manners."

Her face went pink. Good, he thought grimly. In fact, excellent.

"As for your treatment of the doorman, he was simply trying to do his job."

"A useless job."

"A job," Draco said. "Something that puts food on the table, though I doubt if someone in your situation would ever have to worry about that."

Anna felt her color deepen.

He was right, of course, though what a prince would know about putting food on the table was beyond her.

She certainly knew what it was like. How it felt to worry about money. When you refused financial support from your father to get you through university, when you lied to your brothers and said thanks but you didn't need any help paying your tuition, your room, your board…

"You going to get in the car or not? Make up your mind, *consigliere*. I'm not in the mood for games."

What she wanted to do was slam the door in his handsome, arrogant face, but, speaking of jobs, she had one to do and she was going to do it.

Anna tossed her head, slid into the passenger seat and flashed a sickly-sweet smile at the doorman when he reached, warily, for the door.

"Grazie," she said, but when she looked at Draco, the saccharine smile faded. "You," she said, each letter a virtual pellet of ice, "would, of course, be fully cognizant of what it's like to worry about putting food on the table."

Draco thought back to the years he'd spent eating one meal a day so he could put most of what he earned into paying for the exorbitant costs of getting his degree—well, of almost getting that degree—but he'd never told anyone about those years and no way was he ever going to talk about it with someone like Anna Orsini.

Instead, he handed the doorman a tip and then stepped hard on the gas.

"Oh, I don't know," he said as the car shot away from the curb. "Truffles and caviar aren't always easy to find."

Anna glared at him. A joke? For all she knew, a statement of fact.

Not that she cared.

Her temper was at boiling point again, and there was nobody to blame but herself.

She despised Draco Valenti, yet she'd gone to bed with him. She was a modern woman, yes. But she was a discriminating woman. She did not go to bed with men she despised.

Now she was compounding that error by, heaven help her, obeying his regal commands.

What was she doing, sitting in his car like an obedient slave? Why was she letting him take her somewhere without knowing where that somewhere was? Why had she not worn what he'd scoffingly referred to as her lady lawyer outfit? That's what she was. A lawyer, never mind the sexist and demeaning "lady" sobriquet.

And not to dwell on it or anything…

Why had she ever gone to bed with him?

Because you wanted to, a scathing voice inside her purred. *Because he's gorgeous and sexy, funny and smart. He's arrogant, too, and you love his unmitigated arrogance. You love it when he has the balls to stand up to you, love it even more when he takes you in his arms and changes everything you thought you knew about being with a man….*

"…change everything you thought you knew about it," Draco said.

Anna swung toward him, horrified. "I didn't mean to say…"

His eyebrows rose. Okay! She hadn't said anything. She was not so far out of touch with reality that she was speaking her thoughts out loud.

"Never mind," she said quickly. "I, uh, I was just—just thinking about something…."

Draco narrowed his eyes.

Thinking about what? he wondered.

Her eyes had gone blurry; her cheeks had taken on a rosy glow. It reminded him of how she looked in the heat of passion, when he'd held her in his arms, her body warm and yielding as he moved inside her, her moans of ecstasy his, all his...

Damnit, he thought in righteous indignation, what was wrong with him?

"Forget thinking," he snapped, "and try paying attention. And I know it's difficult, but try having an open mind, okay?"

"About what?"

"About my land in Sicily."

"It's Orsini land."

Draco snorted. How had he forgotten, even for a second, that this was Anna Orsini, her father's *consigliere?* Anything else was just an illusion.

They rode in silence for a few minutes. Then Anna turned toward him, frowning.

"This isn't the way to your office."

"No," he said calmly. "It isn't."

"Then where are we going?"

"To a place where we can settle this idiocy."

"If you think I'm going to let you take me somewhere to try and seduce me—"

"Did anyone ever tell you that you have an overblown opinion of yourself as a sexual trophy?"

"You," Anna said through her teeth, "are a horrible human being!"

Draco laughed. That only made her angrier. She was glaring at him, her lips set in a thin, angry line. What would she do if he pulled to the shoulder of the road, pulled her into his arms and kissed her until her lips softened, parted, clung to his?

He would not do it, of course; he was done with kissing her or even touching her. He wasn't interested in her anymore; it was just idle thought...

"And," she said, "I am not letting you drive one more mile until you tell me where—"

"Sicily."

Just as he'd figured, shock replaced the look of fury on her face.

"Sicily? You and I are going to—"

"Right. You and I, and a pilot."

That was when Anna saw the sign. Aeroporto Ciampino. She didn't hesitate, didn't stop to weigh her words. She simply swung toward him and said, "No!"

"In fact…" Draco checked his mirror, accelerated, swung around a black van in the lane ahead. "We're running late. I want to be off the ground before—"

"Listen to me, Draco. I am not flying anywhere with you."

"We aren't flying 'anywhere,' *consigliere,* we're flying to Sicily."

"Forget the word games! And stop calling me *consigliere.*"

"It's what you are, aren't you?"

"I am not my father's counselor. I am not even his lawyer. I'm his daughter, and I am not letting you take me to Sicily."

"Wow," Draco said, his voice thick with sarcasm, "so much information in one breath! I'm impressed."

"Damn you, Valenti—"

Anna gave a little cry as he swung the wheel hard to the right, pulled onto the shoulder of the road and put the car in neutral.

"Frankly," he said, turning toward her, his eyes, his words, cold, "I don't care what you call yourself, lady. You came to Italy to do a job for your old man. You made threats. You—"

"Threats?" Anna laughed. "What, do you think I'm

carrying a pistol? That I'm going to put a gun to your head and—"

Draco moved fast. Too fast for her to protest. One heartbeat, he was sitting next to her; the next, he'd pulled her half over the gear shift and into his arms.

"I know every inch of you," he said in a low voice. His hand swept up her side, cupped her breast; Anna gasped and tried to slap his hand away, but he wouldn't let her. "So, no, I don't think you're going to threaten me physically." His eyes grew dark and hot. "Hell," he growled, "you're already a physical threat, Anna. When you're in my arms, when you're looking at me the way you are now, *Dio,* I can't think straight."

"I don't know what you mean. And you'd better let go of me, Valenti. Let go, or—"

Draco cupped the back of her head and brought her mouth to his. Anna stiffened, tried to twist away…and then she moaned, wound her arms around his neck and sucked his tongue into her mouth.

The kiss was long and deep; it left her shaken. When Draco finally drew back, she was trembling.

"This is crazy," she whispered. "Just plain crazy! We cannot—"

"Yes," Draco said roughly, "we can."

"One minute we're enemies. The next…the next—"

He kissed her again, his lips gentle on hers, so gentle that she wanted to sigh, to melt, to stay in his arms not so much for the sexual pleasure she knew he could bring her but for the simple joy of feeling his arms around her.

The thought was unsettling, and she tore her lips from his. He let her do it, let her turn her head and lay it against his chest.

"Please." Her voice was low, almost breathless. "Please, Draco. Don't."

Draco held Anna close, one hand stroking her hair, the other on the small of her back.

He was a man who'd had considerable experience with women. Perhaps that was putting it modestly. He'd been with a lot of women, all of them willing and eager. Sometimes, despite all the talk of women meaning what they said, women who said "don't" meant just the opposite.

"Don't," a woman might say, even as she put her hand over your fly. "Don't," she'd say, even as she moaned into your mouth and rubbed against you. "Don't," she'd whisper, when she wanted you to tell her why she should be saying "Do."

That was how he knew, with all the instincts of a man holding an aroused woman in his arms, that "don't" was not what Anna really meant.

She wanted him.

He could hear it in her voice, feel it in the way she trembled in his arms, in the way she remained curled tightly against him. One more drugging kiss. One more caress and she would whisper his name, lift her mouth to his, kiss him with all the passion he knew was in her.

But he didn't kiss her, or touch her. Instead, he went on holding her, his eyes closed, his face buried in her hair. Long moments went by before he raised his head.

"Anna."

She sighed. Then she sat up and her eyes met his.

His heart turned over.

Delicate and strong, his Anna. His beautiful, beautiful Anna.

"Anna." Draco stroked back the riot of curls that had come loose from her ponytail. "Something is happening with us, *bellissima*."

Anna shook her head.

"We're attracted to each other," she said quickly. "Why make it sound so unusual?"

She was right. There was nothing unusual in a man and a woman desiring each other. So why did her swift denial anger him?

Draco sat up straight. Checked for traffic, then pulled onto the road.

"We both want more of what happened last night," he said brusquely. "Don't waste time denying it, Anna. You know I'm speaking the truth."

Anna smoothed back her hair, redid the ponytail, folded her hands in her lap.

Damnit, why were they shaking?

"It doesn't matter," she said. "There's still the land."

"Exactly. That's why we're going to Sicily. We'll settle this thing once and for all. And then—"

"And then," Anna said firmly, "I'll go home."

The plane was a small private jet, all leather and luxury inside. The pilot and Draco shook hands, Draco introduced Anna, all of it done with the politeness of people doing business for the first time.

Not Draco's plane, then, Anna thought as she settled into her seat.

"It's a rental," Draco said as if she'd spoken the thought aloud. "Mine is en route to Rome, from Hawaii."

Rome. Hawaii. Sicily, and hadn't some of the documents in her father's file carried a San Francisco address?

The prince knew his way around the world.

Around women, too. That was why she felt so confused. It wasn't him. Or rather it was, but not because of anything special he made her feel. She was confused because he was so suave, so sophisticated, so damned smooth. She knew men who thought they were all those things, but she'd never known one like Draco.

And that was over.

She'd come to Italy on business, and this trip to Sicily wasn't going to change that.

A couple of hours from now she'd have seen whatever earthshaking thing he wanted her to see, and then Rome and Sicily and Prince Draco Valenti would be history.

Wrong. W-r-o-n-g. Wrong, wrong, wrong.

The flight took just a little over an hour. Draco had arranged for a rental car to be waiting at Catania for the drive to Taormina. It was some kind of sturdy-looking SUV, and once they were under way, Anna understood why he'd chosen it.

Put simply, the roads.

Taormina was a tourist destination. She'd had, at least, enough time to determine that before setting off for Rome. And from what she saw of it as they drove through, it was charming. Cobbled streets, winding alleyways, the incredible blue of the Ionian Sea and, of course, the breathtakingly beautiful Mount Etna, the heat of its volcanic breath rising against a cloudless sky.

Then they left the town behind.

The road grew narrower and rougher. It twisted around mountains, clung to rocky slopes, climbed and climbed and climbed.

"I thought the Orsini land was in Taormina," Anna said as she tried to keep from clinging to the edges of her seat.

Draco looked at her.

"My land, you mean."

Anna rolled her eyes.

"Could you just answer the question? Is it in Taormina or isn't it?"

"Sure. More or less. Definitions of what is and isn't a boundary line are a little less stringent here than in Rome. Or Manhattan."

"Shouldn't we have stopped at the town hall? Or wherever it is they keep real estate records?"

"They keep records, all right. Some go back a couple of thousand years."

Anna raised an eyebrow. "Well, then—"

"My lawyers sent copies of all that stuff to your father weeks and weeks ago. Didn't you read it?"

"I did," she said, lying through her teeth. "And nothing I read changed my mind. I only meant it might be helpful to have the deed, whatever, with us right now."

Draco nodded.

"I sent your old man photos, too. Did he pass those along to you?"

Photos. Photos? Anna did a quick mental review of the material she'd seen.

"What kind of photos?"

Draco took his hand off the gearshift and held it out to her. "What do you see?"

What, indeed?

A strong, very masculine hand. Tanned skin. Long fingers. Without warning, she thought of how those fingers had felt, learning the curves of her body.

"What do you see?" he demanded.

Anna looked away.

"A hand. Am I supposed to congratulate you for having one instead of a tentacle?"

He laughed. "Nice."

"Thank you," she said primly. "I thought so."

"Look again."

"Listen, Valenti, you may find this amusing, but—"

He put his hand on her thigh. She swallowed hard. His hand was hot. So hot. She could feel its heat straight through her jeans.

"See this ring?"

Anna looked down. Yes. She saw it. The ring he wore was obviously old. Very old. It was made of gold. And it had a...

"Is that a crest?" She looked at Draco. "I never saw you wear that ring before."

He took his hand away, downshifted, took the SUV through a hairpin curve that left Anna certain they were going to fall into the sea.

"I don't wear it," Draco said, his eyes on the road, his voice low. "I'm not into jewelry. Besides, it is irreplaceable."

"Irreplaceable?"

"There hasn't been another like it for a thousand years."

Anna blinked. "A thousand..."

"*Sì.*"

She looked at the ring again. "And the crest?"

Draco cleared his throat. "The Valenti crest. The mark of my family. The mark that is on the once-crumbling pile of marble my father brought to near ruin in Rome."

"I don't understand. What has that to do with—"

He braked. Hard. The SUV jerked to a stop.

"Look," he said.

It was hard to take her eyes from Draco, but finally she did.

And caught her breath.

Ahead was a castle. Or what remained of a castle. A tower. Wide stone steps. Ancient stone walls. The ruins were stark against the blue of the sky.

Draco opened his door and stepped out of the SUV. So did Anna. He held out his hand; she hesitated. Then she took it and they walked slowly across the clearing.

"Look at the wall," he said. "Do you see what is chiseled in it? There, just above the steps."

Anna looked at the wall. Her breath caught. "It's—it's the crest."

He nodded. "The deed, if you will, and more telling than any piece of paper—though there are those, too."

A falcon called out high above them, its cry poignant and chill.

"This was once a great castle," Draco said softly. "My great-great who knows how many times great-grandfather built it. He was not like my father, or my father's father, who brought dishonor to our name. He was a man others respected, you understand? He cared for his people, defended them and this place against robbers, against barbarians, he and his sons and the sons of his sons. But eventually all things end. Invaders came from across the sea." Draco took a long breath. "The land and the castle were lost. After that, who knows? Somehow a Valenti prince put down roots in Rome. Maybe he forgot this place existed. Maybe he wanted to forget it." Draco shook his head. "I didn't know anything about the castle, the land, or the Valenti connection to Sicily until a year or so ago."

"How did you find out?"

"I was in Palermo on business. After a couple of days I felt the need to get away for a few hours. So I rented a car, took a drive…."

"And ended up here."

Draco nodded. "It was by accident, I know, but I drove around that last curve, saw this ruin…I don't know how to say it. It seemed somehow familiar. Crazy, perhaps, but I got out of the car, walked up to these steps…"

Anna traced her fingers lightly over the crest chiseled into the stone. Then she put her hand on Draco's arm. His muscles were tight as steel.

"No," she said softly, "not crazy at all." She smiled when he took his gaze from the ruins of what had surely once been a magnificent castle and looked, instead, at her. "You walked to the steps, and you saw the Valenti crest."

Draco nodded. "Yes." He shrugged as if it were not important, but the darkness in his eyes told her that it was. "I don't know if you can understand what it was like to discover that I carry the blood of brave, good men in my veins."

Could she understand? Anna wanted to laugh. Or maybe cry.

"I understand all too well," Anna said gently. "And now you're going to restore the castle."

A muscle knotted in his jaw.

"Yes. *Sì*. I am." His smile was fleeting. "Trust me, *bellissima*. My architect and builder assure me that this wish is crazy."

Was this truly Prince Draco Valenti? Did her arrogant, take-no-prisoners aristocrat actually have a heart?

Not that he was hers. Not that she would want him to be hers. There was nothing logical to that idea, nothing rational about it...

"I know succeeding in this is important to you, Anna. Securing the land for your family, I mean. But—"

To hell with logic.

Anna grasped Draco's shirt, lifted herself to him and pressed her lips to his.

CHAPTER ELEVEN

THE drive back to Catania seemed to take forever.

How could it not, when Draco kept pulling the SUV onto the shoulder of the road so he could draw Anna into his arms and kiss her?

He kept telling himself that the exquisite torture would end once they boarded the plane. Then they'd have all the privacy they needed.

He gathered her into his arms as soon as they were in the air.

She came to him with hot eagerness, straddling him, her kisses wild and abandoned, her hands on him and his on hers until he made a sound that was half groan, half laugh, leaned his forehead against hers and said, "*Bellissima*. You're killing me."

"Am I?" she whispered, and the delight in her voice made him laugh again.

"You know you are." He pressed his lips to the hollow of her throat, felt the swift race of her blood just beneath the delicate skin. "Anna. I've never wanted a woman the way I want you." He paused. "But we're going to wait." He wrapped his arms around her, gathered her tightly against him. She was trembling, *Dio,* so was he. He kissed her hair, her temple, her eyes. "We are going to wait until we are alone. Until there is all the time in the world for us."

For us. Anna closed her eyes, buried her face in his shoulder, inhaled the glorious scent of him, of his arousal.

"I want you in my bed, not on a plane, not in a hotel room." He gave a soft laugh. "It makes no sense, I know, but—but that is what I want, Anna. You and me and a quiet place that belongs only to us."

Gently he cupped the back of her head, tilted it so that their eyes met.

"I love having sex with you," he said gruffly. "But it's time to make love."

What he'd said hung between them. He hadn't planned it; he wasn't even sure what it meant. He only knew that it was true. He, the pragmatist, the man who thought *making love* was a phrase used by romantic fools, wanted to do exactly that.

Now he waited for Anna's answer. He stroked his hand the length of her back, soothing her, steadying himself. Waited for her to tell him he was wrong, that sex was sex, that she didn't want to be in his bed, to lie in his arms, that all she wanted was quick, passionate release….

"Yes," she whispered. Her lips curved in a tender smile. "Take me to your bed, Draco. And make love to me."

Something inside him took wing. "Anna," he said, *"il mio amore…"*

He kissed her. Kissed her deeply. And held her in his arms all the way to Rome.

The night was very dark, the ancient Appian Way lit only by a quarter moon and a scattering of stars that some ancient god might have tossed against the firmament.

The tall pines sighed at the caress of a warm summer breeze.

Draco led Anna through the shadow-filled silence of his

villa, to his bedroom, where he turned on a lamp that shed a pale, ethereal glow over the bed.

Then he took her hands and drew her to him.

Dio, how lovely she was! Her hair streamed down her back in long, loose curls of palest gold. Her blue eyes glittered as she raised them to his. She was beautiful beyond any woman he had ever known.

Even her name was beautiful, he thought, and he spoke it now as she came into his arms.

He bent to her and kissed her.

She rose on her toes, wrapped her arms around his neck and returned kiss for kiss.

It was almost as if they had never been intimate before. He knew Anna felt it, too; she looked up at him, her lips delicately parted, her eyes luminous and filled with questions.

The questions weren't hers alone.

Last night had been incredible. Such passion. Such desire. But this—this was not the same. It was a different kind of passion, a new kind of desire. It was a storm, building inside him.

The seconds ticked away. Then Anna stepped back and reached for the hem of her T-shirt.

He caught her wrists, brought her hands to his lips, kissed each with lingering tenderness.

"I want to undress you," he said in a low voice.

A tremor went through her. "Yes," she whispered, "oh yes."

He caught hold of the bottom of the shirt, eased it up, drew her free of it and tossed it aside.

His heart turned over.

Her bra was pale peach silk, almost the color of her skin. Her breasts swelled above the delicate cups. Ripe fruit, awaiting the touch of his hands, the heat of his mouth.

Draco bent his head and pressed a kiss to each curve of

lush flesh within the silken cups. Anna moaned, cupped her breasts, made them an offering to his desire and hers, but he took her hands and brought them to her sides.

Not yet. Not yet.

Her jeans rode low on her hips. He undid the button, opened the zipper, his eyes never leaving hers. He saw the color in her face deepen, heard her breathing quicken. She made a little sound, half moan, half sigh.

He was killing them both.

What an exquisite way to die.

Inch by inch, torment by torment.

There would be no mercy for her, or for him.

He was already hard as a man could be without groaning but this—this was a special kind of pain, and worth whatever it took to endure.

He would not rush this night.

He knelt. Unlaced the laces of her sneakers. Her feet were bare, the arches high and feminine. He curved his hand around one ankle, then the other, and slipped the sneakers off. Then he rose again, hooked his thumbs into the jeans and slowly, slowly eased them down her hips and legs.

Draco got to his feet, everything in him tight and intense, his eyes narrowing to dark slits as Anna stepped free of the jeans.

All she had on now were the bra and a matching thong that cupped her like the hand of a lover.

His hand, he thought. Only his.

A muscle flexed in his jaw.

She was half-naked, all hot skin and cool silk. He took one step forward, his eyes on hers, and curved his palm over the bit of silk between her thighs.

Anna cried out.

He could feel all his good intentions coming apart.

"Anna," he said, the single word hot with warning.

"Draco," she whispered, and she smiled, such a sexy smile, so wicked, so filled with the knowledge of Eve.

He knew she was remembering last night and how they'd said those same words when he'd stormed into her hotel room. He would have smiled, too, but suddenly she was touching him, her fingers at his zipper, dragging it down, and his rigid length sprang free into her hand, her fingers wrapping as best they could around his engorged flesh.

"Now," she said, and any coherent thought he might have still possessed flew from his head.

He swung her into his arms, carried her to the bed. Tore off his clothes. Came down to her and she arched toward him, seeking his mouth, her tongue a sliver of silk against his, her teeth nipping at his lip, her soft cries burning, burning into his brain.

Draco caught her wrists. Raised her arms over her head, his fingers manacles of steel.

"What do you want?" he said thickly. "Tell me."

"You," Anna said, "you, Draco, please, please, I want you. I need you…"

"Only me," he growled. "Say it, Anna."

"Yes, yes. Only you. Only you. Only—"

She screamed as he thrust into her, hard, fast, deep. Her cry filled the night; he felt her muscles contract around him.

"Open your eyes," he said roughly. "Look at me."

Her lashes rose. Her eyes wild and hot, filled with him.

"Draco," she sobbed, "Draco…"

He let go of her wrists, slid his hands beneath her, lifting her into his hard body, into the steady demand of a primitive rhythm. She moved with him, her hair flung over the pillow, her hands clutching his biceps.

He could feel the tension building in his body, in his scrotum. *Wait,* he told himself, *wait for her to come again…*

She did. Once. Twice. He heard Anna cry his name, felt

her fingers dig deep into his buttocks. And then he stopped thinking, gave in to the pleasure that was more than pleasure, let it consume him.

Let it consume them both as they flew off the edge of the world into the black Roman night.

Time slipped past.

A minute. An hour. Anna couldn't tell. It didn't matter. Time had no meaning.

Only this was important.

Draco, collapsed over her, his skin as slick with sweat as hers, his heart hammering the same as hers, his breathing as ragged as hers.

Her arms were wrapped around him. One leg was draped over his hip. She had no idea where she began and he ended, and she sighed and thought she could stay like this forever.

"Too heavy," he grunted, hearing her sigh, but she shook her head, kissed his shoulder, held him even closer and that was a damned good thing because he wasn't sure that he could move.

He sure as hell didn't want to.

"Stay," she murmured, and he grunted again and let his muscles go slack.

After another minute, or maybe another hour, he said something.

"Mmm," Anna said, because she had no idea what it was but she figured that *mmm* would cover all possibilities.

He laughed and rolled onto his side, taking her with him. "'Mmm' what?"

"Mmm to whatever you asked me," she said lazily.

Draco nuzzled a spill of curls off her cheek.

"I didn't ask. I said."

Her lips curved in a lazy smile. "The authoritative prince."

"Damned right." He rolled again, this time onto his back, taking her with him so that she lay sprawled over him like a blanket. *A warm, silken blanket,* he thought, his arms tight around her.

"I said so much for the best-laid plans."

"I am," Anna said primly, "very well laid, Your Highness, and thank you for asking."

Draco laughed. "I'm happy to hear it."

"So what were these plans?" she said, and kissed his shoulder.

"I was going to make love to you very, very slowly," he said, running his hand up and down the length of her spine.

"Ah. *Those* plans." She lifted her head, folded her hands on his chest, propped her chin on them and smiled. "You looking for compliments, Valenti? 'Cause if you are, all things considered, I think we did pretty well."

There it was again, that wickedly sexy smile. Combined with the feel of her draped over him, it was causing trouble with his anatomy.

"You do, huh?"

"Ladies and gentlemen of the jury," she said in her best courtroom voice, "consider the evidence."

He shifted, just a little. "What evidence?"

"The evidence," Anna said. "You know. Exhibit A. And exhibit—" Her breath caught as he shifted again. "Exhibit B," she whispered. "Definitely exhibit—"

He cupped one hand around the nape of her neck and brought her mouth to his. His kiss was sweet and tender; she could feel a honeyed warmth spreading through her body.

No, she thought as his kiss deepened. Not just through her body. The warmth was everywhere. In her lips, as they clung to his.

And in her heart.

The realization made her tremble. Draco rolled her beneath him.

"Anna. What is it, *bellissima?*"

"Draco," she whispered, and his lips found hers, moved over hers with passion and tenderness. "Draco," she said again, and then she wound her arms tightly around her lover's neck, and the world, and reality, fell away.

Sometime between midnight and dawn, long after the moon had set, Anna awoke to Draco's kisses.

"Mmm," she said sleepily, and he smiled and brushed his lips lightly over hers.

"Such an extensive vocabulary, *il mio amore,*" he said softly. "I'm glad we agree."

Anna yawned. "Mmm," she said again, and started to snuggle deeper into his arms.

"Anna. Surely those *mmm*s meant 'Yes, Draco. I agree. I'm starving. I can't even remember the last time we had anything to eat.'"

Anna blinked her eyes open. "You're right. I can't."

"Exactly. We need food. Sustenance. That which gives a man energy to survive the difficult demands put on him by a woman."

That made her laugh. "Such a sacrifice, Valenti."

Draco caught her bottom lip in his teeth, nibbled gently, then ran the tip of his tongue over the sweet wound.

"What would you like?"

Anna toyed with a dark strand of hair that had fallen over his forehead.

"A Big Mac and fries?"

He grinned. "How about some pasta? Tomato sauce. Black olives. Garlic. Anchovies. Freshly grated Romano cheese. And whatever else is in the refrigerator." He raised one eyebrow. "How does that sound?"

"Like takeout from this amazing little Italian place down the block from my office. One problem, though. In case you hadn't noticed, we're a few thousand miles from Manhattan."

Draco tossed back the duvet and sat up.

"I," he said smugly, "just happen to be a world-class cook!"

She sat up, too, and gave him a look. "You, Valenti?"

"Me, *consigliere*," he said as he strode into what Anna assumed was a dressing room.

He was, she thought, a gorgeous man. All hard muscle, taut definition and potent masculinity.

But he was more than that.

So much more.

Charming. Strong. Determined. Opinionated. Arrogant. Tender. Sweet.

He was all those things, some of them total contradictions, and how could that be? How could he be so many different things to her?

He was—he was wonderful. Being with him was wonderful, not only in bed but in so many ways.

She loved talking with him. She loved joking with him. She loved being held in his arms.

She loved—she loved—

"Anna?"

Anna blinked. Draco was back, wearing sweatpants, holding open a deep blue terry-cloth robe.

She stared at him. Her heart was beating fast. No. The idea was insane. You didn't fall in love with a man in, what, forty-eight hours. She certainly didn't. She didn't fall in love at all!

She didn't even know what love was…or maybe she did. Yes, damned right, she did. Love was a trap. It was the way nature reminded you that you were a second-class citizen, that once you gave yourself up to a man, you were whatever he wanted you to be and not what you'd wanted to be.

"*Bellissima?* Why such a shocked look on that beautiful face?"

She took a deep breath.

"Nothing. Well, I mean—I mean, it's terribly late. I—I should get back to the hotel."

"Anna." He came toward her slowly, his eyes locked to hers. "What are you talking about?"

"The time. How late it is. And—"

"I don't want you to leave."

Anna grabbed the robe from his hands, stood up and quickly slipped it on. She didn't want to be naked. As it was, she felt—she felt totally, terrifyingly exposed.

"Well, but it isn't up to you, is it?" Her voice was brittle. She hated the sound, hated the way he was looking at her, the way she felt, confused and desperate, and there was this unpleasant, leaden feeling in her heart… "It's up to me if I want to leave, and—"

She gasped as Draco pulled her into his arms.

"I would not have thought the Orsini *consigliere* would be a coward."

"I'm not a coward. And I told you, I'm not a *consigliere*. I hate my father and what he stands for, and the only *famiglia* I'm part of is the one made up of my four brothers and my sister, and if you don't let go of me, Draco Valenti, I'll—I'll—"

Draco muttered a rough phrase in Italian, hauled her to her toes and kissed her. Anna fought the kiss.

No. Not the kiss. She fought what she felt, the floodgate of emotion opening in her heart.

She trembled as Draco took his lips from hers and drew her close.

"*Lo so, tesoro,*" he whispered. "I know. You don't under-stand this. Neither do I." He stroked her hair, pressed his lips to her temple. "Something different, *sì?* This—this feeling. This emotion…"

She gave a watery laugh.

"Pasta and philosophy. What more could one ask for in the middle of the night?"

He laughed, too, and gathered her to him.

She could feel his heart beating. He could feel hers.

They stood that way for a long time. Then Anna leaned back in her lover's arms.

"Draco," she said softly.

"Anna," he said just as softly.

They smiled, both thinking, again, of that first night together and how he had said her name and she had said his.

He cupped her face. Kissed her so tenderly she felt tears in her eyes.

After a long time he stepped back. Tied the sash of the robe at her waist. Looked at her, from the tips of her bare toes to the top of her tousled curls.

His smile lit her heart.

"Sei cosi bella," he said softly.

He took her hand and kissed it. Then, fingers entwined, he led her through the still-dark villa to the kitchen.

CHAPTER TWELVE

DRACO had told the truth.

Almost.

He wasn't a world-class chef, but he made world-class espresso. Anna pronounced it amazing as they sat drinking it at a small marble-topped table in the garden just off the kitchen.

"Not even my mother makes better coffee," she told him.

"That," he said solemnly, "has to be a world-class compliment."

She grinned. "You'd better believe it."

The sun was rising, shedding streaks of gold through the garden and the pines that surrounded it.

Anna sighed. "It's lovely here," she said softly. "The only thing missing is music."

"The Pines of Rome," Draco said.

Anna looked at him over her coffee cup. "Yes, exactly." She smiled. "And here I thought I was the only person in the world who loved Respighi."

"Got to admit," Draco said solemnly, "for me, it's a toss-up between Respighi and Mick Jagger."

She laughed. He loved to watch her laugh. There was nothing delicate or false about it, the way there was with so many women.

"Well, heck," she said, "why not? I mean, they're both golden oldies."

Draco grinned. And then, because it seemed the most natural thing in the world, he leaned across the table and kissed her.

"Nice," he said. He kissed her again. Her lips parted, clung gently to his. "Very nice. The best possible way to get sugar with my espresso."

Anna's lips curved against his. "Flattery will get you everywhere. But I guess you know that, huh?"

"Me?" Draco said, with such innocence that she giggled.

He grinned, tugged her from her chair and drew her into his lap. They kissed again. And again. His hand slipped inside her robe. She moaned as he caressed her breast, and then she grabbed his hand and clasped it firmly in both of hers.

"We need food, remember?" she said sternly. "Sustenance, Valenti. You said so yourself." She got to her feet. He rose, too, collected their cups and followed her into the kitchen, where an enormous pot of sauce simmered on the stove.

It had turned out that he was not only a world-class maker of coffee, he was also a world-class slicer and dicer of onions, garlic, celery, tomatoes—all the stuff they'd pilfered from the fridge and pantry and combined in a pot.

It had been simmering for an hour. Now Draco took a deep, deep breath.

"Wow."

Anna nodded. "Wow, indeed."

"It smells wonderful."

"That's 'cause I'm the chef," she said smugly, plucking a big wooden spoon from the top of the stove and stirring the sauce. "Maybe not world class, but my-mother's-kitchen class, anyway."

"Hey," he said, "we're both Italian. *Ragù* is in our genes."

"*Ragù,* as in the brand of gravy in a jar?"

"*Ragù,* as in that's the word for… Gravy? What gravy?"

Anna laughed. "If you grow up in Little Italy, this red stuff is gravy."

"Ah." Draco took the spoon and stirred the simmering sauce.

"Ah, what?"

"Nothing. I just—oof! Darn it, woman, that is a very sharp elbow."

"Did you just make a disparaging comment about my ancestry?"

He gave her a look of abject innocence.

"Would I say anything disparaging about a woman who can make a pasta sauce this good? Here," he said, holding out the spoon. "Take a taste."

"From that spoon straight to my hips."

"Your hips are perfect."

"Liar," she said, trying not to smile.

"They're curvy. Feminine. Sexy. In other words, perfect. Now, come on, lady lawyer. Taste."

Anna rolled her eyes. "That is so-o-o sexist."

"Stop complaining and taste the… What did you call it? Taste the gravy."

Smiling, she leaned toward him. Draco whisked the spoon away and captured her mouth with his.

"Mmm," he said softly.

"Mmm, indeed."

Draco swept his arms around her. "*Mmm* is becoming my favorite word."

She reached up and brushed a dark lock of hair off his forehead. "Mine, too."

"In that case…"

He kissed her again. And again.

Anna laid her hand against his jaw, felt the roughness of early-morning stubble beneath the tips of her fingers. So sexy.

So masculine. It felt that way, too. Against her hand. And, God, against her breasts. Her belly. Her thighs.

Had she really thought she didn't like that sensation? That, and coming awake in a man's arms. Why had that always seemed as if it would surely be something to avoid?

Turned out it wasn't.

In fact, there were definite benefits.

Morning sex. Something she'd never thought was all that movies and books made it out to be. But it was. It was lovely. Absolutely lovely when the man was Draco.

"Such deep, deep thoughts, *bellissima*."

She blinked. Draco was watching her with the kind of all-or-nothing intensity that was one of the first things she'd noticed about him.

Liked about him.

Liked very much. Very, very much…

"Anna." He set the spoon aside, gathered her into his arms. "What is it, *cara?*"

She swallowed hard, worked up a smile.

"I was just thinking that this is the first time, the very first time in my life, I'm going to have pasta for breakfast."

Draco watched as she busied herself with the *ragù*. He took the pot he assumed his housekeeper used for pasta from a cupboard, brought it to the sink and filled it with water.

Was that really what she'd been thinking? Pasta for breakfast? A first for him, too…

There were more firsts for him this morning than pasta.

Early-morning conversation with a woman. Breakfast with her. No thought at all of business. That alone was inconceivable, that he should have awakened as he had, his thoughts not on the day's business agenda or how the New York market would open but on, of all things, a woman.

And what, exactly, did that mean?

The water began to boil.

Draco lowered the flame and wished he could lower the boiling point of whatever it was that was happening inside him.

A muscle knotted in his jaw.

Anna was still at the stove, concentrating on stirring the sauce as if her life depended on it.

Was she as confused as he was?

Yesterday he'd told her that something was happening. The question was, what? He needed time and space to clear his head.

"Draco."

He looked at Anna. Her face was pale.

"I have to leave."

He didn't answer.

"Go back to New York, I mean."

Still he didn't respond. Anna expelled a breath.

"I came to do a job and I've done it." She gave a little laugh. "I mean, I came to do a job and now I know there's no job to do. The land is absolutely yours. I don't even know how my father came up with that story, but—"

"I understand," he said politely…and then he looked at her, really looked at her, and felt himself growing angry. At her. At him. At them both. He moved toward her, clasped her shoulders, pulled her to her toes and glowered. "Goddamnit, Anna, you're not going anywhere!"

"Don't be ridiculous. I have to."

"What you have to do is stay here. With me."

"No." Her voice took on a panicked edge. "I can't. My work—"

"I have work, too. Call your office, as I will call mine. Tell them you won't be in for a week."

"Draco. I can't simp—"

He kissed her. Again and again, his arms hard around

her, until she was hanging on to him to keep her knees from buckling.

"Stop," she whispered. "I can't think when you—"

"I am not asking you to think. I am asking you to do."

Oh, he was so sure of himself! So arrogant. So demanding. So certain that because he was a man, he could bend her to his will.

"I have a job," she said. "A life. I have commitments…"

Dark fire flashed in his eyes. "To a man?"

"No! Never. See? You don't know anything about me or you'd never have asked me a thing like—"

"What I know," he said, "is that we aren't done with this."

"Done with what?" Anna gathered herself together. "Look. It's been—it's been—"

"*Sì,*" he said in a low voice, "it has. But it isn't over." He let go of her, reached for the phone, held it out. "Call your office. Call whoever needs to be called. Tell them you'll be gone a week."

Anna looked at her lover. At the phone in his outstretched hand. *Arrogant* wasn't the word to describe him. It didn't even come close. No one had told her what to do since she'd turned eighteen. Hell, she'd stopped listening to those who'd tried long before that.

And now this man, this impossible, tough-and-tender man thought he could step into her life with orders and demands?

"Anna." Draco kissed her. Gently. Tenderly. *"Per favore, mio amore,"* he said softly. "I beg you. Stay with me this week."

Anna stared into his eyes. Took a deep breath. Took the telephone from him.

And made the call.

* * *

They ate bowls of delicious pasta. Showered. Then Draco said he wanted to show her his Rome.

"I hate to say it," he told her, "but it's time to get dressed."

Dressed in what?

Anna groaned as she looked at the clothes she'd left on a chair in his bedroom. "Oh no," she whispered.

Draco, who was zipping up a pair of chino trousers, looked at her.

"What's wrong, *cara?*"

"If there's anything worse than wearing the same stuff two days in a row—"

"Ah," he said. "That."

"Yes. That. I don't even have a change of underwear."

"But you do."

"I do?"

His smile was as smug as any she'd ever seen.

"*Sì.* Your clothes, your makeup—although why you'd put gunk on such a beautiful face is beyond me—all of that is here."

Anna stared at him. "Here?"

"Of course. I took care of it."

"You took—"

"Anna," Draco said gently, "stop repeating what I say. Yes, I took care of it. I arranged for the hotel to pack for you and my driver to bring your luggage here. My housekeeper put everything in the dressing room. Didn't you notice?"

"Well, no. But then, I didn't expect…" She paused. "Let me get this straight. You made all these arrangements without asking me?"

Draco slipped on a white cotton shirt, did up most of the buttons, then folded back the sleeves.

"What was there to ask? I knew you would want your belongings."

"Did you also know I'd be amenable to staying here instead of at my hotel?"

"Amenable. Lady lawyer talk," he said, smiling as he reached for her.

Anna stepped back. "Don't do that."

"Don't do what?"

"Don't try and—and make fun of what I say."

"Whoa." Draco held up his hands. "All I did was—"

"This may surprise you, but I can think for myself."

His smile fled. "Such a mistake," he said stiffly. "A man tries to do a good thing for his woman—"

"I am not your woman. I am not anyone's woman. I am my own…" Anna caught her lip between her teeth. *His woman.* She had to admit there was something special in the words. "Hell," she said softly. "I'm behaving like a fool."

Draco hesitated. Then he sighed and reached for her.

"Yes," he said, "you are."

She gave a little laugh. "Thanks for agreeing with me. I think."

Smiling, he put a finger under her chin and tilted her face to his.

"Let me spoil you a little, *bellissima,* okay?"

"I'm just not used to…" She sighed. "It was very sweet of you to do what you did."

His answering grin was all sexy male arrogance.

"Yes," he said, and brushed his lips over hers. "It was."

Anna laughed as he drew her close. Learning to let a man spoil you, especially a man like Draco Valenti, was going to be a challenge.

He said there were five places you had to visit if you wanted to say you had seen Rome.

The Coliseum. The Forum. The Piazza Navona. The Trevi Fountain. And the Spanish Steps.

Today, he said, they would see the Spanish Steps.

Another of his self-assured pronouncements. This time Anna fought her instinctive—and foolish—reaction. Why should he consult her on something so simple? This was Rome, he was Roman, she wasn't. End of argument.

Besides, the Spanish Steps sounded perfect, and they were.

The stone steps, worn smooth in places by the tread of feet over hundreds of years, climbed from the beautiful Piazza di Spagna to the Piazza Trinità dei Monti. Tourists as well as Romans climbed the steps, stood on them and sat on them, enjoying the sights, the sounds, the balmy weather….

And cups and cones of cold, creamy *gelato*.

Draco took Anna to his favorite *gelateria*.

"So many flavors," she said, looking at the endless list, but it turned out she didn't have to make a choice. He ordered for them both, no questions asked. One chocolate, one *marrone*. The two best flavors, he said with his arm around her, keeping her close to his side.

What about lemon? she almost said, but didn't. The day was perfect. So was the man. The truth was, there was something sexy to this me-Tarzan, you-Jane approach that she had so recently laughed at.

As long as it didn't go too far.

They found places to sit on the steps, one right above the other. Draco took the upper step; Anna took the one beneath it and leaned back against his legs.

She took a long lick of chocolate *gelato*. Draco's eyes followed the motion of her tongue.

"Now try the *marrone*," he said softly.

She licked at the chestnut ice cream, caught an almost-spilled drop at the corner of her mouth with the tip of her tongue.

"You," Draco said in a low voice, "are asking for trouble."

She looked up at him. "What kind of trouble?" she said with a teasing smile, and he laughed and deposited a quick, ice-cream-sweet kiss on her lips.

Anna sat back again, Draco at her back, the Roman sun on her face, the *gelato* cool in her mouth. *Wonderful,* she thought. All of it. The city. The piazza. The *gelato.*

The man.

Most especially the man.

He was so different from what she'd expected, so different from the men she usually dated. He was beautiful to look at, yes, but what made him unique was harder to pin down, that tantalizing combination of strength and tenderness, that old-fashioned belief in honor...

That male arrogance.

Back to that again.

She'd always hated it.

Well, no.

She hated it in her father, where arrogance equated with dominance. In the men who surrounded him. She hated it in a handful of her colleagues, who sometimes spoke to her as if she were a girl and not a woman.

But her brothers were male to the core; they were incredibly arrogant and yet she loved that in them—their assertiveness, their protectiveness...

Her sisters-in-law, independent females every one, clearly loved those same qualities. Maybe whether you thought a man's attitude was caring or dominating depended on what you felt for the man. On whether you respected him and admired him.

On whether you loved him—whatever that meant, because she didn't believe in love. In the very concept of it. In being with one man forever, waking up in his arms, falling asleep with your hand on his heart, feeling peace inside you just because you did something simple like—like sitting in the sun, eating ice cream while you leaned against him...

The cup of *gelato* slipped from her hand.

"Such a waste," Draco teased as he scooped it up. Then he saw her face. "Anna? What is it?"

What, indeed? It wasn't possible. It absolutely wasn't. She was—she was a victim of her own imagination. The beautiful city. The beautiful man. A hundred movies and magazine articles with Rome as the setting, and that was all it was, this—this sudden gallop of her heart.

"Anna. Answer me. Are you ill?"

"No. No! I'm fine."

Draco rose and drew her to her feet. "Are you sure?" His eyes were dark with worry.

"I'm positive. Too much sun maybe." She managed a smile. "Or maybe too much ice cream after too much pasta. I mean, when your usual breakfast is whole wheat toast..."

He was supposed to laugh. Instead, he drew her into his arms.

"I know exactly what you need."

There it was again. That damnable male attitude. No. She could never—

"In fact," he said, his voice a rough caress meant for her ears alone, "I know precisely what you need. A cool drink. A cool bed. And my arms, warm around you."

He was right.

He was right, and whatever that meant was...

It was terrifying.

Over the next few days Draco showed Anna more of his Rome.

The ancient, narrow streets. The magnificent fountains. The green parks. The centuries worth of paintings and frescoes and sculptures. The passageways beneath the Coliseum, where she could almost hear the cries, smell the fear of the men and the animals about to die in the arena.

And he wanted to buy her things. A carnival mask from Venice. A tiny bejeweled heart from Bulgari. Each time, she offered a polite "Thank you, but no."

He tried to overrule that *no* in a tiny, elegant shop on the Via Condotti, where he'd taken her after she said she really, really needed to buy some clothes, emphasis on the *really, really* in a way that told him what he already suspected—that his Anna wasn't accustomed to spending much on herself.

Except for shoes. "My weakness," she'd admitted one night, and he told her he was glad that it was, because the sight of her long, lovely legs in those killer heels, the rest of her clad only in a thong and matching bra, was fast becoming his.

But when she said she needed to get something to wear, that she couldn't live in her lady lawyer suits, one pair of jeans and that T-shirt that made him laugh each time he saw it, Draco took her to the only place he could think of. The Via Condotti, its endless designer shops…

A mistake.

Any of the women who'd passed through his life would have been thrilled.

Anna was horrified.

"Ohmygod, look at the prices!" she'd hissed—at least she'd hissed it when there were prices to see. There were no tags on the things in some shops; when Anna asked, the clerk would ignore her and give the answer to him.

That they would assume he'd pay for her purchases made Anna even more indignant.

"Anna," he'd said softly, *"bellissima,* be reasonable. This is how things are done."

"Not by me."

"But I want to buy these things for you. That dress. This

skirt." He picked up a tiny gold-and-Murano-glass replica of the Trevi Fountain. "And this. Imagine how it would look on your fireplace mantel. Or the desk in your office."

Imagine how it would remind you of this week we spent together, he'd meant, but it was pointless.

"That little figure," she'd said, "costs a king's ransom. Besides, I don't have a fireplace or a mantel in my walk-up, and if I put it anywhere in the hole-in-the-wall I call an office, one of my scruffy clients would try and steal it."

A walk-up flat. A miserable office. Clients who probably spent more time making excuses for their failures than doing something about them. She deserved better than that, but he'd known that telling her so was pointless.

Almost as pointless as their shopping expedition until a clerk had taken pity on her, or maybe on him, and whispered the name of a place blocks away that dealt, she said, in things far less expensive. Anna had dragged him there and left him outside to cool his heels.

When she'd emerged a quarter of an hour later, carrying a huge, plain shopping bag, he'd been surprised.

"So fast?" he'd said.

"I don't need to waste time. I know what I want when I see it."

Yes. So did he. And what he wanted was Anna.

He wanted her all the time, and she wanted him with the same hot desire. And yet the more they made love, the more he felt that heat changing to something else. Something deeper and stronger, something powerful...

And frightening.

It was on his mind all the time.

That he felt something he couldn't comprehend, and that their time together was coming to a close. Only another two days, he found himself thinking one night as they were finishing dinner on the terrace of a small, very quiet, well—off-the-tourist-route restaurant in Trastevere.

Anna was talking. Animatedly.

Draco was listening. More or less. Mostly he was filling his eyes with her.

"…haven't listened to a word," she said suddenly, and he blinked and said, "What?"

She made a face. "See? And here I was telling you all my secrets."

He reached for her hand. "I know all your secrets," he said softly. "That place on your neck that drives you crazy when I kiss it. The taste of your nipples on my tongue…"

"Stop that," she said, but her eyes glittered and her lips curved in a smile. "I'm talking about a different kind of secret. About my hair."

He looked at her hair, hanging down her back like curls of spun gold.

"I love your hair," he said.

"Yeah?" She flashed a smile so smug it made him raise his eyebrows. "I bet you wouldn't have loved it when I dyed it black."

He blinked. "You what?"

"I dyed it. Not just black. Jet-black. So then, of course, I went the whole route. Black nail polish, black lipstick, black T-shirts, black jeans…"

He tried to imagine it. And shuddered. "Why?"

"Teenage rebellion, maybe. I was, I don't know, sixteen, seventeen. Or maybe it was a way to tell my father what he could do with his version of 'young ladies are expected to be quiet, demure and obedient' nonsense."

"Was that what he expected of you?"

"Of course." Anna eyed the tray of tiny pastries that the waiter had brought with their coffee, reached for one, pulled her hand back, reached for another, did the same thing, finally sighed and gave the tray a delicate push away from her. "He had as much chance of me falling into line as a snowball has of making it through hell."

Draco smiled. *Dio,* his Anna was tough!

"And your father said…?"

"He said if this were the fifteenth century instead of the twenty-first, he'd have locked me away in a nunnery."

"I'm starting to understand that T-shirt of yours," Draco said, and grinned. "The fish and the bicycle thing. I'm just trying not to take it personally." Anna smiled. He reached for her hand and enfolded it in his. "So what did he do?"

"Well, what *could* he do?"

"Ah. No nunneries. I forgot."

"He cut off my allowance. Big deal. My brothers made up for it."

"Your brothers liked your black hair?"

"They liked that I'd stood up to our father, the way they had. Plus, I'm pretty sure they thought my Goth phase was cool. See, they're pretty cool themselves." She reached for the tray again. This time she grabbed a pastry and ate it in two quick bites. "They never took a penny from our father," she said after she'd swallowed. "And now they run this humongous investment firm in Manhattan."

Draco slapped his forehead. "Of course! Orsini Brothers."

"Uh-huh."

He chuckled. "It's perfect. A crime boss rendered powerless in his own home. Nice work, *bellissima.*"

Anna's smile broadened. "Thank you, Your Highness."

Draco brought her hand to his lips and kissed it. "Did your sister rebel, too?"

"In the most innocent-seeming way. Izzy took to digging in the soil. Getting her hands dirty. Father found that to be beneath one of his daughters. The more he objected, the more she dug." Anna's eyes danced. "Checkmate."

"Indeed."

"Okay. It's your turn."

"At what?"

"You know all about me, but I don't know a thing about you. What were you like as a kid?"

Draco's smile faded. "I was not—what did you call it? I was not cool, Anna."

Her smile faded, too. "Draco," she said softly, "I'm sorry. I should have realized. It must have been hard. Your father, your grandfather, whatever they'd done to lose everything…"

Had he told her about that? Yes. He had. What for? He didn't talk about his childhood, his family… Except that now, without planning to, he found himself talking about all of it.

About his mother, who'd never been a mother to him at all. About his father, who had, literally, never noticed if he was there or not. About boarding school, and what it had taken to survive it…

Finally he ran out of words.

He fell silent. So did Anna. He couldn't read her face at all.

"Well," he said after a minute, trying for a laugh he couldn't quite muster, "so much for ruining the evening."

Anna shoved back her chair. A second later she was crouched beside him, her eyes suspiciously bright.

Draco looked around. A score of interested people looked back.

"Damnit, Anna," he said.

"Damnit, Draco," she replied, her voice as soft as the petals of a flower, and right there, on the crowded terrace of a crowded restaurant, she clasped his face with her hands, brought it down to hers and put her lips against his.

That was the moment he knew he could not possibly let her leave him at the end of the week.

* * *

He lay awake that night long after she fell asleep.

Two more days. Then Anna would fly to New York. She had a return ticket, she'd said when he'd suggested she use his plane, which was finally back in service. He'd argued, then given in. She was so damned stubborn, too stubborn even to agree to something when anyone could see that doing so would make sense.

As for him, he'd stay on in Rome for a few days, take care of some business. Then he'd fly to San Francisco. And the week they'd spent together, their affair, if you could call seven nights and two days an affair, would be history.

They would still see each other, of course. He'd fly east, she'd fly west. A weekend here, a weekend there. It was doable.

For a while.

Well, so what?

These relationships never lasted. Hell, why would he want them to? The sex lost its excitement. Conversation lost its luster. Yes, this week had been different. Morning conversation. Late-night kisses. Things he'd never even considered with other women had become not just enjoyable but important.

Damnit. He was not ready to let Anna walk out of his life.

New York. San Francisco. Three thousand miles. If only his offices were on the East Coast, or hers on the West. He could not change that. He'd spent years building his company. Hundreds of people worked for him. Anna, on the other hand...

Wait a minute.

What had she said about her work? A hole-in-the-wall office. Sleazy clients. A walk-up flat.

What if she had another opportunity? A much better one? She would, of course, accept it...

And just that quickly, Draco knew what to do. And how

to do it so it wouldn't make her hackles rise. Underhanded? No. Clever, that was all. Clever and logical.

Carefully he eased his arm from her. "Mmm." She sighed, and he smiled, thinking of how now he'd be sure to hear that soft whisper again.

He rose, pulled on his discarded trousers and went through the villa to his study. It took a while to make the necessary phone calls. Two hours, to be precise.

And then the deed was done.

No more East-Coast, West-Coast conundrum. One coast was all they'd need.

A few days from now, Anna would be headhunted by Vernon, Bolton and Andover, a top-flight San Francisco law firm. The firm he used, as a matter of fact. They'd explain that they'd decided to expand their *pro bono* cases and they needed an experienced litigator. They'd offer her four times her current salary, a staff and all the indigent cases they believed had merit.

And, as was often the case, the partner who recruited her would tell her they'd already scouted out an apartment she'd surely like.

By happy coincidence, it would be in the same building as Draco's condo.

Draco had given that lots of thought. He really wanted her living with him, but maybe he wasn't ready for that. Besides, he knew his Anna.

She liked feeling independent.

Having her own place, even if she spent most of her time in his, would make her happy. He'd let her pay the rent— she would believe the owner was renting it out—and Draco wouldn't be fool enough to suggest letting him pay it. But she didn't have to know that he was the owner, and that she was paying only half the actual monthly cost.

Even with her new income, she'd never be able to afford

the flat otherwise, and no way was he going to give her any excuse not to be with him.

A tiny kernel of doubt crept in.

What if it turned out she hated California? What if she didn't want to leave her family?

What if she didn't want to spend her life with him?

Well, not forever, of course. Nothing lasted forever. Still…

Still, maybe some things did. Maybe what he really wanted of her was more than a move to the West Coast. Maybe this wasn't simply about wanting her, but was about needing her. About—about—

Dio, his head was spinning.

Draco ran his hands through his hair until it stood up in unruly little peaks.

Had he acted too impulsively? He couldn't think.

He needed coffee. Or brandy. Grappa. Yes. Excellent. Some good, strong grappa so he could think through this whole thing again.

He walked quickly through the silent house, grabbed the bottle of grappa from the bar in the living room. The phone rang as he was pouring the fiery liquid, but he didn't bother answering it. What for? He knew what it was. A fax from his lawyer, confirming everything they'd arranged: Anna's new job, her new flat, the reduced monthly costs she'd never know about.

He drank off half the grappa.

He'd done the right thing. Surely he had…

Hell.

He had done a stupid thing!

How could he have woven such a lie? You didn't lie to the woman you loved, and he loved Anna. He didn't want her to be his mistress, to be at his beck and call. He wanted to be with her always, for the rest of his life. He wanted—

Something hit him, hard, in the center of his back.

Draco swung around, the grappa flying from his hand… and saw the beautiful, furious face of the woman he loved. She'd slugged him with her fist. A fist that held what were, quite obviously, the pages of a fax.

"Anna. Anna, I know what you must be thinking—"

"You—you son of a bitch!"

"Per favore, bellissima…"

"Do not," she snarled, "do not *bellissima* me, you bastard!"

"Anna. Listen to me."

"Was this the plan all along? To tell me lies and lure me to California after I passed the—the tryout for the part of your new mistress?"

"Look, I know how this must seem. But—"

"Did you or did you not arrange for me to get a new job and a new apartment?"

How had it all come apart this quickly?

"Answer me, damn you!"

"Yes," Draco said, "but—"

"How could you be so stupid? How could you even dream I would ever be any man's mistress? Especially yours!"

"I made a mistake. I know that. I didn't think. I was so—so intent on not losing you—"

"On owning me, you mean." Her voice broke. "What an idiot I was! How I could have let myself think that you—that I…"

She spun away and ran from the room, Draco on her heels, but she reached the bedroom first, slammed and locked the door.

"Anna!"

Draco pounded on the door, but it remained closed until she flung it open. She was fully dressed: sneakers, jeans, the to-hell-with-men T-shirt, the carry-on over her shoulder, the bulging briefcase under her arm.

"I phoned for a taxi. Make sure the gate opens for it."

"Anna—"

"Damnit, Draco, did you hear what I said?"

"Anna. I beg you—"

"It was a great week," she said, her eyes, her voice, everything about her as icy and unyielding as when they'd first met. "I've never had an Italian lover before. Thanks for giving me the chance to add you to my list."

It was a solid metaphorical blow, delivered by a tough street fighter.

He had to admire her for it, even though she had just broken his heart.

CHAPTER THIRTEEN

"So, what do you think, Iz? Too much color? Not enough? What?"

Isabella Orsini stood in the center of her sister's minuscule living room, arms folded, brow furrowed, watching as Anna held paint samples against the wall.

"What I think is, it's Friday night. You want to go to a movie?"

"Answer the question. Too bright? Too dull? Which?"

Isabella sighed. "Try that orange one again."

"Which orange one? Pumpkin Patch? Russet Red? Autumn Peach?"

"That's ridiculous. Peaches are a summer fruit. There are no peaches in autumn."

"Go over to the Whole Foods on Union Square. I'll bet they have peaches."

"For goodness sake, Anna, you know what I mean."

"Just answer the question, okay? Pumpkin? Russet? Autumn?"

Isabella sighed. "You want the truth, I don't like any of them. Tell me again why we're going to paint this room?"

"So it looks different, that's why. To shake things up, that's why. Must there be a logical reason for everything?"

"Just listen to you, lady lawyer. Since when aren't you a stickler for logic?"

"Change is logical. And what's with calling me lady lawyer?"

"I don't know. I just did, that's all."

"Well, don't do it again." Anna edged out from behind the sagging sofa she'd picked up at a Bowery consignment shop the prior weekend. "Ugh! Why did I buy this gross-looking thing?"

"I have no idea. I mean, it sags. It tilts. And baby-poo brown isn't one of my favorite colors."

"Thank you. That really makes me feel better."

"Hey, you asked. Here's an idea. You take one end, I'll take the other, we'll drag it downstairs, put it at the curb—"

"We'd never move it. It weighs a ton. I had to pay the super fifty bucks to get it up here."

"And it cost you how much?"

Anna sighed. "Fifty bucks."

"So a hundred dollars for a pile of sagging baby poo when you already had a perfectly acceptable sofa?"

"It was ugly."

"Not like this." The sisters sank down on opposite ends of the offending piece of furniture and looked at each other. Isabella cleared her throat. "So, you gonna tell me what's happening?"

"You know what's happening. I have an interesting new client."

"Excellent way to describe a nut who shot out all the windows in his ex's apartment so he wouldn't have to see her and her new boyfriend through them." Izzy snorted. "Anybody break the news to him yet? That, hello, you can see through windows even better when the glass is gone?"

"And," Anna said, choosing to ignore the remark, "in addition to an interesting new client, I have a new sofa. New for me, okay? This time tomorrow I'll also have new paint on the walls. And let's not forget the boots I bought last week."

"Right. Not boots. Snow boots. And it's still summer."

"It's the end of summer. That's why they were on sale."

"Uh-huh. Maybe they were on sale 'cause only my sister would be crazy enough to buy snow boots with five-inch heels."

"Four-inch, and what's so bad with me trying to make some changes in my life?"

"Nothing," Isabelle said, "if you weren't doing it to try and bury something you don't want to think about."

Anna snorted. "That's crazy."

"That's accurate. Remember you asked me about psych 101? About sexual fantasies?"

"Isabella. I have no intention of—"

"There was more to psych 101 than that. For instance, chapter twelve of that oversize textbook, remember? Ahem. 'A sudden flurry of change-centered activity is often symptomatic of a desire to obliterate memory of a distressing situation.'"

Anna stared at her sister. "You can remember reading that?"

Iz shrugged. "Heck, no. I just made it up. But see, I'm right. I can tell. Just look at your face."

"Coffee," Anna said briskly. She sprang to her feet and walked the six feet it took to reach the kitchen. "Get out the cream, would you? And the pink stuff."

"Anna. You went to Italy. 'I'll be gone a couple of days,' you said. Instead, you were gone a week. And when you got back, you looked like crap."

"Baby poo. Now crap. What a fine sense for similes my sister has." Anna's words were brisk, but her hands trembled as she filled the coffeepot with water. "Want some cookies?"

"I want some answers. What happened in Rome?"

"Nothing," Anna said. "Nothing at all. I saw the Trevi Fountain, the Coliseum, I did a little shopping and—"

"And?" Isabella said, narrowing her hazel eyes.

"And," Anna said, turning her back to her sister, "and…"

"Anna. Honey, you can tell me anything. You know that."

Anna nodded. She could. And, really, she had to. She couldn't carry this around inside her anymore.

"And," she said in a low voice, "I fell in love."

Isabella all but collapsed onto a wooden kitchen chair.

"Not you. Not you, Anna!"

"I fell in love." A sob broke from Anna's throat. "With the coldest, cruelest, most hard-hearted bastard in the world."

"What's his name?"

"Draco. Draco Valenti." Anna sank into a chair across from Isabella. "Prince Draco Valenti, no less."

"A handsome prince?"

"An ice prince. All sex, no heart."

"Wow. That's quite a description."

"It's accurate. But don't worry. I fell out of love fast enough. I mean, I realized how I really felt two minutes after I walked out on him. I'm just upset, is all. With myself, for having been such a jerk."

"Oh, honey…"

"Really. It's okay." Tears ran down her face as she looked at her sister. "I never actually loved him, Iz. I never would have. Never, not me, not in a billion years…"

Anna folded her arms on the scarred wooden table, laid down her head and sobbed.

Not too far away, in a much trendier part of Manhattan, in a bar that was still a bar and not a cocktail lounge or a club, Raffaele, Dante, Falco and Nicolo Orsini were having their usual Friday-night get-together.

The bar—actually, The Bar—was theirs, which was why it was still a bar despite the fact that the neighborhood, to their enormous distaste, had gone upscale.

Once, this had been the place where they shared talk of dangerous dilemmas and beautiful women.

Now they were all married. Very happily married, but they met anyway and talked sports and business, kids and family, and, yes, once in a while they even talked dangerous dilemmas.

Tonight they were talking about one of their sisters.

"Izzy agrees," Rafe said. "Something's up with Anna."

Nick bit into his burger, chewed, swallowed and nodded. "Yeah. But what?"

Falco lifted his beer to his mouth. "Isabella's going to try and find out."

"Could it be a man?" Dante said. His brothers looked at him, and he sighed. "Right. Not our Anna. There's not a guy alive could bring our Anna down."

There was a sound from nearby. Somebody clearing his throat, maybe.

"Agreed," Rafe said. "A guy tried to upset our Anna, she'd take him out."

There it was. That same sound again. The four Orsinis looked up. A guy was standing next to their booth. He was big, like them. Dark haired, like them. Dressed in an expensive suit and handmade shoes, also like them, but his tie was crooked, his hair looked as if he'd combed it with his fingers and there was a glitter in his eyes that they all recognized as Trouble, definitely Trouble, and with a capital *T*.

The brothers looked at each other. *What the hell is this?* those looks said and, as one, they rose to their feet.

"Service is at the bar, pal," Falco said.

The guy nodded. Did that throat-clearing thing again.

"Listen," Rafe said, "you got a problem with the place or the food—"

"I am Draco Valenti," Draco blurted. "And she's not your Anna, she is mine."

Silence. A heavy, awful silence. Then Nick jerked his chin toward the door that led to The Bar's private office, and the five men marched to it, Draco surrounded by men he figured could grind him into dust if they decided that he was the problem, not the solution.

He could fight back. He was pretty sure he was as tough as they were, but there were four of them, one of him, and besides...

Besides, he had hurt his Anna. Their sister.

All things considered, if they wanted to beat the crap out of him, he wouldn't try to stop them.

A hand shoved him, none too gently, into a small, inexpensively furnished room. Desk. Phone. Chairs. And framed photos on the walls. Photos of these four. And of four smiling women. Babies. A toddler. A woman who had to be the mother of the clan. A slim, beautiful young woman with dark hair.

And Anna. His Anna, smiling and happy and lovely and— and God, how he missed her, yearned for her, needed her—

"So?"

Draco turned around. The Orsinis stood lined up, shoulder to shoulder, arms folded, jaws set. He was a fan of American football and he had a totally irrelevant thought.

He'd seen offensive linemen who looked less threatening than these guys.

"What do you mean, she's *your* Anna?"

He had no idea which of them had spoken the first time, which had spoken now. The only thing he did know was that now was not the time for introductions.

"You want it straight?" he said. "No bull?"

"Straight," one of them growled. "From the beginning."

So Draco told them.

Everything. Okay. Not everything. Not about what had happened on the flight to Rome, or what had happened in her hotel, or, *Cristo,* not what had happened in his bed.

But all the rest… He told them.

How he'd thought this was just going to be a weekend fling. One of them started forward when he said that, but the guy beside him muttered, "Cool it," and the other guy stood still the way a tiger might stand still before it made a kill.

Draco told them more.

He said that weekend fling hadn't been enough, how he'd convinced Anna to stay another week. How incredible the week had been, and how he'd suddenly realized he didn't want her to leave him when it ended.

Now came the hardest part.

He told them of the scheme he'd hatched. All of it. The job offer. The apartment. That what he wanted was to make Anna his mistress.

One of the Orsinis swung at him. He stood there and took the blow, straight to his jaw.

"Damnit, chill," one of Anna's brothers snarled, and glared first at Draco and then at the other three. "Been there, done that," the guy growled, and damned if the rest of them didn't sort of hang their heads.

"And now you're here," said the one who'd slugged him. "What took you so long?"

Draco had expected the question. His answer was blunt and honest.

"She said something that hurt me. About—about having been with other men."

"Let me get this straight," one Orsini said. "You're into a double standard?"

"No. I am not. It was only that—that by then Anna had made me forget every woman I'd ever known. To think that I had not done the same for her…"

"Yeah, okay. No need for specifics."

"I still don't get it. You think we're going to tell you that you can make our sister your mistress?"

Draco narrowed his eyes. It was one thing to be deferential, but quite another to be taken for a fool.

"If I wanted her to be my mistress," he said quietly, "I'd go to her, not you."

"Then what do you want?"

Draco took a breath. "Anna loves the four of you."

"Damned right. And we love her."

"I am Italian."

"If you think that makes this better—"

"I am also a prince."

"Whoopee," one of the brothers said, his tone flat and insulting.

"What I mean is that I carry a name that had once been respected." Hell. This wasn't going well. "But my father sullied that name, and I have spent my life trying to restore honor to it."

The atmosphere in the room eased, if only a little.

"Go on."

"You don't know the half," one of the brothers muttered.

"In Italy, honor demanded asking permission of a woman's family before asking for her hand in marriage."

A muscle twitched in one of those grim jaws.

"Is that why you're here? You want Anna to marry you, and us to tell her that she should?" Four deep, unpleasant barks of laughter. "If you knew anything about our sister, you'd know that nobody can tell her what to do."

"No," Draco said softly. "It's one of the things I love about her. I will do the asking, not any of you."

"And why should she say yes?"

"Because I adore her," Draco said gruffly. "And she loves me." Nothing. Not even a twitch. Draco narrowed his eyes. Eating crow was one thing; eating an entire rookery's worth was another. "I know that she loves me. It is the reason she acted as she did when she found out what I'd done."

"The bastard stood there," one of the brothers said grimly, "and watched her cry."

"She didn't cry. Another woman would have." Draco paused. "Anna hit me."

Silence. And then the Orsinis began to laugh. But as quickly as the laughter started, it stopped.

"Suppose we say no? Suppose we refuse you permission to marry her? Or even to ask her? Suppose we tell you to get the hell out of here and never look back? Then what?"

Enough, Draco thought, and he stood straighter, his dark eyes level with theirs.

"Then," he said quietly, "I am afraid I will have to take you on, one by one, and when I am the only one of us left standing—and I will be, in an honest fight—I will go to my Anna and put my life and my heart in her hands."

The silence that followed was surely the longest of Draco's life. Then Anna's brothers smiled. Grinned. Shook his hand and introduced themselves, and when the introductions were over, they wished him good luck and sent him on his way.

Autumn Peach was too dark, Russet Red was too deep and Pumpkin Patch was just plain insipid.

That was all Anna would talk about when she stopped crying, never mind Izzy's persistent questioning, and finally Izzy threw up her hands and said okay, fine, enough was enough. She'd go to the hardware store and get some more color samples.

"You're a pigheaded mule," she told Anna, and Anna tried to laugh at the impossible image, but she couldn't.

Laughing seemed out of the question.

At least she'd gotten rid of Izzy for a while. A half hour would give her time to regroup.

Unfortunately, Izzy had obviously decided leaving was a mistake, because the doorbell rang not five minutes later.

Anna rubbed her eyes with her fists, pasted a smile on her face and went to the door.

"No," she said as she flung it open, "I will not compromise on Tangerine Twist...." The words died on her tongue. "Draco?" she said, and two things happened at once. Her hand balled into a fist so she could hit him, and Draco said her name and reached for her, and after a hesitation that surely lasted no more than a heartbeat, Anna sobbed her lover's name and went into his arms.

He kissed her, over and over. Her forehead. Her eyes. The tip of her nose. Her mouth. Oh, her mouth, even sweeter than he remembered.

"Anna," he said brokenly, "Anna, *bellissima, mio amante* Anna, *ti amo, ti adoro!*"

Anna didn't speak much Italian, but a woman didn't have to speak the language to understand any of those words.

"I love you, too," she whispered. "I adore you. I've missed you so terribly!"

"*Sì*. I have missed you, too. My heart, my life have been so empty..."

"That night," Anna said, "that awful night..."

"I was afraid to lose you. And afraid to try and keep you." Draco laughed as he framed her face in his hands. "I always thought love was a foolish fairy tale."

Anna smiled, even as tears rolled down her cheeks.

"I thought it was just a way of keeping a woman under a man's thumb."

Draco kissed her again.

"We were both wrong, *bellissima.*"

"Yes. Oh yes, we were."

Draco took a deep breath. And dropped to one knee.

"Anna. Beloved," he said, "will you do me the honor of becoming my wife?"

The smile that curved Anna's lips was, Draco knew, the most beautiful sight a man would ever see.

"Yes," she said, "oh, yes. I will."

He reached in his pocket, took out a ring and slipped it on her finger. It was a perfect copy of the Valenti crest, done in sapphires and diamonds.

Anna looked from her hand to her lover. Her eyes filled again.

"It's beautiful," she said softly. "And I am honored to wear it."

Draco rose to his feet. "Anna," he murmured, "*bella* Anna."

She went into his arms and he kissed her, kissed her until the world floated away. They never heard Isabella come in, never heard her hurried departure.

But when Izzy quietly shut the apartment door, she was smiling.

They were married two weeks later in the little church Anna's mother had always loved, on a street that was either part of Little Italy or Greenwich Village, depending on who you asked.

Sofia Orsini was thrilled with her new son-in-law, but she raised her eyebrows when he came to her at the party that followed in the observatory at the Orsini mansion and said he had a wedding gift for her.

It was the deed to the Sicilian land that sheltered the ruins of the castle that had belonged to his ancestors.

"Now it will belong to two families," he said.

Sofia shook her head and gently gave the document back to him. She said she had no idea what he was talking about, but that it was good to know her Anna had married a man who loved Sicily.

He shook hands with each of Anna's brothers, all of whom

had been his best men— "Just try and talk me out of it," he'd told the wedding planner, who had not been foolish enough to try—and laughed with them in a way that told Anna they shared something, but none of them would tell her what it was.

He kissed his sisters-in-law, who had been Anna's brides-maids, kissed the nephews and nieces he'd so suddenly acquired, and reserved a special hug for Anna's maid of honor.

"Isabella," he said, "Anna says you are the dearest sister a woman could possibly have."

"You next, kid," Rafe said to Izzy as he swept her away and danced her around the room.

"Right," Izzy said brightly, and thought, *Not me, not now, not ever in a million billion years.*

And, finally, he walked up to Cesare.

"Anna thinks she despises you," he said softly, "but the truth, *signore,* is that she loves you because you are her father." He looked the don straight in the eye. "And you made up all that nonsense about your wife's family and my land."

The don permitted himself a small smile.

"I may have had my facts confused. Anything is possible." He paused. "By the way," he continued, as if what he were about to say was unimportant, "I knew your father. He was not the best of men but then, neither am I."

Draco waited. Then he said, "And?"

The don smiled. "And, I suspect your father would be proud of the man you have become."

At last it was time for Anna and Draco to say goodbye and leave on their honeymoon.

They were flying to Venice, on his private plane. It was big and luxurious; the center aisle had been garlanded with white roses.

Draco carried his bride down that aisle to the private bedroom in the rear of the plane and kicked the door shut after him.

"This is how it all began, *cara*," he said softly. "A plane. And you. And me."

Anna smiled as he set her slowly on her feet. She was wearing stilettos, of course. Still, she had to rise on tiptoe to kiss him, and then to put her lips to his ear and whisper something hot and wicked.

His eyes grew very, very dark. Slowly he shrugged off his jacket. Undid his tie. Unbuttoned his shirt.

"Anna," he said in a voice that was pure sex.

Anna laughed and wound her arms around his neck.

"Draco," she whispered. "What took you so long?"

AT HIS MAJESTY'S REQUEST

MAISEY YATES

CHAPTER ONE

"THERE is a science to matching people." Jessica Carter tucked a lock of blond hair behind her ear and lifted her computer, a flat, all-in-one device shaped like a clipboard, so that it obscured her figure. Pity, Stavros was enjoying the look of her. Even if she was starch and pearls, rather than spandex and diamonds.

She continued, her eyes never leaving the screen. "A matching of social status, values, education and life experience is very important to creating a successful, enduring marriage. I think most match services realize that." She paused and took a breath, pink lips parting slightly, her green eyes locking with his just for a moment before dropping back down. "However, I have taken things a step further. Matching is not just a science. It's an art. The art is in the attraction, and it's not to be underestimated."

Prince Stavros Drakos, second son of the Kyonosian royal family, and named heir to the throne, leaned back in his chair, his hands behind his head. "I am not so much concerned about the art, Ms. Carter. The essentials are general compatibility and suitability for my country. Childbearing hips would help."

Her pale cheeks flushed crimson, her lush mouth tightening. "Isn't that what all men want?"

"I'm not sure. And frankly, I don't care. Most men don't

have to consider the entire populace of their country when they go about selecting a wife."

But it didn't matter what most men did. He wasn't most men. Ever since he'd been forced to step into the place of his older brother, he had been different. It didn't matter what normal was, it didn't matter what he wanted. All that mattered was that he be the best king possible for Kyonos.

His methods might be unorthodox, and they might grieve his father, but what he did, he did for the good of his people. It just wasn't in his nature to be too traditional.

She blew out a breath. "Of course." She smiled, bright and pristine, like a toothpaste commercial. She was so clean and polished she hardly seemed like a real woman, more like a throwback from a 1950s television show. In Technicolor. "I… Not that I'm complaining of course, but why exactly have you hired me to find you a wife? I've read the newspaper articles written about you and you seem perfectly able to attract women on all your own."

"When I want to find a suit for an event, I hire I stylist. When I need to organize a party, I hire an events coordinator. Why should this be any different?"

She tilted her head to the side. Her hair was in a low, neat bun, her dress high-collared, buttoned up and belted at the waist. A place for everything and everything in its place. She all but begged to be disheveled.

Any other time, he might have done so.

"I see you have a…practical outlook on things," she said.

"I have a country to run, I don't have time to deal with peripherals."

"I've compiled a list of candidates, to be refined, of course…"

He took the monitor from her hand and hit the home button, tapping a few icons and not managing to find a list. "What is this?"

She took the device back from him. "It's a tablet computer. Shall I put that technologically savvy women need not apply?"

"Not necessary, but you can put down that women with smart mouths need not apply."

Her full lips curved slightly. "Someone has to keep you in line."

"No one has to keep me in line. I'm going to be king." That hadn't kept Xander in line. In fact, he'd pulled himself straight out of line and put Stavros in front. But Stavros wouldn't falter. He wouldn't quit.

One well-shaped eyebrow lifted upward. "Oh? Is that so." She typed something on her onscreen keyboard.

"What? What did you write?"

"Strong tyrannical tendencies. A possible negative in social interactions, possible positive in BA."

"BA?"

"Bedroom activities. It's shorthand. Don't dwell on it," she said, her tone snappy. "I told you attraction is considered. That said, do you require a virgin bride, Prince Drakos?"

"Stavros will do, and no, I don't." He shouldn't be surprised by her frankness. She had a reputation for being bold, brash even. She also had a reputation for setting up unions that had led to successful mergers and increased fortunes. She was a relationships strategist, more than a matchmaker, and he'd been assured that there was no one better. She knew the rules of society, knew the function a practical marriage served.

His marriage, and securing it, meant nothing to him personally, and being able to pawn off the legwork on Jessica Carter had been too good of an idea to pass up. And if the press happened to pick it up, all the better. He had a reputation for doing things differently. Doing things his way. Turning away from how his father had run the country.

And this was as far from something his father would do as he could think of.

"That's good," she said. "It's always awkward to ask women to submit proof of sexual history."

"Do you do that?"

"I have. Though not just women."

"Who?" he asked.

"Ah, now, if I told you I would have to kill you. I operate on the basis of strict anonymity. Unless those involved are seeking publicity, I don't talk about my clients."

"But word does spread," he said. He'd seen an old school friend three weeks earlier, and the smugness had practically been dripping from him as he stood there with his new fiancée. Oxford educated. And a model. She was everything he'd asked for. Beauty and brains. And who had accomplished the feat?

Jessica Carter.

The woman the media called the World's Most Elite Matchmaker. She catered to billionaires. CEOs, tycoons. Royalty. And she was renowned for making matches that lasted.

That was what he needed. He'd given up on allowing himself any sort of personal interest in the selection of his bride ever since he'd discovered that it was likely he would be assuming the throne for his absentee brother. His wants didn't matter. He needed a woman who could be a princess, an icon for his country, an aide to his rule. Aside from that, he had some of his own ideas. Someone beautiful, of course. Someone smart. Philanthropic. Fertile.

It shouldn't be too hard to find.

"This isn't just about me, Ms. Carter, this is about Kyonos. My family has seen too much tragedy, too much…

upheaval. I have to be the rock. I have to provide a solid foundation for my people to rest on, and establishing a solid marriage is essential to that plan."

The death of his mother, nineteen years ago, had shaken his people to the core. The abandonment of his older brother, the rightful heir, had caused months of instability. Stocks had tanked, trade had stalled, the housing market going into a deep freeze.

Why had the future ruler really left? Would he truly abdicate? What secrets were the Drakos family guarding beneath that veneer of polish and old world sophistication?

He had been determined to undo all of the unrest brought about by his brother. And he had done it. He'd revitalized Thysius, the largest city on the island, with posh hotels and trendy boutiques. He'd brought in new revenue by having the seat of his corporation on the island, a country much too small to house companies the size of his, when the owner wasn't the crown prince.

He'd done much to drag his country back from the brink. From the age of eighteen his entire life had altered so that it revolved around his homeland. He hadn't had the luxury of being a boy. Hadn't had the luxury of feeling fear or sadness. He'd learned early on that feeling had no place in his world. A ruler, an effective ruler, had to be above such things.

"I understand that this is a big deal," she said. "Not just in terms of your country, but for you. She *is* going to be your wife."

He shrugged. "An acquisition I've long known I would make."

Jessica let out a long, slow breath. "Mr.…Prince Drakos, will you please stop being so candid? It's remarkably hard to sell a man who clearly has no interest in romantic love."

"Try this for a tagline—marry the jaded prince and receive a title, a small island, a castle and a tiara. That might make up for it."

"Money can't buy love."

"Nice. Trite, overdone, possible copyrighted by The Beatles, but nice. You might consider tacking this onto the end—love doesn't buy happiness."

Something changed in Jessica's eyes, a shard of ice in the deep green that had been warm a moment before. "That's for damn sure, but we're talking about putting together a sales pitch. And you aren't helping."

He shifted. "Can't you put something in my file about my impeccable table manners?"

"I haven't witnessed them, and I don't lie. You're my client, yes, but there is a pool of women I work with on a regular basis, and I have great loyalty to them."

It was intriguing. The way she flashed hot and cold. The way she presented herself, nearly demure, and then she opened that mouth. And such a lovely mouth, too. She was holding it tight. What would it take to make it soften?

The idea made his stomach tighten.

"And you think one of them is my queen?"

"If she isn't, I'll walk through all of Europe beating gold-plated bushes until a member of minor nobility falls out. I won't stop until we get this settled."

"You are supposed to be the best. You did manage to get a confirmed bachelor friend of mine to settle down."

"That's because, in my business, there's no settling. It's all about making the best match possible," she said brightly.

"Somehow, I do not share your enthusiasm."

"That's okay, I have enough for both of us. Now…" She looked back down at her tablet computer. "Your sister's wedding is in just a couple of weeks, and I don't want you going with a date, are we clear?"

He frowned. "I wouldn't have brought a date to a wedding." Weddings were where one picked up women; he didn't see the point of bringing one with him. The thought reminded him that it had been a very, very long time since he'd picked up a woman.

"And no leaving with any of the bridesmaids," she added. "You have to be seen as available, approachable and, oh yes, available."

"You said that already."

"It's important. Obviously, we don't want to put out a call for all eligible women in the kingdom to show up, so we need to go about this subtly."

He frowned. "Why aren't we putting out a call for all eligible women?"

"Look, Prince Charming, unless you want to put a glass slipper on a whole bunch of sweaty feet, you do this my way. That means you behave how I tell you to at Princess Evangelina's wedding."

"I wouldn't have picked up a bridesmaid. My sister's friends are far too young to interest me," he said.

"Ah…so you have an age range," she said, perking up. "That's important."

"Yes, no one as young as Evangelina. I'd say twenty-three at youngest. A ten-year age difference isn't so bad. Maybe cap it at twenty-eight."

She frowned. "Oh. All right." She looked down at her computer, then up, then back down again, her mouth twitching, like she was chewing on something. Her words, he imagined. She looked up at him again. "Why, exactly, is anyone older than twenty-eight too old?"

"I need a wife who can have children. Preferably a few of them. Any older and…"

"Right," she snapped, directing her focus downward again.

"If I ask you how old you are I'll only make this worse, won't I?" he asked dryly.

"I have no problem with my age, Prince Stavros, I'm thirty. Not that it's your business."

"It's not personal."

"I get it," she said. "And I'm not applying anyway."

"A pity," he said, noticing the way color bled into her cheeks.

Jessica set her iPad on the ornately carved table to her right and put her hands in her lap, trying like crazy to stop the slight tremble in her fingers. She was saying all the wrong things. Letting her mouth run away with her. Not a huge surprise since she tended to get prickly when she got nervous.

She'd managed to make that little quirk work for her over the years. People found her bold approach refreshing. And that suited her, since it enabled her to keep all shields up and locked, fully protecting her from people getting too close. Without showing vulnerability.

And now, with Prince Stavros Drakos, was not the time to let her guard down. No, most especially not with him.

"I've managed to finagle three wedding invitations," she said. "They will go to three girls that you and I will work at selecting sometime this week. At the wedding, you will speak to them for twenty minutes apiece, no more. And after that, I want you to pick one to advance to a higher tier. I've made a list of questions for you to consider asking."

"I'm not even getting a full date?" he asked, dark eyebrows lifting.

She shifted in her chair. He was so sexy it was unnerving. Because his aesthetic appeal couldn't be observed in the cool detached manner she might use to look at a nice piece of art. That was the way she'd been looking at men for the past few years. As lovely objects, nice to behold, but nothing that invoked feeling.

She'd let that part of herself go and she hadn't missed it. Until now.

Stavros...well, he made a spark catch in her belly. One that had been entirely absent for so long now she'd thought it had gone out permanently. It was a disastrous realization.

She stood up and took a step away from him, hoping distance would bring clarity. Or at least control over her body.

"You don't need a full date. Not at this stage. I've picked out a few candidates based on what we talked about over the phone. And now I've refined some of that, and I've got a number of women I'd like for you to have an initial meet with. You've been matched with them based heavily on compatibility. The kind we can establish from forms, anyway. Attraction," she said, the word sticking in her throat for some reason, "is actually one of the simpler parts of this stage. But it's not simple, not...not really." She felt her stomach tighten. The way Stavros was looking at her was intense, his brown eyes locked with hers. He was gorgeous.

It was sort of ridiculous how hot he was. It was as if he'd splashed around in the finest end of the gene pool, only collecting the good, the bad rolling right off. Square jaw, straight, proud nose and his lips...they changed a lot. Firm and unyielding sometimes. And other times, when he smiled, they looked soft. Soft and...kissable.

She swallowed and tried not to think about how very long it had been since she'd been kissed. She tried even harder to stop thinking about kissing Stavros's lips.

"Anyway," she said, breathing in deeply. She knew what to say next, knew her system by heart. She could explain it in her sleep. And she could take a few more steps away from him while she did it. "We start with that base attraction. What I call 'lightning bolt' attraction—" like the kind she'd felt when she'd walked into Stavros's office this morning "—or what many confuse with love at first sight. You'll feel a stronger pull of that immediate attraction to at least one of the women at the wedding. As we go on, we'll try and figure out which woman you feel a more lasting attraction for. But that's a different phase of the program."

"And you're accusing me of lacking in romance. You have this all worked out to a cold, calculated system. I'm not complaining, but let's be…what was the word you used? *Candid*. Let's be candid, you and I." A smile curved his lips and he rose from his desk, slowly rounding it. "You're no more romantic than I am."

His voice was like warm butter. It flowed over her body, so good, and so very, very bad for her. She cleared her throat. And took a step back. "All right, I'm not a romantic. Not really. I mean I was, at one time. But not so much now. What is romance? Warm fuzzies and the unrealistic ideals we project onto others when we're first beginning a relationship. Romance is an illusion. That's why I believe in matching people based on something concrete. From these basic principles, love can grow. And when the foundation is solid, I believe love can be real and lasting. It's when people go with that lightning attraction only, with nothing to back it up, that's when you have problems."

He lifted his arm and ran his hand over his hair, the action stretching his crisp dress shirt tight over his well-defined chest. She wondered what muscles of that caliber would feel like beneath her hands. She'd never touched a chest that looked quite like that.

Oh, dear. Wandering thoughts again. And redirecting…

"So, is that what you did?" he asked. "Follow one of those flash attractions, or whatever you call them, and have it end in disaster?"

She laughed and turned, hoping to look like she was

starting to pace and not like she was trying to put space between them. "Something like that." A lot more complicated than that, but she wasn't about to get into it. "The point is, I know what works."

"But you aren't married."

She stopped midstep, wobbling slightly on her sky-high stilettoes. "I'm happily divorced, as it happens." Happily might be overselling it, but she was rightfully divorced, that was for sure. "I just celebrated my four-year anniversary of unwedded bliss."

He arched an eyebrow. "And you still believe in marriage?"

"Yes. But the fact that my marriage didn't work helps with what I'm doing. I understand what breaks things down. And I understand how to build a solid foundation. You've heard of the wise man who built his house on the rock, I assume?"

"It's buried somewhere in the ether of my debauched mind. Memories of childhood Sunday school lurk there somewhere." Oh, he did that charming, naughty smile far too well. It was no wonder he had a reputation as the kind of man who could meet a woman and have her taking her clothes off for him five minutes later.

She found her own hand wandering to the top button of her dress and she dropped it quickly, taking another defensive step back. He answered that move by taking three steps forward.

She cleared her throat. "Excellent, well, I'm helping you build a marriage on a rock, rather than sand."

His eyebrows lifted, one side of his mouth quirking into a smile. He took another two steps toward her. "Different than a marriage on the rocks?"

She stepped back. "Much."

"Well, that is good to know," he said.

"You and I will work together to create a strong partnership, for you and your country," she said, with all the confidence she could pull out of her gut. Confidence she didn't really feel.

He closed the distance between them and she took another step in the opposite direction, her back connecting with the wall. She forced a smile, and a step toward him.

He held his hand out, so large and tan and masculine. She just stared at it for a moment, trying to remember what one was supposed to do when they were offered a hand.

Her brain jolted into gear and she stuck her hand out. He gripped it, heat engulfing her as his fingers made contact with her bare skin. She wished now that she'd worn her little white gloves with the pearls. She'd thought them a bit quirky for a business meeting, but the shield against his touch would have been nice.

She just hadn't realized. Sure, she'd seen his picture, but a picture didn't do justice to the man. He was broad, nearly a foot taller than her, and he smelled like heaven. Like clean skin laced with a trace of sandalwood.

He made her feel small and feminine. And like she was losing her mind.

She shook his hand once, then dropped her own back to her side, hiding it behind a fold in her full skirt as she clenched it into a fist, willing the burning sensation to ease.

"I'll hold you to it, Ms. Carter. And I warn you, I can be a tough taskmaster."

Her breath caught. "I'm… I can handle you."

He chuckled, low and dark, like rich coffee. "We'll see."

CHAPTER TWO

"Are you finding the accommodations to your satisfaction, Ms. Carter?"

Jessica whirled around, her heart thudding against her breastbone. Stavros was standing in the hallway of her hotel, a small smile on his face. "I… Yes, very. I didn't expect to see you here. Today. Or ever."

He looked around them, as though checking to see if he was in the right place. "This is one of my hotels."

"Yes, I know, but I assumed…"

"You assumed that I had no real part in the running of my hotels, casinos, et cetera. But I do. In another life I might have been a businessman." His tone took on a strange, hard tinge. "As it is, I divide my time between being a prince and running a corporation. Both are equally important."

She tried to smile and took a step back. "So, to borrow a phrase…of all the hotels you own, on all the island, you walk into mine?"

His sensual lips curved upward. It was hard to call it a smile. "Oh, this was calculated, but I also had a business reason for coming by."

Her stomach fluttered. *Down, girl.* What was wrong with her? A man hadn't made a blip on her personal radar for a long, long time. And Stavros was a client.

Anyway, she wasn't quite through licking her wounds.

The loss of her five-year marriage, and the circumstances surrounding it, had left her feeling far too bruised to jump back into dating. Which had been fine. She'd left her job, poured everything into starting her own company and perfecting her system of matchmaking.

Those who can't do, teach, those who can't find a match, match others.

That wasn't true. She *could* find a match. Had found one, back when she'd believed in falling in love accidentally with the aid of some sort of magic that might make it stick. As if it were so simple.

And then life had taken her dreams, her hopes, her beliefs and feelings, and it had jumbled them all together until the wreckage was impossible to sift through.

Until it had been much easier to simply walk out of the room and close the door on the mess, than to try and find some sort of order again.

But her ex-husband had no business wiggling into her thoughts. Not now. Not ever, really. That was over. She'd changed.

Her job had always seemed important. At first, being a matchmaker had been all about indulging her romantic streak. She'd been in love with love. With the mystical quality she'd imagined it possessed.

She knew differently now. Knew that relationships were about more than a flutter in your stomach. Now her job seemed essential in new ways. To prove to herself that it could still be real. That people could get married and stay married.

It was almost funny. She created successful relationships, successful marriages. And she went to bed alone every night and tried not to dwell on her broken one.

She'd had mixed success with that. But she'd had phenomenal success with her business. And that was what she chose to focus on.

"All right, what was your reason?" she asked, taking another step back.

"First off, I had to speak to my manager about handling all of the incoming guests for Mak and Eva's wedding. One of my gifts to them. Putting Mak's family up in the hotel. He could do it himself, and he's argued with me about it no end, but I'm insistent."

"And you do get your way, don't you?" she asked. She had a feeling he never heard the word *no*. That if a command was issued from his royal lips everyone in the vicinity hopped to obey him. It wasn't that he had the manner of a tyrant, but that he had such a presence, a charisma about him. People would do whatever it took to be in his sphere. To get a look from him, a smile.

He was dangerous.

"Always." The liquid heat in his eyes poured into her, his husky smooth tone making her entire body feel like it was melting. She was pretty sure she was blushing.

Oh, yeah, dangerous didn't even begin to cover it.

She cleared her throat, "And the other thing?"

"I came to get you. If you're going to be aiding me in the selection of my future bride, you need to understand me. And in order to do that, you need to understand my country."

"I've done plenty of research on Kyonos and…"

"No. You need to see my country. As I see it."

She really didn't relish the idea of spending more time with him. Because it wasn't really her practice to buddy up to a client, though, knowing them was essential. But mostly because, between yesterday and today, the strange fluttery feeling in her stomach hadn't gone away. The one that seemed to be caused by Stavros's presence.

"Are you offering me a tour?" She should say no. Say she had paperwork. Something.

"Something like that."

"All right." She wasn't quite sure how the agreement slipped out, but it had.

Well, it was best to agree with the one who was signing one's very large check when all was said and done with the marriage business. Yes. Yes, it was the done thing. So she really had no choice but to spend all day in his presence. No choice at all.

"Great. Do you need to get anything?"

"I was ready to go and have some lunch, so I think I'm all set." Her cherry-red pumps weren't the best choice for walking, but she'd packed some black ballet flats in her bag for emergencies. And anyway, they were amazing shoes and worth a little discomfort.

His eyes swept her up and down, a lift in his brow.

"What?" she asked.

"Nothing."

"What?" she repeated.

He turned and started walking down the hall and she clacked after him. "Why did you look at me like that?" she asked.

"Do you always dress like this?"

She looked down at her dress. White with black polka dots, a red, patent leather belt at the waist. It was one of her favorites, especially with the shoes and her bright red bag. "Like what?"

"Like you just stepped off the set of a black-and-white film."

"Oh. Yes. I like vintage. It's a hobby of mine." One her new financial injection allowed her to indulge in in a very serious way. Her bed might be empty, but her closet was full.

"How do clothes become a…hobby?"

"Because you can't just buy clothes like this. Well, you can, but they're reproductions. Which is fine, and I have my share, but to actually get a hold of real vintage stuff is like a game sometimes. I haunt online auctions, charity shops, yard sales. Then there's having them altered."

"Sounds like a lot of trouble for secondhand clothes."

"Possibly fourth- or fifthhand clothes," she said cheerfully. "But I love the history of it. Plus, they just don't make dresses like this anymore."

"No, indeed they don't."

She gritted her teeth. "I don't care if you don't like them. I do."

"I didn't say I didn't."

"Oh, the implication was all there."

He paused, then looked hard at her, his expression scrutinizing. "You know I'm royalty, yes?"

She nodded once. "Yes."

"And yet you still speak to me like this?"

She frowned, a slow trickle of horror filtering through her stomach. She wasn't backing down now, though— pride prevented it. "Sorry, my mouth gets away from me. Sometimes I need someone to restrain me."

He chuckled. "Ms. Carter, you have no idea how interesting that sounds."

Oh, but she did. Especially with the wicked grin crossing his lips. And it had been a very, very long time since she'd been with a man.

Longer since she'd missed it. Longer still since she'd enjoyed it.

"Jessica," she said, her dry throat keeping her from speaking in a voice that transcended a croak. "Just call me Jessica." Because for some reason when he called her Ms. Carter in that sexy, sinful voice of his, that Greek accent adding an irresistible flavor, she pictured him calling her that in bed. And that was just naughty. Naughty and completely out of the blue.

She wasn't interested in sex. Not the responsibility of it, not the repercussions of it. And not the pain that resulted from it.

"Jessica," he said, slowly, like he was tasting it.

Well, that didn't help, either.

"Prince Stavros?"

"Stavros. Please."

Her heart pattered, a sort of irregular beat, like it had tripped. "I don't assume you're in the habit of asking commoners to call you by your first name?"

He shrugged. "Titles are fine. In many regards, they are necessary as they establish one's place in society. I like them for negotiation, for the media. I don't really like them in conversation."

"All right then," she said, "Stavros." She put a lot of effort into the name, taking her time to savor the syllables, as he'd done to hers. She saw a flicker of heat in his dark eyes and fought to ignore an answering flame that ignited in her stomach.

"We'll start here," he said, indicating the halls of the hotel as he began to walk ahead. "This hotel, and many others like it, have been essential to my country. After the death of my mother, my father started neglecting the tourism industry. He neglected a great many things. I was fourteen at the time. My brother, the heir to the throne, was sixteen. He left a few years after that. It became clear that Xander was gone, and that we could not count on him to see to his duties." Stavros didn't bother to hide the hint of bitterness in his voice. "That started rumors of civil unrest. And of course tourists don't want to be somewhere that could possibly be dangerous. As soon as I was able I did what I could to start a revival of the tourism industry. I went abroad for college, established contacts. I studied business, hospitality, economics. Whatever I thought might be helpful in getting my country back to where it needed to be."

"You turned Kyonos into a business."

"Essentially. But not for my own gain. For the gain of my people."

"True," she said, "but by all accounts you have gained quite a bit."

"I have. I won't lie. My own bank account is healthy, in part due to the fact that, at this point, the interest it's collecting on a yearly basis is more than most people will see in a lifetime." He turned to look at her. "Do you need my estimated net worth for your records so you can pass it on to the women you're considering for me?"

"What? Oh, no. I think they'll feel secure enough in your…assets. I doubt they'll need anything so crass as actual net worth. A ballpark figure will do."

"You're very honest."

"Yes, well." She took in a deep breath and tried to ignore the tightening in her stomach. "Hiding from reality doesn't fix anything."

"No. It doesn't," he said.

She could tell, from the icy tone in his voice, the depth to each word, that he was speaking from experience. Just like her.

Interesting that she could fly halfway across the world and meet a prince who seemed to have more common ground with her than anyone in her real life did.

She had friends, at least, the ones Gil hadn't gotten custody of after the divorce. But they were still married. They had children.

A hollow ache filled the empty space where her womb had been. The same one that had plagued her so many times before. When she saw babies. Small children on swings.

Women wiping chocolate stains off of their blouses. And sometimes, it happened for no reason at all. Like now.

"No, reality's one bitch that's pretty hard to ignore," she said.

He chuckled, dark and without humor. "A very true statement. That's why being proactive is important. Sometimes you get problems you didn't make or ask for, but hiding doesn't fix them."

They stopped in front of an elevator and Stavros pushed the button. The gold doors slid open and they stepped inside. The trip down to the lobby was quick, and they breezed through the opulent room quickly, making their way to the front.

There was a limousine waiting for them, black and shiny. Formal. It didn't fit with what she'd seen of Stavros so far. He didn't seem like the type of man who would choose to ride in something so traditional.

He seemed to lurk around the edges of traditional, doing everything a man of his station must do, while keeping one toe firmly over the line of disreputable. It ought to make him obnoxious. It ought to make him less attractive. It didn't.

He opened the door for her and they both slid inside. She sighed, grateful for the air-conditioning. Kyonos was beautiful, but if the breeze from the sea wasn't moving inland it could be hotter than blazes for a girl from North Dakota.

As soon as they settled in and the limo was on the road, she turned to him. "So, why a limo?"

"It's how things are done," he said. He pushed on a panel and it popped open, revealing two bottles of beer on ice. "More or less."

She laughed and held her hand out. "You're about fifteen degrees off unexpected, aren't you?"

He chuckled and handed her a bottle. "Am I?"

"Yes. Hiring a matchmaker to find you a wife and drinking beer in a limo. I'd say you're not exactly what people expect in a prince."

"There are protocols that must be observed, responsibilities that must handled. But there are other things that have a bit more leeway."

"And you take it."

He shrugged. "You have to take hold to the pleasures in life, right?"

"If by pleasures, you mean shoes, then yes."

He laughed and took a bottle opener from a hook on the door and extended his hand, popping the top on the bottle for her. "A true gentleman," she said. "And clearly a professional. Get a lot of practice in college?"

"Like most people."

"Where did you go to school?"

"I did two years in the U.K., two in the U.S."

She nodded. "You would be best suited to a woman who's well traveled, who understands a variety of cultures. Probably someone multilingual."

"Because I'm clearly so cultured?" he asked, raising his bottle. He relaxed his posture, his arm over draped over the back of his seat. There was something so inviting about the pose. The perfect spot for a partner to sit and snuggle against him...

She blinked. "Well, yes, you have to be able to communicate with your spouse. Connect with them on a cerebral level."

"Most of the women I've dated have only connected with me on one level, but it's a level I've found to be very important." The suggestive tone of his voice left no doubt as to just what level he was referring to.

She cleared her throat and tried to banish the heat in her cheeks. For heaven's sake. Talking about sex was nor-

mal in her job. It was part of the job, because it was part of
relationships. It never made her…blush. She was actually
blushing. Really and truly. Like a schoolgirl. Ridiculous.

After enough invasive doctor visits for three lifetimes
she thought she'd lost the ability to do that years ago.

"And I consider that important, too," she said, knowing
she sounded stiff and a little bit prudish, and she absolutely
wasn't either thing, so she had no idea why. "But you will
be expected to see each other outside of the bedroom."

"Of course," he said. "But as I said, I have my priorities.
Even sexual attraction takes a backseat to a spotless reputation and the ability to produce heirs."

"Right. And how do we establish for certain if she can…
produce heirs?"

"Most women can, I assume." He said it with such throw-
away carelessness. As though the idea of a woman not being
able to have children was almost ridiculous.

She pursed her lips. "And some can't." Why did the subject always make her feel sick? Why did it always make her
feel like a failure?

Well, discussing the ability to bear children as an essential trait of a queen, a wife, was never going to be easy,
no matter how much peace she imagined she'd made with
her lot in life.

"As we get closer to choosing someone, we'll have to
undergo a medical screening."

"You'll be required to do the same," she said.

"Will I?"

"Well, yes, I'm not allowing any of the women I might
find for you to sleep with you until I establish that you have
a clean bill of health."

"You need me to get tested for STDs?"

"Yes. I do. You're planning on having children with the

woman who marries you, which means unprotected sex. And that means a risk to the health of your wife."

"I assume the women will be undergoing the same tests?"

"All of the women who come to me, all of the women and men in my file, are required to submit those test results to me."

"As it happens, I just got tested. Clean. You can have the results if you like."

"I would like them. And I assume you won't be taking on any more sexual partners while we undergo this process?" She felt her cheeks heating again. The topic of sex and Stavros, in the close proximity of the limo, was just a bit too much.

His eyes flickered over her, leaving heat behind. "Naturally not," he said, the words coming slowly. Unconvincingly. "And I haven't had one in quite a while."

"Good. Also, you will not sleep with the women I introduce to you. They know the rules. I don't allow sex between my clients."

"You don't?" he asked, an incredulous laugh in his voice.

"Not until a match is set and I'm not longer involved. Clearly, the relationship can still dissolve, but I'm not a pimp. I'm not prostituting anyone, and I'm not allowing them to prostitute themselves. This is about creating a relationship, a real lasting relationship, not about helping people hook up casually."

"I suppose, running it as a business, you would have to be careful of that," he said.

"Very. When I was starting the business I was really excited, and then I realized what it could quickly turn into if I didn't lay the rules out. Men...well, and women...could use it to find suitable people to...use. And that's not what I want."

"So, you're not a big one for romance, and yet, this is what you choose to do for a living? Why is that?"

She looked out the window, at the crystalline sea and white sand blurring into a wash of color. "It was what I was doing anyway, though not on this level. But after…when I made some changes in life and started my own business, I knew that somehow…I knew relationships could work."

"So you went looking for the formula."

"Yes. And I don't have the only method, though mine has proven highly successful, but I think the way I go about it works. It also helps to have a disinterested party involved who doesn't have their heart in it. That's me. I help people think things through rationally. I set rules so that physical lust doesn't cloud everything else, doesn't create a false euphoria."

"And why don't you apply it to yourself?"

She laughed. "Because. First of all, I can't be my own disinterested party. Second, I don't have the energy or the desire to do it again. I had one big white wedding and I do not intend to do it again."

"Yet you watch other people do it. Get married, I mean."

"Yes. But I find that it…helps. It's restored my faith in humanity a little bit."

The corner of his lip lifted in a sneer. "Was your ex that bad?"

She shook her head slowly. "Sometimes people change, and they change together. Sometimes one person changes. And the other person can't handle it."

It had been her. She'd changed. Her body had changed. And it had altered everything the marriage was built on. Their dreams for the future. It had been too much.

"You're selling the institution so well," he said dryly. He punched the intercom button on the limo divider. "Stop us at Gio's." He let up on the button.

"I'm not trying to sell you the institution. You *have* to get married."

"True."

"And most people who come to me want marriage, or need it for some reason. My personal story, just one of a sad, all too common statistic, will hardly dissuade them. And I'll admit, most of them don't bother to ask about my personal life."

"I find that hard to believe," he said, as the limo slowed and turned onto a narrow road that wound up a hillside.

"Do you?"

"You're interesting. Your clothes for example—interesting. The things that come out of your mouth, also interesting. You beg to have questions asked of you."

"You would be in the minority in that opinion."

"Again, I find it hard to believe."

"I'm very boring. I have a house in North Dakota. I grew up there. Obviously, I don't work with many billionaires, royalty or socialites in North Dakota. I do a lot of work online, and I travel a lot. I'd say my house is empty at least eight months out of the year. I live alone. Can't have a cat because…well, the traveling. So that's me."

"You skipped a lot."

"Did I?"

He leaned in, his head turned to the side. Sort of like how a man looked right before he kissed a woman. If she could even remember back that far, to when she'd experienced anything close to it. "You didn't tell me why you're so prickly."

She leaned in a fraction. "And I don't intend to. Stop flirting with me."

"Am I flirting with you?"

"I think so." If he wasn't that was just too horrifying.

"I can't help it. You're beautiful."

She swallowed. "Look, I know women melt at your feet and all, but I have a job to do, so best you leave me unmelted, okay?"

He leaned back, his lips curving into a smile. "But you're in danger of melting."

She was afraid she might be. "No. Sorry."

He chuckled and settled back in his seat.

The limo stopped in front of a small, whitewashed building that was set into the side of a mountain. The building was tiny, but the deck was expansive, filled with round tables, most occupied by diners. The tables overlooked the beach, with strings of white lights running overhead.

"Ready?" he asked.

She nodded and put her beer in a cupholder. He got out of the car before her and opened her door. "Isn't your driver supposed to do that?" she asked.

He shook his head. "I always open the door when I accompany a woman."

"Another one for your file," she said.

"I'm not sure whether I'm nervous or aroused at the talk of this file. Makes me feel like I'm in trouble, which leads to the same conflicting feelings."

Heat flooded her cheeks, her stomach. "That's inappropriate."

"You're the only one who can make jokes?"

"No…but I didn't make any that were that bad."

"BA? Bedroom Activities?"

"That was serious!" she sputtered as they walked into the restaurant.

"Prince Stavros." A maître d' walked to the door quickly, her willingness to serve the prince obvious, as was the blush staining her cheeks. "I wasn't aware you were coming today."

He winked. "I'm being spontaneous."

"Of course," the woman said. "Your usual table is available. Shall I bring you your usual dinner? For…two?"

Jessica opened her mouth to correct the woman's assumption, but Stavros cut her off.

"That will do nicely. I can show us to my table."

He led the way through the indoor dining area, and heads turned as they passed. Stavros had a sort of effortless charisma that poured from him, touching everyone who saw him. She could imagine, so easily, the kind of woman he would need.

One who could match his ease. His strength. Someone to create the perfect image for Kyonos. Someone to carry on the bloodline and keep it strong.

She swallowed a strange, unexpected lump in her throat.

They exited the dining room through two glass doors that led out to the deck. There were only a few scattered tables out there, each partly shrouded by draping fabric hung from a wooden frame built over the porch.

Stavros held her chair out for her and she sat, looking out at the view of the ocean, because it was much safer than looking at the man sitting across from her. She wasn't sure why. She had meetings with male clients, and very often they were lunch or dinner meetings, in very nice restaurants.

But being with them didn't evoke this same strange fauxdate feel that being with Stavros did. It was that darned attraction.

She opened her purse and pulled out her iPad. "So, I know we were going to talk about specific women to have come to your sister's wedding."

"Were we? Now?" He curled his hands into fists on the table, his knuckles turning white. It was hard for her to look away from his hands, from the obvious strain. His face remained passive, easy, but his manner betrayed him.

"Well, no, but I wasn't expecting to see you until tomorrow, so…no. But we can talk about it now. I've had a chance to think about what you've told me and I've been through my system. I also called two of the three women I'm thinking of and if you're agreeable to them, they're willing to come for consideration."

"This is like an old-fashioned marriage mart."

"Well, these sorts of marriages are," she said. Strangely, she felt like comforting him. She didn't know why. "Granted, you're the first actual prince I've worked with. But I've dealt with lesser royals. Billionaires with an interest in preserving their fortunes. Women with family money who wanted an alliance with businessmen who could help them make the most of their assets. People have all kinds of reasons for choosing to go about things this way. Some of these women have money, but no title, while others have a title but are…low on funds."

"Ah. A title, but no money and a need for a husband with wealth."

"Some of them. Though this one…" She pulled up a picture of a smiling blonde. "Victoria Calder. She's English, from a very well-to-do family. She's not titled but she's wealthy. She's been to the best schools. She has her own money and she donates a lot of it to charities. As far as my research has taken me, and it took me to the far and seedy recesses of the internet, her reputation is as spotless as a sacrificial lamb. So if a prominent title isn't important…"

"As long as you think she would be suitable to the position, she can be considered."

"So basically fertile and scandal-free. And able to handle public appearances with grace and poise, of course."

Stavros took the tablet from Jessica's hand and looked at the photo of the woman on the screen. She was beautiful. More than beautiful, really. He couldn't find fault with her features. A small, pert nose, pretty, well-shaped lips, rosy cheeks, pale blue eyes.

Yet she did nothing for him. She didn't stir his blood. She didn't interest him. More than that, just looking at her made his throat feel like it was tightening. The impression of a noose.

He preferred Jessica's face. Her longer nose, fuller lips, cat green eyes that tilted at the corners. And her figure… she was like a pin-up girl.

He wondered, not too briefly, if she favored old-fashioned undergarments to go with her vintage dresses. Stockings and garters.

That caused a surge of blood to pump south of his belt. She was a distraction. A temptation. A welcome one, in many ways.

"Yes." He shouldn't be allowing distraction now. He had to focus on finding his bride.

Though, Ms. Jessica Carter would make an intriguing lover. She was all soft curves and pale skin. But her eyes… they showed a fire he imagined she set free in the bedroom. She was spicy, her tongue always ready to flay the skin cleanly off the bone if necessary.

Just as she'd pronounced his commanding personality a plus in bedroom activities, he imagined her sharp mind and bold tongue would earn her points in her own BA category.

It would be so sweet. So good. And a welcome distraction from the marriage talk.

"Anyway," Jessica continued, pulling him from his fantasy, "she's one I would like to invite to your sister's wedding."

"And she's aware of just what she'll be invited for?"

Jessica nodded. "Yes. All of the women I'm working with have come to me, seeking out husbands that are suitable to their backgrounds and financial level, just the same as you."

"I see. So invariably my future wife will be after a title and wealth—" he looked at the photo of the blonde again "—just as I am."

"Fair is fair. You both know just what you're getting into. No false expectations. Not if I can help it."

"No false expectations? Then can I assume you're including a list of my faults in the file you'll be sending on to the women involved?"

"Only if they make it past a certain point in the process. Discretion," she said.

"Of course." He looked at her face, illuminated and washed gold by the afternoon sun. She was beautiful. Not due to perfection of features, or from the expertly applied makeup, though. Her features were beautiful, and her makeup was expertly done. But it was something more. Something deeper.

She was captivating. Different.

Sexy.

His stomach tightened. "And the first wave of the process begins at my sister's wedding."

"That's right. Is that okay? Or do you feel it will detract from—"

"It's fine," he interrupted. It was strange to think of Evangelina married. To think of her as a woman rather than a little girl. "My sister is in love," he said.

"That's good. Since she's getting married."

He gave her a look. "But you know that's not really how things work around here. Not necessarily."

"True."

"She was meant to marry for the good of Kyonos. She is marrying her bodyguard instead."

"Are you angry about it?" she asked, her eyes meeting his, the glittering green light in them far too perceptive.

"Not in the least. Anger is a completely unproductive

emotion." As were most emotions. He's witnessed it first-hand. He made sure he didn't have time for them.

"But that leaves only you."

He shrugged. "Doesn't matter. I can do it."

"And your brother…"

"Might as well be dead. He doesn't care for his country. He doesn't care for his family, his people. He might as well have died with our mother." The words tasted bitter on his tongue and he wished he had some ouzo to wash it out with. Bitterness wasn't helpful, either.

As if on command, a waiter appeared with a tray, laden with food and drinks, and set them down on their table. Stavros took the drink first, while Jessica picked up a stuffed grape leaf and turned it in her fingers.

He took a quick hit of the strong alcohol. "I'm happy for Eva. And her husband does bring a lot to the country in terms of assets and security. Mak is a billionaire several times over. She's hardly marrying beneath herself, even if he isn't royalty."

Beneath Stavros's casual manner, Jessica could sense his dark mood. He was very good at playing smooth, very good at coming across as the genial prince. Ready to smile for a photograph. Never caught scowling by a scandal-hungry public, who would latch onto the salacious headline declaring one grumpy expression proof of some sort of national crisis.

And yet, she could feel that something wasn't right. That there was something beneath it.

He was the last man standing. The anchor. How could he not feel it? Of course he would. His sister had abandoned her duty for love, his brother had abandoned it for selfish, personal pleasure. It was only Stavros now.

She felt added pressure. She couldn't imagine that he didn't.

"Well, we'll find you a royal bride who suits the needs of Kyonos, and you, perfectly," she said, injecting a confidence and enthusiasm into her voice she wasn't sure she felt.

A half smile curved his lips, a shaft of sunlight hitting his face, that single moment displaying the breathtaking quality he possessed to its very best effect.

She certainly felt as if her breath had been taken. Ripped straight from her lungs. Why did he have to be so hot? More to the point, why did she have to suddenly care how hot he was?

She looked back down at her iPad, at the picture of Victoria Calder. And for the first time ever, she felt her stomach curl in with jealousy in connection with a client.

It was the first and last time it would happen. She couldn't afford it. Not financially, and most especially not emotionally.

She'd already had everything drained from her in that department. She would never put herself through it again.

CHAPTER THREE

JESSICA tried not to die of despair as she watched one of her favorite potential brides, Dominique Lanphier, standing by the buffet table looking like a deer in the headlights. She was sort of fidgeting, looking as if she was ready to dart away from the table at a moment's notice and grab Stavros from Corinthia, the petite redhead he was currently engaging in approved conversation with.

This wasn't her best idea. She could see that now. It was just a pity she was realizing it far too late to change anything. Her prospective brides, normally so well-behaved, were a bit giddy over the chance to compete for a prince and all of the good manners that had been bred into them seemed to have been knocked from their heads the moment they'd entered the palace.

Jessica was sweating. Actually sweating. And trying not to look like anything more than a guest. Which, in the grand ballroom, filled to maximum capacity with nearly one thousand people, shouldn't be too hard.

Victoria, her best hope for Stavros, had been unavailable for the wedding, which had forced her to bring in Dominique as a last-minute replacement. Something she was bitterly regretting.

"Just stay there," she whispered, begging Dominique to

go with the program, hoping the other woman would absorb the command from across the room.

It just seemed to be getting hotter in the ballroom now, and she could swear the sweetheart neckline of her flirty cocktail dress was about to slip and go from sexy to burlesque. And that would draw far more attention to herself than she wanted.

She gripped the sides of the bodice and tugged at it slightly. Feeling, for a moment, every inch the unsophisticated North Dakota girl she was on the inside. Feeling her persona start to slip.

No. You are not unsophisticated. You are a businesswoman. You are in a castle. Own your inner princess!

Yes. Inner princess. She was sure she had one of those.

She took a deep breath and felt a bit of her anxiety ease as Stavros checked his watch and disengaged Corinthia right on time. Any longer and there would be speculation. And now, he would go to the buffet and it would be Dominique's turn.

This sort of brief, public meeting, was, in her experience, the perfect way to open. To see people interact in a social situation, to prevent a feeling of enhanced intimacy too quickly.

She had to remind herself of all the reasons it was a good idea now, since she was on the verge of panicking and eating her weight in wedding cake to try and stave off the anxiety. This was what she did. This was her one area of confidence, of expertise. And watching it go very much not according to plan was crazy-making.

The transition went smoothly and she watched Stavros engage Dominique in conversation. So casual it could have been accidental. He was good.

She watched as he leaned in, his body language indicating interest, the smile on his face warm. Genuine. Her throat tightened a bit, and cut off the flow of air entirely when he brushed Dominique's arm with his hand.

Such a brief touch. And yet, it spoke of attraction.

He hadn't touched her. Not more than a handshake. And that brief touch at the restaurant. She shouldn't have a list of the times his skin had made contact with hers. It shouldn't matter that he was touching someone else.

It shouldn't matter. It didn't. She was here to try and match him with one of these women. This choking jealousy had no place in it. Jealousy was an awful emotion. Consuming. It brought out the worst in people, in her particularly.

When she'd found out Gil was getting married again. When she'd found out his wife was pregnant.

A prickle of shame spread from her scalp through her body.

She shouldn't be jealous of Gil's wife. Of her ability to give birth. It was small and petty. If he couldn't find happiness with her, he should be free to find it with someone else.

The thing that sucked was that he'd found the happiness she'd wanted. He'd been able to move on and get all of the hopes and dreams they'd built their marriage on. He'd been able to leave her.

She couldn't leave herself.

Her body was her body. Her limitations wouldn't change with a new partner. Moving on for her meant something very different than it had for her ex. Moving on meant rebuilding, finding new dreams. She was happy. She had a successful business. She was financially solvent and she was matchmaking for a prince, for heaven's sake.

A prince she should have no feelings for at all. And certainly not any kind of longing type feelings.

Crazy was what it was. Crazy.

Stavros's time with Dominique closed and he made a

polite exit, not lingering for a moment longer. Which suggested he couldn't have gotten too lost in her eyes or anything.

She should not feel satisfied by that.

She felt her stomach free-fall when Stavros changed course suddenly and started walking toward her. His movements easy, his manner approachable. And several people did approach him. He managed to make everyone feel he'd expended attention on them without actually taking much time, barely halting his movement. Every so often, his dark eyes would land on her, leaving her in no doubt that she was his destination.

And, well, he was a prince, and he was a client. So she wasn't going to dodge him.

She stood, rooted to the spot, until Stavros stopped in front of her. "I'd love a word with you in private," he said.

She looked around. "As long as we don't draw attention. I'm hardly the most recognizable face in the world but…"

"Come," he said. Taking her hand and striding toward the ballroom's exit, his gait much more purposeful than it had been a moment ago.

She snagged a glass of champagne off of a passing waiter's tray and followed him out. "Wait. I'm in heels," she said, taking quick, tottering steps out into the corridor. She flashed a passing guest a smile and tried to match Stavros's pace. "Hey, Tarzan. Me not Jane. You no drag me out by the hair."

He ignored her, continuing to walk down the hall until he came to an ornate wood door that she recognized as the entrance to his office. She never would have found it by herself. Not in the maze of halls the Kyonosian palace boasted. He released her hand, entered in a code and pushed the door open. "Come in," he said.

She shot him a look and walked into the room, wiping

her hand on the tulle skirt of her gown, trying to get rid of the heated feeling that his touch had left behind. She crossed her arms beneath her breasts, pushed her cleavage up into prominence, then thought better of it when she realized just how prominent it was.

She put her hands on her hips. "What's up?"

"None of them were acceptable," he said.

"None?"

"No."

"But…but…" she sputtered. "What about Dominique? You touched her arm."

He shrugged. "I know how to flirt."

"Well, yeah, I know, I yelled at you for it a while back. But why flirt if you aren't going to follow up?"

He frowned. "Did you just imply that I am a…tease?"

"Yeah. A marriage tease. Why feign interest if you don't feel any?"

"I'm not seeking to hurt anyone's feelings," he said dryly. "I could hardly stand there and act bored. And anyway, that begs the question why you would send me such dull women."

"Dull? Dominique is a beauty queen, Corinthia is a doctor, for heaven's sake, and Samantha…"

"Had the most annoying laugh."

"All right. Yes, her laugh is kind of annoying. But it's sort of endearing."

"No. It's not."

"You're being unkind."

"Maybe. But I don't have forever to find a wife, and you were supposed to be the best."

"I am," she said. "I can find you a wife. Anyway, I didn't think your personal preferences came into it."

"I don't want to be…irritated into an early grave by a woman who laughs at all my jokes, even when they aren't funny, or by one who can't seem to make conversation about anything other than the weather."

"That's called small talk. It's how people get to know each other," she said.

"Boring." He waved a hand as if dismissing the concept. "Talk about world events. Something other than the 'balmy evening.'"

"So marriage is more to you than you said. Glad to hear it."

"I am not glad that you presented me with unacceptable candidates. This is not about…meaning, or emotions. This is about… I have to be able to stand the woman I marry."

"You really are being ridiculous. They weren't unacceptable. What's the problem? You didn't find them attractive?"

"They were attractive. But I was not attracted *to* any of them."

"You say that like it's my fault."

"It is," he said, whirling around to face her. His dark gaze slid down to her breasts and her own followed.

She looked back up at him. "Elaborate," she said, teeth gritted.

"You expect that you can show up in that dress, and I can focus on other women?"

"What's wrong with my dress?" She gripped the full, tulle skirt reflexively.

"Other than the fact that you're showing off much more of your breasts than any straight man could be expected to ignore? It also shows your legs. This was a formal wedding. Every other woman, including the ones I was speaking to, had on long gowns. You…you…"

"This dress comes to my knees. And I didn't realize you were a fourteen-year-old boy masquerading as a prince."

The insult rolled off her tongue, because what he was saying felt far too good. She wanted to turn it over in her mind, to savor it. To pretend that it was for her and that it mattered. To bask in being seen as pretty instead of broken.

The thought made her so annoyed with herself she wanted to scream.

He took a step toward her, and she sucked in a breath, holding her ground. He leaned in, his face close to hers, dark eyes intense. "I can assure you, I am not a boy."

She swallowed, fought the urge to put her hand on his cheek and see if the faint, dark shadow there was rough yet. "I believe it."

"Then do not test me." His eyes held hers, her heart threatening to beat clean through her chest. She pulled away, her breathing shallow.

Stavros turned away from her. She stood in the middle of his office as he paced, each movement languid and deadly. Her heart was pounding, her body shaking. She'd known that he couldn't possibly be so easy, so relaxed. Beneath that charm lurked the soul of a predator. The deadliest sort, because he knew how to portray an air of complete and utter harmlessness.

Stavros Drakos was anything but harmless. How had she not seen it? How had she assumed he was all flirtation and ease?

And had he…had he really just confessed to finding her cleavage distracting? She looked down again and felt a small flush of pride creep into her cheeks. It had been a long time since she'd been able to feel anything overly positive in connection with her body.

It was nice to have a man look at her and simply see a woman.

It might be a facade, a trick, but it didn't really matter. Stavros would never have to get closer. Would never have to know the truth, or deal with the fallout of it.

But that didn't mean she wouldn't enjoy it. Just for a moment.

"I wasn't intending to," she said.

He stopped moving. "You cannot be ignorant of how you look. You outshone the bride."

She couldn't believe that. Not seriously. Princess Evangelina was a great beauty. Olive skin, long dark hair and a slender figure. In her wedding gown, she was unsurpassable. Plus, the princess was only twenty-one. She didn't have the years Jessica had on her body. Didn't have the scars.

"I doubt that," she said.

"My eyes were on you most of the time."

Heat rushed up her neck and into her face, then spread down over her breasts. "We should not be having this conversation."

"We should. Because if you're going to be present at all of my meetings with potential fiancées, you need to dress more suitably."

"I will dress how I please, Prince Stavros," she said, feeling her hackles rise. She really didn't do backed into a corner well, and, at the moment, she felt backed into a corner.

Stavros felt his pulse pounding in his neck, all of his blood rushing south of his belt. He'd been fighting to urge to go and pull Jessica into his arms and kiss her lips, kiss the swells of her breasts where they rose up over that gown. That ridiculous gown that made her look like every man's midnight fantasy.

He'd tried to focus on the women, the bridal candidates. But they'd seemed…insipid. Young. They hadn't interested him. They certainly hadn't stirred his body. Not in the way Jessica did. And that was not part of tonight's plan.

But when she'd walked into the ballroom tonight, it was as though a switch had flipped inside of him.

Lust had ignited in him like fire, the need to see her curves, those gorgeous curves, without a dress covering them. It made him want to press her against the wall and push all that frilly netting aside. To make her scream with the kind of desire that seemed to be actively trying to eat him alive every time she was around.

He was better than this. He mastered his desires. He directed them where he wanted, when he wanted to express them.

"Has anyone ever told you that you are very stubborn?" he growled.

"It's probably been said to me as many times as it's been said to you. Actually, I imagine I've heard it more, since people probably don't stand up to you very often."

That much was true. But she stood up to him, and she did it without compunction. Yes, she had a reputation for being this bullheaded, but he hadn't expected she would truly treat him in the same way she did every other client.

His expectation had been wrong.

"Fair enough then," he said. "But I do expect you to do as I ask."

"Then I expect you might find yourself disappointed."

"You are supposed to be working for me," he said, not sure where this urge to push her was coming from. But that was what he was doing. Pushing her. Daring her.

"If that's how you feel, you can hunt for your own wife. But we both know you don't want that."

"I'm not sure I want this." The closest he'd ever come to voicing the truth to anyone.

"But you will." She was so certain. And she was right. Emotion had no place in this. It had no place in him.

He crossed his arms. "You have other candidates?"

"You still haven't met Victoria. And there are others."

She shifted and so did her cleavage. A flame licked at his body, igniting desire. Arousal.

"We can discuss it further later. Shall we go back to the wedding?"

"Yes."

She pursed her lips and raised an eyebrow. "And will you be civilized?"

A loaded question, and one he was certain applied to more than just tonight. An answer he wasn't certain of. "I suppose you'll have to take your chances. Are you willing to do that?"

He extended his arm and she didn't move for a beat. Then she took a step to him and looped her arm through his. "You don't worry me too much, Stavros."

He felt a kick in his gut, a purely masculine part of himself taking her words as a challenge. He stopped, turning to face her. Her green eyes widened, lips parting.

"You trust me?" he asked, his heart thundering.

Her eyes drifted to his mouth before raising up to meet his. "Yes."

"Ah, but, Ms. Carter, I'm not certain I trust myself. You certainly shouldn't be putting any trust in me."

It was nothing. Just a little lust. Nothing deeper than any other attraction he'd felt. It was a direct result of his long bout of celibacy. He would meet more women. Find the one he was supposed to marry, and then he could focus all of his desire on her.

But *Theos* help him if he could think of marriage without feeling like he was choking. The attraction to Jessica at least made him feel…well, he could breathe.

"I'm going to be in Greece for the next few weeks and I want you to arrange my meetings with prospective brides there. I have business to attend to." Flexible business, but he needed to get out of Kyonos. Now.

Jessica blinked. "I...I can do that. But I have other clients and I..."

"Not right now you don't. I need you to put everything else on hold. I need you with me, organizing meetings and whatever else I might need so we can simply get this done."

"What will people think if we just up and go to Greece the day after your sister's wedding?"

"Perhaps that we're embarking on a wild affair?" The idea made his body harden. The idea certainly had merit. Merit he might have to seriously consider. Just the idea of lowering her dress, revealing those luscious breasts...

She laughed. "Oh, I doubt that. More than likely they'll wonder if you're looking for a Greek wife."

"I'm not opposed." Not any more opposed than he was to the whole idea.

"I guess it doesn't matter if we operate from Greece or Kyonos."

"Good. Then we'll leave for Greece first thing tomorrow." He opened his office door and held it for her. Tomorrow he would get out of Kyonos, get his head on straight.

For now, he was determined to go back to the reception and enjoy the happiest day of his sister's life.

CHAPTER FOUR

WHAT did one wear on a private jet headed to Greece? With a prince as cabin-mate. That last part was important.

That had been the first question in her mind that morning, and it was still plaguing her even as she boarded the private jet, decked out in a yellow halter-top sundress and a matching wide-brimmed hat.

Because seriously, dwelling on anything more important than that might make her head explode. And she didn't want to risk it. Aside from the fact that the interior was far too swanky to chance getting brain matter on it, she had too much work to do and she couldn't function without said organ.

Stavros was already on the plane, lounging in one of the spacious leather seats, hands behind his head. It was like his go-to mess-with-her-composure position. Exposed bulge at the apex of his thighs? Check. Hard, muscular chest on display? Check. Washboard abs on show? Double check.

He was going to drive her insane.

And what would you do about it? Even if you could act on your attraction to him?

Nothing. The answer was an absolutely nothing, because while attraction, flirtation and sexual desire were all fine and fun, going any further than that would only result in pain. Emotional pain if not physical pain.

Probably both.

"Good morning," she said.

He stood, his posture straight as she moved into the cabin and sat down in a chair that was positioned as far from his as was polite. He didn't sit until she had settled herself.

"I like that," she said. "Very chivalrous."

"Etiquette is, of course, important for a prince to learn," he said, humor lacing his tone.

"It's a dying art form these days, trust me. With both men and women."

"I imagine you would have a greater insight into that than most." He buckled his seat belt and she followed suit as the plane readied for take-off.

"Probably. I deal with people on a pretty regular basis. And I have to ask a lot of…intimate questions. But people also tend to be on their best behavior when they're looking for a relationship, or just beginning one. So I see a lot of the polished squeaky clean veneer, too."

He nodded. "I suppose I do, too."

"I'll bet not many people let loose in front of royalty."

"You don't seem that bothered by my position."

The plane started down the runway and a bubble of excitement burst in her stomach. It had taken a while, but she liked flying now. She liked how free it made her feel. If she wasn't happy where she was, she could hop a plane and escape for a while.

It was liberating; providing some of the few real moments of freedom she felt. It was superhuman to fly, and it took her mind off the fact that she really was just human. With all kinds of shortcomings.

"Well, unlike my clients, I don't see the point in hiding who I am." Lies. She absolutely hid who she was. Behind a suit of armor that was a lot tougher than she was. But what was the point of armor if you admitted you had it on?

"Really?"

"Really."

"I don't believe you," he said, his dark eyes far too perceptive for her liking.

What was he? A mind reader? "Why is that?"

"Because you have secrets. You won't tell me why you're prickly."

She bit the inside of her cheek. "I told you not to flirt with me."

"You tell me that when I start to get close to things you don't want to talk about," he said, leaning over slightly. He was still across the aisle from her, but she felt the move. Felt the increased closeness.

She shifted the opposite direction. "Having secrets is normal. I imagine you have them."

"Not one. Every detail of my life is published in the archives and kept in my father's office. My more public exploits are in the news, in tabloids, on royalty stalker websites."

"So that's it then, you're an open book?"

"I have nothing to hide. More to the point, I can't have anything to hide. If I did, it would be put out in the public eye. I'm a public commodity," he ground out, a bitterness tingeing his words. "I exercise discretion in certain areas of my life, naturally. I don't announce when I take a lover, for example, though all tabloids will imply it. You, on the other hand—you have secrets."

"You think you have me figured out?"

A smile curved his lips. Wicked. Dangerous. "No. Not at all."

"Well, that's good. I would hate to be thought of as predictable."

"You aren't predictable in the least. Not down to what you'll wear on a given day," he said, his eyes on her hat.

"That makes you interesting. It makes me wonder." His eyes met hers and she felt a jolt in her system. "It makes me want to discover all of your secrets."

His made goose bumps break out on her arms. Low and husky, with the kind of accent usually only found in her late-night fantasies. And his eyes…dark and rich, like chocolate. A bitter, intense sort of chocolate.

Her favorite.

She swallowed and tried to slow the beating of her heart. "I live in North Dakota when I'm not traveling, as you already know. I don't own pets. I like clothes. And I do a really dorky celebration dance when I beat my own high scores on computer games." She tried to smile. "Open book."

"I would like to see the dance. But I also don't believe you."

"I do the dance. But I won't do it for you."

"No, I believe you do it." His eyes locked with hers, the perception in them, the sudden seriousness, unnerving her. "I just don't believe you're an open book."

"And I can't believe you care. You don't have time to worry about me or my idiosyncrasies, Prince Stavros, you have a wife to find."

"No, *you* have a wife to find. Deliver her to me when you do."

She laughed, trying to dispel the tension. "That's the plan. Although, I have to do a bit more than deliver. You have to agree with my selection."

"I admit I liked the look of…Victoria, was that her name?"

"Um…yes." She bent down and picked her purse up, hunting for her iPad.

"It's fine. You don't need to get her picture out. I remember."

Was that jealousy? That hot, burning sensation in her stomach? Yes. It very likely was. Ridiculous. She wanted him to like Victoria. Victoria was a fabulous candidate. "Victoria would probably like to meet you here in Greece. She was disappointed that work conflicted with the wedding."

"What happened to your speed-dating idea?"

"I'll get a couple of other girls out as well, just to keep the pressure off. But if I—and by I, I mean you—fly them to Greece they deserve more than fifteen minutes of your time."

"Agreed."

"When will you have time?" She looked back down at her bag.

"Get it out if you have to," he said, his tone grudging.

She leaned down and took her tablet out of her purse and opened the flap on the cover. She opened up the calendar and sat poised with her finger at the ready.

"In the evenings. Dinner dates will do."

She typed in a quick note. "Would you like to see photographs of the other women I'll be asking?"

"Not especially."

She let out an exasperated breath. "If I don't show them to you, you'll only accuse me of picking women who aren't attractive again."

"You can't hear a laugh in a picture. And that laugh was unforgivable."

The look she shot him would have been fatal to a lesser man. "You really are being unkind about the laugh."

"She sounded like a nervous mouse. And she even lifted her hands up and wiggled her fingers. Like she was waiting for cheese."

Jessica tried, and failed to suppress a laugh. "That... you...well."

"I'm right."

"You're mean!"

"I'm not mean. It's one of those things that would eat at me. Day in and day out until one day I divorced her over her laugh and that would be a much bigger unkindness than just not pursuing things from the get go."

She expelled a breath. "Fine. I won't push the laugh issue again. You're entitled to your judgmental opinion."

"I am," he said, lowering his hands so that they were gripping the armrests on his chair. He had such big hands. Very big. Oh…dear. What was her problem?

She lowered her head and focused on her computer. "Anyway, I was thinking of asking Cherry Carlisle and Amy Sutton over." She looked at Stavros, who was affecting a bored expression and staring out the window. "Cherry is a brunette. Amy is a redhead. And Victoria's a blonde." He kept his gaze off of her. "It's actually pretty good because it's like the setup to your own, personal joke. A blonde, a brunette and a redhead go to Greece."

He looked at her, the corners of his mouth tipped upward. "To marry the prince. You really are selling this well."

"I try. Once we land in Greece I'll coordinate with them and hopefully we can get them there ASAP."

"You like speaking in acronyms, don't you?"

She shrugged. "It's faster."

"Speaking of, by my very fast math, you'll be involving six women in this so far. And while I'm under no illusion that we'll keep the press out of this entirely, I wonder what might happen if one of them ends up feeling…jilted."

"Oh, they've signed a gag order."

"A gag order?"

"I take my business very seriously and yes, this is tabloid bait. Serious, serious tabloid bait. And I have no interest in feeding you, or me, to the wolves. So I've taken pretty big precautions."

He leaned forward, his interest obviously piqued now. "And what are the consequences if they break the gag order?"

"Their firstborn child. All right, not quite but there are some monetary fees."

"You are quite deceptive, Ms. Carter."

"Am I?" she asked, leaning back in her chair and crossing her arms beneath her breasts.

"Yes. You seem so sunny. Soft," he said, his dark eyes settling on her breasts. "And yet…you are cynical. More so even than I am, I think. Which is really quite something."

She swallowed and angled her face away from him. She could still feel him looking at her. "Call it cynical if you like, I call it realism. Human nature is what human nature is. No matter how much someone thinks they love you, if being with you starts to conflict with their ultimate goals… well, it won't take much for them to start believing that they don't love you anymore. That's why I work to find people who have united goals and interests. Things that are concrete. Much more concrete than love. Whatever that is. I'm a realist, that's all."

"Cynic. Realist. Whatever the case, you certainly aren't soft."

She shook her head. "No. Being soft hurts too much."

She had no idea why she was telling him so much. What was inspiring her to give away any of her tightly guarded self to this man. She only knew that it was easier to talk around him than to hold it in. That was new. Strange.

She'd always found it easier to just keep it all stuffed inside. Locked behind a wall of iron, defended by her sharp wit. Easier to have an off-the-cuff, half-serious response to everything than to let someone see her true self.

And yet, with Stavros, she had shared.

So pointless and silly. Irritating even, because there was no reason for her to choose him as a confidante. No reason at all. She didn't have a confidante. She didn't need one.

So stop it, already.

"You're right about that," he said, his voice different now. Serious. Lacking that mischief that was usually present. "Emotion…it can eat you alive. Steal every good intention. Every concept of responsibility. We'll be staying in my private villa," he said, changing the subject neatly. And she was grateful.

"We? As in…the two of us?"

"What did you imagine might happen, Jessica?" he asked. Her ears pricked and her heart stuttered at the use of her first name. It felt…intimate.

"I thought maybe we'd stay in a hotel and I'd have my own room." Perhaps a floor or twelve away from his.

"I prefer not to stay in hotels, if I can help it, and you may reserve your comments on the irony of that."

She arched an eyebrow. "How did you know I had a comment ready?"

"You always have a comment ready."

"True," she agreed.

"The villa is big. You won't have to run into me at all, unless it's work-related. If you don't want to, that is."

His voice dropped a step when he said that last part, his words a husky invitation that her body was aching to respond to.

"Why…why would I want to?" she asked, her voice a bit shaky.

"You're the only one who can answer that," he said.

She knew what her answer would be. And it would be completely inappropriate. "Well. I won't. Come looking for you, that is. For anything besides work."

He nodded slowly and leaned back in his seat. "Probably a wise decision."

Probably. And she shouldn't regret making it. But she did.

CHAPTER FIVE

THE villa was everything a prince's Grecian villa should be. Windows that stretched from floor to ceiling and ran the length of the room, offering views of the Aegean that were incomparable. Everything was washed in white and blue, reflecting the pale sun and glittering sea.

"You have a room on the second floor. Ocean view," he said.

"Are there any non-ocean views available?" she asked.

"Not many. But I like to be near the sea. The product of my island upbringing, I would imagine. I used to..." A strange expression crossed his face. "I used to like watching the ships come into harbor. Or sail out to sea." He cleared his throat. "Until I became a teenager, and just enjoyed watching women walk around in bikini bottoms. Either way, I've always liked the beach."

"North Dakota's not by the ocean. It's landlocked."

"I know. And the idea of it makes me feel claustrophobic. How do you stand it?"

"I leave. A lot." Her hometown made her feel claustrophobic more often than not, in truth. Especially since she always ran the risk of seeing Gil and Sarah if she went grocery shopping. And now it was Gil and Sarah and Aiden.

Suddenly the fresh ocean air seemed too briny, too harsh. Her throat tightened against it.

"That's one solution," he said.

"A temporary one."

"Why not make it permanent?"

Because then she really would have to let go. "I own a house. It's nice. I have…petunias."

"And I have bougainvillea. There are flowers everywhere."

"But they're my flowers." And it was the place she could go and rehash where her dreams had started. And where they had ended.

No. Not ended. Changed. She was just hunting for some new ones now. Well, that was total garbage. She had a bunch of new ones. She was successful. She had awesome shoes. She helped people find…well, lasting marriage if not love.

"You could transplant them."

She sighed. "Oh, come on, Stavros, they're only petunias."

He laughed, the sound rich and genuine, catching her off guard. "Perhaps find me a woman *you* wouldn't mind spending time with."

His suggestion caught her off guard more than his laughter. "What do you mean by that?"

"You're funny. Quick. I imagine you don't hang out with people who bore you."

"I don't hang out with much of anyone these days, outside of a working relationship, but you're right, I don't."

"So, find me someone you would be amused by. Someone who has better things to talk about than the weather."

"The weather here is lovely," she said, unable to resist.

"Things like that," he said, amusement lacing his tone. "Find a woman who does things like that."

"So someone who's like me, but not me."

"Exactly."

He was teasing. And even if he weren't, there was no

way she could be suitable. She wasn't sweet and demure. She didn't know how to do a royal wave. And she wasn't fertile. Not even maybe.

The only requirement she met was being a woman, a broken one. And that just wasn't enough.

Still, when she looked at her ex-husband's curvy, blonde new wife, she felt like he had gone and done that same thing. A woman who was her, but not her. He'd found a replacement model with a working, intact uterus.

It was something that still burned no matter how hard she tried to pretend it didn't. She didn't love Gil anymore. She didn't want him back. But the way it had all gone down... that was the really hard thing to deal with.

That was the part she had to process. So she just had to move forward. Inch by inch, day by day. Breath by breath.

Some days were more successful than others.

"Charming," she said, turning and heading toward the staircase.

"Jessica." Stavros caught her arm and turned her to face him, his dark eye intense. "I'm sorry. That came out... It was a bad joke."

She shrugged and tried to pull away from him. Away from his touch. His heat. "It's nothing. I'm just tired. I'll think about what we talked about today and I'll get back to you, okay?"

He released his hold on her, her skin still burning where his flesh had touched hers. Scorched hers. How long had it been since someone had touched her? And by touch, she didn't mean handshakes. Didn't mean brushes of fingers, or even a proprietary male hand on her back as she was guided into a building.

Really touched her. Personal. Caring, almost.

It had been so long. Even longer since she'd felt a real connection with someone. That was actually worse than not being touched. Being touched, being skin-to-skin with someone, and knowing that there was no connection at all.

This wasn't like that. She didn't want to crave it. She'd let go of those desires and had done her very best to replace them with new ones. He was ruining it.

Reflexively, she brushed her fingers over the spot where his had rested. "It's nothing. I'm fine."

"You don't look fine."

"Stavros, I'm fine," she said, finding it easier to use his first name now. Here in the villa and not in the palace. "I'm not vying for the position of wife to the future king of Kyonos, remember? I'm helping you find her. And I will. Promise."

"Have dinner with me," he said.

"Where?"

"Here, at the villa."

The thought of it made her stomach feel all fluttery. It made her palms sweaty, too. She was seriously out of practice when it came to dealing with men. Except she wasn't, not really, she just never got asked to have dinner with them in a way that went beyond business.

And you think this is more than business?

No. Of course it wasn't. She was here, in the villa, and he was being hospitable to someone who was working to find him a wife. And she was not that wife.

She didn't want to be anyway. Not even tempted.

The only reason she'd forgotten, for a moment, that his invitation wasn't meant to be an intimate one, was because he'd touched her arm. It had caused a momentary short circuit but she was back now.

"That would be lovely. We can discuss some women who might have more advanced conversation skills…"

"Leave your computer in your room."

"B-but…"

"Come on, Jessica, I think we can have a conversation without your piece of technical equipment between us."

Did he? Because she didn't think so. She wasn't sure what she would do with her hands. Or what she would look at when she started to melt into those dark chocolate eyes of his and she needed a reprieve.

"Of course. I don't have a problem with that. None at all."

"Good. See you in a couple of hours. That will give you enough time to unpack and freshen up?"

She frowned and touched her hair. Freshen up? Did she need it?

"Not everything I say is a commentary on you. Or me finding you lacking in some way," he said, his tone sardonic.

"Pfft. Of course not," she said, dropping her hand to her side. "And not everything I do is connected to something you say making me feel like I'm lacking in some way."

One dark eyebrow arched upward. "Touché."

"Oh…which way to my room?"

"Pick any room you want. Top of the stairs and turn left. I'm to the right."

Then she would be picking the room at the very, very far end of the hall. Left as left could be. "Great. Thanks. See you down here at seven?"

He cocked his head to the side, that charming, easy grin curving his lips. "Sounds good to me. I'll have your bags sent up soon."

"All right. See you at dinner."

She turned and started up the stairs, the marble clicking beneath her heels.

She wasn't going to change her dress before dinner. Because that would mean she was treating it like it was special. Like a date.

No. She definitely wasn't changing her dress.

* * *

She'd changed her dress. That was the first thing he noticed when Jessica descended the stairs and stepped into the living area.

She'd traded in the cheery, yellow, low-cut halter-top dress for a slinky, red, low-cut dress, belted at her tiny waist. The skirt hugged her rounded hips and fell just to her knee, showing those shapely, sexy calves that he was starting to fixate on.

Not as much as he was fixated on the creamy swells of her breasts. But close.

"Hello," she said. Her posture was stiff, her elegant neck stretched up as tall and tight as possible. Her cherry-painted lips were thinned. Which was a waste in his mind. If a woman was going to wear red lipstick she should pout a little. Especially this woman.

But it wasn't the sexual feelings she stirred in him that disturbed him. It was the way she'd looked at him earlier… sad, hurt. And how he'd wanted to drop everything, the wall he put between himself and everyone he interacted with, to comfort her.

That feeling, that desire for a true connection, was foreign to him. And if not entirely foreign, connected to the distant past. Back when he'd believed he had a different future ahead of him. Back before he'd realized the importance of erasing any feeling that could root itself inside of him too deeply.

That might control him. Weaken him. As emotion had weakened his father.

"Good evening," he said, inclining his head. "Have you started settling in?"

"Yes. It's lovely here." The corners of her lips turned up slightly. "Very…balmy."

The small talk was too crisp. Too bland. And Jessica Carter was neither of those things. What she was, was

prickly as a porcupine and likely making inane talk to ir-
ritate him. It shouldn't. With women he was all about connecting on a surface level. With people in general. Why did
he want more from her?

Why did she make him want more for himself?

Talking to that woman with the mouse laugh…it had
been grating. Insufferable. Just the thought of being shack-
led to her for the rest of his life… It had seemed personal
in a way it hadn't before. Whether that was due to Jessica
or the wedding being more of a reality, he didn't know.

"Tell me about your dress," he said, because he knew
it would catch her off guard. It would also redirect his
thoughts to her delicious figure, and that was acceptable.
The rest, the feeling, was not.

She blinked rapidly a few times. "My dress?"

He started to walk toward the terrace, where dinner was
waiting for them. "Yes, your dress. What's the story behind
it? A woman who makes clothing her hobby surely has a
story for each item."

"Yes. Well, but I didn't think you would be interested."
She was walking behind him, trying to keep pace in her
spiky black heels.

He hadn't thought he would be interested, either.
Strangely, he was. "I live to surprise." He paused at the
table and pulled her chair out. "Sit. And tell me."

She arched one well-shaped brow. "I don't respond to
one-word commands."

Heat fired through his veins, pooling in his stomach.
His answering remark came easily. And it was welcome as
it served to mask the intense need that gripped him. "I'll
bet there are a few one-word commands I could get you to
respond to."

She sat quickly and picked up the glass of white wine
that was waiting for her, taking a long drink before setting

it down and saying, far too brightly, "I found this dress at a charity shop."

He rounded the table and sat across from her, keeping the chair pushed out a bit. He didn't trust himself to get too close. And clearly, Jessica didn't, either. Her change of topic had been about as clumsy and obvious as they came.

She'd picked up the meaning of his words. And he'd driven her to drink. That was an ego boost.

"Go on," he said.

"It's from the late forties or early fifties. Sort of business attire."

"That was business attire?" It was a wonder any work got done.

"Clothing then was so feminine. It didn't have to be obvious to be sexy, and it didn't have to be boxy to be respectable. That's one reason I like it."

It was certainly that. But then, Jessica would look feminine in a man's suit. She had curves that simply couldn't be ignored or concealed.

"It suits you," he said.

"I'm glad you think so. You looked at me like I had two heads the first couple of days we were together."

"Did I?"

"Yes."

"I hope you like fish," he said, indicating the plate of food. He always opted for simple when he was at the villa. Something from the sea, vegetables from the garden on the property and a basket of bread and olive oil. He had all the formal he could handle in Kyonos. Ceremony and heavy custom, though he'd been born into it, had never seemed to fit him. Just one reason he was always skirting the edge of respectability.

That and a desire—no, a need—to control something about his life.

"I do," she said. "I didn't always, but as we've discussed, my home state is landlocked, so seafood wasn't that fresh. And fish out of the river just tastes like a river and it's not a good experience. Not for me, anyway. Traveling has expanded my horizons in a lot of ways."

"Was your husband from North Dakota?"

A crease appeared between her eyebrows. "Yes."

"Is that why you aren't with him anymore?"

Her mouth dropped open. "No. What's that supposed to mean?"

"Nothing," he said. But he had wondered, when she spoke of travel, of not spending time at her home, if her ambitions had grown bigger than the life of a housewife.

"Are you asking if I traded my husband in for—" she waved her fork over her plate "—for fresh seafood?"

"Not in so many words."

"Well, I didn't." She released a heavy breath. "If only it were that simple."

"It's not simple?"

"It is now," she said, stabbing at the white flesh of the fish on her plate. "Because we're divorced, and he's my *ex*-husband, not my husband. So whatever happened between us doesn't really matter. That's the beauty of divorce."

An unfamiliar twinge of guilt stabbed at him. "You wouldn't be the first person to run from an unhappy situation. To try and find peace somewhere else." He thought of Xander when he spoke those words. Xander, who had been so miserable. Who had been blamed for the death of their mother. By their father, by their people. And sadly, in the end, by Stavros himself.

"I'm the one who left, if that's what you want to know," she said, her voice cold.

His stomach tightened. She'd walked away. He didn't know the story, he didn't know her pain. But still, it was so easy for him to judge her. It was his gut reaction. Because he knew what happened when people walked away just because it was too hard.

"Did he mistreat you?" Stavros asked.

She met his gaze, her green eyes glittering. "That's a loaded question."

"Seems simple to me."

"All right, I think he was an ass, but then, I'm his ex-wife." She looked down. "Really? He's a moral paragon. You know, he could have taken a lot of money from me. I was the main breadwinner. And he didn't. He didn't want it. He just wanted to be free of me. He took the out I gave him and ran." She pushed her plate back. "I'm not hungry." She stood and put her napkin on the table. "Thanks, but I'm going to go to bed now." She turned and walked away, her shoulders stiff.

Stavros wanted to go after her. To grab her arm like he'd done earlier. To soothe her. With a touch. A kiss.

He sucked in long breath, trying to ease the tightness in his chest. To kiss those ruby lips...they would be so soft.

He wanted to offer comfort. To hold her in his arms.

He couldn't do any of those things.

So he let her go, while his body bitterly regretted every step she took away from him.

Jessica flopped onto the bed and growled fiercely into the empty room. "Way to spill your guts there, Jess," she scolded herself.

Why had she told him that? Any of that. Yes, he'd pushed the subject of Gil. And yes, it had gotten her hackles up because she didn't want any judgment from him about her marriage.

But it was hard to talk about it without talking about everything. About the reason things had crumbled. About the pain, the embarrassment. About the bitterness and disappointment laced into every word. About how going to bed at night had been something she'd dreaded. To have to share a bed with someone, maybe even make love with someone, when they were distant at best, disdainful at worst.

About how in the end she'd had to face the hardest, scariest thing she'd ever endured on her own. About how her husband had let her have major surgery without his support, without him there. She'd had to just lie by herself in a hospital bed. Her body had hurt so bad, and her heart had been crumbling into pieces, the victory over her chronic condition costing her her dearest dreams.

And that was when she'd called a lawyer. She hated that. That he'd made her do that. She honestly believed if she hadn't he would have stayed. Would have punished her by making her live with a man who had grown to hate her.

She closed her eyes and blocked out the memory. As much as she could, she just tried to pretend those moments were a part of someone else's life. Sometimes it worked. Just not right now.

She stood up and started pacing the length of the room. She was pathetic. And pitiful. And where was her armor when she needed it?

There was a knock on the door and she paused midstride. "Yes?" she asked.

"It's me."

The very masculine voice was unmistakable. As was the shiver of excitement that raced through her.

She turned and flung the door open, putting her hand on her hip and shifting her weight so that her hip stuck out, exaggerating the roundness of her curves. "What?"

He only looked at her, his dark eyes glittering. A muscle in his jaw ticked, his shoulders flexed.

They stood for a moment and simply looked at each other.

Then Stavros moved, quickly, decisively, and pulled her up against the hard wall of his chest. He dipped his head and his lips met hers. Hot. Hungry.

So good.

She clung to the door with one hand, her other hand extended next to her, balled into a fist as Stavros kissed her, his hands roaming over her back, his tongue tracing the outline of her lips. And when it dipped inside, slid against her tongue, that was when she released her hold on the door and locked her arms around his neck, forking her fingers through his hair.

He turned her so that her back was against the door frame, his hands moving to her waist.

Oh, yes, she wanted this. All of it. More.

She moved her hands to his shoulders, let them roam over his back. He was hot and strong, his muscles shifting beneath her fingertips. His shirt felt too thick, scratchy on her skin. She wanted to pull it off of him. She arched against him, her breasts pressing against his chest, and she became aware of just how present her dress was. How much of an impediment it was.

They needed to get rid of their clothes.

She moved her hands around to his chest, toyed with the first button on his dress shirt. He growled, a masculine, feral sound that she'd never associated with sex, but that made her entire body tighten with need.

Being with Stavros wouldn't be like any experience she'd had before. Not even close. Being with Stavros would be…

A really bad idea.

She froze, their lips still connected, her fingers curled into the fabric on his shirt. "Stop," she said.

He did. Immediately. He moved away from her, his expression as dazed as she felt. "That's not what I came up here for."

"What did you come up here for?" she asked, her words shaky, her entire body shaky.

"I…don't know." He sounded shocked. Dumbfounded. She wasn't sure if it was a comfort or an insult.

"But not for…that?"

He shook his head. "I'd ruled that out as a possibility."

"But you'd…thought about it?"

"Not a good question."

"You're right about that."

He took a step away from her. "It's understandable that we're attracted to each other."

"Totally," she said.

"But that doesn't mean we can act on it."

"No," she said, while her body screamed at her to change her answer.

And what would happen if she did? Professional suicide. And for what?

Sex for her had become all about failure. About shortcomings. All of hers on display when she was literally naked and as vulnerable as she could possibly be. She couldn't get pregnant. She couldn't even orgasm properly. As her husband had told her during one particularly ugly argument, there was literally no point in having sex with her. He'd said at the time his right hand was better company.

"I'm sorry."

"Oh, don't," she said, her lip curling in disgust, her body rebelling. "Don't apologize for kissing me, please, that's just… I'm not going to let you do that. Act like there was something…wrong with it." There was always something wrong.

"It was inappropriate."

Annoyance spiked inside her. "You're acting like you

compromised my maidenly virtue, or something. That's long gone so you don't need to worry."

"You are working for me right now."

"Not exactly."

"No matter what, it was wrong of me to do it. You're trying to help me find a wife, I'm paying you to do it. I have no right to charge in your room and kiss you."

"I kissed you back," she said, crossing her arms beneath her breasts, unwilling, unable to back down. Because she would not be treated like she was a victim in this. She was tired of being a victim. And she would not show him how much she was affected by it, either.

His expression was almost pained. "Don't remind me."

"That good?"

"If you keep talking I'll be tempted to kiss you again simply to quiet you down."

"You say the sweetest things, Prince Stavros. I am pudding at your feet." Oh, she could have cried. She was so relieved to have those sassy words fall out of her mouth. She needed them. Needed the distance and protection they would provide.

His jaw tensed, his lips, so soft and sensual a moment before, thinned. "You are...infuriating."

"And you like it," she said. "Wonder what that says about you?"

For a moment, he looked like he might grab her again. Might pull her up against his hard body and press his lips to hers.

Instead, he turned away from her.

"I'm going to call the girls. See when they can come out here. You're paying, naturally," she said. She didn't know why she'd chosen to tell him that. Only that the temptation to make him stay a bit longer had been stronger than it should have been.

He stopped and turned. "Naturally."

"See you tomorrow then."

"I'll be busy."

"So will I. I have other clients to do consultations with." She was still stalling. Still trying to keep him close.

He ignored her last statement and turned away again, heading down the hall. She let out a breath and walked back into her room, shutting the door behind her.

She picked up her iPad and opened up her file for Stavros. *Good kisser. Amazing body.*

She deleted both as soon as she wrote them. If only she could delete it from her memory so easily.

CHAPTER SIX

THE women had arrived. Victoria, Amy and Cherry. Beautiful, polished and royal. They were wearing sleek, expensive-looking clothing, their hair perfectly coiffed, their makeup expertly applied.

They were perfectly beautiful. Perfectly boring.

Stavros surveyed the three women in their spot on the balcony. He felt like he was being featured on a bad reality television show. It was suddenly hard to breathe.

He'd been around some in his thirty-three years. Some people might call him a playboy, he preferred to think he was taking advantage of the physical while ignoring the emotional. Even so, facing three women who had marriage on their minds was out of his realm of experience.

Jessica was not out there with him, not there to run interference and give him a time limit for how long each woman could speak to him.

Victoria spoke first. "It's nice to meet you," she said. "I apologize if you weren't expecting me…us." He could tell she was irritated to be sharing the terrace with the other two women, who clearly felt the same way she did.

"Of course you were expected," he said, opting for diplomacy. Though he hoped, fervently, that they were staying at a hotel in Piraeus and not in the villa. Two was company, five would be a nightmare.

Especially considering that kiss he'd shared with Jessica and all the options it was making him contemplate. Again.

Victoria smiled, saccharine and a bit false, though, again given the situation, he hardly blamed her. His own smile was just as fake.

Cherry—at least he was assuming she was Cherry based on Jessica's description—spoke next. "I waited down at the airport for quite a while."

"I apologize," he said.

"I didn't have to wait," Victoria said, her expression a bit superior as she looked at the other two women.

"Because your plane landed last," Amy said, sniffing slightly.

He heard the click of high heels behind him and turned, a rush of heat filling him as Jessica came walking out onto the terrace.

"Sorry, ladies, I didn't realize you'd arrived." She smiled widely and he could sense the women in front of him relaxing as Jessica drew closer. She put her hands on her hips, pushing her full skirt in, revealing a bit of those luscious curves. "I had told the driver to bring you to your hotel. I apologize for the confusion."

Efharisto con theo.

He didn't want three women, all vying for position as queen, under the same roof. At least not one he was beneath. Not a very good thought to have, since it was very possible one of the three could be sharing his home, his bed, for the rest of their lives.

They could spend the rest of their lives smiling falsely at each other. He didn't know where the thought came from, and he didn't know why it filled him with an emotion that he could only identify as terror.

He appraised the three sleek women in front of him. All different in coloring, height and shape. He tried, he tried very hard, to find one that appealed to him more than the others.

A blonde, a brunette and a redhead…

He could not find anything especially appealing.

Until Jessica appeared on the balcony. That made fire in his blood, heat pooling in his gut, coursing down to his groin. His lips burned with the memory of her kiss. Just a kiss. Something that, for a man of his experience, should mean nothing. And yet, it had seemed the height of sensuality. The pinnacle of pleasure.

More than that, his heart had burned. And it hadn't hurt. It hadn't been unpleasant at all. He didn't know what that meant.

"Since you're here, I think we should have a drink before you're taken back into the city." Jessica was in control, her smile unshakable, her composure solid. "Does that suit?"

Amy looked like she might protest, about the drink or being taken back into the city, but instead, she nodded along with the others. Jessica turned and went back into the villa, undoubtedly to give the order for drinks to be served.

The three women stared at him, doe-eyed. An indistinct blur of beauty that meant nothing more to him than the scenery. Possibly less. "Excuse me for a moment," he said, turning and following Jessica. "Jessica…"

She whirled around, hands on her head. "I am so sorry."

"You are?"

"Yes. I don't really like all the three of the women to be together and…this…all right, this isn't really going according to my system. But it's okay. We'll improvise. We'll all have a drink, we'll chat, tomorrow you can choose one to go on a dinner date with. Does that work?"

"Fine," he said, amused by how quickly her composure had evaporated once they were out of sight of the other women.

"Really, this just makes it all seem a bit…"

"Like a reality television show?"

"Yes. And also a bit crass. And I'm sorry. But they all know the drill, so while it's awkward, they knew that they weren't the only people who had put in to be considered for this match."

He leaned against the wall. "So how exactly do women find you?"

"I advertise. In a discreet manner of course, but I've managed to put together a select group of men and women. When someone comes to me looking for a match, I let those who meet the qualifications know, and then they respond and let me know if they're interested. Simple."

"In a complex sort of way."

She raised both eyebrows, her expression haughty. "Well, it works anyway."

"So how many of these women you've shown me haven't made the final cut with other men?"

She sniffed. "Almost all of them. Where is the wine?"

"Which ones?"

"Only Victoria has never asked to be entered in for consideration yet. You were the first one she showed interest in."

"Setting her sights high?"

She kept her focus on her hunt for beverages. "Wine?"

"I mean that as far as status goes, not really saying I surpass the other men in terms of other qualities."

"Right. Where is the wine?"

He chuckled and reached behind her, pulling a bottle from the built in rack above her head. "Will a merlot do?" He took glasses from the rack as well, holding them by the stems.

"Fine." She reached up and took the bottle from his hand, then tilted it in his direction. "We should…" She gestured in the direction of the terrace. "Because I don't want them to scratch each other's eyes out or anything."

"Remind me again why you thought this would be a good idea?"

She frowned. "Well, it seemed logical. It sort of followed how I do things…it's just…it not being a big event sort of closes everything in a bit more."

"Yeah."

He took the bottle from her hand and led the way back out onto the terrace. Victoria, Cherry and Amy were standing at the far end of the terrace, a healthy bit of distance between each them so that they didn't have to engage in conversation with one another.

He set the glasses down on a small round bistro table and opened the bottle, pouring a substantial portion into each glass.

"Drinks," he said, lifting one for himself. They would need them.

The women advanced and each took their wine. The silence was awkward, oppressive. He hated this, he was starting to realize. It was the first thing he could remember hating in a long time. He hadn't had an emotion so strong in…years.

He hadn't thought he would mind this situation. Because he didn't want a wife, not in a particular sense. Marriage for him would be something he did for his country. A distant affair, and that was how it had to be. He knew—he'd seen—that love, emotional attachment, could overpower strong men. Bring them to their knees. And if those men were in control of the country, they could bring the country down with them.

That was why he had to do it this way. That was why he had to keep everyone at a distance. Why he had to find a wife who would matter to the country, not to him.

Still, even with that in mind, being in the middle of the matchmaking process was as enjoyable as being boiled alive. His flirtatious manner was harder to hold on to than he could ever remember it being before.

Ultimately, it was Jessica, her quick wit and sparkling laugh, that saved the night. She engaged everyone in conversation and managed to make things seem easy. Easier at least.

By the time his marriage candidates had been sent off in the limo, the knot in his gut had eased. Though, it could have been due to the wine and not just Jessica's lightning-quick wit.

As soon as the women were out of sight Jessica let out a loud breath and lifted her wineglass to her lips, tilting her head back and knocking the rest of the contents in. "That was vile. Worse than vile."

"You're good at covering up how you feel."

"So are you," she said. "Image. It's important to both of us, right?"

"I have to put on a good front for my people." Except he hadn't thought of it as a front before. He'd simply thought of himself as empty of anything but confidence. Empty of anything unimportant. If something needed to be done, he saw it done.

"And I have to put on a calm front for my clients."

"Then why is it you're letting me in on just how stressed out that made you?"

She grimaced. "Well, for all intents and purposes, we're roommates at the moment and I have to let my hair down at some point in the day, so to speak. For another, you've licked my lips and that puts you slightly over the line of 'usual client.' Slightly."

"You don't let all your clients lick your lips?" he asked. A strange tightness invaded his chest, his stomach. Jealousy.

Possessiveness. The image of all of her clients getting the sort of special treatment he had been on the receiving end of made him want to pull her to him again, to make sure she didn't forget what it was like to be kissed by him. To make sure she never forgot.

That was as foreign as all the other emotions she'd brought out in him over the past few days. Jealousy implied some sort of special connection, and a fear of that connection being threatened.

He gritted his teeth, fought against the tightness in his chest. Flirting. That would put the distance back between them. Something light. Sexual.

"Hardly," she said. Unable to read his mood, she kept her tone casual. "Indulge me, though, since I've now confessed that I don't kiss my other clients. What exactly are you hiding?" She tilted her head, her green eyes assessing. Far too assessing for his taste. Too sincere.

It made it impossible to find that false front. Made him feel something shift deep inside himself.

"No skeletons in my closet," he said. "But of course I have to live a certain way, conduct myself in a certain way."

"You aren't exactly a traditional ruler."

"It's not just tradition. It's about instilling confidence. Showing stability. Emotion…that has no place. I must be charming, confident, at ease at all times."

"I've never heard a whispered rumor that you were anything but."

He looked out into the darkness, at the black ocean, moonlight glittering across the choppy surface. "I know. Because I don't slip up. Ever."

He had, though. He had slipped up with her. He had let go of his control, control he'd been forced to cultivate when he'd been named heir to the throne. He'd let go of it completely in those moments his lips had touched hers. Not control against physical desire, but the control he kept so tightly over his feelings.

Jessica laughed, a sad, hollow sound. "I'm certain I do. Sometimes."

"What about you, Ms. Carter?" he said. "What are you hiding?" He turned to her, studying her face in the dim light. It seemed imperative to know her secrets. And he wasn't certain why it would be. But just like last night, he was going to let his guard drop. Just for a moment. Just to follow that heavy, aching feeling in his chest. To give it some satisfaction.

The corners of her mouth twitched slightly. "If I told you, I'd have to kill you."

Warmth spread through him. In him. An alien feeling. One he was compelled to chase for the moment. "And that would create an international incident."

"It would prick my conscience as well, so maybe I should keep it to myself," she said, a small curve in her lips. It wasn't really a smile, though. It was too sad for that. "Better question, if you could be anything, I mean, if the whole world was open to you, what would you be?"

He frowned. "If I wasn't in line to rule Kyonos?"

"If you weren't royal at all. If you could have anything you desired, without obligation, what would you do?"

It was the thing he never let himself wonder. The alternate reality that wasn't even allowed in his dreams. But he was cheating now. Cheating on his own standards for himself.

For a fleeting moment, he had a vision of a life that was his own. A life with a woman of his choosing, in a home of his choosing. With children who wouldn't know the pain, the responsibility of a royal lineage depending on them. With love.

He shoved the image aside. "I would run my corporation," he said. He had a sudden image of sailing a ship around the world and wondered if he'd told the truth.

"Would you get married?" she asked, a strange tone to her voice.

"Yes," he said, the answer almost surprising him. But in that little, warm hint of fantasy, there had been a wife. There had been kids. And it wasn't hard to breathe. "Yes," he said again.

"Hmm." She turned and walked to the end of the terrace, resting her hands on the railing.

He followed her, standing behind her, watching the sea breeze tug wisps of hair from her updo, letting them fall around her neck. He wanted to brush them aside. To kiss her shoulder. Her neck. Not just because he wanted her, but to feel connected to her.

A deadly desire.

"Why do you do it?" she asked. "Why is this so important?"

She was asking for more honesty. For answers he wasn't sure he had. "I... When my mother died things fell apart. And the one thing that seemed real, that seemed to matter, was Kyonos. It was the one thing I could fix. The one place I could...matter."

As he spoke the words, he realized that they were true. That every change he'd made, every effort he'd put forth, had been not just about helping his country, but about finding new purpose for himself.

"What about you?" he asked, ready to shift the spotlight off of himself.

She didn't speak for a long time. When she did, she spoke slowly, cautiously. "In this scenario, reality isn't playing a part, right?"

"Right," he said, voice rough. He waited for her next words, anticipated them like a man submerged beneath the waves anticipated breaking the surface, desperate to take a breath.

She lowered her head, her eyes on her hands. "I would be a wife. A mother..." Her voice broke on the last word. "And maybe I would still do this, or maybe not. I don't know if I would...need it. But...I would be a mother."

She pushed off from the railing. "Back to reality," she said, trying to smile. Failing. "I'm going to bed."

He nodded, watching as she walked past him.

I would be a mother.

There was something so sad, so defeated in the admission. It made his chest tighten, and he couldn't pinpoint why. He'd never had someone else's feelings inhabit his body in this way. But he was certain that's what was happening. That the oppressive weight that had just invaded him was the same sadness that filled her.

Maybe Jessica wasn't as happily divorced as she appeared to be. And maybe she wasn't quite as hard as she appeared to be, either.

She was running interference for Stavros and his harem today, and she wasn't all that thrilled about it. It was getting harder to chuck other women in his direction when she just wanted to throw herself at him.

Not happening, but still. She was so envious of her clients that she was developing a twitch.

And for heaven's sake, she never should have said all that about being a mother. Should never have asked him what he wanted. Should never have tried to get to know him. Because it didn't matter. It just didn't. There was no point in suspending reality, even for a moment.

There was no escaping reality. You couldn't outrun it. You could try but eventually it would bite you in the ass. She knew that. She knew it really, really well. She'd tried to ignore how often she and her husband went to their separate corners of the house. She'd tried to ignore his touch at night, and when she couldn't, she tried to ignore his total disregard for her pain. She'd even tried to ignore his outright berating of her. The screaming and anger and hateful words.

No, there was no point in ignoring that kind of thing. The facts were simple. Stavros needed certain things, she didn't have any of them.

Why was she even thinking about that crap? She didn't have time for it. She had a gaggle of women to manage for the whole day.

She blew out a breath and slipped her oversize sunglasses onto her face, tightening her hold on her latte. She had gotten them all booked into a luxury salon in Piraeus, and they were all safely getting massaged and waxed as she stood out on the crowded, narrow streets drinking her coffee.

Stavros was coming soon. He was meeting the group of them for a quick lunch and tour around the city, and then he would be selecting the woman who would accompany him on a private date for the evening.

And it would be up to Jessica to send the other two off without making them feel like it really was some low-rent reality television show.

Jessica wasn't used to feeling like things were out of her control. Not since that moment four years ago when she'd taken back the reins of her life. She liked to feel like she had everything managed. Like her little universe was in the palm of her hand.

It was an illusion, and she knew it, but she still liked it.

Since Stavros, she didn't even have her illusion.

What was it about him that reminded her...that reminded her she was a woman? Not just on the surface, but really and truly. With a woman's desires, no matter how hard life had tried to wring them out of her.

Oh, dear…right on time. The master of her rekindled sexual needs was striding toward her. Cream-colored jacket and trousers, shirt open at the collar. She did love a man who knew how to dress. A Mediterranean sex god with very expensive taste.

He also had two dark-suited members of security flanking him and discreetly parting the crowd so that His Majesty wouldn't be jostled.

Not that Stavros ever behaved that way. He didn't act like a spoiled prince who would be able to feel a pea through fifty mattresses, not even close. He acted like a man who carried the weight of a nation on his shoulders.

More than that, he acted like a man who intended to support the weight of that nation for the rest of his life. A man prepared to tailor his every decision to suit that responsibility.

"Hello, Jessica," he said, a smile curving his lips.

"Prince Stavros," she said, reverting because last night had gotten a bit too intimate and she had no desire to go there again. Well, that was a lie. She did want to go there again. But she couldn't.

"Demoted, I see."

"What?"

"Back to a title."

"Oh…" Why did he have to notice all these little things about her? Why did he have to care at all? "Sorry."

"How are things going?"

"Good. Great. Looking forward to you thinning the herd tonight."

"You make it sound like there are a lot more than three."

She sighed. "They feel like more than three. In my experience, the women haven't been so catty. But then, I normally don't do this with them in such close proximity to each other. I've also never tried to match a crown prince."

He looked past her, into the spa. "Let's leave them in there."

"What?" She looked behind her.

"If we hurry, they won't know I was here."

She laughed. "You're not serious."

He frowned. "No. I'm not. Things are getting… I need to make a decision."

"Because of Eva?" she asked, remembering his mood at his sister's wedding.

"Everyone in Kyonos was happy for Eva. They love to see their princess in love. But I have to be sure that I make them feel like there's stability."

"You've been the rock for Kyonos for a long time," she said, not quite sure why she felt compelled to offer him… not comfort…support, maybe.

"And I will continue to do it. With a wife by my side."

"A most suitable wife."

"Yes." He looked back in the spa. "Will they be done soon?"

"Soon.

"It's not too late to go another route," she said, not sure why she was offering her client an out from a program she publicly professed, and privately believed, to be the best way to find a mate.

He shrugged. "Why would I?"

"You could still fall in love." She wrapped both hands around her paper cup and hugged it close to her body.

"No. I can't."

"I'm sure you could. What if you met the perfect woman and she was wholly suitable?"

He shook his head. "It isn't that I don't think it's possible. It's that I won't. Love weakens a leader. You know of Achilles and his heel, I assume?"

"Of course."

He frowned, his expression intense. "One weakness is all it takes to crumble a man who is strong in all other areas. And a weak leader can destroy what was a strong nation. I will never have part in that."

He was serious again. Like last night. Not a hint of flirtation. She was starting to wonder if that was really him at all. Or if it was who he thought he was supposed to be.

"Is that really what you think?"

"I know it. I saw it happen, in my family, in Kyonos. When my mother died everything fell apart. My father could not function. He... We made Xander the scapegoat for it, all because grief could only give way to anger. I had to set it aside. I had to move on for the good of the country. It took my father years to do it. He is a king, he did not have the luxury of grief, or pain. It's different for us."

She studied his face, so hard and impassive, as though it were carved from marble. "Feeling pain is the only way I know to deal with it." Sometimes she wondered if she clung to pain. If she turned it over and dissected more than she needed to. If she used it to protect herself.

"I have gotten to the point where I don't feel it at all. Kyonos comes first, and everything else comes second. That will include a wife. She'll have to understand that. She'll have to understand that her role is not to love me, but to love my country."

Bone deep sadness assaulted her. He deserved more than that. More than this.

Her phone buzzed and she pulled up her text messages.

We're done. Where are you?

The message was from Victoria.
Out front. She typed out the note and then hit Send.
"They're done," she said. "Brace yourself."

He straightened his shoulders, his expression changing, that wicked charm back in place. She had to work hard to suppress a smile.

As if on cue the three women walked out of the spa, sunglasses fixed firmly on flawless faces. Victoria was the first to spot Stavros, the first to smile widely. "Prince Stavros. How lovely."

Like she was surprised. Like she hadn't been briefed by Jessica early that morning.

"Lovely to see you, Victoria," he said, inclining his head. "Cherry, Amy."

Cherry and Amy didn't look thrilled at being after-thoughts, but they managed to smile, too, and offer platitudes about what a lovely day it was.

"I've made reservations at a café down by the water," he said.

"Sounds lovely," Amy said, taking her chance to be the first to speak.

"My car is just this way," he said, leading down the narrow street and to a black limo idling at the curb. The security detail opened the back doors on both sides. The women slid in and took their positions on the bench seats that ran the length of the car.

Jessica got in and sat on the bench facing them, and Stavros slid in beside her. The doors closed and the air-conditioning provided immediate relief from the heat. Or, rather, it would have, if Stavros himself wasn't so hot.

A thick, awkward silence settled into the air and Jessica worked to find her social ease. She was good with people. It was one of her strengths. But Stavros had her in the throes of her first sexual attraction in years and his potential brides were sitting a foot away.

It was more awkward than any situation had the right to be.

"I…" She cleared her throat. "I'm really looking forward to lunch."

"I'm looking forward to dinner," said Cherry, flashing Stavros a smile.

From awkwardness to greater awkwardness.

"I imagine everyone will be eating dinner tonight," Jessica said, a bit too brightly. *Some will be eating alone, though.*

Stavros laughed…easy, charming. False. He did that so well. No matter the situation he seemed to be in control. More than that, he seemed to distance himself. The flirtier and friendlier he seemed, the less present he actually was. And that seemed to be his default setting.

Not always. Her mind flashed back to the kiss. That hadn't been emotionless at all. Or distant. That had been… amazing. And wild. She sneaked a peek at him from the corner of her eyes, her line of sight connecting her with the strong column of his throat. She was willing to bet he tasted like salt. Clean skin and man.

"I'm certain everyone will," he said, earning a delicate blush from Cherry.

The limo stopped and Jessica nearly said a prayer of thanks out loud. "We're here!"

The doors opened and they filed out. The restaurant was at the harbor, the seating area extending over the pier. Boats, ranging in size from dinghies to yachts, filled the horizon. Seagulls screeched nearby, landing near tables, fighting over crumbs, showing no respect for their otherwise elegant surroundings.

Jessica made sure everyone ordered wine with their

lunch. Heaven knew they would need it to get through the afternoon.

They made appropriate small talk while they waited for their orders to be filled and Jessica cringed inside as she watched the patented disinterest in Stavros's eyes grow more and more pronounced.

She wanted to pinch him. She couldn't fix him up if he didn't even try to like the women she introduced him to.

She caught his gaze and treated him to a hard stare. A glimmer of amusement appeared in the depths of his dark eyes. She didn't even want to know what he was thinking.

When everyone had their food, Stavros leaned in, his very best charming-politician smile on his face. How had she not noticed before? How fake it was. How much it wasn't him at all. "I know this is a bit unusual. But I think it's best to think of it as a job interview. I hope no one finds that offensive. We have all signed up to have Jessica's help finding a suitable spouse, have we not?"

Jessica wanted to hit him. Except none of the women seemed offended at all. They should have been. His mercenary assessment should have made them all angry. They should have poured wine in his lap.

They didn't, they simply nodded.

"The reality is, my country needs very specific things from a queen. That's my top priority."

"Naturally," Victoria said. "We're all far too practical to think this is going to be a love match."

Cherry nodded, and Amy only stared into her glass.

"Then the rejection should not be personal, either," he said, his charm never slipping. He was firm, yet still perfectly engaging. She didn't understand how he did it. She didn't understand what he was doing, and yet, he was doing it.

"This is really lovely," Jessica said, looking around them. "Isn't it lovely?"

Amy nodded. "It really is."

She chattered on about the scenery and the food, anything to dispel the lingering scent of that horrible honesty of Stavros's. They managed to make it through the meal and get the women deposited at their hotel without it appearing again.

That left just the two of them alone in the limo for the ride back to the villa.

"And what was that?" she asked.

"What was what?" He was positioned across from her, and he still felt too close, because now there was no one in the back with them to help diffuse the tension.

"That. The whole thing about it being a job interview. Didn't I tell you to keep your candor to yourself? Or just tell me if you have something so honest to say."

"They didn't seem to mind. Anyway, I had to make a choice about tonight, about which one of the three to continue seeing. If that, the clinical nature of this, is going to bother them, they should leave now. I'm not doing this for romance."

"I know…"

"And now so do they. If any one of them wants to leave they better do it now, I don't have time to mess around with the future of my country. I told you already, I need a queen who understands that her loyalty will be to Kyonos."

"Still…geez. Don't underestimate the power of a little sweet talk."

"I of all people know about sweet talk, as you should know. I do have a reputation. But I'm not going to deceive anyone that's involved in this."

"I appreciate that. I wasn't talking deceit. Just…sugar-coating."

"I didn't think you did sugarcoating," he said, his dark eyes locked with hers.

"Um…well, I don't…I mean not with you, but you have to know how to talk to women."

"You think you know how to talk to women better than I do? How many women have you dated?"

She crossed her arms beneath her breasts. "Zero, but I *am* a woman so I win."

"This isn't about tricking someone into marrying me because they want to be a princess and live in a castle and have their happily-ever-after. They can want a title, but they have to be worthy of it. They have to know what it means. They have to realize I'm a busy man and that love isn't high on my list of priorities. It's not even on the list of options. For that reason, I thought it was important I spelled it out."

She looked out the window, her throat tightening. For one moment, just for a moment, she pictured Stavros without the obligations. What would it be like for him? If he could have been free to do what he wanted? If he could have had that wife and the children that he'd seen in his mind's eye last night while they were talking? Would his expectations be different?

Would he have loved that wife? If he didn't feel like a nation was dependent on his emotional strength, would he have given himself over to love? Would he have focused his fearsome loyalty on his family?

The thought of it, of what it would be like to be the woman on the receiving end of all that intensity, filled her with a kind of bone-deep longing.

Get a grip, Jess. Even if he was free, she wouldn't be the woman for him. He had goals, dreams and desires that weren't about his wife, or who she was, but what she could offer. And they were things she couldn't offer. She knew all about trying to be perfect for someone when she fell so far short of it. She could never do it again.

"I respect that," she said.

"Victoria."

"What?"

"It's Victoria. She's the one I want to see again." His voice didn't hold any particular enthusiasm.

She felt like she'd been sucker punched. And she wasn't sure why. "Did you...have a lightning-attraction thing?"

A muscle in his cheek jumped. "She's lovely. More than that, I think she's a bit...well, she seemed unemotional." He didn't sound too enthusiastic and she hated the small, ridiculous part of herself that liked that. The part that wanted Stavros to be dwelling on their kiss, and not on his attraction to another woman.

Even if that other woman was the one he might potentially marry.

"Victoria is... She's very smart. And I'm certain she would do a lot of good as queen." Victoria wasn't just smart, she was brilliant. And, Stavros was right, a bit on the unemotional end of things. She was looking for an opportunity to better herself, and to make an impact on the world.

Jessica had been trying to talk Victoria into considering a few of her previous clients, but Victoria hadn't been interested. Because she'd clearly been holding out for better. And had found it in Stavros.

Well, nice for some.

For you, too, she tried to remind herself, but herself wasn't listening. Herself was sulking a little bit.

"Great, I'll call down to the hotel later."

"I'll do it," he said. "If you give me her room number."

"Can't," she said, the word escaping before she could think better of it.

"Why?"

Her stomach tightened to a painful degree. "No sex, remember?"

"I'm not going to have sex with her, not at this point. I'm going to call and ask her to dinner."

She cleared her throat, ignoring the little surge her heart had taken when he'd said the word *sex*. Because when he said it was so…evocative. Husky male tones wrapped in an exotic accent. It made her think of tangled limbs and heavy breathing and…

And what? Like she was some great sensual goddess? Like she would be able to enjoy being with him? Like he would enjoy being with her? Her throat ached and she couldn't fathom the sudden onslaught of emotion. What was wrong with her?

"Yeah, I'll call Amy and Cherry then and just let them know that…I'll let them know they can return home."

"At their leisure. They can stay in the city for a few more days if they wish. I'll continue to pay their expenses for as long they remain here. An extended holiday doesn't seem too unreasonable."

"Ah, so you'll ask Victoria out but I have to break it off with the other two?"

"As I said earlier, it's just a job interview. And only one candidate can get hired, so to speak."

"Right." She leaned back in the chair and flexed her fingers, curling them into fists and letting her manicured nails dig into her palms.

There was no reason at all the thought of Stavros going on a date with Victoria should make her feel like she might be sick.

But it did. She couldn't deny that it did.

She was seriously losing it.

"Well, if I don't see you again before your date...break a leg."

He smiled, but his eyes held a strange, unreadable expression. "I'll see you. After at least."

No. "See you then."

CHAPTER SEVEN

THERE was nothing wrong with Victoria. She was beautiful, she was pleasant. Smart. She would make a wonderful queen. Over dinner she'd talked at great length concerning how passionate she was about charities, starting foundations and visiting hospitals.

She possessed all the qualities he required for a bride.

Yet as he thought of binding himself to her, he felt nothing. No matter how hard he tried. He felt like he was being suffocated. As if the weight of the crown would physically crush him.

Don't think of marriage. Think of sex.

If he could find a connection with her on that level, then maybe nothing else would matter. If he could flirt and put them both at ease, put a wall between them, maybe the tightness in his throat would abate.

When the limo stopped in front of the hotel she looked at him from beneath her lashes, her open, friendly expression changing. Seduction, he decided, was her intent. Good. He knew the game. Often, he relished the game.

So, why didn't he feel anything? Nothing. Not even the slightest twinge of interest in his stomach. When she cocked her head to the side and licked her lips, there was no answering tug in his groin. Indeed, there was no signal coming from south of his belt at all. It was as though that member of his body hadn't registered her existence.

He was a man, a man with a healthy appetite for sex. And she was, on paper, a sexually attractive woman. What he should be doing was pressing her back against the soft leather seat and claiming her soft pink lips.

His body rejected the idea while his mind replaced the image of a rosy pink mouth with one painted in temptation red. And with that image came a tightness in his chest, his heart pounding harder, his mind suddenly filled with Jessica.

"I had a nice time at dinner," he said.

"So did I," she said, cocking her head to the side even farther. Why was it that some women thought affecting the mannerisms of a cocker spaniel was sexy?

Except, usually, he would find this sexy. He just didn't now. No use pretending he didn't know why.

"Good night," he said, opening the door to the limo and stepping out into the cool night. He held the door for her, giving as strong of a hint as he could.

She frowned and slid out, her body on the opposite side of the door to his. "I had a…a really nice time." Her blue eyes were locked with his, her intentions obvious.

"So you said."

"I appreciate you taking me out."

"We'll go out again. When I'm through with my business here." Where was the flirtation? Why couldn't he even pretend that he was interested? Whatever he felt for Jessica, it shouldn't have the power to reach him here and now. It shouldn't be able to control his thoughts and actions. That was the sort of thing he'd spent most of his adult life fighting.

"Oh…okay." She smiled. "That's good, right?"

It should have been. But he didn't have any sort of positive feeling about it. "You're a…nice woman, Victoria."

Nice? Where the hell had his seduction skills gone?

"Thank you. You're a nice man, Stavros." She cleared her throat. "Good night, then?"

"Good night," he said.

She stepped out of the way of the door and he closed it firmly. He would walk her into the hotel, as was the appropriate thing to do, but that was all.

She looked at him one more time in the lobby of the hotel, requesting a kiss, and when he took a step back he could have sworn he saw a fleeting hint of relief in her eyes.

"Hopefully we'll see each other again soon," she said.

"Hopefully," he said, turning and leaving her in the lobby.

He felt no such hope. He would see her again though. Just because something in him was off at the moment didn't mean she wasn't the right candidate for the job. For the marriage.

He grimaced, lifted his hand to loosen his tie, which suddenly felt like a hangman's noose.

Victoria was a sound choice.

He gritted his teeth. Yes, she was a sound choice. It didn't matter that he desired someone else. Desire, no matter how strong, did not have a say in the future of his country. Desire could not shake his resolve.

He closed his eyes for a moment, clenched his hands into fists to disguise the unsteadiness in his fingers. It was only lust. Nothing special. Nothing important. A picture of Jessica flashed through his mind and there was an answering kick in his gut.

In spite of his intentions, desire seemed to be shaking

him from the inside out. And what he really didn't want to believe was that a whole lot more than desire was making him tremble.

Jessica wrapped her arms around herself and turned away from the view of the ocean, leaning against the rail of the terrace, the salted breeze blowing at her back, tangling in her hair. She wondered what Stavros was doing. If his date with Victoria has been successful.

Part of her hoped that it had been. He could marry her and they could have gorgeous, royal babies that could inherit the throne of Kyonos. They could be all sexy and royal together and she could go back to her empty house and contemplate the merit of getting a cat.

Yes, that was a good plan. A solid plan. She could name her cat Mittens.

"And how was your evening?"

She turned and her breath caught in her throat, forcing a sharp, gasping sound. Stavros was in the doorway, his black tie draped over his shoulder, the first three buttons of his shirt undone, the sleeves pushed up to his elbows.

He looked like he'd been undressed. She tried to smile while her stomach sank slowly into her toes, jealousy an acrid thing that ate at her insides, working its way out.

"I think that's my line," she said. Her words scraped over her dry throat.

"Lovely. Not nearly as lovely as you are. But lovely." A smile curved his lips and he stepped fully onto the deck, closing some of the distance between them.

There was something strange about his manner. Something too slack. Too easy. "Have you been drinking?"

"Not even a little. But you do make me feel a bit lightheaded."

"Seriously. What the heck, Stavros?"

"Careful, *agápe,* you'll make me think I've lost my touch."

"What did I tell you about not flirting with me?" Rather than the sort of shaky, sexy unease she usually felt when he flirted with her, she only felt anger. He had no right to do this to her. No right at all. He had been on a date with another woman. A date that, ideally, would be the beginning of a 'til-death sort of relationship.

"You told me not to." He stepped closer to her, his movements lithe. Graceful. Like a panther. "But I find I can't help myself."

"Then get some help from an outside source," she growled, tightening her arms around herself.

"You are upset with me?" he asked, a boyish, teasing glint in his eye.

"Yes, I am upset with you. I don't understand you. You kiss me, you act mad about it, you apologize, you go on a date with another woman and now you're flirting."

"Victoria was fine."

"Fine?"

"Adequate. I should like to see her again."

"What? That's all?"

"I would like to marry her," he said between clenched teeth.

"And you came out here flirting with me?"

He shrugged. "I told you why I'm doing this. It has nothing to do with personal feelings or excitement on my part and everything to do with getting things in order for Kyonos."

"Great," she said, annoyance deserting her, replaced by a sadness she had no business feeling.

"I prefer it when you smile," he said, injecting a playful note to his voice.

"I don't feel like smiling." She turned away from him, her focus pinned decidedly onto the scenery.

"Why do you do this?"

"Why do I do what?" she asked, not looking at him as she responded.

"Why do you make it impossible for me to reach you?"

"Why are you trying?"

"Because I can't take a breath without thinking of you," he said, his voice suddenly real. Raw.

"I don't…"

"Jessica," he said, regaining some of his composure, "you know my situation. My obligations. But that doesn't mean we can't see where our attraction takes us."

"Yes, Stavros, yes, it does mean that," she said, panic fluttering in her chest. Panic and a desperate desire to believe the words he'd just spoken.

His dark brows locked together. "That kiss…it haunts me. It's eating at me. I need…" He sucked in a sharp breath. "I need you. Tell me you need me, too."

"I…" She shook her head. "It doesn't matter if I do."

His expression shifted, a veil dropping, revealing unguarded hunger. Stark and nearly painful to witness. "Let's pretend that it does." The desperation in his tone, the raw need, was beyond her. And yet it called to her, echoed inside of her. "Let's pretend, like we did the other night, that none of the other stuff exists. That I am just a man. And you are just a woman. A woman I desire above all else."

She sucked in a breath that tore at her lungs, leaving her raw and bleeding inside, and tried to keep the tears from falling. How could he tempt her like this? "Stavros…that's the problem, all of that, that stuff we tried to ignore? It is real. And we can't pretend it's not. It won't change anything."

"Tonight it doesn't have to be real," he said, his voice dark, tortured.

"I am not your best bet for a last-minute, commitment-phobic fling," she admonished. "I am the last woman you should want for that."

"Why? The attraction between us is real. And you said yourself, it isn't as though you're a virgin. You're an experienced woman who knows what she wants."

There was no ease now. No flirtation. And he was harder to resist now because of it. Because this was real. What she'd witnessed when he'd first come out onto the terrace, that had been the fake. This was her evidence that he really did want her.

It was unfair. It was too much.

Anger, unreasonable and not entirely directed at Stavros, spilled over. "I'm pointless, don't you know? Can't you tell? I can't have a baby. I am a testosterone killer. I make a man feel like he isn't really a man. I can't be pleased sexually. Don't I know what that does to a man?" She knew she sounded crazy, hysterical. She didn't care. "I am cold. And frigid. A bitch who cares more for her own comfort than the dreams of her husband, than the hope of a family. Does that sound like the sort of woman you should have a fling with?"

She stood, her hands clenched at her sides, her breathing harsh. Speaking those words, giving voice to every terrible thing she'd been called, every horrible feeling that lived in her, made her feel powerful. It made her feel a little sick, too.

"Jessica...who said those things to you?" he asked, his voice rough.

"Who do you think?"

"Your husband?"

"Ex," she said, the word never tasting so sweet.

"He was wrong," he said.

"You don't know that. I just turned you down, didn't I?"

"And my ego remains intact."

"Just go."

"No. Help me understand," he said. It was a quiet statement, a simple gesture. It was more than anyone else had ever asked from her or offered her.

"This is one of those things men don't like to hear about. And by that I mean it contains the word *uterus* and pertains to that particular 'time of the month' that means a man can't get any action."

"Try me," he said, his dark eyes never leaving hers, his jaw tense. "Scare me, Jess. I dare you."

She forced a laugh. "Fine. I'll give it a shot. I had endometriosis. I might have it again someday, since it's still possible to have a flare-up. I don't know if you really know what that is but it's incredibly painful. I was one of the lucky ones for whom it was especially bad. It causes bleeding and…pain. Lots of pain. Lots of blood. For me it caused pain during sex. After orgasm. It could last for days for me. And…I started just not wanting to have desire anymore. I didn't even want to want sex. The reward was too fleeting for what I had to go through and…I rejected my husband. Often. I made him feel undesired. And you know what? He was."

She was sure that had to have done the trick. That had to have scared him. "I think that's your cue to turn and run."

He crossed his arms over his chest, his eyes never leaving hers. "I'm not a runner. Did it hurt you all the time?"

"Most of the time. I've had…" She always tripped over the word *hysterectomy* because there was something so defeating about it. "I had a procedure done to help, and it has, but…I haven't tested how well it worked in terms of… it still scares me."

"Jess…"

She was the one to take a step back. She shook her head. "It's not worth it, Stavros. For one night? It's not worth it. I'm way too much trouble. If you want one more fling before you get married make it with someone who's easy. And I don't mean that in the general sense. Make it with someone who actually wants sex."

The idea of trying it again, of failing again, destroyed her. It was more than just what it might mean to him. It was that she wanted it so much, and the thought of desiring yet one more thing that remained out of her reach was too painful to even consider.

She'd made success. She'd left her failures behind. There was no point repeating the same mistakes.

"I'm tired." She turned away from him and headed back to the house.

Stavros watched Jessica walk back into the villa, her arms wrapped around her body as though she were holding herself together with her own strength.

He felt numb. Numb and in pain all at once. He'd come out with the express purpose of seducing her. Of finding a way to put her in a category he was comfortable with. To embrace his sexual need and ignore the strange ache in his chest that seemed to appear whenever she was around.

It hadn't worked. She hadn't allowed the distance, and he certainly hadn't been able to retreat behind the security of flirtation, not after that admission.

What an ass he was for making her confess something like that.

She was right, he should run. He should take her advice and focus on his upcoming marriage. Or find a woman to help him burn through his pent-up sexual desire.

He took a heavy breath and walked into the house, heading for his office. He closed the door behind him and sat at his computer desk. He ought to email his father, at the very least, to let him know he was almost certain he was close to finding the future queen of Kyonos.

Instead he opened his internet browser and stared at the blinking cursor in the text box of the search engine.

Then he typed in *endometriosis.*

She wanted to cry, and she couldn't. She'd spent so long forcing herself to keep it together that now she actually wanted to take a moment to fall apart, she couldn't.

It was impossible to force tears.

She just lay on her bed and stared out the window at the moon glimmering on the surface of the ocean. It was the perfection of nature, beautiful and unspoiled. She would never understand why some things were fashioned so perfectly when she wasn't.

Why her body seemed to have been put together wrong when so many other people were made just right. Why she hadn't been able to just buck up and deal with it. Why the shame and failure still ate at her like a parasite.

And she wanted Stavros so much she could hardly stand living in her skin. She wanted to touch him, wanted to taste him. She wanted to kiss him again, to have all that passion directed at her. Mostly she wished she could go back and not tell him about her endometriosis. It had been so nice to have a man look at her like she was beautiful. To have him not see her as different from other women, not in a bad way, but in a way that made her seem special rather than damaged.

When he said she was different, he hadn't meant broken. He hadn't meant pointless. Worthless as a woman or a partner.

His perception of her had been a lie, sure. But it was one she would have been happy to live in for just a little while.

She closed her eyes and let their kiss play through her mind again. Allowed herself to relive what it had been like to feel the pressure of his hard body against hers. To feel his lips against hers, so hot and demanding. So unlike any man she'd ever kissed.

Desire coiled in her stomach, her heart beating faster, her body begging her for some sort of release. Release she'd denied herself for so long. Too long, maybe.

She sat up and balled her hands into fists, pushing against her closed eyes. Without thinking, she stood, her heart hammering as she slipped out into the hall and looked in the direction of Stavros's room. He would be in there by now, asleep.

And he wanted her. He'd said he did. It was such a rush. Such a shot of adrenaline. Pure, feminine pleasure. To be wanted. To want someone.

Her hands trembled and she shook them out, trying to steady them. Trying to steady herself. Easier said than done. She breathed in, then out again.

What if she could have a little bit of it? Something guaranteed. Something she couldn't fail at. She tried to swallow but the motion stuck in her dry throat. The idea of sleeping with Stavros was the most elating and terrifying thing she could imagine. To be so vulnerable to a man who was so perfect. To take a chance at failing again. At being revealed as not good enough.

Blood roared in her ears as she made her way to his room. She stopped and wiped her hands, damp with sweat, on her skirt. She knocked lightly on the door, not pausing to think because, if she did, she would have just turned and scurried back to the safety of her bed.

"Yes?" She heard Stavros's sleep-roughened voice from the other side of the door and she pushed it open.

He was propped up on his elbows, the sheets riding low

around his waist, revealing his chest. The moon glanced off the hard ridges of muscle, the valleys cast into shadow, giving his body the impression of cut stone.

He was utter perfection. Just as she thought, that was not the sort of chest she'd ever touched before. And she was dying to touch him. Aching for it. His beauty drew her in, but it also intimidated.

"I couldn't sleep," she said. So lame. "Obviously *you* could so maybe I shouldn't have come."

"I wasn't sleeping well," he said.

"That's good, I…" She took a step forward. "Can I?"

"Please," he said, his face half-hidden in shadow, his voice strained.

She sat on the edge of the bed and held her hand out in front of her, curling it into a fist, then flexing her fingers as she fought against indecision. Then she placed her palm on his chest and her breath caught as a shock of fire streaked through her veins.

He was so hot, his hair rough on her skin, his muscles hard, his skin smooth. She let her fingers drift down over his sculpted muscles, lightly skimming, following the ripple of his body.

She leaned in and kissed his lips. He remained frozen beneath her, his stomach rock-hard beneath her hand, his body wound tight. She could feel his tension, flowing from every tendon and into her fingertips. Hers to command. Hers to enjoy.

Maybe she couldn't have everything she wanted. But she could have some of it. He wanted her. And she could satisfy him. Without having to give up any power. Without being vulnerable. Without failing.

"What are you doing?" he asked, his forehead resting against hers, his lips a whisper away.

"If you have to ask, I must not be doing it right. It has

been a while, maybe protocol has changed?" She kissed his neck, tasted salt and sweat on his skin.

She let her hands slide down beneath the sheet, where she found him hard for her, a whole lot bigger than she'd anticipated. An involuntary rush of air hissed through her teeth, matching time with Stavros's sharp intake of breath as she curled her fingers around his erection.

In this, she was certain. Giving a man pleasure without taking any for herself had been a necessity in the latter days of her marriage. A desperate attempt to hold things together. A way to keep intimacy without having to deal with any physical discomfort.

She could do the same now, with Stavros. A way to have him without risking anything. It seemed so easy.

Except she was getting a lot hotter than she'd anticipated, and it made the thought of leaving his bed unsatisfied a lot less…satisfying than it had seemed a few moments earlier. Still, even without an orgasm she was enjoying this. Enjoying wanting him. Enjoying exploring his body.

It was a slice of what she wanted, and she'd learned to accept that that was how life was for her. Little tastes here and there of true pleasure, while the full experience stayed out of her reach. It would be enough, because it had to be.

She pressed a kiss to his pectoral muscle and down to his nipple, sliding her tongue over it, feeling it tighten beneath her touch.

His hand came up to the back of her head, fingers sifting through her hair. She smiled against his skin and continued to pepper kisses over his body. "You have the most incredible chest," she said, "among other things." She squeezed his shaft lightly. "I have never, ever, seen a man like you. Much less been close enough to have a taste. And I was really looking forward to it. You do not disappoint." She lifted her head and tugged the sheet down, exposing him. "Oh, no, you don't disappoint at all."

Her heart beat hard, echoing in her temples, at the apex of her thighs. He was amazing. Everything she'd imagined and so much more. She leaned in and trailed her tongue over his stomach muscles, then flicked it over the head of his shaft. He jerked beneath her tongue, a rough groan escaping his lips as he tightened his hold on her hair.

She felt like she'd been let loose in a candy store. Every delight she could imagine spread before her. And she wasn't planning on employing restraint.

She slipped her hand lower, took as much of him into her mouth as she could, reveling in the taste, the feel of him. She could feel the muscles in his thighs shaking, feel the tension in his body as he tried to maintain control.

She didn't want his control. She wanted him to lose it. She wanted him to lose it in a way that she couldn't. She wanted him to do it for her. She more than wanted it, she needed it. Needed his strength to dissolve beneath her, needed to be a part of his undoing. She wanted to exercise the power she had over him. And she did have it. She could feel it. Could feel just how close he was to losing it completely.

That was what she wanted. Needed. Craved. To have victory tonight, in his bed. To be perfection for him. For herself.

"Jessica," he said, and he tugged lightly, trying to move her away from him.

She didn't stop. She ran her tongue along his heavy length and she felt his ab muscles contract sharply beneath her hand.

"Jess," he said again. His tone a warning.

She lifted her head, her eyes locking with his. His gaze was clouded, sweat beaded on his forehead. A surge of power rushed through her. "This is for me," she said. "I want you like this. And I intend to have you."

She leaned in again and his fingers tightened, tangling deep in her hair, the slight sting of pain heightening the pleasure that created a hollow ache between her thighs.

A shaky laugh escaped his lips. "Doesn't it matter what I want?"

"Not in the least. But you like this, don't you?" She traced the head of his shaft with her tongue. "Don't you?"

"*Theos,* yes," he breathed his consent.

She continued to pleasure him with her lips and tongue. And she took everything. His ecstasy, every broken breath and trembling muscle, every curse, every word of praise.

This was her moment. Her pleasure. Her power.

Her taste of what she truly wanted. A hint of the feast she couldn't have.

She didn't stop until he found his pleasure, his body shaking, his skin slicked with sweat, every vestige of control stripped of him as he found his release.

He lay on his back after, stroking her cheek. She rested her head on his stomach and closed her eyes. Just for a moment.

She felt him stir beneath her. He sat up and brought her with him, kissing her on the lips. The kiss intensified, his tongue sweeping across her bottom lip, arousal pouring through her.

When she felt like she was on the edge, she pulled away. Her body trembled, her breath shaky and uneven. She had meant to push him to the brink. She hadn't realized that she would go with him. She needed sanctuary. Needed escape.

"That was it," she said, her voice choked. "I mean…I'm going back to bed now."

He frowned. "What do you mean 'that's it'?"

"Just what I said. Most men would be pretty happy with that."

His face was hidden in shadow, his tone dark. "Then why did you come to me tonight?"

"Because I wanted you. And I got to have you."

"You didn't have an orgasm," he said, his words blunt in the quiet of the room.

"I know, but that wasn't what I came for. I got to have a taste, no pun intended." She slid off the bed and crossed her arms beneath her breasts. "We can talk more tomorrow about how we're going to handle all this."

"This?" he said, indicating the bed.

She shook her head, heat prickling her cheeks. Not embarrassed heat, but anger. She was so mad at…everything. At her body, at Stavros, at herself. At the fear that lived inside of her. A tenant she couldn't seem to evict. "No. About Victoria and where we intend to go from here with that part of our arrangement. You wanted a night. This was a good night. Let's not ruin it now."

"I wanted more," he said. "I still want more."

She nodded. "I know." She wanted more, too. But any more would be far too much. She would have to be too vulnerable. She would have to give too much. Far more than she'd given tonight.

"Stay with me. Just sleep," he said.

That was tempting. Beyond. To sleep in his arms with her head on his chest. To listen to his breathing all night… it surpassed almost every other desire that lived in her.

Which meant she had to say no. "I need to go to bed."

His expression changed, hardened. "We'll talk tomorrow," he said.

"Okay."

She had a feeling that he wasn't going to stay on the topic she wanted to stay on. If there was one thing she'd learned about Stavros it was that beneath all that charm lay a stubbornness that rivaled her own.

Stavros's body still burned. It had been six hours since his late-night visit from Jessica and he couldn't get it, or her, out of his mind. The way she'd taken him, so confident, so bold and sexy. And the way she'd retreated, arms wrapped around her middle, looking like she wanted to disappear.

His feelings on the matter didn't make sense. He'd wanted her to stay. Even if it just meant holding her all night. He'd wanted…he wasn't sure what he'd wanted.

Her actions didn't make sense to him, either. Sex was all about pleasure and release, and she'd taken none for herself. She hadn't removed any of her clothes, he'd barely touched her, and yet, she'd acted as though it was what she wanted.

And then she'd acted like they weren't going to talk about it. She was so very wrong on that count.

His housekeeper refilled his mug of coffee and retreated from the terrace as he lifted the cup to his lips. There was another mug placed across from him and the contents were getting cold, but they were ready for Jessica, when she decided to show herself.

"Morning." He turned and saw Jessica, buttoned up into a yellow dress that covered her from knee to throat, a white belt spanning her tiny waist. She was clutching her little computer in her hands. Her tiny electronic shield.

"Good morning," he said, not bothering to be discreet in his appraisal of her. Her cheeks flushed as she sat down across from him.

She took a sip of her coffee and frowned, not swallowing, not spitting it back out, either.

"Cold?" he asked. She nodded, her frown intensifying. "Bitter?" She nodded again. A smile tugged at the corner of his mouth.

She swallowed slowly, her lip curling into a grimace. "I'll need fresh coffee."

"Leda will be back soon," he said.

"So, things went well last night?"

He said nothing, simply looked at her until the double meaning of her words hit her. He could tell when they did, because she blushed, her lips pulling into a pucker.

"With Victoria," she said sharply.

"Very well." He leaned back in his chair. His heart was beating faster than usual, and that surprised him. He was always in control of himself. Although, Jessica tested that, at every turn she did, and right in this moment, what he had to say to her made him feel…nervous. What her reaction might be made him nervous. "But there is a problem."

"What's that?"

"The same problem we discussed last night. I am currently…obsessed—" he hated the word, but it was the only one that fit "—with another woman, and I can't possibly get engaged to Victoria, much less marry her, while I'm still wrestling with it."

Her face paled, her green eyes looking more vivid set against waxen skin. "Me? This is me you're talking about? Good grief, Stavros, what does it take for a woman to scare you off?"

"A blow job at midnight might not be the best way to go about scaring a man off."

"Granted," she said tightly, some of her color returning.

"I did some reading on endometriosis last night."

Her mouth dropped open, a perfect, crimson O. "You did what?"

"I wanted to understand it more. To understand what you were telling me. I'm embarrassed to say I didn't know anything about it."

"I… Why should you?" The utter confusion on her face puzzled him.

"Because it…it seems like it's not uncommon and like I should. But now, I especially wanted to know about it because of you."

"I don't really have it anymore, like I said. At least I'm not symptomatic."

"You mentioned that, but you still don't want to have sex?"

"It's not that I don't want to. I do, I just…don't. I'm aware that that sounds stupid. But it's…complicated. It's wrapped up in a lot of little problems that you really don't want me to get into." Her green eyes chilled, hardened. "Like I said. I'm not fling material. Too many issues."

"It's understandable. But you also said you had a procedure that fixed most everything for you. Maybe it won't hurt now. Maybe…"

"You know, if it was only physical pain it wouldn't bother me. I've been through hell and back with physical pain. A little more would hardly wreck me. But the point is, I don't know if I can deal with that kind of relationship again. I don't know if I can deal with a man looking at me like I'm the living embodiment of his every crushed dream."

"Jessica, I am not your ex. I don't want anything from you but…"

"Sex. You want sex. And I suck at that, too. My own pain was offensive to him," she said, her words coming out harsh, bitter. "I just had to bite my lip and deal with it because it hurt his feelings. Because crying when it hurt made him feel bad. I had to hide anything I bled on because it disgusted him. And then even when I took steps to fix the pain, when I couldn't take it anymore, that was a failure in his eyes, too. I can't do this right now…"

Stavros felt sick. He pushed his coffee back into the middle of the table. "Tell me."

She looked away from him. "The bottom line is that he wanted kids, I can't have them."

She'd said as much last night. "I saw that endometriosis can effect fertility," he said.

A smile curved her lips. "Yes. It can. But not for everyone. And it doesn't mean it can't happen. But I can't. Because in order to try and fix my endometriosis, I opted to get a hysterectomy. He didn't want me to. He wanted to keep trying to conceive first and I…I couldn't take it anymore. In his mind, I gave up. Can't very well get pregnant if you haven't got an oven to put the bun in, right? To him, I gave up on kids. I gave up on us. I killed our dreams for my own comfort. I'm a selfish bitch. I told you that, remember?" She stood up. "Sorry. I have to go."

She turned and walked back into the house, her expression pale and set as marble. His stomach burned, acid, anger, eating away at him.

Not at her. Never at her.

He stood, and looked out at the ocean for a moment before walking back into the villa. He was more determined now than he'd been a few moments ago.

He needed Jessica. And she needed him. Even if it was only for a while, he was determined to have her. Determined to heal some of the wounds her husband had left behind.

Determined to have a stolen moment of time that belonged solely to him.

He had not been born to be the king. He had taken hold of it when it became clear that Xander would not. He had let go of so many things. So many desires he wouldn't let himself remember now. He had consigned himself to a marriage that was to be little more than a business arrangement.

He had given it all. Would continue to give it all for the

rest of his life. He would embrace the hollowness he had carved out inside of himself, let it fill with all the duty and honor he could possibly stand.

Just now, he was filled with Jessica. With whatever it was she made him feel. Something foreign, all-consuming. Something he wanted to embrace with a desperation he couldn't put into words.

For now, for just a little while, he would. If only she would allow it.

CHAPTER EIGHT

IF POUNDING her head against a wall and repeating the "you are an idiot" mantra would have made any difference to the outcome of her morning conversation with Stavros, she would have done it. Unfortunately, no amount of self-recrimination would fix the fact that she'd vomited her emotional guts up for him to dissect whether he wanted to or not.

Yes, he'd asked. But he hadn't known what he was asking.

I did some research on endometriosis.

Replaying those words in her mind made her eyes sting, made her skin feel tight. When had anyone in her life done that for her? Her mother, her husband, her friends? When had anyone cared enough? Or been brave enough? As far as everyone in her life was concerned her condition only mattered in terms of how it affected them.

Only Stavros had asked. Only he had made that extra effort. Why? Why did he care for her at all? It didn't make sense.

The commanding knock on her door could only come from Stavros. She knew it by now.

"Come in," she said. There was no point in avoiding him. He wouldn't go away. He was like that.

The door opened and Stavros walked in, closing it behind him. "Why don't you let me decide what's too much work?"

She blinked. "What?"

"Can I be the one to decide if you're too much work? Because you keep telling me you are, and that I don't want to deal with you but...the thing is, I do."

He looked so sincere, so deadly serious, and she couldn't help but laugh. "Why? It doesn't make sense. Go...have a fling if that's what you need before you get married. There's a whole lot of women in bikinis down on the public beaches. Or hurry up and marry Victoria, so you can get to your wedding night. But why would you want to waste your time with me?"

"I want you. And if you don't want me, that's fine, but I'm pretty sure your actions last night mean that you do. So if you want me, take some time with me."

"I...I don't think I understand."

"Four weeks. Four weeks and I'll ask Victoria to marry me, and until then, I want you." He looked down. "I understand it's not the world's most romantic proposition, but it's all I can offer."

Her stomach seemed to be cold inside, and she knew that wasn't possible. "Yes, I know. I'm over twenty-eight, I can't have children, I probably have an annoying laugh. The reasons why I'm wrong for you are many and varied. Those are just the obvious ones."

"Yes," he said, the word flat, honest. "But that hasn't stopped me from wanting you."

"I...I don't know whether I'm flattered or insulted. Actually, scratch that, I don't know if I'm supposed to be flattered or insulted. I think I'm flattered, I'm just not certain I should be."

"Because it's a temporary offer?"

She lifted her thumb to her lips and gnawed the corner of her nail, nodding.

"I would never insult you by pretending I could offer something I couldn't. My responsibilities won't change. They are what they are. But I can't get you out of my head. I can't force myself to want Victoria when it's you that I see every time I close my eyes."

"No one's ever said things like this to me," she said, looking up at him, trying to see some hint in his expression that he was joking because…it didn't seem real.

"Not even your husband?"

"No. He uh…he was a college student when we got together. So was I. Young and stupid and very sincere, but not very poetic." She cleared her throat. "It didn't last, either, for all that we thought it would."

"Neither will this," he said.

She nodded. "But we won't pretend otherwise, will we?"

"No. I won't pretend with you, ever. Promise to do the same with me?"

"Yes," she whispered, not sure if she was agreeing to his last request, or his request for the four weeks. She was lost anyway. No matter how much she pretended she was undecided, she was lost to him. To her desire for him. Her curiosity. Yes, she was afraid, but she wanted him more than she wanted to keep hiding.

Because that's what it really was. She wasn't afraid of the pain of sex. She wasn't even as afraid of failing as she'd thought. She was more afraid that she would have sex, and that it would be good. And then she would lose her excuse to hold men at arm's length. She would lose that thing that kept her from seeking out another relationship.

She swallowed, trying to push her fear down. Fear she didn't want. Not now.

"I need you," he said, the words raw, lacking charm,

flirtation, any kind of artifice. "I'm not sure if you realize how much. I'm not sure you could, as it's something I don't entirely understand. But I need…you. This. I hope you want me."

She did understand. She needed him, too. As much as she needed to escape from the confines she'd put herself into, as much as she needed to move on. He felt like a necessity.

She hadn't ever thought of herself as a temporary kind of woman. But then, when sex was such an ordeal it was hard to think of it as something she might do recreationally. Still…Stavros made her want a taste of the illicit.

Of something she'd never really had, first because she'd met her husband at such a young age, and then because she'd developed endometriosis. And after that, because clinging to the past, wrapping herself in the memories of the pain, had become a shield against any sort of future hurt.

It also kept her tied to her old life. Tied to who she'd been.

She needed to be free of it. She finally felt ready to be free of it. It was all well and good to wish she could fully embrace her new reality. But she wasn't. And that was no one's fault but hers.

"Yes," she said again. "I want you, too. And now that you've given up on that fake flirting business I actually find you a lot more irresistible."

"What fake flirting business?"

"You know. That's not you, Stavros. This is. This is the man I can't resist."

He swallowed visibly, a muscle in his jaw twitching. "As long as you can't resist me."

"I could. But I'm not going to anymore."

He laughed, the sound as raw and ragged as his expression. "I couldn't resist you. That's why I'm here."

Her stomach contracted, her heart pounding faster. To

have such a big, strong man admitting he couldn't fight his attraction to her was…it was beyond her. And it restored something in her. Something she'd thought was so mangled beyond recognition it could never be fixed.

"This is stupid," she said, laughing, because if she didn't she thought she might cry.

"I know," he said, taking a step toward her, cupping her cheek in his palm. "I know." He rested his forehead against hers, his eyes closed.

She tilted her face and touched her lips to his, a gentle kiss, a question. One he answered with his own kiss, stronger, more certain. His tongue teased her, and she parted her mouth for him, sliding her tongue against his, the friction igniting a wave of heat in her stomach that spread to her breasts, down to her core.

"Wow. You really are an amazing kisser," she said, a shiver sliding down through her.

"And you are very honest."

She shook her head. "I'm not usually. I just do my very best to seem tough all the time and no one questions what I do or say too closely. They don't want me to kill them with snark. And that way I don't have to be honest. But for some reason, I am honest with you. I'm not sure why."

"You have the same effect on me," he said. "I can't fathom it."

"It's the lust thing. It's scrambling our brains."

A smile turned up the corners of his mouth. "Is that it?"

She nodded. "I'm not familiar with it on quite this level, but I remember feeling this way in college a couple of times."

"Yes, that sounds about right. You'd think at our age we would be impervious." He smiled slightly and it made her knees feel a little weak.

"Hey, watch it. No age jokes."

He kissed her again. "You are a beautiful woman. I cannot imagine you being any more attractive to me. Your dress today is lethal."

She looked down at her demure yellow dress. "This?"

"It has buttons," he growled. "And all I can think of is undoing all of those buttons."

Her face heated. "Really?"

"Oh, yes, really. I want to do it now, but I don't want to move too quickly."

"It's not even noon."

"So?"

"Isn't there a no-sex-before-noon rule?"

He laughed. "Sex isn't like alcohol. And if that's been your experience with it, I can tell you, you need your experience broadened."

She swallowed. "I'm a little nervous. A lot nervous." She wasn't sure what he would do to her, and that fear wasn't rooted in the fear of physical pain, but over how complete the loss of control might be. Over whether or not she would be able to hold onto her defenses.

He smoothed his thumb over her cheek. "Tell me, is there a specific act that causes worse pain?"

She nodded, finding that focusing on the physical was helpful. "Orgasm can cause pain, which…sucks." She breathed the last word with a shaky laugh. "The worst of it always came from…penetration. In the end at least."

He nodded slowly. "No sex. Not now. I want to take your dress off. I want to touch your breasts. Taste them, too. Nothing more. Nothing more until you're ready."

She could hardly breathe. His promises, so husky and sensual and perfect, had her body wound so tight she was certain she would break. "You really do have a way with words."

"Funny you should say that. My speechwriters usually

handle my words. I pride myself on being a man of action. What are words if you can't back them up?" He slid his hands down to the first button on her dress and slowly slid the little fabric-covered bead through the hole, letting the neck of the dress gap.

She wished she could capture the bravado she'd felt last night. But then, last night had been her game. She'd been in control, in her element. She'd been giving pleasure and feeding off of the residual. Here and now, Stavros had command of her. A reverse on last night, and she found she actually liked it.

He moved to the next button, then the next, pressing a kiss to her neck for each button. When he reached the button just beneath her breasts, he slid his tongue along the line of her collarbone, then down a fraction. He paused at her belt, sliding it through the buckle slowly, then letting it drop. He continued down, until her dress hung open, until his tongue was curving around the line of her bra, teasing her sensitive flesh.

She shivered as he pushed the dress from her shoulders and let it fall to the floor, leaving her in her white pumps and matching bra and panties.

"You are amazing," he said, dropping to his knees to press a kiss to her stomach. Tears filled her eyes and she couldn't stop them. She didn't want him to take her panties off, not this time. He would see her scars and she wasn't ready. Not yet.

She tugged on his shoulders, urging him up, and he complied, his hand on her back, toying with the catch on her bra, teasing them both. He took a step, his arms wrapped around her still. She stepped backward. They made a slow, smooth dance to the bed and he undid her bra as he laid her down, pulling it off and casting it aside.

He was half over her, his breathing harsh, his eyes on

her bare breasts. Thankfully, she knew they were one of her best features, so this was the easy part. It was made even easier when she caught the feral light in his dark eyes. "You are so much more beautiful than I imagined. Much more beautiful than I *could* have imagined. I have never seen a woman as exquisite as you." He cupped her, slid his fingers gently over her tightened nipples.

She arched into him, pleasure making her breath catch.

"Tell me if I do something you don't like," he said. "Tell me, and I'll stop."

She didn't want him to stop. Not ever. She reveled in his touch, in the feel of his rough, masculine hands on her tender skin. And when he replaced his fingers with his mouth, with the slick friction of his tongue, she felt a sharp tightening in her core, waves of pleasure, of pending release, rippling through her.

She gripped his hair, arched her body. She was close. She'd never been so close, so fast. She couldn't remember ever wanting anyone this badly, either.

"Oh, yes." She sighed, letting her head fall back.

He raised his head. "More?"

She nodded, biting her bottom lip. "Yes."

He moved his hand down her stomach and she was certain he would feel the line of scar tissue that ran just below the waistband of her underwear, but she was past caring. Past caring about anything. About the future. About possible pain. Even about the loss of control.

How could something that felt so amazing end in pain? Any kind of pain was worth it, surely.

He slipped his fingers beneath her panties, grazed the scar and continued down to where she was wet and ready for him. He teased the entrance to her body with his fingers, before sliding them over her clitoris. The sensation was like fire, burning heat from there throughout her body.

She gritted her teeth, her breath getting sharper, uneven. She curled her fingers into the sheets as he continued to touch her there. Soft, even strokes that brought her closer and closer to the edge.

He leaned in and kissed her mouth as he increased the pressure of his touch, and everything in her seemed to release at once, a flood of pleasure roaring through her, drowning out thought and sound. She cried out, not caring if she was loud, not caring that it was daylight, not caring that their relationship would only last a month.

Because there was nothing else. Not in that moment. There was Stavros. And there was what he made her feel.

Only when reality started piecing itself back together, did fear assault her. But there hadn't been any pain yet. Still, she waited. Waited for the low, dragging sensation that rivaled stories she'd heard about childbirth to begin.

And there was nothing. Nothing but a feeling of being replete. Nothing but a feeling of total bliss and satisfaction. She didn't feel as though she'd given her body away, didn't feel as though she was lost. She felt as though she'd gained a part of herself back.

A sob shook her body and she felt a tear slide down her cheek. The tears she couldn't find earlier. Tears she hadn't been able to find for a long time. Something in her shifted, changed. Like a dam had been broken inside of her, one she'd walled up to protect herself. One she felt she didn't need. Not now.

Stavros cupped her face, his expression fierce. "Did I hurt you?"

She bit her lip and shook her head. "No. You didn't. I can't…I can't remember the last time… Thank you."

He wrapped his arms around her and pulled her to him so that her head was rested on his chest. "Don't thank me.

I can't accept thanks for that. I took far too much pleasure from it for that."

"Realistically," she said, trying to escape from some of the moment's intimacy, impossible when she was mostly naked and cradled in his arms, but worth a try, "you have to see Victoria a couple more times before you propose."

He nodded. "All right."

"I know that will run during our…relationship. But I suppose as long as you don't…"

"I will be faithful to you, you don't have to worry about that. And I will be faithful when I am married," he said.

She swallowed. It was the right thing for him to say, the right thing for him to do. He should keep his vows. She believed in marriage, respected it. For all that she and Gil had screwed up their marriage, neither of them had cheated.

Still, a part of her died when he said it. "I'm glad. For all of that."

"This might not be the best idea. But I don't regret it."

"I can't, either," she said. It was the absolute truth. How could she regret what had passed between them? How could she regret the loss of a fear? There were others, of course. But she was free of one, too. And that wasn't a small thing.

"So, tell me," she said, attempting a subject change, in a bid keep things from getting too heavy, "what does a woman expect when she signs on to be your temporary companion?"

"I'm not sure. I've never had a relationship quite like this. Of course, I've never met a woman quite like you."

"What do you normally do?"

"There's that sort of coyness to it that one employs in a sexual relationships. Gifts, shallow conversation, references only to the here and now, nothing said of the future one way or the other. And with you, there's no coyness, that's for sure."

She smiled. "I don't do coy."

"I noticed." He tightened his hold on her. "All of my life has been devoted to fulfilling the needs of others. Right now, just now, I want to meet my own."

So this was for him, as much as for her. She liked knowing that. Felt empowered by it. Because there was something he needed to, and maybe she could provide it. Maybe she could be the one to give him moments of bliss. Moments that were purely his own, so that he would have the memories years later when his life was no longer his at all.

"What do you want?" she asked.

He sifted his fingers through her hair. "I want to sleep with you tonight. Just sleep, if that's all you want."

"That's too easy. What else?"

"To go to the beach. Which should be easy, since we're on an island. I am a man with the world at my fingertips in terms of the material. The thing I often find myself lacking in is a companion who makes life interesting. Who makes it fun. You be you, and I will simply enjoy it."

"Really, you're too nice. I feel outmatched."

"I like your prickles," he said. "Even more now that I understand them."

She sat up and wrapped her arms around herself. "I should get dressed."

"I'm in no hurry."

"I have some work to check on, just real quick, and then…and then we can do whatever we want. Because that's what we've decided to do, isn't it? Whatever we want for the next month."

He smiled at her and her heart felt like it tightened in on itself. She could do a month. A month was short enough. Short enough that he wouldn't start wishing she could be a million things she could never be.

CHAPTER NINE

ANYTHING he wanted turned out to be much more low-key and much less in bed than she'd imagined it might be.

Stavros took her on a tour of the ruins just outside the city, and then down to the open-air markets to shop. The market ran just outside the boundaries of the packed harbor, small stalls crammed between buildings, the ocean just beyond them.

Stavros could have taken her anywhere in Piraeus. To the more modern quadrants of the city, to exclusive boutiques with cutting-edge fashion.

But he'd taken her here. Because he knew what she liked. He understood what she enjoyed. She did her best to ignore her constricted lungs and turn her focus to the items for sale.

There was an eclectic mix of trash and truly exquisite treasure on offer. Things she would have found at an average yard sale in her home town, fresh seafood and antiques all mingled together. She bought a necklace fashioned from fishing line and glass beads, and earrings made from old coins.

"It's certainly vintage," Stavros said, eyeing her purchases later at an outdoor restaurant.

"Yes, most definitely."

"You need a *pallas* to go with it."

She pulled her necklace out of the bag and held it up so

that the afternoon sun filtered through the glass beads. "All right, what's that?"

"The traditional draped dress. It would look beautiful on you."

"Not my typical style though, draped clothes."

"No. Not at all." Today she was in a full white skirt that went down past her knees and a red button-up top. All very crisp and tailored.

"It makes for an intriguing thought."

"Yes, but you don't like my clothes."

"No, I like your clothes very much, it's just that I find them a distraction. And now that I have permission to be distracted...well, I like them even more."

Her cheeks heated. He made her feel...he made her feel so new. Like this was fresh. Flirting, and eating together. The anticipation of sex. And she was anticipating it. Bigtime. She smiled and looked down at her plate.

She ignored the little hint of fear that pooled in her stomach. If she felt so close to him now, what would happen after? She really hadn't ever been a fling girl. She'd been one and done. She'd met her husband right out of high school, and he was the man she'd married.

"What is it?" he asked.

"Nothing."

He reached over and took her chin between his thumb and forefinger, tilting her face up. "What?"

It was hard meeting his eyes. Intimate, suddenly. "I'm happy. I haven't...enjoyed anything like this in a long time."

"I haven't, either."

"Stavros, why is this marriage so important to you?" She wasn't sure where the question came from, only that it seemed essential, suddenly. "I mean, I know why you need to do it eventually. But it's more than that, I can tell. I just...want to know why."

He frowned. "I'm the only one, Jessica."

"I know."

"When Xander left, everything was chaos. My father was a wreck, my mother was gone. Eva was just a child. There was only me. My willingness to step in. I was a teenager, but just that show of strength and solidarity, and the years I spent after building up the economy, that made the difference. I need everything to be as it should be. I need it to have balance and order. I want it to."

"And Victoria will help with that."

"Victoria is only a piece of the puzzle. I've been setting all of this in place for years."

"I know," she said, looking away from him again. "Plans...I wish sometimes that some of mine had worked out. And sometimes...I'm glad they didn't."

Really, today was the first time she was honestly glad to be in a different place. With a different man. She hadn't loved her ex for years. But very often she'd longed to go back to a time when she did love him.

A time when her life had been full of possibilities. Instead of a time when so many of her dreams had died.

"Mine have to work out," he said. "For my people."

"Has Xander officially abdicated?"

"No. And he won't until after my father dies, which doesn't look like it will be soon. I am thankful for that."

"But you're playing chess," she said.

"What do you mean?"

"I actually suck at chess, but I have a brother who plays very well, and he used to talk me into playing when we were younger. I could never win, because I was always responding to his moves. He knew all of his moves from the beginning. And he had back-up maneuvers just in case I failed to be predictable, but mostly, he just followed the strategy he'd had since the opening move. You already know your checkmate."

He laughed and placed his hand over hers, his thumb blazing a trail of heat over her skin as he moved it back and forth. "But this is a move I did not see making."

"Do you regret it? Because we haven't done anything we can't take back."

He shook his head. "I don't. I should, I'm certain of that. This is unfair to you."

It was her turn to laugh. "How? I'm not some young, inexperienced girl. I've been married, I've been divorced. I've done love and loss. I'm a bit too cynical to get hurt by a temporary affair." She hoped that was true. She'd certainly believed it of herself before she'd met Stavros. Before she'd started caring for him.

How had that happened? He was so far removed from her. A prince, for heaven's sake. And a client. They shouldn't connect on any level. Yet, she felt like he was the one person who had a hope of understanding her. She felt she understood him. How had he started to matter so much?

He nodded. "I know. But your husband hurt you. I don't want any part of that. Of hurting you."

She forced out a laugh and lifted her wineglass to her lips. "By that logic, you should worry about yourself. Yes, he hurt me. But I hurt him, too. Marriage is a two-way street, and very rarely is everything the fault of one person. I'm capable of breaking a man's heart, Stavros, so perhaps it's me who should be giving you an out."

"I don't have a heart to break, Jess."

"I don't believe that."

"When have I had time to worry about my feelings? I have to take care of Kyonos. While my father took his rage and grief out on Xander, while Xander wallowed in his guilt, someone had to push it aside and stand up. I have made it my mission to never allow emotion to dictate what I do. It has no place in me." His eyes met hers, the blankness in them frightening. She was so used to his charming glimmer that seeing him now, flat, empty, made her feel cold. The problem was that it rang far truer than the charismatic charm ever had. As though this was really him. The real depth of him. "It is what I must do, to be the best king I can be. To be better than my father."

"I get that." If she hadn't been able to hide behind her wall of snark, she could never have done her job. Could never have gone on matching other couples, trying to help them find their happily ever after. She couldn't have done it if she'd allowed the wound from the loss of her own to keep on bleeding.

She'd learned to shut it off. To protect herself. That was all deserting her now.

Not the time.

The darkness in his eyes changed, warmed. "But for a while, I'm going to focus on this." He leaned over and pressed a light kiss to her lips. He'd barely touched her since their encounter in the morning, and it was so very welcome.

"I appreciate your focus," she said, her breath coming in shorter bursts now. She tried not to be so obvious, tried to regain control.

But she could tell, from the expression on Stavros's face, that he didn't have any more control than she did. And that made it all seem a little bit more acceptable. Made it feel better that she couldn't stop her stomach from fluttering and her heart from thundering, hard and fast.

Neither of them had command of the attraction. The fact she was a part of it, that she was able to drive a man to this point, it did wonders for her completely squished ego.

It affected more than that, but she didn't really want to ponder it on a deeper level.

"I can't focus on anything else when you're around," he said, sliding his fingers through her hair.

"It's hard to believe you needed my help finding a wife. You seem to have the romance thing down."

He shook his head. "Romance is an area I've always found myself lacking in. Not in seduction, or flirting, but that's a different matter, isn't it? It requires no sincerity. And the matter of my marriage…that's separate from either of those. You know that."

His eyes were intense on hers, desperation evident in their depths. Desperation for her to understand. She didn't know why, and she was willing to bet he didn't, either. Only that she felt it echo inside of her.

"I know," she said, covering his hand with hers. "But we aren't worrying about that, right?"

"I see you've finally gotten on board with the denial tactic."

"Reality has its place. But it's not here."

"Normally, I would disagree. I would disagree with the entire concept of this relationship. But I don't have the strength right now." The words were rough, a hard admission for a man who lived his life by his strength. Who had based every action on being stronger than those around him.

He was Atlas, with the world on his shoulders. Or at least a country.

He deserved to set it down for a second. To have some relief.

"The only reason you don't have the strength right now, is because you've had to be stronger than any man should have to be. You've given up too much." she said.

"Maybe. But until now I hadn't missed anything. But if I passed up the chance to be with you…I think I would miss it for all of my life."

His words hung between them, thick and serious. And

far too true. They'd always spoken with honesty, it seemed like they couldn't help speaking with honesty. But this was a hard truth to take. Mostly because it was true for her, too, and admitting he was that important, that essential, scared her.

She swallowed, blinking to try and dispel the stinging in her eyes. "I would certainly hate to miss this." She looked at the view, at the sun glinting off the crystalline water. It was easy to look at the scenery and say it. Easy to let him think she might mean something else.

Far too difficult for her to let herself be vulnerable to him. To let him know how much he was starting to mean to her. It was almost harder to admit to herself how much he was starting to mean to her. Because she was tired of wanting the impossible.

"Jess." He whispered her name and he turned to look at him. His expression stopped her heart. He looked so hungry, so sad. And just as quickly as the emotions became evident on his face, they disappeared. "I do have some work to complete today, and then I would like to see you again. After dinner?"

She nodded. "Yes." She was grateful for a break, a reprieve. Because her chest felt so tight, far too tight, and she was finding it difficult to breathe.

This was supposed to be about her. About reclaiming a part of herself she thought was lost. About letting go of her past, not clinging to someone else. And she couldn't lie and say Stavros meant nothing to her. Of course he did. She liked him. She wanted him to have this, this last thing that he desired, before he gave himself over to his country.

But she was going to try to lie and say that was the end of it. She was going to try and do that for as long as she could.

She would use the time apart to try and get a grip on the other emotions, the unwelcome ones.

"Then I'll see you back to the villa."

She nodded, trying to ignore the fullness inside of her that was keeping her lungs from expanding all the way. "That sounds good."

Yes, she needed to get a grip, and she needed to get it badly.

She'd gone into her marriage a naive idiot, and she'd learned a lot about the reality of life since then. That, coupled with the fact that she knew her relationship with Stavros wouldn't last, should be enough to keep her head on straight.

Sadly, she wasn't certain it was.

"Jessica?" The villa was empty when Stavros returned later that evening. It was later than he'd intended. Mainly because he'd spent the evening sitting in his Piraeus office, staring out at the ocean and trying to get a grip on his rioting libido.

And the strange twinge in his heart that seemed to hit him hard and radiate down to his stomach whenever he pictured Jessica's face.

He was much later than he should have been, and he half expected her to be in bed. He prowled the halls for a few moments, opened the door to her room and confirmed that it was empty. He'd known right away.

He could feel that she wasn't here. A strange sensation, an impossible one, and yet, he had complete certainty in it. Strange how she'd done that. How she'd opened him back up to feeling.

Stranger that he wasn't fighting it.

Just for this month. Just a little while.

He walked out onto the terrace and looked down at the beach below. He could see her by the shore, her silhouette outlined by the silver moon. He walked down the terrace stairs, and out to the beach, pulling the knot on his tie and letting it fall somewhere in the sand. He discarded his jacket and kept moving to her.

No matter where she was, he felt compelled to find her. To go to her. He could feel her absence nearly as keenly as he could feel her presence. And he wasn't certain what that meant. Only that he had to be near her. And that if the force of his physical desire weren't so powerful, weren't so all-consuming, the need that came with it, the need to be with her, would be frightening. At least with the lust there, he had something else to focus on. Something to take the edge off the unfiltered emotion she called up in him with so much ease.

He walked soundlessly on the sand, discarding his shoes, not caring about their fate. Jessica turned sharply, and he wondered if she could feel him, too.

"Hi," she said, her voice barely audible above the sound of the waves on the shore.

"Sorry I'm late."

"You didn't give me a time. It's okay."

"Still, it's pretty late."

She shrugged. "It's okay. I had a nice evening. I called Victoria and told her to expect an invitation to an event in Kyonos. I hope that was okay."

"It was the right thing to do. No matter how I feel about it."

"It's not exactly ignoring it, I admit. But we both know you can't just not contact her at all over the next month."

His stomach tightened. "I know."

"Don't you have a celebration ball coming up for when Eva and Makhail return from their honeymoon? It's on the copy of your schedule I received and I thought it would be the perfect opportunity for you to be seen with Victoria."

"Oh, yes. I had forgotten."

"She should go to that. With you. Give a hint as to your

developing relationship. That way your people can really look forward to the engagement announcement."

His people. That was what all of this was about. His country. His heart. He had thrown himself into it, completely, into planning what he would do to make it better, to heal it. And that was why he was marrying Victoria.

He couldn't lose sight of it. But it was so easy to do when Jessica filled his vision. So easy to simply let his desire for her color everything. That was emotion. That was weakness. He could not afford it.

Just right now, it was okay though. Just for this moment in time. He moved to her, unable to stand apart from her any longer. Unable to be so close yet not touching her.

He sifted his fingers through silken strands of blond hair. "I missed you," he said. He wasn't sure why he said it, even though it was true.

He wasn't certain that level of honesty had a place in their arrangement. But he wasn't sure what else he should say, either. Wasn't sure what to hold back and what to give.

Holding anything back when Jessica was around seemed an impossibility. He wasn't sure he wanted to, and that was a new feeling entirely.

Lust he'd dealt with. He'd put it aside when he had to, embraced it when it was convenient. He'd never been controlled by it. But it had never before been accompanied by this strange…ache. An ache that seemed to spread through his body, sink down deep into his bones, beyond, down into his soul.

Wanting Jessica was painful. And it was more real than anything in his recent memory. He craved it. Because it was better than not being near her. Than not wanting her. He wasn't sure what kind of madness it was, only that for now he wanted to drink it in.

"Jessica, I want to kiss you."

She nodded, her gaze level with his. "I'm game. I like it when you kiss me." She had a bit of her false bravado in place, but it was all right. One of them needed to keep their guard up, and he wasn't certain he could.

When his mother had died, he had been the only one to hold himself together. He had been the one to pick up and move forward. He hadn't been allowed to grieve. Hadn't had time to feel. He had closed down.

But he couldn't shut these feelings off. Couldn't staunch the flow of emotion that seemed to bleed inside of him like a hidden wound. When he looked at Jessica, he had no control.

"I want to do more than that. I want to make love with you tonight. But you tell me, if it hurts. And I'll stop. I don't care how hard it is for me to stop, I will. I would never hurt you." Even as he said the words he feared they weren't true. Not that he wouldn't stop making love with her if it hurt, he was confident he would do that.

But he feared he might hurt her emotionally. That he might have a part in causing her further pain that way. He didn't want to, but to avoid it he would have to turn back. And at this point, even that would hurt her.

More than that, he feared what would happen to himself. Selfish, maybe. But he felt like he was standing at the edge of a fire, toying with the idea of touching the flame. Then throwing himself into it.

They were in too deep to escape unscathed. But then, maybe they had been from the beginning. That connection—instant, seemingly physical—had been more from the moment they'd met.

She nodded slowly. "I want that. And I'm not even nervous. Which is crazy but I just…know it will be good. That I'll be good."

"Something I have no doubt about," he said, forcing words through his tightened throat.

She laughed. "I'm glad."

"Oh, Jess, you are the most beautiful woman. The most fascinating. Bewitching." He kissed her. Her lips were so soft, so warm. They heated him, all the way through his body, his blood burning in his veins, his body getting hard.

She parted her lips and angled her head, her hand pressed to his cheek. He took advantage of the move and slid his tongue into her mouth, sliding it against hers, the intimate action sending a hard kick of lust through him.

It roared in him like a beast, one that demanded satisfaction. That demanded he lay her down in the sand and take what he needed. That he use her to fill the emptiness inside of him. Because she could. She was the only one who could.

He put his hands on her hips, braced her. Braced him. He curled his fingers in, gripped the full skirt of her dress tightly in his palms. He wouldn't do that to her. He wouldn't make this hard and fast, he wouldn't make it about his satisfaction.

He would give to her. He would control his own need. He would master it.

It was Jessica who changed the game. Jessica who moved her hands over his chest, down to where he was hard and ready for her. She was a mass of contradictions, his Jessica. So confident in giving pleasure. So hesitant to receive it.

So afraid to release control.

She cupped him and he nearly lost his head then and there, her palm sweet and knowing on his erection, sliding over the length of him.

"Oh, yes," she whispered against his lips. "I'm so ready for this."

He took her hand and moved it away from him, his body

protesting. He lifted it to his lips and kissed her palm. "Not like that, Jess. Not this time."

"Stavros…"

"You aren't in charge. I know you don't like to hear that. But that's the way it's going to be."

Her eyes rounded and he wondered if he'd taken her a step to far. But she didn't move away. She moistened her lips and slid her hand around to the back of his neck, her fingers sifting through his hair. She kissed his jaw, his ear.

He chuckled when he felt her teeth scrape against his earlobe. "I see how it's going to be," he said.

"Do you?" she said, her voice trembling, betraying a hint of nerves.

"Well, that isn't entirely true. I can't really guess how it's going to be. Because I have never felt this way about a woman before." As he said it, he realized how true it was. "I have never wanted a woman as I want you."

"Glad we're on the same page there. I've never felt like this, either, not even before…not even before…not ever."

"Then we're both equal. And for that I'm glad. I would hate to be standing here, ready to lose my mind with wanting you, with you feeling completely calm and certain."

"Oh, no sweat there, Stavros. I'm shaking," she whispered.

He swore. "Sorry, I'm losing my finesse."

"Good. I don't need your finesse. You're a very charming man, Stavros, and you seem to come by it effortlessly, no matter how you really feel. I would much rather have something real."

"You have it." He kissed her again, through with talking. Words were too difficult now. He just had to show her. Because it was the absolute truth. With her there was no artifice. He had tried to put distance between them with his charming persona, and he hadn't been able to. She made him real.

She made him real in a way he could never remember being before.

He wrapped his arms around her and pulled her flush against his body, sighing when her full breasts made contact with his chest. She was soft and perfect, everything a woman should be. He ran his hands over her curves, the indent of her waist, the fullness of her hips, the round curve of her butt. He palmed her, his body shuddering.

"Buttons," he growled, taking his hands from her backside and turning his focus to the front of her dress. Most of her dresses had buttons, but he was half convinced she'd chosen this one to torment him thanks to his earlier comments.

Her wicked smile confirmed it. He moved slowly, pushing each button through the hole at half the speed he could have done it in. Teasing them both. It was worth it. She bit her lip and watched him work. Even in the dim light, he could see the color mounting in her cheeks. He could feel her breath shorten, her breasts rising up against his fingers as he worked at the buttons there.

He was hard, burning with the need to take her, to join with her.

He pushed the top of the dress down, letting it fall around her waist. She had a lace bra on beneath it, thin and sexy. He slid his thumb over one breast, felt her nipple harden beneath his touch.

He moved to the next set of buttons on until the skirt loosened enough to fall down her hips and pool in the sand.

She was barefoot already, and now she was wearing nothing more than a pair of lace underwear and bra. He'd had her this undressed before, but not all the way. He unhooked her bra in one deft movement and consigned it to the sand with the dress.

"You're perfection," he said, cupping her breasts, teasing her nipples. She closed her eyes, her lips parted slightly. He took advantage of the moment and kissed her, then moved to her neck, her collarbone, before drawing one tightened bud between his lips and sliding his tongue over it. "And you taste amazing," he said.

She shivered beneath him, and he felt an answering tremor echo in his own body. He'd never felt so connected to a lover before. He'd always been committed to giving pleasure, because sex was only satisfying if all involved got what they needed. But he'd never felt dependent on his partner's response. Had never needed to draw the pleasure out like this, to be sure it was superior to his own. To be sure it was superior to any she'd had before.

He got on his knees in the sand, not caring about his suit, not caring about anything but the need to taste her everywhere. He slid his tongue along the waistband of her panties and he felt her stiffen.

"Come on now, Jessica, don't get shy on me."

She gripped his shoulders, the cold from her fingertips seeping through his shirt. She didn't stop him. He hooked his fingers into the sides of her underwear and tugged them down her legs.

She stepped out of them, her movements unsteady. He looked up at her and saw a shimmer of tears in her eyes. When he looked back down, it wasn't simply the gorgeous triangle of curls at the apex of her thighs that caught his attention. It was the scar that ran just above it. A thin line, an imperfection that meant very little to him in terms of how it looked.

But one he knew held a wealth of pain. Her pain. He could not remain unaffected by that. He was grateful he was on his knees, because the hard punch it delivered to his stomach might have taken him there had he not been down already.

He could hear her teeth chattering. "Stavros…"

"Oh, Jess." He leaned in and pressed his face to her stomach, kissing her there, just beneath her belly button. "You are amazing to me."

He lowered his head and traced the same line the surgeon's knife had followed, pressing kisses to the depressed section of skin. He didn't give her a chance to protest. He moved lower and flicked the tip of his tongue over her clitoris. A raw sound escaped her lips and she clung more tightly to him, her nails digging sharply into his shoulders.

He held her hips tightly and continued his exploration of her body with his lips and tongue. He could feel her shaking beneath his touch, and that was good, because he was shaking, too. He couldn't remember wanting a woman more, couldn't remember if the taste of woman had ever been essential. He was certain it never had been before.

Jessica was utterly unique. Comparing her to other experiences, comparing this moment to other experiences, was an impossibility.

He slipped his hand between her thighs and pressed a finger slowly inside her body, she froze for a moment, her hands gripping at his shirt and he felt her muscles contract around him as she found her release. It was her orgasm, her pleasure, and yet he felt spent. Satisfied.

But still in need of more. He was so hard his body burned.

She slid down to her knees, kissing him, her body pressed against him, her hands tearing at the buttons on his shirt. He was sure more than one was made a casualty in her haste, but he didn't care. Nothing mattered now. Nothing but being joined to Jessica. Nothing but finding some solace from the ache. From the emptiness he'd never been cognizant of until she'd walked into his life.

He helped her with his pants, shucking them off as quickly as possible. She pressed lightly on his shoulders, pushing him back into the sand. She slid her hands down his chest, his torso, along the side of his erection, teasing but not touching.

"Careful," he groaned.

She smiled, a sassy, sleepy smile of a woman who'd been satisfied, but who was still hungry for more. The big difference between the two of them right now was that she'd had the edge taken off, and she had the time to tease. He feared he did not.

She moved over him, and he put his hands on her waist, tilting his face up to pull one nipple into his mouth. She arched into him and he slid one hand down her back, guiding her so that his erection was pressing against her slick entrance.

"It's up to you now," he said, words nearly impossible to force through his tightened throat.

She bit her lip, her eyes on his. He could see her fear and he wished there was something he could to ease it. He kept his hold on her steady, kept his body still, gave the control back to her. He didn't want to move too quickly, didn't want to do anything to ruin the moment.

She lowered herself onto him, taking him inside an inch at a time. It took all of his strength not to thrust up into her. He kept his focus on her face. Her lips parted, her expression intense. And when she had him inside all the way, she let her head fall back, a slow breath escaping her lips.

"Oh, yes," she whispered.

"Good?" he asked.

She looked down at him, a smile touching her lips. "So good. And not enough."

She tilted her hips and pleasure flashed through him like a flood, pouring over him, taking over him. She set the pace, but he moved with her, thrusting up into her body, encouraged by the sounds of ecstasy coming from her lips. She planted her hands on his chest, her face tilted down, her hair covering them both, shielding them.

He could feel his orgasm building, taking him to the edge. He clung to it, every ounce of his willpower channeled into keeping his control. He had to give her more. One more. One more graceful movement and she tossed her head back, her breasts thrust forward. He captured one with his lips and she froze, her mouth open on a silent scream.

And then he let go. He was falling, lost, unsure if he would ever come back to earth. Back to himself. But Jessica was there. And that meant nothing else mattered. Nothing but the pleasure that bound them together, nothing but the all-consuming sensation that was washing over him like a wave, drawing him farther and farther away from shore.

She collapsed over his chest, her breath hot on his skin, her breasts pressed against his stomach. He wrapped his arms around her and smoothed his hand over her hair.

He could feel her tears on him, dampening his skin. "Jess…don't cry."

"It's good crying," she said, sniffing.

"No pain?"

She shook her head. "No pain. You're amazing, by the way."

"That was all you."

"I don't think so," she said. "It's never been quite like that for me before."

He wound a silken strand of her hair around his finger, then released it, watching as the ocean breeze caught it. "Well, it hasn't ever been quite like that for me, either."

"You've never had to deal with a neurotic woman who had mass amounts of sexual hang-ups and cried afterward?"

He laughed, so strange because he had her naked body pressed to his front and he was becoming increasingly aware of the sticky, itchy sand at his back. And he couldn't remember ever wanting to laugh after sex. Sleep. Go back to his own bed, yes. But not laugh.

He sat up and brought her with him, holding her on his lap. "You are truly unique." He kissed her, drank her in. Would he ever feel like he wasn't starving for her?

He stood and swept her into his arms, looking out at the waves, the breeze warm on his bare skin. "Hang on," he said.

He ran toward the water and she tightened her hold around his neck, making a sharp, squeaking sound as they hit the waves, the water spraying around them. He walked out into the surf and spun them around. He set her down gently, the water lapping around her hips. She was laughing, breathless. He was shocked to discover that he was laughing and breathless, too.

She didn't just make him feel. She made him feel everything. All at once. And in such a big way he was sure he would burst with it.

"You're crazy," she said, kissing his mouth, her lips tasting of salt water and Jessica.

"Maybe a little." He looked at her face, so pale and lovely in the moonlight. "Yeah, maybe a little." He couldn't stop the smile from spreading over his face, couldn't fight against the strange, expanding feeling in his chest.

She wrapped her arms around his waist. "You're like Prince Charming's hot cousin. Prince Sexy."

"No nicknames," he said.

She laughed against his chest. "All right, fine. No nicknames." She smoothed her hands over his back. "You've got sand all over your back, Prince Sexy."

"I wonder whose fault that is?"

She looked up at him, the expression on her face impish. "No clue."

Something in his chest seemed to break, causing a release. Like a bird escaping the confines of a cage. A strange sensation assaulted him. Happiness. Freedom. Things he didn't have a lot of experience with.

If only he could hold on to it forever.

This month would have to do. Four weeks to carry him through the rest of his life.

CHAPTER TEN

"STAY in bed with me tonight." Stavros tightened his hold on her hand when they reached the top of the stairs back at the villa.

"You want me to sleep with you?"

"Eventually." A wicked smile spread over his lips and her heart expanded. Sex, lovemaking, whatever it had been, with him was like a whole new experience.

She should feel...some sort of awkwardness. It was their first time together after all. Walking back from the beach with him completely naked, her beautiful 1950s-secretary dress discarded and uncared for, should have left her blushing.

The memory of what it had been like to ride him, to be filled with him, to lose her mind completely when she orgasmed, rushed over her. How vocal she'd been both when he'd gone down on her and when he'd been in her, should have made her want to hide under the covers.

But she felt...surprisingly relaxed. And also still turned on.

She'd never experienced this sort of comfort in her own skin before. Even when she'd been younger with nothing medically wrong with her, she'd had insecurities. Her hips were a little wide for her body, her stomach not perfectly flat.

It had taken her a long time to let Gil make love with her with the lights on. And earlier she'd let Stavros touch her with the sunlight filtering through the window. Maybe it was her age. Maybe she'd finally hit that point where she just didn't care. With Gil she'd been an eighteen-year-old virgin, after all. A couple years later and they'd gotten married. Then things had started going wrong with her body.

And now things were so much better. The sex had been so good she didn't think she could have felt anything but good about it if she'd tried. His pleasure had been obvious. He'd had no insecurities, no anger to project onto her. And she'd just basked in her own pleasure, in the way they'd been connected, like one person. She hadn't had to wonder if she'd been right, because she could feel that she had been. That they'd been in perfect sync.

And that was a new experience. She didn't feel like there were ghosts hovering in the background anymore. She hadn't realized how much of herself had still be wrapped up in things from the past. How afraid she'd been of letting it go. Because clinging to it had been less scary than moving on.

"I just want you to know, that really was the best ever," she said.

He smiled. "You're very good for my ego."

"As if your ego needed inflating."

"It may not have needed it. At least not from just any woman. From you it means a lot more than that. So much more than empty flattery."

She cleared her throat, tried to deny the tender feelings that were swirling in her stomach. "I'm definitely staying in your bed tonight."

"Good." They walked down the hall hand in hand and he pushed the door open to his room, scooping her into his arms again as he had at the beach. "Shower first though. I'm still sandy."

He carried her into the bathroom and set her down on the bright white marble floor before turning on the water in the shower.

She turned and caught her reflection in the mirror. There were red splotches on her body, from sand and Stavros's whiskers. Her cheeks were pink from the sun, her hair tumbled beyond reason, stringy from the salt water. Her scar was still there. Still impossible to ignore.

But her eyes…they looked so happy.

She lowered her hand and ran her fingertips across the line that ran below her belly button.

"It's nothing to worry about," he said, wrapping his arms around her from behind and lowering her hand. "You're beautiful."

"Do you know…you're the first person besides my doctor to see me since I've had that scar."

"I didn't know," he said.

"Well, that was… This," she said, moving her hand back to the scar, "was the end of my marriage."

"He divorced you because you got a hysterectomy?"

She but her lip and shook her head. "No. I divorced him after he wouldn't come to the hospital to see me. To sit with me. After I came home and all he would do was look at me like…like I'd betrayed him."

"Bastard."

She shook her head. "I don't know. Maybe not. Maybe… maybe I did the wrong thing. Maybe if we would have kept trying it would have worked. Maybe the first four years of trying weren't enough. Maybe if there would have been four more years, or IVF or something…it would have worked. I was the one who couldn't take it anymore. My doctor told me the hysterectomy would make my pain go away and so I jumped at the chance."

"What about adoption? Why wouldn't he adopt a child?"

She swallowed. "It wasn't the same to him. It…wasn't what he wanted." She would have done it. Gladly. Happily.

"Jessica—" he turned her so that she was facing him "—how can you think you made a bad decision? And what business did he have making you feel bad for dealing with pain the way you had to? It wasn't his pain. It wasn't his right to make the decision. You said yourself he did his best to ignore your pain. It wasn't his right to make you suffer for trying to make it stop."

"Sometimes I think so, too," she said, her voice breaking. "A lot of the time I do. For the last couple months before the procedure I was on a steady pain-pill diet. That made me feel a bit happier, but it also made me sleepy. Made my brain foggy and made me unable to do my job."

"That's unacceptable. I can't believe you were in so much pain. I can't believe he didn't care." He shook his head. "That's too much," he said, his voice rough.

"I know," she whispered. "And he never…he never wanted to know how bad it was. He just didn't…he didn't want things to change. He didn't want a sick wife that couldn't stand to be touched. Didn't want a woman who was broken. It wasn't what he signed on for."

"He *never* asked you how badly you hurt?" Stavros touched her cheek. "He didn't care?"

"I don't know. I don't…I was so convinced he loved me. He was my husband. But on this side of it, I get angry. I wonder how you could watch someone suffer and only care about how it made you feel. I… And he said I was a bitch. But I wasn't." Her voice caught a sob sticking in her chest. "I wasn't. He was a bastard. And he didn't love me.

He didn't even have the decency to divorce me. He made me do it so he could hate me for that, too."

"And you did what you had to do. For yourself. And it was right. You know that, don't you?" His expression was so earnest, so impossibly sincere. It made her heart ache.

"I do. But then sometimes I think I gave up too quickly." *I would be a mother.* Her own words echoed in her head. "I'll never know if I could have conceived if…"

"And then you would have stayed with a man who loved the ideal better than he loved you. You don't deserve that."

She laughed. "Funny you should say that. About the ideal. I always think his new wife looks too much like me for comfort."

"He's remarried?"

"Yes. And they have a baby. The sad part? I cried for two days when I found out she was pregnant. I hated her. I hated her so much. And that was so stupid. So wrong."

He shook his head. "Not wrong. You're human."

"Yeah. I am. Too human. But you're right. I do deserve better than him. Better than being the vehicle for his dreams. Better than being his failed dream. He was able to move on and have the exact same thing. I can't. I am who I am. I have the body I have."

"You say that, that you can't leave yourself, but that he can move on, but you overlook something."

"What?" she whispered.

He cupped her face, his thumbs moving over her cheekbones. "He can't leave himself. He's a sad, selfish person. And that's who he is. He won't grow or change. He'll never understand what he lost. His punishment is living with himself. And living without you."

"Oh," she breathed, words failing her completely.

"Come here." He took her hand and led her into the shower. His hands slid over her curves, the water making his touch slick. It wasn't sexual, even though it did arouse her. His touch was comforting.

She had him turn around so she could rinse the sand from his skin. Kiss the place a rock had bit into his flesh while they'd made love. They helped dry each other off, and then they got into bed.

He pulled her against the curve of his body, his arms so strong, his heat warming her.

It was so intimate. It felt far more intimate than anything she'd ever experienced. Because for the first time she felt like the man in her bed understood her. That there wasn't a secret thought in her mind she knew he wouldn't approve of.

Stavros felt like her ally. Sadly, most of the time her husband had felt like an enemy.

Her pain had caused him pain, so he hadn't allowed her to talk about it. Her escape from pain had been unacceptable to him, so he hadn't supported it. His words had wounded her. Flayed the skin from her bones.

But Stavros's words were healing.

"He really let you go through that by yourself?" His fingers grazed her scar.

"Yes. He didn't want me to do it."

He swore, a truly foul word in Greek that she knew roughly translated to something that would be physically impossible for her ex to do to himself. She laughed. "I appreciate how strongly you feel about it. But I've been my own champion for long enough that I don't need your anger." Was it so wrong that she wanted it? That it soothed her?

He turned her so she was facing him. "I need to be angry at him. For me."

Her throat tightened and tears stung her eyes. "Oh."

"He should have been there for you."

"He couldn't do it. He couldn't stand that I was killing our dreams. And without those dreams…there was no point."

"I don't believe that, Jess. You're enough to fulfill a man's dreams all on your own."

His words hung between them. She couldn't speak. She didn't bother to wipe away the tears that were falling down her cheeks. Tears it felt so good to finally be able to cry.

When Stavros woke up the next morning, Jessica was lying across the end of the bed, playing a game on her iPad. Her lips were pursed in concentration, her focus on the screen. She must have gone back to her room to get both the computer and a set of pajamas that consisted of a thin T-shirt and some very short shorts.

But she'd come back to his room. That thought brought him more pleasure than it ought to. "What are you doing?" He sat up and leaned over to get a good view of the screen.

"Oh." She turned and looked at him, the impact of her smile carrying all the force of a prize fighter's right hook. "Waiting for you to wake up."

"How do you play the game?"

"You shoot these little birds out of the slingshot and try to hit the pigs." She demonstrated by drawing one slender finger over the touch screen and aiming her feathered bullet at its target. "Yes!" She sat up after she hit her target, pumping her fist.

He laughed, this moment, this one where she was so happy, so relaxed, where he felt the same things, was one he would cling to always. One he would hold inside of him to keep. To treasure.

You are weak. You find it too easy to grow attached to this woman.

He had always feared as much. That he was as weak, as

governed by his emotions as his father, as his brother. That it would be his ruin, the ruin of his country.

But he didn't see how it could be. Looking at Jessica now, being with her, he felt strong. Stronger than he had in his life. More vulnerable in some ways too, but he wondered if it was good.

Then he wondered about his sanity.

"High score!" she said.

He smiled. "Don't you do a dance when you get high scores?"

She treated him to a bland look. "I told you, you don't get to see my dance."

"So, I can see you naked, but I can't see you dance?"

She stood on the bed and looked over her shoulder. "Don't tell anyone about this."

"I wouldn't dare."

She swayed her hips from side to side, her arms moving in time, her lips pulled to the left. She twirled in a circle, continuing in the same motion. He felt, for a moment, like he was watching himself from a distant place. An observer rather than a participant. Like it couldn't be real. This snatch of happiness, this moment of pure connection and silliness with another person. He had never felt anything like it.

His heart seemed to draw tight around itself and squeeze hard. The same heart he had professed not to have.

She plopped back down onto her knees in front of him. "There. Now I've done it."

He leaned in and kissed her. "Amazing."

She was amazing. What she made him feel was amazing. He felt different. He wanted to fight against it. He wanted to embrace it, and all the changes he could feel her making inside of him.

Just take this time. Just this time.

He put everything into the kiss, into losing himself in it. In her.

For once, he didn't want to think. He only wanted to feel.

They spent the next week in Greece. Jessica handled clients remotely, and Stavros went to work in the city, or worked from his office in the villa. And mostly they had a lot of sex.

Jessica was pretty sure she had a perma-grin from all the ecstasy she'd been exposed to over the past seven days. She was a little worried, though, because she didn't seem to be getting tired of him. Worse, she missed him a lot when he was working, or when she was working. And if he got up to work on his computer at night, she would wake up, feeling his absence almost immediately.

She'd been sleeping in her own bed since well before her divorce, but it had been so easy to get used to having someone again. No, not just someone. Because even after eight years of sharing a bed with Gil he hogged the covers and pushed her to the edge of the bed.

Stavros hogged the covers sometimes. And he certainly took up more than his half of the king-size bed. But she was content to curl around him and let him hold her. And she didn't really mind that he kept most of the blankets. Because she liked having him there. Liked waking up and seeing his face first thing. Liked having him be the last thing she saw before she went to sleep.

That was a bit of a problem. Because this was temporary. They had three weeks left.

That sucked big-time.

They were also going to have to figure out how to make it work in Kyonos, which would be its own problem.

She walked into Stavros's—now their—bedroom just in time to see him walking out of the bathroom with a white towel slung low on his lean hips, his muscles shifting pleasantly as he ran his fingers through his dark, damp hair.

"Hey, stranger," she said.

He turned and looked at her, his smile making her heart stop beating for a moment. "Did you get any work done?"

"Uh…yeah. I had a woman from India contact me. She's from a very wealthy family and she wants to use my contacts to find someone better than the guy her parents are pushing her toward. She seems fun. I'm looking forward to it."

She was looking forward to matching anyone except Stavros, really.

"You sound excited."

"I am."

"I understand if you have to travel once we're back in Kyonos," he said. "If you need to go and meet this client."

"I probably will." She didn't really like to think about it. To consider wasting nights away from him when their time was already so limited.

"You can use my plane."

"Oh, no, I don't want to do that."

He put his hands on his hips and her eyes were drawn to the cut lines that ran down beneath the towel, an arrow to an even more interesting part of his anatomy. "Jessica, don't be difficult."

Annoyance coursed through her, battling against the arousal being near him all damp, fresh and half-naked had caused. "Tough luck, Prince Sexy, I am difficult, if you hadn't noticed. And I'm not going to take advantage of you. My expenses are all worked into the fees I charge my clients. I'm a businesswoman. A very successful one. Maybe not quite on your level, but I do very well for myself."

"I know that. But if you use airports, it will all take longer. I can have you flown any time, day or night, in superior comfort in half the time."

"Well. Yes. But still, it's not my plane."

"Then I'll sell you a ticket."

She narrowed her eyes. "For?"

"If I say sexual favors will you knee me in the groin?"

She bit the inside of her cheek to keep from smiling and offered him a deadly glare. "Yes."

He named an insultingly low figure.

"No dice," she said. "I'll be flying out of Kyonos International. Deal with it."

He reached out and grabbed her around the waist and tugged her to him. "You are a pain."

"Yeah, so? You like it." She grabbed his towel and tugged it, letting it fall to his feet.

He smiled down at her, then kissed her nose. "Maybe."

"What time are we headed back to Kyonos?"

"This afternoon." His tone said what his words didn't. That it was too soon. That even though they still had time together, the real world would be intruding. That he didn't want that.

She didn't, either. She wanted to freeze time and live in the bubble for a while. Where reality wasn't such an intrusive force. Where chemistry was enough of a reason to be with someone. Where her ability to produce children, to be a figurehead and not just be Jessica, wouldn't be essential to her being with Stavros.

But that wasn't real. That couldn't last. And they both just had to buck up and deal with it.

"All right. I guess I should get packed then."

He kissed her lips. "Later." He kissed her neck, her shoulder.

"Yes. Later."

Reality could have a turn later. She'd spend another hour in the fantasy.

CHAPTER ELEVEN

Stavros idly wished he felt a sense of homecoming when he walked into the Kyonosian palace. He didn't. It felt like the walls had started to close in. A sensation he wasn't very fond of. Somehow, even the high ceiling seemed to reach down to him, as though it was trying to crush him.

Apt indeed.

He walked down the empty corridor and to his father's office. He pushed the door open. "Your Highness," he said, inclining his head.

"Stavros." His father stood, his hands clasped behind his back. "How was Greece?"

"Everything is in order. My hotels there are doing well."

"And your marriage?"

"Have I arranged it? Is that what you mean?"

"For all the money you've spent on that matchmaker I should think it would be settled by now," his father said, his voice gruff, his focus turned back to the papers spread over his desk.

Ah, yes, his matchmaker. His lover. The woman who held his body and his soul captive. The woman who made him feel more than any one person had ever made him feel in his life. The woman who made him question the core of his existence. That matchmaker.

He tightened his jaw. "Ms. Carter introduced me to several outstanding candidates."

"And?"

"And I've selected one." The words threatened to strangle him.

"Name?"

"Victoria Calder. She's English. Beautiful."

"Fertile?"

That made his stomach clench. "According to all of her paperwork, yes. That's part of why I hired Jessica. She handled that unpleasant pre-screening process for me. No potential scandals. No nasty medical surprises." It galled him to say the words. Because it made him feel no better than Jessica's ex. A man looking for a woman who met his terms. A man choosing a woman who was a mere placeholder, rather than a person.

Was that what he was? What he was doing?

Yes. It was.

"Excellent. When do you announce?"

"Not for a while." Not until he had to. Not until he'd taken the chance to draw out every possible moment with Jessica. "We'll make an appearance at Eva and Mak's ball."

"Excellent. I'm looking forward to it. This will be a good thing for, Kyonos. I'm certain of it."

"Yes," Stavros said, feeling no certainty at all.

Stavros nodded and exited the office. And fought the urge to punch the stone wall. Of course he was the only one to never disappoint his father. To never dishonor the Drakos name.

No, but his father had. His father had given up. Receded behind a veil of grief after his wife died. After he drove his oldest son away.

Stavros had never had the option of letting anyone down. He'd had to fix everything. Had had to pretend that everything in him was fixed because someone had to stand firm. He'd never had the luxury of feeling. Of falling apart.

He wanted to now. He wanted to give in to himself. He wanted to follow the emotions Jessica had brought back to him. Wanted to hold on to them forever.

He strode out of the palace and got into his car. He liked to drive himself whenever he could. He needed it. Because it was one of the few times he was able to be alone. When he was able to stop putting on a show.

Alone and with Jessica. Those were the only times that was possible. He shook his head and started the engine.

The streets in Thysius were crowded, but it didn't take long for him to get to his penthouse apartment. It was fortified with security, of course, but for the most part he didn't worry. Kyonos was a small country, and he'd always felt safe there.

He parked his car in the underground garage and touched his fingerprints to the scanner on the elevator. He would have to move into the palace eventually. But for now he would relish his freedom.

The doors to the lift slid open and revealed his penthouse, open and stark. It was a man's home, for sure. And it was modern in the extreme, his rebellion against the ultra old-fashioned stylings of the castle. One of his many small rebellions. Rebellions that, he could see now, were the lingering bits of a man he'd thought long banished. The man Jessica made him feel like again.

He looked on the couch and saw a cream-colored chenille blanket draped over the black leather. He smiled and picked it up, running his fingers over the soft fabric. There was a romance novel on the glass coffee table. He picked it up and flipped through a few pages, careful to save the spot it had been left open to.

"You're home."

He looked up and saw Jessica standing in the entryway of the living room and his breath stopped for a moment. She was so beautiful. She added something to his home, something soft and feminine, something it had been lacking. Something he'd certainly never thought it lacked before.

"Yes. How was your day?"

"Great. I spoke with Harneet on the phone for a while, and that was nice. Got an idea of the type of man she was looking for. I think I'm going to fly out and have lunch with her sometime during the weekend."

"The ball for Mak and Eva is coming up in a couple of weeks."

She nodded. "I know."

"Will you be there?"

"I... Probably not."

He nodded. "I wish you could be."

"Gee, not to hurt your feelings or anything, Stavros, but watching you make your public debut with Victoria ranks right up there with shoving glass under my fingernails for fun." She crossed her arms beneath her breasts and cocked her hip to the side.

"That isn't why I want you there."

"No? But that's what you'll be doing there. I know...I know that's what's going to happen. We both know. But that doesn't mean I want to watch it."

She turned away from him and he caught her arm. "Why are you suddenly mad at me?"

"For having all the sensitivity of a bull elk."

"I want you with me. If I could, I would fly to India with you and hover around the lunch table while you talked to Harneet. But I can't do that, can I? Because that's when the press would wonder, and since I am about to try and show that I'm making a move toward marriage we both know that can't happen."

"I know. So what do you want me to do at the ball? Hover around the edges and stare longingly at you?"

"No, I want you to hover around the edges so I can stare longingly at you."

She frowned. "That doesn't make any sense."

"None of this does. None of it. It hasn't from the moment I met you. You make me want things, Jessica. And I can't have any of them."

She closed her eyes. "Neither can I, Stavros."

"Jessica…"

"You know? I think I'm going to call Harneet and ask if I can meet with her earlier. I might leave tomorrow. I should be back in to help arrange any future endeavors with Victoria." She opened her eyes, her resolve clearly set, her chin pushed out at a stubborn angle.

"You're still helping me with Victoria?"

"It's my job, Stavros. And nothing changes that. Because nothing changes what has to happen."

"True enough." She was right. No matter what, he had to marry. And really, given her qualifications, Victoria was the woman he needed to marry. "I have to work early."

He knew what she was doing. Getting them both some distance. And they desperately needed it. They'd been in each other's pockets during their time in Greece, and she was staying in his home now. They needed space.

She nodded. "I'll probably be gone when you get home." She took a deep breath. "And I should probably sleep in my own room tonight."

He shook his head. "No. Sleep with me." Because even if they needed that kind of distance he wasn't sure he could stand it. "Please."

She nodded. "Okay."

Tomorrow they would take a break. He could clear his head.

He could set his focus back on what had to be done, and not on the insidious little fantasy that had burrowed beneath his skin over the past few weeks.

A fantasy that was simply impossible, no matter how badly he might want it.

Jessica felt like something that had washed up on the beach back at their Grecian villa by the time she got back from India a few days later. Definitely more bedraggled seagull than mermaid.

Their Grecian villa. What a silly way to think of it. It was Stavros's Grecian villa. She had simply shared his bed there for a while.

And now the idea was for her to share his penthouse for the next few weeks. She sighed. She'd done a lot of thinking on her out-of-town days, about whether or not what they were doing was a good idea.

The conclusion she'd come to was that it was a very bad idea, but then, she'd known it was a bad idea from moment one. They both had. They just hadn't been stronger than the desire.

She closed her eyes as she lifted her hand to the fingerprint reader on his elevator, one he'd programmed to accept her touch, and she knew that no amount of realization about the badness of their arrangement had made her any stronger.

She had a feeling Stavros was just as aware of the folly of it as she was. And that he was just as unlikely to stop.

She stepped inside and leaned her head against the metal wall as the doors slid closed and the lift carried her up the penthouse.

She'd strongly considered staying over in India for a while longer, if only to miss the ball. She didn't want to see Stavros with Victoria. She couldn't play disinterested party anymore. She couldn't separate Stavros her lover from Stavros her client. It was impossible.

Everything inside of her seemed to be tangled around him, and he seemed to be completely tangled up in her life.

The doors to the lift opened and she stepped out into his immaculate living room. She knew the housekeeper had been in, because if there was one thing she'd learned about Stavros, it was that his neat-as-a-pin modern-looking homes weren't kept in that fashion by him.

He left his clothes on the floor. And very often he left dishes in the sink.

He's not perfect.

No, he very much wasn't perfect, but she wasn't sure she cared about that, either. The reminder meant nothing, because if anything, being so aware that he wasn't perfect only gave validity to the feelings that were eating her from the inside out.

She stalked over to the fridge and pulled out a bottle of milk. It was nearly empty. She could add that to his list of sins. Putting a nearly empty milk bottle back into the fridge. And he'd probably forgotten to tell his housekeeper that he needed milk.

She padded down the hall and pushed open the door to his office. It was empty. He wasn't here.

It was easy to pretend, standing in his house, walking around as thought she belonged. Like they belonged together. But she'd had a lot of time to think while she'd been away. Even if she could have him, if he gave it all up for her…she couldn't let him.

Because she'd been the broken dreams of one man already. Stavros would only grow to resent her, too, as she tried, once again, to fit into a position she simply wasn't made for.

She took her phone out of her pocket and saw that she

had three new text messages. She'd put it on silent and forgotten about it.

She opened the first one.

Will you be back in time for dinner?

It was long past dinner so the answer to that was no. She opened the next message.

Call me when you land so I know you're safe.

A smile curved her lips and she ran her fingers over the screen of her phone. Why did he have to do things like that?

She scrolled to the next one.

Jess, I miss you.

A tear slid down her cheek. Had she really mourned how hard it was for her to cry only a few weeks ago? Now it seemed so easy. What had he done to her?

She curled her fingers around her phone and thought about calling. She wasn't sure it was a good idea. In fact, she was almost certain it was a bad idea. She would probably cry all over him. Maybe blurt out things she had no business thinking, much less saying to him.

She hit the reply button and typed in: I miss you, too.

She deleted it. And took a breath.

I'm here. Where are you?

Her phone pinged a second later.

Can I send a car for you in an hour? I want to show you something.

She'd wanted to rest for a while, but that didn't seem important anymore for some reason. The only thing that mattered was seeing him.

Sure. Give me time to get the travel grime off.

His return message came quickly. I'll be waiting for you.

CHAPTER TWELVE

The car stopped in front of a lighthouse. The tower was dark, no signs of life anywhere in the small stone house. Jessica gathered up the skirt of her white, flowing gown, the one she'd purchased in Greece with Stavros in mind, and stepped out into the warm evening.

She looked up and saw Stavros, standing in front of the whitewashed building, his hands in his pockets, the top button of his shirt undone. He looked different. And so wonderfully the same. She had the strangest sense of being home. A feeling she hadn't had in so long she hadn't realized the absence of it.

"What's this?" she asked.

"A place I'd almost forgotten about. The palace is there," he said, pointing to glimmering lights on a hill. "Technically, this is part of the grounds. It hasn't been used for years. I used to come here whenever I could sneak away. I wanted to see it again and then, when I did...I wanted to show it to you."

"Why?" she asked, the tightness in her chest spreading, climbing into her throat, making it hard to breathe.

"Because you... Come with me, maybe then I can explain." He held his hand out and she took it, his fingers warm and strong as they closed around hers. He led her into the house. It was cool inside, the thick stone walls providing protection from the heat that still lingered in the air.

There was no furniture in the house. Not even a chair. "No one lives here?" she asked. "Well, that's actually obvious."

"No one has lived here in years. It's been vacant since I was a kid. Come with me." He led her through to the back of the house, to a small, rounded doorway with a steep set of stairs. She followed him up the curving staircase, her fingers laced with his.

They ended at the top of the tower, a small, clean room with a lantern at the center. Here there was a chair. And blankets laid across the floor.

"I used to come here and watch the ships," he said. "Imagine where they had been. Where they were going. Dream I was here, keeping them from hitting the rocks. Keeping watch."

"You've always been protecting people, haven't you?" she whispered.

He walked over to the lantern, pressing his hand against the glass case. "It was different. It wasn't real, first of all. And second…I remember caring more then for imaginary ships and dangers, feeling more for created peril, than I've cared about anything since. It was a child's game. Silly. But I had a passion for it. I felt something. I…I lost that. I lost it very purposefully. I…I wanted to show you, because I thought you might understand."

"If I ask what I'm supposed to understand does that mean I fail?" she asked, her heart pounding, her stomach weighted down. With desire. Fear. Longing.

"I want to feel again, Jess. For the first time since I was a child…I want it back. I want to care. You brought it back to me. Passion. I hadn't felt a passion for anything in so long…."

"Sure you have. I know you've had a lot of lovers besides me," she said, trying to steer the conversation away from where she feared it was going.

"Lust isn't the same as passion. It's not the same as… It's not the same as this. I used to think…I have thought for so long…that emotion was weakness. That caring for something, for someone, made you weak. And then I kept thinking of this place. Of how much I cared. Of how seriously I took even an imagined responsibility…because of love, really."

"Stavros…"

He moved to her, his eyes locked with hers. "You look like a goddess," he said, reverting to the physical. And she was so very glad he had.

"I had a layover in Greece and I remembered you saying… I remembered you saying I should wear a *pallas*. It's really vintage," she said, trying to force a smile. "Nearly a hundred years old, or so I was told."

He closed his eyes and leaned in, pressing his forehead to hers. She thought her heart might burst. "I need…I need you. Now."

His body was shaking with desire and that was something she could handle. This was what they both needed. The physical. To remember that this was about desire, mutual lust that they were both trying to satisfy.

It had been the reclamation of her sexuality. Of her body. A release of the things in her past, letting go of any remaining desire to be the person she had been. And she could never regret that. She wouldn't let herself.

She also wouldn't let it be more. There were so many things Stavros needed. So many responsibilities he needed a wife to help him fulfill. Things she couldn't possibly do.

"Are we… No one will come up here, right?"

"I told your driver he could leave. I drove myself." He

moved his hand to her hip, then slid it around to her lower back, to the curve of her bottom. "This dress is not fit for public. It's far too erotic."

"There isn't a single button on this dress to fuel your fantasies."

A strange expression crossed his face. "No. But I don't think it was ever the buttons." There was a heavy undertone to the statement, a meaning she didn't want to search for. Because there was no point. "I think it's been you all along."

She sucked in a sharp breath, ignoring the pain that lodge in her chest. This had to be about sex. Only sex.

If she let it be more…she just couldn't let it be more. Because it had to end.

"*You* have buttons, on the other hand." She put her hands on his chest and started working at the buttons of his dress shirt, revealing teasing hints of his perfect chest. She parted the fabric and slid her hands over his bronzed skin. "Oh, Stavros, I don't think I could ever get tired of this." The words were far too candid, far too honest, but she couldn't have held them back if she'd tried.

They were true. She could never tire of him. Not of his body, not of his humor, or his drive. Not of that spark of rebellion in him. That glorious bit of himself that could never be fully tamed.

She swallowed and pushed his shirt and jacket from his shoulders, leaving him nothing more than a pair of dark slacks.

He leaned in and pressed a kiss to her bare shoulder, his hand searching for where her dress was held together, at the waistband, taking the end of the fabric and tugging it from its secure place. He let it fall and she felt the top of the dress loosen.

He stepped back, his eyes appraising.

She put her hand on her shoulder and pushed the large

swath of fabric that crossed her body down, exposing her breasts to him. She watched his face as she slowly unwrapped herself, memorized the agony and ecstasy she saw there. No one had ever looked at her like that before. No one had ever made her feel so vulnerable and so powerful at the same time.

Stavros did it as effortlessly as most people drew breath.

He removed his pants and underwear quickly and shoved them to the side, naked and aroused for her enjoyment. And she did enjoy him. He was a sensual feast, amazing for all of her senses. To touch, to taste, to see. Stavros never disappointed.

She was about to go to him, to wrap her hand around his erection, but he moved first, dropping to his knees before her. He kissed her stomach, pushed her panties down and slid his finger through her slick folds, drawing the moisture from her body over her clitoris.

"You're so very good at that," she said, holding tightly to his shoulders. It was so much more than sexual skill, and she knew it.

Because her response to him went well beyond a basic physical reaction. It grabbed her, low and deep, and held her in thrall, no matter what was happening. Whether they were naked, alone on a beach, or fully clothed in a crowded ballroom, Stavros held her. All of her.

"The pleasure is mine," he said, rising back to his feet and kissing her mouth. "You have no idea."

He walked her backward to the blankets that had been spread on the floor, and held her tightly as he lowered them both to the soft surface.

"I've been expertly seduced," she said. "You planned this."

"I very much did," he said, not a hint of apology in his tone.

"One of the things I…" She stopped herself before she could say the words that were ringing inside of her head, her heart. "You and I think alike," she said. No feelings. No love. Oh, please not that.

He cupped her face and kissed her again while his other hand teased her breasts.

"You don't get to have all the fun," she said, sliding her hand down so that she could cup his erection.

He closed his eyes, the expression on his face one of a man completely given over to pleasure, completely lost in it. She memorized that, too. Watched him until her own pleasure became so intense she had to close her eyes.

She clung to the image of his face. Made sure it stayed in the forefront of her mind.

She clung to his shoulders, wrapped her leg around his hips, and he angled himself so that he slid inside of her. She bit her lip to keep from crying out. To keep from crying period.

He rolled her to her back and she parted her legs. He pushed in deeper and she arched into him, rocking her body in time with each of his thrusts.

There was no sound in the room beyond fractured gasps and short breaths, echoing from the stone walls. She dug her fingernails into his shoulders, trying to find something solid to keep her on earth. To keep her from losing herself completely.

If it wasn't already too late.

A sob climbed in her throat and burst from her as she fell over the edge, her orgasm stealing control of everything, drowning her in pleasure. She couldn't think, she could only cling to Stavros as wave after wave of bliss crashed down over her.

"Stavros," she said, tears spilling from her eyes.

He shuddered his own release, his muscles tight, her name on his lips.

After he pulled her against him, pressed kisses to her cheeks, her forehead, her mouth. His hands, hands that had been demanding in their pursuit and deliverance of pleasure, were gentle as he smoothed them over her curves.

She rested her head on his chest, tears drying on her cheeks, her eyes getting heavy in the aftermath of her release.

"I love you, Jess."

The words hit like a blow. She closed her eyes against the pain. Against the regret. Against the desire to turn and say them back to him. She couldn't. And he didn't mean it. He couldn't. He had responsibilities, responsibilities that far surpassed getting imaginary ships to the shore, and she knew that fulfilling those obligations meant the world to him.

And if he tried to put her in that position of being the one to fulfill them with…she could do nothing but fail. Could do nothing but watch the sweet tenderness in his eyes flatten into a cold, bitter hatred.

You're such a selfish bitch, Jessica. The words were always there. So easy to hear. So easy to remember.

She wouldn't be. Not now. No matter how much she wished she could. Tonight, though…she had to let herself have tonight.

She curled tighter into Stavros's embrace and hoped he wouldn't notice the tears that fell onto his chest.

Stavros knew the revelation should terrify him. But it didn't. Not even hours later, after he drove them back to his penthouse. After he laid her down in his bed and made love with her again. And now, as he lay in bed with Jessica curled up at his side.

He loved her.

He waited for something in him to crumble, for it to break and reveal his weakness. But it didn't. He felt reinforced. As though everything in Jessica, as though loving her, was shoring up his strength. Fueling it.

Love was different than he'd imagined. But then, Jessica was a different woman than he ever could have imagined.

He stroked her silky blond hair and watched her sleep, her cheek pillowed on his chest, and he wondered how he would ever face a future without her.

And he knew that if he was truly going to be the king, the man, he was meant to be, he needed her to be the one at his side.

CHAPTER THIRTEEN

IT WAS the coward's way out. To sneak out while he was sleeping. While the first edges of light were peeking over the mountains. But men did it all the time, didn't they? And wasn't it supposed to save everyone from a big emotional scene? She certainly needed to be saved from it.

Because he'd said he loved her. Loving her, being with her, would stop him from finding everything he'd said he wanted. She would never, ever allow herself to be blamed for a man's ruined life and broken dreams.

Never again.

She held her suitcase tightly to her body and walked across the apartment, heading for the elevator.

"What are doing?"

She turned and saw Stavros, still naked, his pants in his hand.

"I'm...I'm going."

"Why?"

She let out a breath. "Because it was now or in a few weeks, and I decided it should be now. We both knew this wasn't permanent, and the four-week time frame no longer works for me."

"Put your suitcase down." He tugged his pants on quickly, leaving the belt undone.

She shook her head. "No. I'm leaving."

"I love you."

"You don't want love. You told me that already. You don't believe in it…you don't."

"I love you," he repeated, the words breaking.

"Stop it," she said, her voice shaking. "Just stop."

"It's true, I do. I love you, Jessica." He sounded tormented, his voice raw and pained. And she had caused it.

"It doesn't matter, don't say it like it does. Like it ever could. So you love me? What does that mean?"

"What does it mean? You want to know what it means? It means that my world stops turning when you aren't in it, and when I see you I feel like I can breathe again. That's what it means. It means I've found my passion again. That I'm not hollow anymore."

She dropped the suitcase then, pressing her hand to her chest. "No. What does it mean? Practically. In the real world. Because we both know that loving me doesn't make me able to have your royal babies, which means I'm not good enough to wear the royal crown. We both know it, so what's the point in any of this?"

"The point," he said, taking a step toward her, his expression deadly, "was to make me forget you. To make me get over this…need that I feel for you. To make it so the thought of a future without you didn't make me feel like my guts were being torn from my body. That was the point. We failed on all counts. I have…feelings, Jessica. I was so dead for so long and then you came into my life. And I couldn't put you at a distance, and I couldn't stop myself from being me when I was with you. I love you, and it's not simple, but it is so damned important because it changed me."

"You just think that, Stavros. Because of the sex. Because you love skirting the edge of convention as much as you possibly can and oh, how shocking would a divorced infertile queen be? But it's not real. It's temporary. Victoria is real. She can be your princess, your queen. And she can give you everything that you need. I can't."

"That is unfair, Jessica. Don't tell me what I feel."

"You would hate me in the end, Stavros. You would."

He stood there, his dark eyes pinned on her. "Tell me you love me, too."

She shook her head, the words tearing at her throat, struggling to escape. She wouldn't let them. She wouldn't make it worse.

He crossed the room in three strides, cupped her face, his hands so gentle, his expression so dark and fierce. "Tell me."

"No," she whispered, taking a step back and picking up her suitcase again. "I'm glad that you…found yourself with me, or whatever you want to call it. But you don't need me to feel passion. You don't need me to have emotions. I hope that things with Victoria go well. I hope you…I hope you love her some day." She didn't. She never wanted him to love her. She wanted his love forever, and if that made her small, she didn't care. But she would lie now. She would preserve what pride she had left now. "Please don't pay me. Not for any of it."

He didn't say anything, he only stood there, his body tense. He looked like he might try to physically stop her from leaving. But he didn't. He only watched her as she turned away. And she didn't look back. She couldn't.

Stavros could only watch as Jessica walked into the elevator, as the doors closed behind her. He could only concentrate on taking breaths, each one causing raw, physical pain.

She was wrong. She was wrong about everything. At least as far as he was concerned. He did need her. He needed her more than he needed air. She had brought something back to him. Something he'd long thought dead. Something he'd been glad was gone.

He hadn't allowed himself to feel the pain of his mother's

death. There had been too much to do. The people around him had fallen apart and his country had fallen into chaos. He had vowed he would never let that happen again.

But now...now he felt as though his insides had broken apart, that each breath dug a shard of the destroyed pieces into his flesh.

He looked at the wineglass sitting on the counter. Something Jessica must have had earlier. He walked to the kitchen area and released a growl as he picked up the glass and hurled it at the wall. It exploded into a million unfixable pieces.

And it didn't heal anything inside of him.

He feared nothing ever would.

CHAPTER FOURTEEN

STAVROS stood in front of his father's desk and looked down at the ring, nestled in a velvet box, glittering at him. The old-world vintage style of the piece mocked him. Made his heart feel as if it was shattering. Which should be impossible since it had shattered days ago.

"You have chosen then?" his father asked, looking at him from his seated position, his grey brows raised.

"Victoria is a wonderful choice for Kyonos. She will be a good queen." He reached out and curled his fingers around the box, lifting it from the desk. He raised it to his eyes, studied it.

"Your mother's ring," his father said. "She loved the unusual antique setting."

He laughed, a bitter sound. "I know a woman like that."

"I get the feeling she is not the woman you will be offering the ring to?"

Stavros shook his head. "Jessica Carter is not fit to be queen of Kyonos. Not by the standards set out for me. If I were to marry her, it would cause great scandal." Something in his chest burned, spread through his blood like fire. The thought of life without her, day after day, faded and brittle, devoid of color, of beauty.

"And if you weren't going to be king, Stavros?"

Stavros looked at his father. "But I am going to be king. And that means I have to think of more than just myself."

King Stephanos paused for a moment, his expression grave. "If you care for nothing, you'll never be able to care for your people. Not as you should."

"Love makes you weak," Stavros said. "I've seen it." He'd never condemned his father to his face. For some reason, now it poured from him. His renewed passion came with a renewal of every emotion. Happiness, and anger. Deep and hopeless sadness.

"What made me weak was the absence of love," his father said slowly. "I cared for nothing after your mother died. Not the country. Not even my children. And so I left it all abandoned. Which is easy to do when you no longer care."

Stavros had never seen it that way before. And yet, it rang true in his soul. Jessica made him feel real again. In touch as he hadn't been for years. She brought passion out in him, to be better, do better.

He looked at the ring again and an image flashed into his mind. One of him sliding the ring onto Jessica's finger. He tried to make the image turn into Victoria. He couldn't. There was only one vision for his future. Only one woman he could have at his side.

"If I marry Jessica there will be scandal," he said, his voice rough. "We will not have an heir. Her past will be fodder for the papers." He raised his focus to his father, who was regarding him silently. "And I don't give a damn. I love her. That's all that matters."

He turned away, his heart pounding hard.

"And that is why you will be twice the king that I have been, Stavros. You are a man who should follow his heart. Because your heart is strong."

He curled his fingers more tightly around the ring box. "It is now. Because of her."

* * *

"Jessica." She heard Stavros's voice through her hotel room door and she froze.

Why was he here? Why was he tormenting her? She'd been miserable for the past forty-eight hours. And she was planning on being miserable on the plane ride home. And then she was planning on being a sopping, miserable mess in North Dakota, so really, she didn't need his help.

Her entire body was heavy. The effort of dragging herself out of bed that morning had been nearly not worth it. Putting on pajamas last night hadn't been worth it, and she was still in yesterday's clothes because dressing hadn't seemed like it was worth it, either.

And now he was here. And she wanted to run to him and ignore reality so much it was nearly impossible to stop herself from flinging to door open and huddling against him.

"What do you want?" she said, knowing she sounded whiny and not caring. She felt whiny. She felt crushed.

"You. Open the door."

Her heart slammed against her breastbone. "Why?"

"Because I can tell you what it means now."

She swallowed and walked to the door, turning the dead bolt and unlinking the chain before pulling it open. "What?"

He gripped the edge of the door and the door frame. "I'm not marrying Victoria."

"What?" she asked again, taking a step back.

"I can't. I can't because you are the only woman that I want. I see you in my dreams, I see you when I'm awake and I close my eyes. I can't forget you. I don't want to forget you. I want you."

"But you…Victoria is perfect for you. She…she…" Jessica reached for her tablet computer, sitting on the arm of the couch, and swiped through a few screens until she found Victoria's file. "She is graceful, and wonderful and she can have your babies. She's beautiful and she does charities for homeless children. She's *perfect*."

"Yes, she is. There—" he pointed at her computer "—in writing, yes, she's perfect for my country. But you, Jessica Carter, you are perfect for me. And I don't care what you can't do, I only care what you do for me, what you give me. I care that when I'm with you I'm a better man. I have been closed off for years. What does it matter if I can give my people charm, an empty smile if I can give them nothing deeper than that? It doesn't matter. But you...you make me feel. You have forced me to find something in myself that's...real. To be more than a shell. I can't go back. I won't."

"Stavros, I... You can't do this. You can't. You have to have these things," she said, pointing to her computer again. "You have to. And if you don't..."

"If I don't, I'll be a better man for it. For pursuing what I want. For finding real passion. For ruling with everything I have in me. You, you helped me find it. Yes, I am expected to have a wife who can have heirs...but I won't. And that will have to be fine, it will be perfect, because my wife will be you. Unless you don't want me. Then...well, I'm not sure what I'll do then."

"Stavros—" her voice broke "—I want you. But I'm not going to be the cause of your unfulfilled vision. You want this so much. To be this perfect figurehead for your people. And I can't be the one to stop you from doing it. I've been that. I have been a man's broken dreams and I won't do it again. I can't. I can't watch love turn into resentment, and anger. I can't be more than I am. I am in this body, and I can only give so much."

A tear slid down her cheek, then another. Tears she realized had been stored up for the past few years of her life.

Anger and pain, and the anguish of being limited. Of not being enough.

Stavros moved to her, brushed her tears away with his thumb. "You are *everything*," he said, his voice rough. "You have given me everything. I didn't want love. Because I was so afraid of it, so afraid of the pain it could cause. Losing my mother devastated me. I just…shut down rather than dealing with it. I shut it all down. But you brought me back, you brought a part of me back and you restored it. I talked to my father. He told me the reason he let things fall apart was that he didn't care anymore. Not about anything. I wanted so badly not to be like him, not to lose myself to love, and I didn't realize I was him. Caring for nothing, going through the motions. But not now. Not since I met you."

He kissed her cheek. "Maybe on paper this doesn't work. But I don't think marriage is as simple as I believed it was. I can't just hire a wife the way I'd hire an assistant. I need a woman who will challenge me, who will push me, to be better, to do better. I know you are that woman. Most of all, I need the woman I love by my side."

"I love you," she said, letting the words come out. Finally. They felt like balm on her soul, healing old wounds that had never truly gone away. Until now. Until Stavros.

"I told you that once that you were enough of a dream for any man, and I stand by that statement now. I want nothing else. I want you."

She bit her lip. "I'm afraid you'll regret it. That you'll look at me every day and see…holes in me. All of the things I'm missing."

"Jessica, there are holes in me," he said, pressing his hand flat to his chest. "I am not perfect. But I believe you're the one who can fill the holes. The one who can make me stronger. Certainly the one who brings me joy."

She let out a sob. "I…I'm afraid you'll regret not having children."

"We can adopt children."

Shock bloomed in her stomach, making it hard to breathe. "But…adopted children couldn't take the throne, it doesn't solve the problem of heirs, it doesn't…"

"I'm not trying to solve a *problem* with adoption. If we want children, if we want to expand our family, we can adopt. We won't be the ones to produce the heirs. That's all right. I don't want another woman's children, I want yours. And by that I mean you're the one I want by my side raising my children. That's what matters anyway." He rested his forehead against hers. "That and if you love me. Because if you really love me, then nothing else matters."

"I do. I really do love you. But when we met you told me all the things you wanted and…"

"Because I was scared. A coward. I was trying to make things easier on myself. Going through life without caring is vain, but it's simple. I was going to marry a woman who would have been a placeholder, and you'll never be that. You make me want to be the king, the man, I didn't know I could be. You make me strong. Be my wife, Jessica. Please."

Every word, every line in his face, spoke of his sincerity. And if she thought back to their time, to the moment they'd first met, she knew it had started then. That every look, every touch, every kiss, had brought them to this point.

That every bit of pain before they met, had made them strong enough to stand here. Made them strong enough to make marriage work. To have love that lasted.

"I… Yes." Her heart lifted, happiness, true happiness, filling her, flooding her. Every place inside of her that had felt empty, incomplete, seemed filled now, with love.

"Don't ever feel like you aren't enough for me. You fill me. All the empty places in me."

She nodded. "I believe you."

"Jessica, this life won't always be easy. There will be press to deal with, and there are big responsibilities, long work hours and a lot of traveling. But I want you by my side for all of it. My queen, my lover, my partner."

"Yes," she said again, her voice stronger this time. "Stavros, I've loved before. But this is different. Because I feel like you're a part of me. I feel like you want me, and not me wrapped up as part of a dream, a fantasy. I truly believe that you love me, and not who you wish I was."

"I do. You aren't a dream. Far from it."

"Hey!" she said, laughing through her tears.

"What I mean is, you are too special, too unique for me to ever have dreamed up. I wrote down all the things I thought I needed in a wife, and I was delivered something completely different. I didn't truly know myself at all, or what I needed. Not until I met you."

"I must be the worst matchmaker in the world. I matched a woman to a prince and then…and then I got engaged to him. We are engaged, right?"

"Yes, we are. In fact—" he reached into his pocket and pulled out a white satin box "—this was my mother's." He opened the box and revealed a platinum, pear-cut diamond with intricate detail etched into the band. "It's been in our family for hundreds of years. When I saw it…when I saw it I knew there was only one woman I could give it to. It's perfect for you."

"You're right," she said. "You're so very right."

He took her hand in his and slid the ring onto her third finger. "It's like it was made for you."

She shook her head. "No, I think you were made for me."

Jessica leaned in and kissed him, pouring all of her love into the kiss. Now that she had Stavros, she didn't feel like she was missing anything.

"You fill all those places inside me that used to feel empty," she whispered.

He stoked her hair, his touch so warm and perfect. Even more perfect now that she knew she would have him forever. "As you do for me. I think you must have been my missing piece."

She closed her eyes and leaned into him. "For so long I felt like I was made wrong."

"No, *agápe mou,* you weren't made wrong. You were made for me."

* * * * *

LET'S TALK
Romance

For exclusive extracts, competitions
and special offers, find us online:

f facebook.com/millsandboon

◎ @millsandboonuk

🐦 @millsandboon

Or get in touch on 0844 844 1351*

For all the latest titles coming soon, visit
millsandboon.co.uk/nextmonth